No Roast For the Weary

No Roast For The Weary

CLEO COYLE

BERKLEY PRIME CRIME
New York

BERKLEY PRIME CRIME
Published by Berkley
An imprint of Penguin Random House LLC
1745 Broadway, New York, NY 10019
penguinrandomhouse.com

Book design by Kristin del Rosario

Library of Congress Cataloging-in-Publication Data

Names: Coyle, Cleo, author.
Title: No roast for the weary / Cleo Coyle.
Description: New York: Berkley Prime Crime, 2025. | Series: Coffeehouse mystery
Identifiers: LCCN 2024047236 (print) | LCCN 2024047237 (ebook) |
ISBN 9780593642283 (hardcover) | ISBN 9780593642290 (ebook)
Subjects: LCGFT: Detective and mystery fiction. | Novels.
Classification: LCC PS3603.O94 N67 2025 (print) | LCC PS3603.O94 (ebook) |
DDC 813/.6—dc23/eng/20241105
LC record available at https://lccn.loc.gov/2024047236
LC ebook record available at https://lccn.loc.gov/2024047237

Printed in the United States of America
1st Printing

The authorized representative in the EU for product safety and compliance is
Penguin Random House Ireland, Morrison Chambers, 32 Nassau Street,
Dublin D02 YH68, Ireland, https://eu-contact.penguin.ie.

To our excellent editor, Tracy Bernstein,
for her kindness, patience, and astute guidance
in our continuing quest to brew up something new.

AUTHOR'S NOTE

No Roast for the Weary is the twenty-first Coffeehouse Mystery in our series. As our longtime readers know, our caffeinated crime fiction is often inspired by the highs and lows of our New York life. This book is no exception. Until our full-time professional writing careers kicked into gear, we spent years laboring in this big, crowded, astonishing city, working regular jobs while writing on the side, which is why we know how exhilarating and exhausting life in the arts can be. The city hasn't changed in that regard. Creative artists continue to toil here, striving to secure a foothold on a never-ending climb. For many, gig-economy jobs pay the bills; and when the shift is over, the real work begins. While we admire all such tireless dreamers—aspiring and accomplished—this is a work of fiction, and any resemblance to actual persons, living or dead, is purely coincidental.

For this story's coffee inspiration, we thank Land of a Thousand Hills (landofathousandhills.com) for their superb Rwandan beans as well as their admirable work uplifting coffee farming communities. Like our Village Blend, they're "dedicated to crafting specialty coffee that makes a difference and is delicious too." As for other practices and procedures in this tale, we researched standard as well as atypical examples, but we also plead the author's defense that in the service of fiction, rules occasionally get bent.

A caffeinated shout-out goes to our publisher and everyone who worked on transforming our manuscript into this beautiful book. We're especially grateful to our brilliant editor, Tracy Bernstein, to whom this novel is dedicated. She not only held our hands throughout the writing process, suggesting good ideas to strengthen our work, but did so with humor and grace.

We applaud our talented cover artist Cathy Gendron for creating another gorgeous Coffeehouse Mystery cover (her twenty-first, too) and our literary agent, John Talbot, for his many years of unwavering support and consummate professionalism.

Finally, we extend our gratitude to those we could not mention by name, including friends, family, and so many of you who read our books and send us notes via email, our website's message board, and social media. Your encouragement always lifts our spirits, and we cannot thank you enough for that. Whether you are new to our world or a devoted reader, we invite you to join our Coffeehouse community at coffeehousemystery.com, where you will find bonus recipes, our latest book news, and a link to keep in touch by signing up for our newsletter. May you eat, drink, and read with joy!

—Alice Alfonsi and Marc Cerasini
aka Cleo Coyle, New York City

The one dependable law of life—
everything is always worse than you
thought it was going to be.

—Dorothy Parker, "The Waltz"

As long as there was coffee in the world,
how bad could things be?

—Cassandra Clare, *City of Ashes*

No Roast For the Weary

PROLOGUE

~~~~~~

THE late-autumn morning arrived with unpredictable clouds and a brisk wind off the Hudson River. Frosty gusts whipped through the Village streets, and the sidewalks were nearly deserted, but inside our cozy coffeehouse the buzz of happy customers promised a robust winter season.

I could hardly believe that only a few weeks ago, our tables were empty, our revenues wrecked, and I feared all was lost.

The heartbreaking slide started earlier this fall when the location filming of a hit television show in and around our Village Blend had disrupted our daily revenue stream and brought a distressing deficit to our bottom line. That calamity had no sooner ended when a devastating drop in foot traffic clobbered us anew, threatening our very existence.

As the manager and master roaster of this historic shop, I refused to watch it suffer a sad, slow death. I owed my family of baristas and beloved octogenarian mentor more than that. So, instead of giving up, I began to fight for its life.

A remedy came in the form of an idea from the Village Blend's own bohemian past: an upstairs writers' lounge. Resurrecting that simple vintage concept jump-started our traffic faster than a triple-shot red-eye with a Red Bull chaser.

Looking around me now, our financial problems appeared to be solved. Outside our wall of French doors, the chilly sidewalks were still far too barren. But inside, our coffeehouse was no longer empty.

Our marble-topped tables were packed with contented customers sipping our drinks and nibbling our pastries. The air was filled with the scent of freshly roasted coffee and the buzz of conversation. Our espresso machines hissed, our fireplace crackled, and our speakers resonated with smooth jazz.

With a fresh tray in my hands, I climbed the spiral stairs to our second floor. All the spots in our lounge were occupied, and every person was a writer. They came here for a place to create and collaborate, and they had my admiration. Many of them balanced multiple part-time jobs, squeezing out extra time in their schedules to type out the music of their imaginations.

As I moved among them, most were lost in the process, fingers dancing across their laptop keyboards, pens twirling on notebook pages. In the corner, I noticed a slumped figure. The poor soul had fallen asleep across their work, head down on the table, cobalt blue hoodie pulled fully up, arms sprawled out beside them.

No rest for the weary, I thought, a phrase I'd heard often among the writers who gathered here—including those who sometimes napped between gig-economy shifts.

As I drew closer, I sensed something was off about this writer's slumped form. Another few steps and I nearly dropped my tray.

"Hey, are you okay?"

No response.

I shook the writer's shoulder, and one limp arm slipped off the table. I saw the waxy flesh and curled fingers.

Oh, no. No, no, no—

Praying I was wrong, I shook the figure again. This time, the whole body toppled off the chair and onto the floor. Seeing the collapsed corpse sent an icy shock through me. Realizing what it meant chilled me to the bone.

In the next few minutes, chaos descended—the call to 911, the uproar in the shop, the desperate attempts to revive a person who could not be saved. As the inevitable whirlwind struck, the gears of my mind worked, putting pieces of a puzzle together with sickening swiftness.

Over the past few weeks, I'd learned things that had spiked my suspicions. Now I feared this poor dead writer had not died of natural causes. And there was something else. Something worse—

There could be more deaths to come.

To stop the killings, I would have to reach back to a dark night from the Village Blend's past and predict the future moves in a murderer's mind. I'd need to recount a dozen micro dramas, sort out specifics, and consider all the suspects: from the eccentric old poet and the bestselling author to the crazy young professor and this shop's chief competitor.

Everyone was involved in this story, practically from the start—and it all began when our financial woes were at their worst. When I feared the end was near. Not the end of any writer's life, but the existential end of our Village Blend.

One

⚰️⚰️⚰️⚰️⚰️⚰️⚰️⚰️⚰️⚰️⚰️⚰️⚰️⚰️⚰️⚰️

Greenwich Village, New York
Two weeks ago

THE bell above our front door jingled.

"Hey, I'm back! What's with the snow?! It's too early for snow!"

Looking up from behind the counter, I found my ex-husband and current business partner struggling with a bulky backpack. Snowflakes clung to Matteo Allegro's dark beard and crimson windbreaker—a jacket far too light for such a frosty morning.

"Don't blame me for the weather," I called. "Tell it to the polar vortex."

As I pulled Matt a speedy pick-me-up from our espresso machine, he made a shivering beeline for the blazing brick hearth and slipped the big pack off his strong shoulders. It hit our restored plank floor with a loud thud.

"I've been gone for ten days, Clare. Don't I deserve a 'Welcome back, partner, how was your trip?'"

"Sorry. I was up at five AM redecorating the upstairs lounge, so I'm all out of enthusiasm. How about a caffeine welcome instead?"

Stifling a yawn, I brought over Matt's usual, one shot with a lemon twist. He drained his cup like a busy Roman, while still standing.

"Thanks, I needed that. I'm just off a red-eye from Kigali. Fifteen hours without a decent drop."

Stripping off his now-dripping windbreaker, he revealed a short-sleeved

Brazilian soccer jersey (which explained why he was freezing). After shaking the snow out of his unruly dark hair, he moved one of our (far too many) empty café tables closer to the fireplace, plopped down in a chair, and rubbed his bare hands near the flames.

I took a seat across from him and waved two fingers at my youngest barista. With a toss of her yellow braids, Nancy Kelly gave me a grinning thumbs-up. She knew what we needed.

"So how was your trip?" I asked. "I hope you found some promising cherries this year."

"Wait till you taste the Burundi!" Matt flashed me a smile, a dazzler of white teeth against his black beard and deep tan. "First shipment arrives next week. The Rwandan's already in our warehouse—and thank goodness you're the one roasting it."

"I appreciate that," I said and truly did.

My ex-husband was one of the most respected coffee brokers in our trade, and he never flattered lightly. He knew how superb Rwandan coffees could be, but they were tricky. Experienced roasters knew how to fire those green beans long enough to develop a rich mouthfeel without letting the cherries turn to charcoal. Like a lot of things in life, getting results came down to the art of nuance—not only knowing when to push, but when to back off.

"Here you go!" With fresh-faced enthusiasm, Nancy served up a demitasse for me and a new one for Matt. "I felt your pain all the way across the room, Mr. Boss, so I made yours a double."

Matt nodded his thanks, took a satisfying hit, and leaned his tanned forearms on the Italian-marble tabletop.

"I'm back early, Clare, yet you don't seem surprised."

"I would have been more surprised if you were a customer."

Matt's tired eyes scanned the coffeehouse floor. "What day is it?"

"Are you really that out of it?"

"My phone ran out of power, and my watch is still on Central Africa Time."

"It's Monday, nine forty AM Eastern."

Matt frowned. "Where's your midmorning rush? This place should be packed, but it's deader than my phone battery."

"The shop is dead every day after nine AM. Even our early-morning business is nothing like the old days. Unless we turn things around soon, I'm afraid the Village Blend will be dead, too."

My unhappy news hit my ex-husband with a force harder than his bulky backpack smacking our polished floorboards.

"You can't be serious!" he cried.

"Lower your voice," I whispered. "You'll upset our baristas."

Matt stared at me. The impact of the word *dead* (in relation to our century-old shop) had produced more than a booming response. A crimson color flushed the man's olive skin.

"This couldn't have come at a worse time," he said. "I took out a million-dollar loan to build our Red Hook roasting facility. It's almost ready to open—"

"Calm down. Our wholesale business is doing fine. We're moving more freshly roasted beans than ever. Restaurants are ordering so much that I can hardly keep up with demand."

"Then what's the problem?"

"Foot traffic. It barely came back after the pandemic. And the disruptions we endured during the location filming in our shop sealed the deal. Midmornings and afternoons are the worst."

"Why didn't I see this coming?"

"Because your focus has been on your coffee-importing business. With all your traveling, you've failed to notice that New York City has changed. People don't pop in and buy a morning cup before they head to the office anymore or drop in during their office lunch break."

"What did they do? Switch to bone broth?"

"They stopped going to the office. Remote work has emptied most of the commercial buildings around us."

Just then, Esther Best, our resident raven-haired slam poet, emerged from our pantry. As she tied an apron around her ample hips, she spotted Matt, pushed up her black-framed glasses, and cried—

"Hey, Mr. Boss! Welcome back from the Mother Continent, birthplace of the magic bean. You look tired. How 'bout an espresso? Mine are supreme!"

Matt smirked at me. "Now *that's* what I call a greeting."

"Esther is just happy to have a *customer*. Like all of us, she's worried. The whole staff is sweating. Nobody wants to be cut loose."

"You know you can't do that. These people are family."

"It's the last thing I want to do. But your mother put both of us in charge of her legacy, and I can't pretend it's not in financial jeopardy. Our place should be packed at this hour, but it's completely empty. You can see for yourself. Not one customer has come through that door."

Then the bell rang and made a liar out of me.

Two

ﾠ⊙ﾠ⊙ﾠ⊙ﾠ⊙ﾠ⊙ﾠ⊙ﾠ⊙ﾠ⊙ﾠ⊙ﾠ⊙ﾠ⊙ﾠ⊙ﾠ⊙ﾠ⊙ﾠ⊙ﾠ⊙ﾠ⊙ﾠ

A SINGLE soul stepped into our shop.

The older gentleman was slight of build with shaggy white hair. Wrapped in a dark green puffer coat that reached down to his knobby knees, he looked like a grandpa elf who'd lost his way to the North Pole.

An old red cap, too small to cover his prominent ears, sat on his head, and a cashmere scarf dangled from his neck. Like a remnant from better days, the elegant, camel-colored scarf looked out of place with the ragged cap, inexpensive puffer coat, and dog-eared spiral notebook tucked under one arm.

When the newcomer spotted Esther's Goth-girl bouffant behind the counter, his pale, blank features visibly brightened. He hailed my zaftig barista with a wave of his worn notebook, and though he was small of stature, his voice was loud and strong.

"Esther, it's a cold autumn day, but seeing you makes me feel like my spring has sprung!"

Esther put her hands on her hips and exclaimed, "Give it to me!"

The man touched his heart with one hand as he replied, "Courtesy of Robert Burns." After clearing his throat, he began to recite—

> *O my Luve is like a red, red rose*
> *That's newly sprung in June;*
> *O my Luve is like the melody*
> *That's sweetly played in tune.*

With a slight blow, he pointed at her in challenge.

Esther put a finger to her round cheek, taking a moment to think. Then her voice boomed—

> *Yo! My love be like a new red tat*
> *Inked in freshest fashion.*
> *Yo, my love be like my slammin' rap*
> *Brash and full of passion!*

Matt leaned across our table. "What's going on?" he whispered.

"It's a game they play every time he comes in. He throws out a classic stanza of poetry, and—"

"Oh, I get it," Matt said. "Esther translates it into urban rap."

"He hasn't stumped her yet. Maybe today's the day . . ."

As Matt and I watched with interest, the elderly man pointed at Esther and recited again—

> *So fair art thou, my bonnie lass,*
> *So deep in luve am I;*
> *And I will luve thee still, my dear,*
> *Till a' the seas gang dry.*

This time, Esther replied immediately—

> *So hot you are, my freaky boy,*
> *For work you made me late;*
> *My twisted heart will beat for you,*
> *Till all gangsta crews go straight.*

The man laughed. "Very good effort, though your meter was off on that last line. One syllable too many."

"It was worth a little freestyle, wasn't it?"

"All right, my dear. I yield. You win again."

Esther grinned wide, her dark eyes sparkling for the old boy as he sidled up to the coffee bar and placed his order.

Matt turned back to me. "So who is this grandpa poet?"

"He's become a regular. Lately, he's the only dependable morning customer we have. Esther calls him Mr. Scrib."

"Scrib? That's an odd name."

"He told her to call him that. He said it was his nickname. The staff thinks it's appropriate because he spends so much time scribbling things in that notebook of his."

"He seems to love Esther."

"Yes, there's a special bond between them. I've seen him walk in and walk out again because Esther wasn't on duty. She's the only one he'll trust with his order."

"Have you tried to engage this oddball in conversation?"

"Don't call him an oddball. He's a sweet man, though I admit he is quirky. And maybe a little paranoid. Tucker thought so, too—"

Tucker Burton was my trusty assistant manager. A part-time actor and downtown director, he'd dealt with plenty of artists who (as he put it) danced to show tunes only they could hear.

"One day when Tucker was working with Esther, he noticed that Mr. Scrib hardly spoke except for that poetry game. Tuck tried to engage him in wordplay, opening with a Shakespearean sonnet."

"How did that go?"

"Mr. Scrib just gave him a dead-eyed stare until poor Tuck slinked away. Nancy once said that if it wasn't for Mr. Scrib's little rituals, he wouldn't have a personality at all."

"What little rituals?"

"Just watch."

As he did most days, Mr. Scrib ordered a large "Coffee of the Day." Instead of simply grabbing a take-out cup, Esther turned to the stack, asking, "What's your special number today, Mr. Scrib?"

He closed one eye, as if calculating. "Let's try number seventeen."

Esther patiently counted down the stack, pulled cup number seventeen, and filled it. Scrib opened his mouth, but Esther was way ahead of him.

"I remember. No lid!"

Mr. Scrib pulled out a wallet and paid with cash. Then, as he did every morning, the old man slowly climbed the spiral staircase to the second-floor lounge.

"There's no one else up there," I whispered to Matt. "But he'll sit, all alone, in our lounge and write in his notebook for hours."

"A freeloader?"

"Oh, no. Mr. Scrib will pony up for a refill every thirty minutes or so, but he refuses a fresh paper cup and insists on using the one he selected. And if Mr. Scrib comes down and finds Esther is gone, he'll leave, too."

Matt raised an eyebrow. "Another Greenwich Village eccentric."

"And this neighborhood was built on them," I reminded him. "Anyway, Mr. Scrib never gives us any trouble. He's respectful, polite, quiet—"

"AAAAAHHHH! NOOOOOO!"

The bloodcurdling howl barreled down from our upstairs lounge in a wall of shocking sound. The shriek of earsplitting terror was so unexpected that Matt and I froze, mouths gaping like sculptures in a haunted icehouse.

That's your quiet customer? Matt's eyes seemed to say.

Once again, the man upstairs made a liar out of me.

THREE

「**D**ID you hear that?" Esther cried, rushing around the counter. "Something's wrong with Mr. Scrib! We have to help him!"

Matt reacted quickly, moving so fast that he nearly collided with Esther at the base of our spiral staircase.

"Look out!" I shouted as an object careened down from above. When it hit the ground floor, I realized it was a take-out coffee. Esther recoiled as the liquid splattered her and Matt.

At the top of the steps, Mr. Scrib was raving. He gripped the wrought iron banister with one white-knuckled hand and hurled something else with the other. Whatever it was landed with a slap somewhere on the floor. Then another object came flying—the vintage metal sign that I'd hung early this morning. It clattered face down on the table beside me.

The three of us watched, paralyzed, as Mr. Scrib screamed, his eyes wide with terror.

"Stay away!" he cried. "I knew you'd come back for me!"

His first coherent words were followed by an agonized groan. Then Mr. Scrib began to descend the spiral staircase. Instead of gripping the railing, the man's arms waved wildly in front of his face, as if he were fending off an attacker.

Though Mr. Scrib's eyes were open, he seemed oblivious to his actual surroundings. Whatever imaginary terror was playing out in his mind, it created a very real danger for him on those stairs.

"He could break his neck!" I cried. "Matt, help him!"

My coffee-hunting ex had dealt with countless dangers around the globe, which is why I called on him while physically pulling Esther back in case the old man fell.

Matt darted up the stairs and intercepted the ranting man just as he lost his balance. As he righted Mr. Scrib, the old man dipped a hand into his coat pocket and whipped something out. I caught a flash of silver—

"Knife! Matt, watch out! He has a knife!"

But I was wrong. The old poet was slashing the air with a silver pen.

"Don't hurt him!" Esther pleaded.

Matt ducked the pen point and grabbed a firm hold of Scrib's skinny flailing arm. The pen clattered down the metal steps.

After that, it was easy. Matt simply grabbed Mr. Scrib by his waist, slung him over one muscular shoulder, and carried the distraught man to the bottom of the stairs. Dropping to his knees, Matt laid Mr. Scrib on the hardwood floor, but kept a firm grip on his shoulders, holding him down.

The old man's arms still waved, but weakly now, and his shouting melted away into mumbled moans. As his energy waned, his fingers curled, as if he were trying to grasp some object visible only to him.

Esther knelt beside the man and touched his cheek. "It's me, Mr. Scrib. It's Esther."

At first, he didn't respond, but she kept talking to him. Miraculously, her voice and her touch calmed him. Scrib's frenzied eye motions ceased, he lowered his arms, and some semblance of sanity seemed to return. Focusing his watery gaze on Esther, he pleaded—

"It's the Kismet. Stay away from the Kismet!"

Kismet? I thought. *What in the world could that mean?*

Finally, Mr. Scrib squeezed his eyes shut. But instead of falling into a merciful unconsciousness, he began to shiver.

"He's going into shock." Matt turned to me. "We need to cover him."

I ran to the back and had Nancy help me bring out a stack of folded aprons.

"I already called 911," Nancy assured us. "They're on the way."

"Good job," I told her, and together we cocooned the man in our Village Blend aprons. Mr. Scrib seemed almost comfortable now, though he looked feverish.

As Esther continued to talk to him, his convulsions slowed. While she remained by his side, whispering verses of poetry, Matt finally released his grip and rose.

"I wonder why he freaked out like that," Nancy whispered. "Maybe he forgot to take his medications."

"What the screaming was about I can't imagine," Matt said. "But I've seen the onset of sudden chills and fever many times—like last year, when I was hunting Kivu cherries along the eastern border of the Congo."

"I doubt it was the same cause," I said.

"Right. Those were cases of cerebral malaria. The quinine that the coffee farmers needed had to be airlifted on a government helicopter. It arrived too late in many cases."

"That's awful, Matt, but I'm guessing Mr. Scrib hasn't visited the tropics lately."

"No, I know." He shook his head. "I'm still orienting myself back to the States."

"Maybe the shivering was just because he was cold," Nancy offered.

The sound of sirens came next. Then a red-and-white FDNY ambulance pulled up to the Village Blend's front door. An NYPD patrol car parked right behind it.

As I took a relieved breath, Matt scooped up the pen and waved it.

"Let's not report this, okay? The poor SOB has enough problems without facing a charge of assault with a deadly writing implement."

Four

〰〰〰〰〰〰〰〰〰〰〰〰〰〰〰〰〰〰〰〰

As police and paramedics filed into the coffeehouse, I pulled Esther away, giving her a hug and reassuring her as the first responders went to work.

Mr. Scrib was not the first customer to suffer a medical episode inside our coffeehouse. But our fondness for the old guy, coupled with his disturbing emotional breakdown, had shaken us all.

So, while my report to the police officers was fairly routine, my feelings about the episode were not. I felt as confused and troubled as Esther and Nancy.

Even Matt, with all his experiences, looked distressed. As the paramedics loaded Mr. Scrib's stretcher onto the ambulance, I touched his shoulder.

"Come to the coffee bar. I'll get you something to eat, and you can recharge your phone."

While Matt sipped a hot cup of my Breakfast blend, devoured two of our fresh-baked Cinnamon-Sugar Doughnut Muffins, and read my copy of the *Times*, I joined Esther and Nancy on the shop floor to clean up.

Leaving Nancy to swab the spilled coffee off the plank floor, I climbed our spiral staircase to rehang the vintage sign that Mr. Scrib had thrown down. Then I roped off the steps. With our dearth of customers, we didn't need to open the space—and after what happened up there with Mr. Scrib, it didn't feel right.

"Hey, look what I found!" Esther called.

For a moment I couldn't see her. Then she popped up from behind a café table.

"It's Mr. Scrib's notebook. He must have thrown it over the railing."

"What should we do with it?" Nancy asked.

"That's easy." Esther held the battered book to her ample breasts. "I'll keep it safe until he returns."

"What has he been working on anyway?" Nancy asked. "He spends so many hours writing. Is it a novel? Poetry? Is he jotting down great philosophical thoughts? I've always wondered, haven't you?"

"He told me it was a true story that would shake up the whole city. A tale of crime and no punishment."

"Crime and *no* punishment?" I asked.

"That's the way he put it—"

"Oh, then we have to see!" Nancy insisted.

Esther started to open the notebook. Then suddenly she hesitated and shut it again.

"I don't know if we have the right to pry," she said. "This notebook might be full of very personal stuff."

"True," I said, "but his real name and phone number might be in there, too. Maybe the name of a friend or next of kin, in case he—"

"All right," Esther said. "Let's take a peek."

Mr. Scrib's notebook was a common type, the kind my daughter, Joy, had used in high school with a spiral binding, brown cover, and the words *500 lined pages* emblazoned on the front. Though the cover was worn and stained, there was no writing on it.

Slowly, with an air of anticipation—or was it dread?—Esther lifted the cover. Seeing the first page, she gasped. Immediately, she turned to the second page and made another distressed sound. Then she flipped through page after page, and an expression of distraught confusion twisted her features.

"What's wrong?" Nancy asked. "What does it say?"

Esther shook her head. "It doesn't say anything!"

Too curious to stand back, Nancy and I moved in close and peered over her shoulder. Both of us were stunned into silence.

"Maybe it's code," Nancy whispered.

"It's not code," Esther said, looking devastated. "It's . . . It's nonsense. Gibberish."

FIVE

~~~~~~

ESTHER'S stunned assessment seemed exactly right. Despite plenty of scrawled words, numbers, and even symbols, nothing appeared to be connected. Almost half the notebook appeared to be jumbled doggerel and random drawings and doodles.

"I can't believe it," Esther murmured. "Mr. Scrib spent hour after hour, day after day, diligently filling this notebook with drivel."

"But why?" Nancy asked. "Could there be a reason for scribbling nonsense?"

Esther closed the notebook. "Nonsense or not, it means something to Mr. Scrib, and I'm going to keep this safe until I can give it back to him . . ."

AN hour later, Matt's phone was recharged, his plate was empty—and he'd seen firsthand how empty our tables remained.

"Would you like another coffee?" I asked.

"No, I should head out." He lowered his voice. "How's Esther doing?"

"She's okay. The paramedics told us Mr. Scrib's vitals were strong, and we're all hoping for the best."

"With luck he'll pull through," Matt said, then forced a smile. "After all, you need all the morning customers you can get."

"So not funny."

"Neither are these empty tables. What has my mother said about all this?"

"I haven't told her yet."

"Do you have an action plan?"

"I'm holding a staff meeting tonight to break the bad news, although I'm pretty sure they know already. Maybe if my baristas and I brainstorm together, we can find a solution."

"I have faith in you, Clare."

"Is that your way of saying this is my problem to solve?"

"My mother made you the manager of her treasured shop for a reason. She knew my strengths—and weaknesses. Unreliable airlines, coffee rust, locating a Rundi translator, those issues I can handle. Reviving a dying customer base?" He shook his head. "No clue."

Matt pulled on his windbreaker and shouldered his backpack.

"I'm heading to the Red Hook warehouse for a crash landing. If you need me, leave a message and I'll get back to you when I regain consciousness."

SIX

Many hours later, the sun sank into the Hudson River, and the polar vortex dropped its unseasonably cold temperatures over the city like a frost giant's blanket. Glacial gusts whipped off the Atlantic and through our West Village streets, turning mounds of plowed snow into curbside blocks of ice.

As I sprinkled our sidewalk with a fresh layer of rock salt, I shivered and nodded at the few pedestrians hurrying to their destinations. Wherever they were going, it wasn't our coffeehouse.

With no customers left inside, I locked our doors for the evening. Then I climbed the spiral staircase to our second-floor lounge, where the hearth was still blazing. Our second floor was more private. I didn't want late-night passersby gawking at tonight's staff meeting through the French doors, especially if our conversation became tense or emotional—which was more than likely.

My crew had put fresh logs on the flames, and seeing their familiar faces in the firelight's warm glow touched something inside me. These talented baristas had worked hard for me and stood by me. They always had my back, and I had done the same for them.

Together, we celebrated good times and struggled through tough times. It had made us more than coworkers. We'd become a family, just as Matt said, and I couldn't bear the idea of letting any one of them go.

For tonight's special meeting, I asked Esther to brew up some late-harvest beans that Matt had sourced in Peru and I had freshly roasted.

Beside the steaming French presses, I laid out a tray of assorted cookies and treats, which my crew had already started nibbling as they openly admired the artwork I'd brought down from our attic this morning—not that I thought changing up the wall art would make a difference to our bottom line. But I routinely refreshed our shop's displays, and I saw no reason to stop.

Of course, after today's "incident," we roped off the second floor, which meant the only other person to see my handiwork was Mr. Scrib. And I never got his opinion (for obvious reasons).

Clapping my hands, I finally called the group together for my straight talk about our financial woes, their future employment, and (with luck) the miracle marketing idea that could solve both. My reasoned managerial speech boiled down to a single sentence—

"We've got to solve this problem fast, or everyone is going to feel the pain."

It was Nancy who jumped up first. With youthful enthusiasm, she flipped back her blond braids and faced our group. "I think loyalty cards could bring in a lot of business."

"Loyalty cards?" Esther looked skeptical.

"Loyalty cards are great because they reward repeat customers," Nancy argued.

"But we need *new* customers," Esther pointed out.

"Yes, and if we show our appreciation, word will get around, and we'll attract new business. Just imagine a Village Blend loyalty card with fancy lettering and our logo on the front. It would be amazing!"

"How do you propose our loyalty cards work?" Esther asked.

"We could give out a card on the first purchase of the week. If the customer makes so many purchases by Friday, they get something free."

"No, no," Esther pressed. "How do they *work*?"

"You would punch a hole in the customer's card—"

"Oh, no." Esther raised her palm. "That can't happen. If I wanted to punch tickets, I would've become a conductor on the Long Island Rail Road. You should see their benefits package!"

"Then we could do it digitally," Nancy insisted. "With a mobile phone app."

Dante paused from devouring his second slice of Double-Chocolate Espresso-Glazed Loaf Cake. A transplant from Rhode Island with an athletic build and razored head, Dante depended on our paycheck to survive in the city as a fine artist. He painted murals on concrete and plywood fences as well as traditional canvas. He had even designed the tattoos on his muscular forearm. And here at the Blend, espresso was his canvas for award-winning latte art.

"Everybody gives out loyalty cards," he said. "If we decide to give them out, we have to do things differently."

Esther folded her arms. "Define differently."

"I can't, and that's the problem with loyalty cards."

"Glad we agree, Baldini," Esther replied. "Because I'm against anything that involves punching tickets."

"Enough with punching down on my hole punch idea!" Nancy cried.

"How about special deals?" Dante suggested. "One for every day of the week. Like that ice cream chain."

"That's good!" Nancy clapped. "We could start with Mocha Monday, Breakfast Blend Tuesday, Flat White Wednesday . . . Then something else that starts with a *T* for Thursday, and for Friday . . ."

As her voice trailed off, she scanned our blank faces. "Come on, coffee peeps. Help me out here!"

Esther groaned. "What's next? Macchiato Monopoly?"

Nancy's eyes lit up. "Wow! I never thought of game tickets—"

"Forget game tickets," Esther said. "Cheap ploys won't work. Premium coffee drinkers are more sophisticated than most consumers—"

"And gimmicks will cheapen the Village Blend brand," Tucker Burton cut in, speaking for the first time.

My lanky, floppy-haired, Louisiana-born assistant manager loved the Village Blend and adored the theater. Since he had performed in dozens of off-off-Broadway shows and directed countless cabarets, his solution was not a surprise.

"We should try entertainment. Maybe a live musician—"

"Like a folk singer?" Nancy said. "A guy or girl with a guitar or banjo?"

"Banjo!" Esther smacked her forehead. "Does this look like the Magic Kingdom's Country Bear Jamboree!"

"Steve Martin plays the banjo!" Nancy pointed out. "And he attracts huge crowds."

"Slow down," Tucker said, waving his hands in the air.

"No banjos!" Esther insisted. "And no stand-up comics. Can you say cancel culture? Hello, stupid joke. Goodbye, Village Blend!"

"That's why I said banjo! You don't need a trigger warning with a banjo!"

"Will you two SHUT IT!" Tucker shouted.

They did.

Then the entire room fell into an awkward silence.

I just knew this discussion was going to get emotional.

Seven

❦❦❦❦❦❦❦❦❦❦❦❦❦❦❦❦❦❦❦❦❦❦❦

"Okay, everyone!" I said in a voice I hadn't used since my adult daughter had playdates. "I think we need a time-out. Let's all calm down and have a cookie."

To my relief, everyone did.

Fortunately, the copious snacking off my cookie tray, and sipping of the freshly roasted Peruvian, relaxed the room's tense vibe.

After munching a few crunchy bites of our Almond Biscotti, Tucker finally resuscitated the strangled discussion—

"When I said musician, I didn't mean for us to go all retro Greenwich Village, à la Bob Dylan and Woody Guthrie. I was thinking more of a pianist."

"Good," Esther said, "because Woody Guthrie is dead!"

"A pianist with a grand piano and a classy tux?" Nancy asked, ignoring Esther. "Or were you thinking more of a Liberace type with a rhinestone Vegas vibe?"

Tucker shrugged. "Just a Billy Joel–type 'Piano Man' sort of player, you know, to liven up the atmosphere. They could take requests. We could even do sing-along nights."

"Like karaoke?" Dante asked, grabbing a Chocolate-Stuffed Peanut Butter Cookie and refilling his coffee cup. "That might be fun."

"Unless the customers who insist on singing can't carry a tune." Esther reached for her third Mocha Blossom Kiss. "A bunch of banshees howling off-key? That'll empty the place for sure."

Nancy spoke up. "If it's quiet entertainment you want, why not hire that mime on Christopher Street? Mimes are quiet and classy."

"What's a mime going to do?" Esther asked. "Moonwalk between the café tables? Pretend to tightrope walk on the coffee bar? That's not going to help business—"

"I think we're missing the biggest issue," Dante interrupted. "There's a lot less foot traffic on the sidewalks nowadays, and if the streets are empty, then there isn't anyone to lure inside."

"The Leonardo of Lattes is right," Esther said. "People go to a *destination*. They may or may not stop somewhere else like a deli or coffee shop along the way, but the destination is key. Their destination used to be the office, their place of work—"

"That's it!" Tuck practically jumped out of his chair. "*We* need to become the destination—"

I could feel a rush of excitement. My staff was finally starting to cook. It only took a single statement from Nancy to deflate us.

"We're a coffeehouse, not the Statue of Liberty. How do we become a destination?"

Everyone fell silent.

Finally, Nancy yelped, "I've got it!"

"Oh, no," Esther groaned.

"Just listen!" Nancy said. "We should be posting social media videos!"

"Of what?" Esther asked.

"Of Dante!"

"Me?" Dante nearly choked on his French-pressed Peruvian. "Videos of me? Doing what exactly?"

"Making lattes. Maybe even with your shirt off. Your latte art wins awards. And you're certified hot! That should attract some IG fans, don't you think?"

"Only the ones who prefer tattoo-armed hottie guys with exceptional latte art skills," Esther pointed out. "What about the ones looking for eye candy of the female kind?"

Nancy blinked. "What do you mean?"

"If you're willing to pimp Dante, then how about we put you in a skimpy outfit with fake eyelashes, six-inch stilettos and have you suck on a coffee stirrer. That should bring in the other half of the Internet."

Nancy looked horrified. "I'm not doing that!"

"Exactly," Esther huffed.

"We do get a social media boost for our holiday specials," I pointed out. "But it's a narrow window. We need something more reliable than a spike from a social media gimmick. We need steady, daily business, and Dante is right about the foot traffic problem."

"It feels insurmountable," Tucker said with a sigh. "What we need is a miracle marketing idea."

"Or a magic wand," Nancy said.

"Magic is right," Dante said and flipped his thumb in the direction of two of the many framed works of art I'd hung on the lounge walls this morning. "Too bad we can't get those two to help."

Nancy frowned at the portraits. "I don't get it, Dante. Who are those old dudes? Magicians?"

"Old dudes?" Esther's hands went to her hips. "They're only two of the most influential writers of the twentieth century."

Nancy folded her arms. "Then I should have heard of them. What did they write?"

"Well, that *dude* wrote *The Lord of the Rings* and *The Hobbit*."

"Oh, wow." Nancy blinked. "I loved those movies!"

"They were adapted from his novels," Esther said.

"I know that!" Nancy said. "I just didn't know what he looked like."

"And the other *dude* was a quirky Oxford don who wrote his manuscripts longhand and had his brother Warnie type them up for him, using two fingers, no less."

Dante nodded. "*The Chronicles of Narnia*. I read them as a kid."

"So did I!" Nancy said, drawing closer to the portraits. "But I don't understand why they're on our wall. Or that bunch of guys—" She pointed to another picture.

"Those are the Inklings," Esther said. "They were a group of writers who met regularly in the back room of an Oxford pub. And those two dudes in the portraits, J. R. R. Tolkien and C. S. Lewis, were the most famous members."

"What about that one?" She pointed to a work of pen-and-ink, done in caricature. "Who are all those people sitting around that big table?"

"Oh, honey," Tucker chimed in. "Even I recognize the Algonquin Round Table, and they weren't just authors. They were journalists, theater critics, composers, playwrights, and actors—that's Robert Benchley, George S. Kaufman, Noël Coward, Harpo Marx, Tallulah Bankhead—"

"And don't leave out the most important member," Esther cut in. "Dorothy Parker, queen of the caustic comeback, and one of my literary heroes."

"What a shocker," Tucker said dryly.

Esther smirked. "'I'm one of the glamorous ladies / At whose beckoning history shook. / But you are a man, and see only my pan, / So I stay home with a book.'"

"And I'll bet you wake up every morning like Dorothy, too. After you brush your teeth, you sharpen your tongue."

"Nice try. But that bon mot came from Oscar Levant, not Dorothy Parker—though it's often attributed to her."

"Hmm," Tucker said. "I guess I stand corrected."

"Even though you're sitting?"

"Fine. I *sit* corrected."

"Which is appropriate," Esther said. "Because when it comes to dodging my wit, you're a sitting duck."

"Keep it up, Acid Annie, and you'll have to duck, because I'll start throwing things."

Here we go again, I thought and was about to suggest we return the discussion to resuscitating our retail when Nancy interrupted.

"What about that one? I don't recognize it. Do any of you?"

She pointed to another item on our wall, a rectangular metal sign covered in azure blue enamel and embossed in white letters that formed three simple words:

WRITER'S BLOCK LOUNGE

EIGHT

~~~~~~

THAT old sign was the start of our solution, and the beginning of big problems. Of course, I didn't know it at the time. The night of our staff meeting, when Nancy asked for help identifying the embossed steel plate, I simply answered—

"It's a vintage sign, Nancy."

Esther stepped up to it. "I don't remember seeing it before. Where did you get it?"

"Upstairs in our attic. It was time to rotate the art on our walls, so I went through our collection, as I usually do. The sign was in a big blue trunk, packed together with all the writers' portraits and the rest of the pieces that I hung up this morning . . ."

It was also the very sign that Mr. Scrib had hurled down the stairs during his heartrending breakdown. But I didn't see any reason to remind Esther of her friend's bad day.

"What is the Writer's Block Lounge exactly?" Esther pressed, examining the antique. "Is it a real place? Or is this sign some kind of archaic meme? A joke someone made for a college dorm?"

"It's no joke," I said. "The Writer's Block Lounge was real. It existed right here at the Village Blend."

"Here? When? How long ago?"

"Several decades, at least. Back when Madame was running the place . . ."

Everyone in the Village knew "Madame" (as we all affectionately called her). French-born Blanche Dreyfus Allegro Dubois wasn't just my employer. She was my mentor as well as my former mother-in-law, long esteemed in the specialty coffee trade—and in Greenwich Village. She'd spent more than half a century caffeinating and caring for the artists, actors, and writers who'd flourished in this bohemian neighborhood, which was how she'd acquired the shop's vast collection of art and artifacts in the first place. Much of it was sketched, painted, donated, or doodled by the talented customers who'd patronized our Village Blend over the decades.

"Tell me more," Esther urged.

"I don't know much more. I remember Madame mentioning that a group of writers once used the Village Blend's second-floor lounge to meet and collaborate."

"Like the Algonquin Round Table?" Nancy asked. "Or those Inklings?"

"Not at those levels, but—well, I guess it was the same idea."

Esther frowned in thought. "So these writers formed the group themselves?"

"I assume so. Madame said they met each other here in the coffeehouse. She also told me she'd never served up so many double espressos."

"Writer's fuel," Esther cracked.

"Writer's *what*?" Nancy asked.

"Writer's fuel," Esther replied. "Definition: noun. A beverage nonwriters refer to as 'coffee.' Often consumed in large quantities to stimulate productivity toward a fast-approaching deadline. Also see: Magic Beans; Hallelujah Juice; Antidotes for Writer's Block. Usage example: 'If it weren't for the *writer's fuel*, my WIP would have been DOA.'"

"Sounds like the writers I know," Dante said. "And the artists."

"And the theater people," Tucker said.

"I think we're onto something . . ." Esther began to pace. "Do you all realize there's a modern version of this writers' lounge concept?"

"Oh?" Tuck leaned forward. "Where?"

"In Tokyo. One of my slam friends, who spent a year in Japan, told me about it. He said they call it a 'Writer's Café,' and the people who work there help customers reach their writing goals."

"How do they do that?" Dante asked.

"They use proctors, and timers, and prompts. Some customers want the help meeting deadlines, and others just prefer a quiet place to concentrate on their work without distractions."

Esther paused. "In fact, I have another friend—well, she's more like a competitor, really. Anyway, procrastination is her middle name, which is unfortunate because she's up for a big slam competition in two weeks."

"Is the problem writer's block?" Tuck asked.

"More like lack of concentration," Esther said. "Lachelle works nights as a bartender, and she can never seem to get enough work done during the day. Too many distractions, she says. I told her about that café in Tokyo, and she said she'd sign up in a heartbeat if the place was local."

"I know someone like her," Tucker said. "Howie's a playwright—or fancies himself one. For now, he works as a Broadway usher. The boy is young and ambitious, but he's been writing the same play for more than a year."

Tuck dropped his voice an octave. "The poor kid is stalled on the third act."

"I know a comic book artist who keeps missing deadlines," Dante said. "He was so late with his last project that he nearly blew a gig with one of the twin giant publishers. They're giving him a second chance, but it looks like he's about to blow that one, too."

"Artist block?" Tuck asked.

Dante shook his shaved head. "Tony earns his rent as an Uber driver. He works nights and has two roommates who do remote work in the afternoon when he's trying to sleep or work on his art. With phones ringing and constant chattering going on a closed door away, he could use privacy and some motivation, too."

"Sounds like they all need a *destination*," Tuck said with a little smile.

"Exactly!" Esther exclaimed. "And that destination should be the Village Blend's new and improved Writer's Block Lounge."

"Interesting," I said.

"Are you sure we can manage it?" Dante asked.

"Sure, I'm sure," Esther said. "In fact, I'm better than sure. I'm positive. You may not know this, but I am great at poking and prodding people."

Nancy rolled her eyes. "You don't say."

"But do you think that's enough?" Dante pressed.

"Poking and prodding is the easy part," Esther said. "This space is comfortable, cozy, and has a great history of inspiring artists—so it's got excellent vibes—"

"And coffee!" Nancy noted.

"You're right," Esther said. "Our coffee drinks are superb, and creative types always need caffeine. But let's think about this, because we can offer so much more—"

"What do you mean by more?" Tuck asked.

"Pastries?" Nancy guessed.

Esther shook her head. "I was thinking more along the line of our own expertise."

"In what?" Nancy asked. "Making latte art?"

Esther ignored her roommate and turned to Tucker. "You have years of acting and directing experience, right? Enough to give good feedback and tips to your Broadway usher friend and others who aspire to write for the stage or screen."

Tuck shrugged. "I guess I do, come to think of it."

Esther pointed at Dante. "Our resident *artista* can handle coaxing and encouraging the budding comic book, manga, and children's picture book illustrators. And I can turn up the heat for writers, poets, and even lyricists who have deadlines."

"That all sounds great," Nancy said. "What do I do?"

Esther rested her hand on her roommate's shoulder. "You have the most important job of all. You, Nancy, will help *caffeinate* them!"

Nancy's head bobbed. "I can do that!"

Esther faced me. "So, what do you think, Ms. Boss?"

Suddenly my staff of baristas was staring at me, waiting for an answer. They understood the decision was mine, that the Village Blend was not a democracy. If it were, I knew by the excited expressions that the vote would be a unanimous "yes." In the end, Esther not only won over her fellow baristas, but she'd also convinced me.

And that night the Village Blend's Writer's Block Lounge was officially reborn.

Nine

~~~~~~

The staff meeting broke up around ten o'clock.

We agreed on a few logistical details, like setting up a proctor station on the second floor, along with shift changes. On the subject of getting the word out, Esther and Tucker were the most vocal.

Esther insisted that "old-school, legacy" advertising would not be necessary. Tucker agreed that posting in the right social media groups, along with word of mouth through their writing and theater communities, would work wonders.

When the news comes through "just the right screens," Esther insisted, that's when viral magic can happen.

Dante agreed and said he'd share the news with the graphic novel community. Nancy nodded enthusiastically and offered the idea of doing Instagram and Facebook posts showing writers at work in our lounge.

"You mean once we actually get some writers up here," Esther cracked.

"Um, yeah," Nancy said. "Or I could record empty chairs and invite people to fill them."

Tucker made a face. "Honey, take it from me, empty theater seats never make a good impression."

I ended the meeting there. The night was turning colder, and I wanted my staff home, safe, and rested for what I hoped would be busy days ahead.

After everyone helped straighten up the future home of the Writer's Block Lounge, I shooed them out the front door. Their excited chattering went with them, bouncing into the cold night and down the shadowy city street. I threw the lock and drew down the shade. When the whole place went dead quiet, I released a bottomless breath.

Could this one crackpot idea really save our shop?

Suddenly, I wasn't so sure, and I was glad to have some time alone to consider my next move.

The calming routine of loading the dishwasher and listening to its rhythmic swishing while I wiped down the marble counter soothed my anxieties. Restacking the clean cups and reordering the pantry seemed to reorder my thoughts, which is why I decided to channel my remaining worries into reviewing our balance sheets.

After putting another log on the fire, pulling a fresh espresso, and grabbing the last of our Chocolate-Dipped Almond Biscotti, I settled in with my laptop near the crackling flames.

Using creative accounting, I'd used our wholesale business profits (from sales of our freshly roasted premium beans to restaurants and caterers) to cover our shop's losses and retail staff's wages. But it wouldn't work much longer. And, given the outcome of our staff meeting, I knew what I had to do.

With a tense inhale, I pulled my phone out of my apron pocket.

It was time to tell Madame. I knew it. I just didn't want to do it.

Now, at least, I could say we had a possible solution to our drop in traffic. I also wanted to learn all I could about the first Writer's Block Lounge. Who better to give advice on how to make it work than the woman who'd managed the original?

At this hour, I wasn't sure she'd pick up. But I dialed anyway . . .

One ring.

Two rings.

By the third, I was starting to feel relieved—

I'll just leave a voicemail message, I decided, *and ask her to drop by in the morning.*

When the ringing stopped, I waited for the recorded message, and—

"Clare! Hello!"

"Madame?" I froze for a moment. "You picked up?"

"Yes, I know. I'm usually snuggled up in bed at this hour, but I'm in my car tonight."

"You're going somewhere?"

"Returning, my dear, from the Pierre."

"Oh, that's right. I forgot about the charity ball. Was it glamorous?"

"The Pierre is always charming and its service superb. I also heard quite a few compliments on the coffee you supplied for the occasion. Exemplary job, my dear. But I'm afraid, overall, the annual Fall Fantastique was a crashing bore."

"That's too bad."

"Far too many tedious speeches, not enough entertainment. Things were much livelier last year when the Gotham Ladies ran the event. We knew enough to put the pizzazz of premier performers onstage *between* the tedious speeches."

"Didn't your friend Babka attend with you? That acerbic wit of hers is usually a good cure for boredom."

"Alas, no." Madame sighed. "She and the other Gotham Ladies opted out this year. But I felt our group should be represented, so I went myself, and I'm glad I did. Near the end of all the dull ball business, the night took an intriguing turn."

"You mean you *met* someone intriguing, don't you?"

"I'd love to dish, but let's do it in person."

"Of course. You must be tired. Tomorrow morning, we can—"

"Morning? Oh, no! The night is young! Are you still in the shop?"

"I just put another log on the fire."

"Perfect. I'll have my driver drop me at the Village Blend. I'll release him for the night and cab it back home—as long as I'm not keeping you from that delightful blue knight of yours . . ."

That "delightful blue knight" as Madame referred to him was my fiancé, Lieutenant Mike Quinn, head of the NYPD's OD Squad.

Mike and I met the very day I'd returned to Manhattan to manage the Village Blend. Madame had persuaded me to come back after my decade-long exile to New Jersey.

Why Jersey? Back then, her son's penchant for extracurricular love-making in practically every country of the world's coffee belt had split us permanently, at least in my mind. (Matt's argument for an "open marriage" never did win me over, though, by his nature, his flirtations would likely never end.) Anyway, as a young single mother, I felt my little daughter would be safer in the suburbs, which is why I'd made the move.

And then Joy grew up.

When she was accepted at a prestigious culinary school here in the city, I accepted Madame's offer to return to her coffeehouse, not only as manager and master roaster, but also as an equity-earning partner and co-inheritor of the business (along with her wayward son).

As for Mike Quinn, the connection between us was immediate and grew to a level neither of us had ever felt before. Given our similar burned backgrounds—of entering our marriages with a sense of sacred commitment and having those commitments casually betrayed—we proceeded with caution. But step by step, the two of us built bonds of trust and love.

Now I couldn't wait to marry the man, and I just knew the wedding we were planning for the spring was going to be beautiful.

Madame was certainly all in. And while it might seem surprising that a former mother-in-law would be happy to see her ex-DIL wed another man, the truth is, she'd been more of a mother to me than the real one who'd left me in my childhood.

Since the day Madame and I met, she'd supported me, encouraged me, mentored me, and scolded me like the mother I'd never had. And like a good mother, what she wanted most for me was to be happy. Still, her affection for Mike wasn't solely based on my feelings.

Over the years, the lieutenant had stuck his neck out for all of us, risking his career so many times to help me, Joy, and everyone at the Blend (even Matt) that Madame already thought of him as family, which is why I wasn't surprised when she wondered where the man was this evening.

"Since you asked," I informed her, "Mike texted me earlier. He's still up the street, at the Sixth Precinct, working with his squad on what he called 'paperwork'—lab results and official reports, most likely. But he should be here soon . . ."

"The poor man is overworked! But I guess I shouldn't be surprised. The stream of illegal pharmaceuticals seems limitless. Heroin. Crack. Fentanyl, and that new narcotic I read about in the *Times*. The one called Tank—"

"Tranq," I corrected. "And you're right. There is always something new, but sadly they always lead to the same tragic result."

I could almost feel Madame shiver through the phone screen.

"What a conversation for a freezing cold night. I'm sure he'll be happy to warm up in your bed—"

"Madame!"

"What, dear? We're all adults here, aren't we?"

"Yes, but we don't have to talk about it."

"It?"

"The fact that Mike and I are on intimate terms."

Madame laughed. "Both you and the lieutenant were married before. You're both passionately in love. Frankly, if you weren't on intimate terms, I'd be worried."

"Well, don't worry. At least, not about *that*."

"Oh?" Madame said, suddenly serious. "What *should* I worry about?"

"We'll talk when you get here."

"I am here, dear. My driver just pulled up."

Ten

~~~~~~

"MADAME! Wow!"

As I held open our shop's front door, my mentor placed her gloved fingers in her chauffeur's proffered hand and exited her sleek black limo with the poise of a duchess.

Swathed in a stunning gown of midnight violet and matching wrap (fittingly silk-screened with a print of Van Gogh's *Café, le soir*), she practically floated over the threshold of our landmark coffeehouse. Her gently wrinkled face greeted me with a warm smile. Then she leaned close to peck my cheek, and I caught a whiff of a sophisticated scent, no doubt imported from Paris.

"You look like royalty," I gushed as her limo drove away. She threw me an impish wink, and I marveled how the rich colors of her floor-length dress brought out the violet of her eyes.

As she moved farther into the shop, her silver pageboy seemed to shimmer in the soft firelight. And when she reached our marble-topped coffee bar, she slid into a seat and slipped off her stunning wrap with the smoothness of a Broadway star joining her party at Sardi's.

Survive everything, Madame once told me, *and do it with style.*

If anyone was a living example of that, she was . . .

Even as a young woman in a more conservative time, Madame knew her own mind—and heart. Although she was raised with a strict upbringing, her love of a passionate, young Italian man gave her the strength to refuse her family's stern directive to wed a wealthy, connected gentleman more than twice her age. Instead, she married Antonio Allegro and gave him a strong, handsome son (Matt, of course). That son and this century-old shop became her pride and joy, and she'd helped her husband run his coffee business until the day of his premature death.

After Antonio died, Madame soldiered on, refusing to sell the Village Blend, even when pressured by unscrupulous competitors. All by herself, she navigated a capricious stream of changing city regulations, shady vendors, and the occasional corrupt inspector. The woman not only survived but thrived, teaching all she'd learned to Matt—and eventually me.

Her air of sophistication was real, primarily due to her aristocratic Gallic roots. Her wealth, however, was mostly show. Her second husband, Pierre Dubois, had been a successful French importer based here in Manhattan. His children inherited most of his fortune, leaving Madame with a Fifth Avenue penthouse near Washington Square Park, as well as an annuity, which allowed her to maintain an upscale lifestyle, but just barely.

Most of her gowns and jewels were remnants of her high times with Pierre, and though she often refreshed her wardrobe and always traveled in style, she was far from wealthy enough to write a blank check where the Village Blend was concerned.

In other words, no bailout was coming. Not from Madame. This shop had to be profitable to survive. I knew it. Matt knew it. And so did his mother . . .

"You're certainly dressed to kill," I told her as I relocked the door and pulled down the shade.

"Well, my dear, given the dreadfully dead atmosphere of tonight's ball, if I had killed someone, it might have livened things up!"

Even at her age, Matt's mother was still a knockout (literally). Her sharp wit and those violet eyes disarmed more than a few of her inamoratos over the years.

As she continued with quips about the disappointing ball, I primed a French press with our freshly roasted Peruvian and set my phone beside it with the timer running.

"Didn't your escort entertain you?" I asked. "Surely, you didn't go without one?"

"I did, and I'm glad of that because I met the most interesting gentleman."

"I knew it! Your night's 'intriguing turn' turned out to be a man."

"Yes, a captain, no less, retired from the United States Navy."

"A sailor?" I raised an eyebrow. "How did you manage that? Fleet Week is months away."

"Trolling for sailors at my age?" Madame arched an eyebrow. "The very idea . . ."

"So how *did* you meet?"

"The captain approached me and introduced himself, right after he bought the Village Blend's Golden Ticket at the charity auction."

"Golden Ticket?" I said. "Back up. What exactly is a Village Blend Golden Ticket?"

"Honestly, it was something I dreamed up at the very last minute. I had agreed to contribute an auction item, and what could be better than an open tab at the Village Blend?"

"Open tab!" I nearly gagged. With our finances so tight, this news wasn't exactly thrilling.

Madame waved her hand. "Don't look so worried. It's nothing, really. For the next twelve months, anything Captain Siebold wants, he gets, gratis."

"In other words, it's a loyalty card on steroids?"

"If you like . . ."

I gritted my teeth. If Nancy heard this conversation, she'd never stop saying *I told you so.*

"Well," I said. "Let's hope he doesn't invite his entire crew."

"If he does, it wouldn't be a large one."

"What do you mean? Don't Navy ships hold hundreds of sailors?"

"Yes, but when I asked Captain Siebold what ship he commanded, he told me he was never in command. He served as a meteorologist aboard the *Enterprise.*"

"Are you making a *Star Trek* joke?"

"I never joke about our men in uniform, especially the dashing ones."

Madame winked again and my phone timer dinged. I pushed the coffee press plunger and served. In silence, my mentor sampled her cup. Then she took a second sip and shared an approving nod, a little gesture that still gave me a big rush of pride. That's when it hit me—

"Hey, wasn't *Enterprise* the name of a NASA space shuttle?"

"Now you're catching on."

"Wait. Do you mean to tell me the 'intriguing' man you met tonight is an astronaut?!"

"He *was* an astronaut. Past tense."

"And a meteorologist? I never knew they needed a weather forecaster aboard a space shuttle."

"I assume he was a mission specialist, dear, on board to study weather from space. Unless, of course, I misunderstood, and his job was to tell the crew *whether* or not to land."

"Touché," I said. "Now when do I meet your astronaut friend?"

"Soon. He says he very much looks forward to visiting the Village Blend—and he spent five thousand dollars for the privilege of doing it all year long."

"He must really love coffee," I said. "Or maybe his generous auction bid was simply a ploy to meet you."

"Oh, bosh."

"Hey, you're the one who dropped in to tell me about your new friend and his Golden Ticket. Sounds like you're interested, too."

Madame silenced me with a raised hand.

"I'm also here to see how your staff meeting went."

"Our staff meeting?"

I stared in surprise at Madame's expectant expression. "How did you know we held a staff—" I caught myself. "You spoke with Matt, didn't you?"

"Indeed, I did."

Eleven

~~~~~~

I DID my best to hide my annoyance, but my spine was already rigid.

When I told Matt about the slow traffic and plunge in revenues, I knew he was upset, but I thought he wanted me to deal with it, including breaking the news to his mother.

Madame patted my hand. "Don't fret, Clare. My son simply mentioned that you had troubling news to convey. He also said that you and your staff are on top of the situation."

"I believe we are now," I said, forcing my jaw to unclench.

"Matt also told me how well you handled an emergency this morning. A customer with a medical issue?"

"More like a mental health issue. And Matt did most of the handling. The rest of us simply kept the poor man comfortable until the ambulance arrived."

"Well, he assured me that you managed everything professionally. He has great faith in you. As do I."

I thanked her and wondered what else Matt had said.

Instead of guessing, I came clean, confessing everything I'd been holding back: the devastating drop in foot traffic, my creative accounting to keep the shop going, and finally my decision to call a staff meeting to brainstorm solutions.

"Esther proposed an idea that could increase our business exponentially, if we can get the word out—"

"Word out?" Madame looked slightly horrified. "Surely you're not suggesting we resort to *advertising*."

"Uh, no . . . Nothing so extreme." I did my best to sound convincing, while keeping the staff's ideas about karaoke and coupons to myself. "Our approach will be smart and dignified, and we have you to thank for the idea as much as Esther."

"Me?"

I explained how I found that old metal sign for the Writer's Block Lounge hidden away in the Village Blend's attic.

"Once Esther saw that sign, she was hooked on bringing the concept into the twenty-first century. She was so enthusiastic that she managed to reel in the rest of us."

Madame frowned—not the reaction I was expecting.

"What's wrong? I thought you'd be happy."

"Are you sure you can manufacture something like that? The original Writer's Block Lounge was organic, not organized by me or the staff. It was created spontaneously among a group of customers."

"But the sign. Didn't you have it made?"

"Not me. One of the members created it as a joke. A play on words. *Writer's Block*—as in a block of writers coming together to help writers who are blocked."

"Well, I think it's worth a try. The staff does, too—"

"But you know how difficult creative people can be," Madame argued. "You just saw that firsthand with all those Hollywood people who filmed here."

"True, but we're not talking about anything like that. The location filming disrupted our business for weeks, limiting our traffic and revenue. This idea would enhance it."

"I don't see how."

"My baristas do. And the same way you have faith in me, I have faith in them. Now tell me, Madame, what do you remember about the original Village Blend writers' group?"

"They had disagreements regularly. Loud ones. There was so much drama in the original group, it eventually fell apart."

"How many members were there?"

"It fluctuated. There were nine or ten regulars. They gathered on the second floor several times a week—until the tragedy."

"Tragedy?"

"There was a death," Madame said and looked away. "After that, the Writer's Block Lounge ended forever."

"What happened?"

"I don't recall the details."

"Really? About a death that broke up a group meeting in your shop. Nothing?"

"It was so long ago—" Her tone was short as she waved her hand. "What does it matter, anyway? It's over and done with. Ancient history."

I got the strongest feeling that it wasn't.

For one thing, Madame was usually a very curious person, especially when it came to unsolved mysteries. Did she really not remember? Or was there a reason she didn't want to?

I could tell pressing her wasn't going to produce any answers. Like with those precious Rwandan cherries in my roasting room, knowing when to turn down the heat was as important as knowing when to apply it. So I shifted my focus . . .

"Do you still know anyone in that original group?"

"One member. She and I hadn't seen each other for decades, but we crossed paths recently on the charity circuit. Actually, I have a chance to see her tomorrow evening. She's one of the honorees at the Wordsmyth Awards Dinner. I was going to pass, but . . ." She paused to think. "This might be an opportunity to call my retired captain back to active duty."

"Ah, so you have an ulterior motive as well."

"You know what they say? Strike while the iron is hot—"

"Not to mention the astronaut."

"Touché, yourself," Madame said. "Oh, all right, I won't deny it. The man is attractive, and we women should go after what we want. Isn't that what I've always told you?"

"Absolutely. If you're going to go, go boldly! See? Now I even sound like a crew member of your captain's *Enterprise*."

"Then it's settled. I'll RSVP for the Wordsmyths in the morning and invite Captain Siebold as my plus-one."

"Yes, order him to do his duty. I'm sure he'll be thrilled to hear from you. And while you're at that awards dinner," I gently pressed, "do me a favor and try to persuade your writer friend to pay us a visit. I know my baristas will appreciate connecting with someone from the old Writer's Block group . . ."

I didn't say it, but I was also curious about the whole tragic death thing. If Madame didn't remember the details of why the group broke up, maybe her writer friend would—

Just then, a sharp electronic buzz rattled the shop and both of us.

Madame looked around. "Is that the night delivery bell?"

"Yes," I said. "But who makes a delivery in a dark alley at midnight?"

"Quite right," Madame said. "Amazon stops delivering at ten, though it could be DoorDash."

"I didn't order from DoorDash!"

"Then who could it possibly be?"

Twelve

~~~~~~

A SECOND frantic buzz rang out, followed by a third. Then silence.

I quickly moved toward the back door and realized that I'd left my phone on the counter.

"Madame," I called over my shoulder. "Grab the—"

"I know what to do," came her firm reply.

I hoped that Madame wouldn't jump the gun and call 911.

"Just keep it ready!" I told her. Though a delivery made no sense at this late hour, it was *possible*.

As I hurried through our back pantry, I considered the crime rate in our city and paused at the door. I wasn't crazy enough to throw the lock and simply open up to goodness knows what. First, I peered through the tiny security peephole.

Outside all was darkness—a good thing because a motion-sensor LED array was mounted above this entrance. If someone was out there, then that light would illuminate the alley and area around the door.

Behind me, Madame's heels clicked lightly as she approached.

"Be ready with that phone," I whispered, still peering through the peephole.

"What phone?"

I turned to find Madame not with my phone, but a baseball bat!

We kept the thing stashed under our coffee bar for emergencies, and I'd forgotten about it. Obviously, Madame hadn't. Now she stood there, resplendent in her formal ball gown, poised to swing like Babe Ruth at home plate.

While it surprised me, I didn't object. After all, a ticked-off octogenarian raising a bat in real time was a better option than a 911 operator asking me to "describe your emergency." And I didn't even know if there was an emergency. Not yet anyway—

"All right," I said. "Get ready!"

Leaving the lock's chain in place, I threw the dead bolt. Now all I had to do was crack the door to activate the motion-sensor lights—except there were no lights. I peered through the crack and spotted the shattered glass on the cold ground.

I was about to slam the door shut when I heard a new sound. The booming thump that our dumpsters made whenever a heavy bag of trash was tossed inside.

Was somebody dumping illegal garbage in our alley?!

The very idea made my blood boil because it exposed our business to hefty fines. I filled my lungs with righteous air and was about to let loose a stream of verbal broadsides to scare away the garbage-dumping jerk when I heard a voice. A man's voice—

"I don't have it! That's why I'm here. That's what I'm looking for!"

The voice was loud, almost shouting, and oddly familiar. I strained to listen for a reply, but if there was one, it was too soft for me to hear. Then the loud voice spoke out again.

"It must be here," the man insisted. "I've got to find it."

Another pause, then—

"NO! It's mine. I would never give it to you! Never!"

His words ended in a choked scream, a fearful, hysterical cry that I finally recognized.

It's Mr. Scrib!

I threw the chain off the steel door and yanked it fully open. An arctic blast instantly smacked me in the face. Light from our shop spilled into the alley, but the darkness quickly absorbed it. I could see my breath rise in curly clouds, but our two dumpsters and beyond were nothing but vague shapes in the gloom.

Suddenly, a strong beam of illumination stabbed through the darkness. Madame found the flashlight!

"Careful, Clare," she warned as she passed the light to me.

"Wait here," I replied.

I was sure Mr. Scrib was still in the alley, maybe deranged and needing help. Maybe even hurt. I listened for his voice but heard nothing—only the traffic on Hudson.

As I approached the first trash bin, the light that seemed so bright a moment ago was suddenly inadequate. So was my attire—a thin cotton sweater, black slacks, and an apron were no protection against the chill. I began to shiver.

When I heard a piteous groan, I directed the beam at the cry and found the man. Mr. Scrib was slumped over, his eyes closed, and his body completely still against one of our two metal dumpsters amid a heap of cups, napkins, lids, newspapers, and shredded plastic bags. On the icy ground I spied blood.

As I approached Mr. Scrib, someone burst out from between the two dumpsters. Startled, I took a step backward. Then someone grabbed my arm and I screamed.

"Clare!" Madame said. "I have the phone!"

"Call an ambulance," I replied, pointing to Mr. Scrib's inert body.

At that moment, a car turned off Hudson Street. Its headlights flashed across the alley, briefly bathing a fast-moving silhouette. I spotted the running figure just before that glare blinded me.

The attacker was fleeing the scene!

I didn't know if Mr. Scrib was unconscious or dead. And if he was dead, then I was the only witness to his murder. But what did I witness? I saw next to nothing to help the police ID the old man's attacker.

Maybe someone else would have been afraid. But I wasn't. The very idea of someone getting away with an assault—maybe even murder—right here in my back alley infuriated me.

And that fury fueled my feet.

THIRTEEN

⊚⊚⊚⊚⊚⊚⊚⊚⊚⊚⊚⊚⊚⊚⊚⊚⊚⊚⊚⊚⊚

MR. Scrib's attacker was too clever to run up or down Hudson, a heavily trafficked and well-lit avenue. Instead, the stranger bolted across the wide intersection and down Leroy, a narrow cobblestone street, leading away from the Village and toward the river.

I could see the figure was wearing a shapeless dark puffer coat with the hood up. *What color? Black? Navy? Dark green?* I couldn't tell—and I was so distracted trying to nail some ID details that I nearly ended up under the wheels of a city sanitation truck.

The driver blew his horn. "Look out, lady! You crazy?!"

I kept going.

Moving out of the treacherous intersection, I dodged mounds of plowed snow and hit Leroy. Unfortunately for me, construction on this block left scaffolding running up and down the narrowed sidewalks.

Scrib's attacker was moving so fast, and the shadows under the endless construction overhang were so deep that I could barely make out more than a silhouette.

Finally, the scaffolding ended, and I could see the figure was still running. Commercial buildings, their windows dark at this late hour, rose on either side of us. Then the solitude of the street was broken by a raucous crowd up ahead.

The laughing, chattering group of college-aged men and women surrounded an unmarked doorway of a newly opened nightclub. The figure I'd been chasing appeared to be heading straight for the mob in front of that club. Fully focused on my target, I followed.

As Scrib's attacker rushed into the cross street, darting in front of a passing car, I could tell the figure was wearing jeans and the color of that bulky coat was black, but the hood was still pulled up, so I still couldn't see a face, hair color, or much else!

As I hurried into the street, my only concern was losing this person in the crowd. If Scrib's attacker peeled off that coat, I would have no way to identify them!

I'd nearly made it to the sidewalk when three things happened in quick succession—

A familiar male voice shouted: "CLARE, WATCH OUT!"

I spied a flash out of the corner of my eye. And when I turned to see what it was, an electric scooter slammed right into me.

The blow to my body was an unhappy shock. The next thing I knew, I was airborne.

Fourteen

~~~~~~

For a few seconds, blackness descended. Not sleep, just a bleak, disconnected darkness. Death without the afterlife.

As the nothingness lifted, the cold seeped in. I felt the hard frozen ground beneath me and heard the traffic sounds around me, along with the voices of strangers—

"Wow! What happened?"

"That scooter hit her and just took off!"

"Is she okay?"

"Clare? Can you hear me?"

Wait. The last voice didn't come from a stranger. Low, steady, and firmly commanding, that one came from a man I knew—and loved.

"People, back up. Give her air."

Opening my eyes, I found myself looking into the worried face of my fiancé. Mike Quinn's arctic blue eyes, usually cop-cool, were now staring at me with open concern. And though the chilly night air barely ruffled the man's trimly cut sandy brown hair, his crow's-feet dug deeper than usual, and his angular jawline appeared rigid with tension.

I could see his tall body folded in half and crouched beside me. I just couldn't make sense of it. *How could Mike be here? How could he have possibly found me so quickly?* Swallowing dry cotton, I rasped—

"Am I delusional?"

Mike responded by pulling off a glove. "How many fingers am I holding up?"

"I don't understand," I croaked. "How did you—"

"Clare, answer me. How many fingers—"

"Three. Press them together and you've got my old Girl Scout salute."

"Do you know your name?"

"Of course. Clare Cosi."

"Do you know who I am?"

"For heaven's sake, I should know my own fiancé. You're Michael Ryan Francis Quinn. And I have a question for you. Did you teleport here? How else could you find me so fast?"

"I was walking to your shop from the Sixth Precinct when I saw you tearing across Hudson. You almost got hit by a sanitation truck, and you kept going. I assumed you had to be running like that for a reason, so I followed, just in time to see a scooter turn you into a hit-and-run victim."

"I'm not a victim. It was my fault. I darted out in front of that scooter—"

"Doesn't matter. The driver should not have left the scene."

"That's true. But I'm all right—"

"No, you're not."

"Yes, I am!" I began to get up.

"Stay down."

"Are you kidding? This ground is freezing!"

"You're shivering," Mike said, looking even more alarmed—and annoyed at himself for not figuring that out sooner.

As I got to my feet, he shrugged off his heavy overcoat. When he draped it around me, the heat of his body came with it. Then he pulled me close, and the bundled warmth felt better than an electric blanket.

"Thanks," I said with a sigh of relief.

Mike's steady blue gaze stayed on me. "Let's get you inside that club. We can wait for the ambulance there."

"I don't need an ambulance. You didn't call one, did you?"

"Not yet, but—"

"No buts. And no ambulance. I got the wind knocked out of me, that's all. Nothing feels broken or sprained. My head is fine—it never struck the pavement. My arm hurts from what feels like a bad scrape, but that's the worst of it."

"You should still be checked out."

"Then walk me back to the Village Blend. The paramedics should be there by now."

"Paramedics? Why?"

"I asked Madame to call 911. That's the reason I was running. I was chasing someone who attacked a customer in our alley. And, no, I'm not crazy. I had no intention of confronting the person. I only wanted to ID them for the police."

Mike nodded, finally understanding. "All right, okay. Then we'll deal with your runaway perp and that hit-and-run scooter driver later. Right now, let's get you home."

I didn't argue, though I did give one last, long look at the street.

By now, the crowd of curious onlookers had melted back to the entrance of the club, and Scrib's attacker in the black hooded puffer coat was nowhere to be seen.

Fifteen

⊶⊶⊶⊶⊶⊶⊶⊶⊶⊶⊶⊶⊶⊶⊶⊶⊶⊶⊶⊶⊶⊶⊶⊶

AMBER flashes strobed the intersection as Mike and I crossed Hudson and approached the Village Blend. Several police and emergency vehicles were on the scene. As we drew closer, we saw paramedics load Mr. Scrib into an ambulance, slam the doors, and speed off screaming into the night. One of the two police cruisers left with the ambulance.

That alone was good news. If Mr. Scrib had been killed, the medical examiner would have been contacted to handle the situation. Instead, he was on his way to a hospital, where I hoped he would recover.

Though Mr. Scrib was gone, the area was still active. Headlights from the remaining police car and a second EMS truck bleached our back alley white. In that harsh glare, I could see uniformed officers were still mingling with a few EMTs.

"Let's get you inside," Mike said, pulling me toward the Blend's front door.

On the walk here, I was glad to be inside the cocoon of Mike's overcoat. Every step of the way, he kept his arm wrapped around me, pulling me close to his body for warmth. But now I needed to pull away.

"Let's go to the alley," I said. "I want to find out what happened to Mr. Scrib."

Mike went along with my request, though I quickly discovered that he had an ulterior motive. As soon as we arrived, he greeted the two remaining uniformed officers, both longtime customers of the Village Blend. Then Mike turned to a young emergency medical technician, flashed his shield, introduced himself, and surprised me by saying—

"My fiancée here was just struck by a hit-and-run scooter. Can you check her for a concussion?"

"Sure, Lieutenant," she replied.

"Honestly, I didn't hit my head," I told her. "I'm fine except for a scraped arm."

But my wounded wing was ignored. Instead, the woman asked me to sit down inside the back door of her EMS truck and I was blinded by a sudden flashlight beam.

"Hey!"

"Hitting your head isn't the only way to get a concussion," the EMT informed me. "A violent shake can do it, too . . ."

She asked me more questions, checked out a few more things, and said—

"There's no sign of a concussion, ma'am. But if you develop a head-ache or a feeling of pressure in the head, experience any nausea, have bal-ance problems, dizziness, blurry vision, or confusion, get to an ER and ask for a CT scan."

"Thank you," Mike said from behind her.

She turned to him. "Watch her tonight. Try to keep her awake for the next few hours to monitor her symptoms. No alcohol. And no aspirin or ibuprofen for pain. Acetaminophen only. You got Tylenol?"

"Got it," Mike said.

I read the woman's name tag—*Alvarez, M*, followed by a whole bunch of numbers.

"Ms. Alvarez, my head is fine," I assured her. "It's my arm that got slammed against the concrete. But it doesn't even hurt that much anymore."

"Let me look." She slipped Mike's coat off my shoulder.

After examining my forearm, she made a tsk-tsk sound. Then she slapped on a pair of latex gloves, pulled a sprayer and some swabs out of a first aid kit, and began to treat the scrape.

While she was getting me fixed up, I realized this was an opportunity to get some questions answered.

"If you don't mind, Ms. Alvarez, can you tell *Lieutenant Quinn* and me how Mr. Scrib is doing?"

I took a chance, emphasizing Mike's name, and hoping she'd be more willing to release personal information if an NYPD officer was involved in the asking.

For a moment, she hesitated. Then she glanced at Mike and replied—
"Scrib? You mean the man who was just taken out of here?"

"Sorry, it's a nickname," I said. "He's a regular customer of ours. I consider him a friend, though I never knew his real name."

"He didn't have a driver's license, or even a wallet," she said. "But he wore a hospital wristband, so we IDed him with that—"

I held my breath as she pulled a very large phone from her pocket and danced her fingers across the screen.

"His name is Van Dyne," she announced. "Jensen Van Dyne."

My gamble paid off.

Sixteen

∿∿∿∿∿∿∿∿∿∿∿∿∿∿∿∿∿∿

Finally knowing this mystery man's real name would be a huge help in finding out more about him. But there was one thing that didn't make sense to me. I addressed Ms. Alvarez again—

"If he was still wearing a hospital wristband, why wasn't he *in* the hospital? Did he escape?"

"Escape?" She laughed. "He probably just signed himself out and didn't bother to take off the band."

"He signed himself out?" I said. "Is that even possible after a complete mental meltdown?"

"It is," Mike interrupted. "Only a judge can order detention at a psych unit. It usually happens when that person is charged with a crime or becomes a danger to themselves or others."

"If you want to know more about Mr. Van Dyne and his condition," Ms. Alvarez said, "you should talk to my partner. He helped the crew in the other ambulance perform triage."

She pointed to the dumpster where Mr. Scrib was attacked. Two uniformed officers and a paramedic were chatting. Even from this distance the splash of blood staining the side of the dumpster was visible in the stark glaring light.

"I'll talk with the paramedic for you," Mike told me. "You stay here and get that arm bandaged."

I watched the group's demeanor switch from informal to all business as Lieutenant Quinn approached. One of the uniforms touched the bill of his cap. Quinn nodded back.

As he buttonholed the paramedic, the two officers departed. They were already heading for their squad car.

"Where are you going?" I called. "Don't you want my statement?"

The officers approached me, and I explained why I wasn't on the scene when they arrived.

"I heard the argument in the back alley before Mr. Scrib was attacked. Then I chased his attacker . . ."

Officers Langley and Demetrios took down my full statement and description of the perp (as limited as it was), thanked me, and were about to depart when I pressed—

"There will be an investigation, won't there? I'm sure I can help the detectives who are assigned."

"That's not our call," Demetrios replied, glancing away.

"Honestly, Ms. Cosi," Langley said in a kind of verbal cop shrug, "the poor guy was probably looking for food or a warm place to sleep when another homeless guy attacked him. We see it all the time . . ."

Langley's attitude didn't surprise me. In a big, bad city like New York, a simple assault on a man like Mr. Scrib could very well fall into a departmental black hole. The officers knew that. I knew it, too. But I also believed this wasn't as simple or random an assault as they assumed it was.

"Listen," I said, "Mr. Scrib . . . I mean Mr. Van Dyne isn't homeless. At least, I don't think he is, and I'm sure he wasn't scrounging for food."

Demetrios shook his head. "Sorry to disagree, Ms. Cosi, but someone ripped into those trash bags, whether it was your friend or the man who attacked him. You can see for yourself. There's garbage all over the place."

"Mr. Scrib left some property here," I explained. "I believe that's what he came back looking for."

"And what would that property be?" Langley asked. "Must be pretty valuable."

"It's a notebook," I said.

Demetrios glanced skeptically at his partner. "A notebook?"

"Not much value in a notebook, Ms. Cosi," Langley informed me, as if I needed advice on what not to take to an *Antiques Roadshow*.

"I realize a notebook in itself has little value," I said, "but it was important to him. And I think—"

"All finished," Ms. Alvarez declared.

I'd almost forgotten about my injury. While I was speaking with the officer, the earnest EMT had mummified my arm with gauze from wrist to elbow.

"You have some nasty scrapes," she announced. "Nothing deep, but you've got to keep the area clean to prevent infection."

I thanked her, assured her I'd take care of it, and turned back to the officers. Both were already gone, and in an awful hurry. The pair either had another call—or wanted one. The police cruiser was already backing out of the alleyway. As it drove off, it took half the light with it.

Meanwhile, Mike was still chatting up the paramedic.

I was about to join them when I spied something even more worrisome— Madame's silhouette, framed by the light of the open back door. Heedless of the cold and the shattered light at her feet, she stared into the alley. Black blood stained her beautiful gown. She didn't even acknowledge my presence until I touched her arm.

"Madame, are you okay?"

Her focus returned. "I'm fine, Clare. But when I tried to help that poor man, I saw his blood on the ground and the dumpster—"

"Mike is speaking with one of the paramedics now—"

Madame waved me off. "That's not what I mean. When I saw that blood, I *remembered* something. Something important. Something you must know if you're determined to go through with your plan."

"Plan? What plan?"

"To restart the Writer's Block Lounge."

"I don't understand."

"You will."

"All right, then," I said. "Let's go inside and talk."

Seventeen

~~~~~~~~~~~~~~~~~~~~~~~~~~~~~~~~~~~~

Fifteen minutes later, the police and medical technicians were gone, and the alley behind the Village Blend was dark and quiet once more. Outside our wall of French doors, the frigid Manhattan streets looked all but deserted.

At a table near the hearth, Mike stoked the fire, and I set down fresh cups of hot coffee for all three of us along with a plate of Vanilla and Praline Sablés. Our baker made these tender, buttery cookies for our pastry case from Madame's own recipe. During my pregnancy, she'd baked up dozens of batches to comfort me, and they still conjured up happy memories for us both.

When she saw the sablés, Madame gave me a weak smile. But, as we nibbled the sugar-crusted rounds, she began to share a story from her past that was far less sweet . . .

"It happened so long ago," Madame told us. "I don't remember many of the details. Some things I never knew. But the original Writer's Block Lounge ended in tragedy—"

"You said there was a death," I prompted.

"Yes, Clare. And I turned a blind eye to it . . ."

Madame released a deep sigh of regret. Then she took a long sip from her coffee cup and closed her eyes, as if my rich brew were giving her a warm hug. Seeing the distressed look on her face, I felt like giving her a real one.

"I'm sure you're being too hard on yourself," I said softly.

Her eyelids snapped open. "I know you mean well, Clare, but I'm sure I'm not."

An uneasy silence followed her sharp words, until Mike gently said, "It sounds like what you need, Madame, is to process these events, whatever they were. Try to make sense of them. We're here for you. We're listening. Why don't you start at the beginning?"

I knew Mike Quinn had great affection and respect for my former mother-in-law, but his years of honing that "you can trust me" interview-room purr didn't hurt, either.

Madame was no pushover, but even she melted into the pools of his concerned blue eyes. With a nod, she patted his hand, and resumed her confession—

"As I told you before, the group formed spontaneously. They first met each other in our coffeehouse. Most of them worked low-paying part-time jobs while they struggled to achieve their dreams. I was happy to serve them . . ."

I didn't doubt it. For decades, the Village Blend had been a safe place for artists and performers to gather. Madame had staunchly believed in that mission. It didn't matter to her whether they were successful, struggling, impoverished, or intoxicated. She mothered and protected them all with hot pots of French roast, delicious food, encouraging words, and (when some needed it) a place to crash.

"After the Writer's Block members formed their group," she went on, "they got together regularly to toss around ideas and critique one another's work. Their gatherings became so boisterous that I asked them to meet in our upstairs lounge to avoid disturbing my other customers."

Mike raised an eyebrow. "Define *boisterous*."

"Nothing sinister, Lieutenant. They were simply young, enthusiastic—and loud. When things were going well, they laughed and joked and talked over one another."

"And when things weren't going well?" Mike asked.

"Each member had strong opinions. Sometimes, those opinions clashed."

I spoke up. "You mentioned being invited to an awards dinner where one of these writers is being honored. Is that right?"

"Yes, Addy's receiving an award for supporting literacy programs."

"Addy?"

"A. F. Babcock."

"You're *friends* with Addison Ford Babcock? She's one of my favorite authors! When I was raising Joy alone in New Jersey, I tore through her *New Amsterdam* novels."

"That's nice, dear, but I'm not bosom buddies with the woman. We're only passing acquaintances."

"But you knew her for so many years?"

Madame shook her head. "Addy and I only recently reconnected at a charity event. She claimed to have fond memories of the Village Blend, but when I tried to reminisce, she didn't recall much. Never fear, however. I shall try to engage her on the subject tomorrow night."

"That doesn't sound promising. Is there no one else?"

Again, Madame shook her head. "I knew most of them only on a first-name basis, and to be honest, I've forgotten the rest, except one—the very one who recently returned to our shop."

"Do you mean . . . ?"

"I barely remember him as a young man, but I do recall the distinctive name of one member. It was Jensen—"

"Jensen!" I broke in. "That's Mr. Scrib's real name, Jensen Van Dyne."

"Yes, Clare. Mr. Scrib was indeed an original member of the Writer's Block Lounge all those years ago. When I gave my statement to the officers and heard his name, my memories began to return. Seeing the blood on the ground and on the dumpster, well, that jarred my memory even more."

She lowered her eyes. "They stirred up other emotions as well."

"Go on," I urged.

"That's the trouble. I can't go much further. My memories returned, but I never did know much about what happened in the first place, so some of what I share may simply be speculation—"

"Just talk," Mike counseled with an easygoing shrug. "You might be surprised at how many details you can recall just by talking."

Madame took a breath.

"I remember there were arguments, lots of them, sometimes very heated. There were jealousies and romantic entanglements. One night, a young woman from the group fled the coffeehouse in tears and never returned."

"Do you remember why?"

"They kept their private business among themselves, but the cause was most likely, you know . . ." She waved her manicured hand. "*Mauvais roman.*"

"Bad romance," I translated for Mike.

"Over time, the bigger group whittled itself down to a core of regulars. And as the group got smaller, it became more intense, more focused, less boisterous. They continued to meet upstairs, and I relegated the task of serving them to my best barista at the time, which meant I had less and less to do with the group. At that point, the membership was down to maybe half a dozen. A small, mixed group of people . . ."

She paused to sip her coffee, taking her time before setting the cup back on its saucer. Mike calmly waited, exchanging a little warning glance with me. *Be patient,* he seemed to be saying. *Give her the time she needs.*

"One evening," Madame finally continued, "the last evening they met in our lounge, they threw a celebratory party of some kind. Someone had a breakthrough success. There was a cake. And they added spirits to the coffee we served them—they often did that."

"So they were drinking," Mike noted. "What happened next?"

"There was an argument that escalated to a physical altercation between a few of the people in the group—"

"Inside the shop?" Mike asked.

"Outside, in the alley," Madame said. "I wouldn't have known about it except that night I emptied the trash while my baristas were busy with customers and discovered the blood on the dumpster and on the ground."

Mike leaned across the table. "How much blood are we talking about?"

"There seemed to be a lot of it."

"Did you find out what happened?" Mike gently pressed.

"The barista who served them told me that two of the men had taken their fight down the back stairs and outside, and more from the group joined them. He swore the scuffle ended with two people getting a bloody nose, and then everyone went their separate ways. After that, none of them came back."

Mike nodded slowly. "You know, drunken fights were a dime a dozen in the old Village. What you're describing sounds like a typical Saturday night back then."

"It does. Except for one thing. Several weeks later, the authorities made a discovery. Human remains in an empty lot in Brooklyn. The victim had been killed elsewhere, moved to that spot, and covered with discarded furniture and loose debris. The timeline of the death put it around the same night as that scuffle in my alley."

I leaned forward. "And who was this person they found?"

"I can't recall the young man's name, Clare, but I remember he was an actor. That's why the *New York Post* ran the headline *Curtain Call on Columbia Street*. I also remember the police came to question me."

"Why?"

"Because that murdered young man was a member of the Village Blend's Writer's Block Lounge."

Eighteen

~~~~~~

An hour later I was upstairs with a wide-awake Mike.

After finishing our discussion with Madame, he and I made certain she got home safely. Then I locked the shop up tight, set the security alarm, and together we climbed the service stairs to my duplex.

That's when Mike seemed determined to start a fire in my bedroom. No, not *that* kind of fire. I was far too exhausted for any sort of physical intimacy. Mike's fire was literal—at first, anyway.

After kindling a blaze in the bedroom hearth, he helped me undress. Because of my bandaged arm, I was glad to have assistance getting into my favorite nightshirt. The familiar softness of the garment against my skin, the luxurious warmth of the crackling hearth, and the quilt Mike tenderly wrapped around me opened the door to dreamland.

Mike slammed it shut.

"I've never seen Madame so upset," he said, loud enough to startle me.

I opened my eyes and realized time had passed. Mike had shed his jacket and tie. His service weapon and shoulder holster hung over the back of an antique chair.

"Of course she's upset," I said, still stretched out on the four-poster. "She feels guilty, and somewhat responsible, that a killer got away with murder on her own coffeehouse property all those years ago."

Mike sat down on the edge of the bed with a glass of water in one hand and two pills in the other. "Here, take these."

"What are they?" I asked through a yawn.

"Tylenol. Remember what EMT Alvarez advised?"

"Mike, I don't have any symptoms. No headache, no nausea, no confusion—"

"Staying up a little longer won't kill you."

"No, it will just make me *feel* like someone killed me."

"And taking painkillers will help that poor arm of yours."

I flapped my bandaged wing. "It's not impoverished. Just mummified."

"If you take the pills, I'll let you sleep."

"Deal." I propped myself up, choked down the pills with a sip of water, and flopped back on the pillows. "Crap!"

"What is it?"

"I squashed my banged-up arm."

"Aw, honey."

"I'll live."

"See? Aren't you glad you took the painkillers?"

"I'm going to kill *you* if you keep talking."

"There's not much more to talk about." Mike finished the water and set the glass on the nightstand. "She was obviously overwrought—"

"She?" I echoed. "Wait. Are you still talking about Madame?"

"I am. Tonight's assault in your alley agitated her. Threw her back to a time when she blamed herself for something that was beyond her control. But I think that's all there is to it. Now that her confession about her long-standing feelings of guilt is out of her system, she should feel better."

"Back up. You don't think what Madame told us tonight about the past has any relevance to the present? That a killer, who murdered a young actor in our back alley, was never brought to justice—and could still be walking around this city, free as a bird?"

"Everything she recounted happened long ago, Clare, and she could be conflating or misinterpreting events—"

"Is that cop speak?"

"It's basic psychology."

"Are you baiting me, Lieutenant?"

Mike folded his arms. And I got the distinct impression that he was trying to prevent me from sleeping by starting a verbal firefight.

"Okay," I said. "Since you seem determined to keep me awake because of some overzealous medical advice, then fine. Let's talk."

Nineteen

∂ᗢ∂ᗢ∂ᗢ∂ᗢ∂ᗢ∂ᗢ∂ᗢ∂ᗢ∂ᗢ∂ᗢ∂ᗢ∂ᗢ∂ᗢ∂ᗢ∂ᗢ∂ᗢ

I sat up in bed, adjusted my twisted nightshirt, and hit Mike with the physical evidence—

"What about all the *blood* that Madame saw in the alley on the night of the writers' fight? How exactly could she be 'misinterpreting' that?"

Mike shrugged. "A smashed nose bleeds a lot. As a patrol officer, I was in brawls that looked like Iwo Jima when they were over."

"And what about the body that was found in a vacant lot? And the follow-up by the police who came to the coffeehouse to question Madame?"

"I have no doubt that she was questioned by detectives," he conceded. "It's standard procedure. The dead man was a member of a writers' group that met regularly in her café. Detectives would have pursued any leads they could, including gathering background on the man's routines. And since weeks went by before the body was found, well . . ."

"Well, what?"

Mike rubbed his square chin, now darkened with stubble. "Madame's memory about the victim's estimated time of death—or what she was *told* about it—could have been off. I mean, her own barista claimed that what took place in the alley that night was just a scuffle."

"Unless he was lying," I said.

"Why would he do that?"

"To protect her."

"Is that likely?"

"I don't know," I said. "I admit there was some conjecture on her part—"

"Exactly," Mike cut in, "and don't forget where the victim was found. She recalled that newspaper headline word for word."

"*Curtain Call on Columbia Street*," I recited.

Before Madame had gone home, I was able to use that headline to locate that story in the digital news archives. But it was basically just a police blotter report with no more information than Madame had given us. The name of the actor was withheld, pending notification of his next of kin. I found no other stories, and Madame said the murder remained unsolved.

Given the headline, Mike now told me that he wasn't surprised by this—

"Curtain call," he said, "was a reference to the fact that the young male victim was a working actor. *Irrelevant*. Columbia Street, on the other hand. Now that is highly relevant."

"Why?"

"Because Columbia Street is in Red Hook, Brooklyn, and back then the area was a mob dumping ground."

"Oh, come on." I waved my good arm. "You're telling me the murder victim—a Greenwich Village actor and aspiring writer—was involved with the Brooklyn mob? Does that even make sense?"

Mike arched an eyebrow. "You see? You're making my argument for me. It's highly possible, maybe even probable, that the blood in the alley and the murder aren't connected at all. It's more likely that all Madame saw on the night of this writers' group kerfuffle was the result of two bloody noses."

I released an uneasy breath. "You really think there's nothing worth pursuing?"

"I think your Mr. Scrib's connection to the past brought that ugliness up for her again, and her feelings of misplaced guilt overwhelmed her. Madame might feel differently after a good night's sleep . . . Now, do me a favor and move closer . . ." He waved me to the edge of the bed. "That's good. Turn a little . . ."

After adjusting my position, he began to rub my shoulders. I didn't realize how much tension was still in my body. I closed my eyes and moaned. Mike's warm hands and gentle massage felt heaven-sent.

"You *could* be right," I murmured. "When she called to tell us that she got home safely, she did sound better. She even apologized for snapping at me, which wasn't necessary, though her shortness did surprise me. She's rarely like that."

"Bad memories can torture a person. So can feelings of guilt about the past."

"Oh, Mike, I know that. And I wish I could help put her mind at ease. She's done so much for me over the years . . ."

"Believe me, I understand what she means to you."

"Then you should know how I feel. I can never repay her for all she's done, but I can at least try to find some answers for her. These questions about what happened in that writers' group have gnawed at her for years. She prided herself on protecting her Village community, giving her vulnerable customers a place where they could feel safe. If only I could help her understand what really happened that night in her back alley . . . and maybe relieve those awful, nagging feelings that she could have done something to prevent a murder—or, if not prevent it, at least bring the killer to justice . . ."

"But you can't," Mike said.

Those two words straightened my spine.

YOU CAN'T.

I loved Mike, and I knew he meant well, but all my life, I'd resisted those words. I'd taught my daughter to resist them, too, which is why my response was physically automatic. I tensed under my fiancé's massaging hands. I knew he felt it because I hadn't said a thing, yet he reacted as if I had.

"Look, Clare," he tried again, "I'm just being a realist. The best thing you can do in this situation is focus on what happened tonight, not something that may or may not have happened decades ago. The here and now is what matters."

"Okay, then. *Now* I'd like you to tell me more about Mr. Scrib's injuries. You talked to that paramedic. I know you wanted to spare Madame the gruesome details, but you can tell me."

"The old guy got knocked around a bit, which is serious for a man of his age. He had a bloodied nose and a laceration on his scalp. That's where most of the blood came from—"

"Was he slammed against the dumpster? I think I heard that."

"You probably heard right. Your friend then either fell or was pushed to the ground. Somewhere in there, he hit his head."

"No wonder Madame was shaken up."

"You got shaken up as well." Mike gently touched my bandaged arm and pressed his lips to my neck.

"I was so angry at what happened. And then felt so frustrated. If I'd only gone outside a few moments earlier, maybe I could have stopped the assault or—"

"You did all you could and more. One of my instructors back at the academy would have awarded you the Diogenes the Cynic Honest Citizen Award, if there was such a thing."

"I doubt Diogenes would have been impressed. In fact, I probably would have reinforced his cynicism. All I did was get run over."

"You provided the uniforms with a statement, a description, and a path to track the perp by camera, if it comes to that. And it may not. The paramedic said the victim's vitals were still strong. Your Mr. Scrib could regain consciousness as soon as tomorrow morning. Then his testimony should fill in all the blanks on his attacker. He may even give us a name and address."

"I hope so."

"We'll check on him in the A.M., okay? Try to stay positive . . ." Mike glanced at his watch. "Okay. Time's up. You're clear for bed."

A microsecond later, my head hit the pillow.

"Finally," I muttered, "rest for the weary."

"You earned it," he said as he unbuttoned his dress shirt. "Sweet dreams, sweetheart."

As my eyelids drifted closed, a smile of affection crossed his tired face. Before drifting off, I returned it—and that's what the sweetest dreams were made of.

Twenty

〰〰〰〰〰〰〰〰〰〰〰〰〰〰〰〰

MORNING came far too early, but there was no sleeping in. I had two of the most reliable alarm clocks in the world to wake me. One was chewing on my hair; the other was kneading my stomach.

I rolled out of bed, taking care to protect my bandaged arm, and led Java and Frothy to the kitchen before their feline antics woke Mike.

Blinking away the last shreds of grogginess, I dished up their favorite food. They purred their approval of my breakfast selection, and my heart warmed a little. Then their two tails—one coffee-colored, the other white as milk foam—swished like those balloon clowns in front of a used car lot, and I stifled a laugh.

I would have liked to linger, brew a pot of coffee, and check headlines on my phone, but duty called.

I showered, dressed, and gasped at the time. The bakery delivery was nearly due, and I was running late; but, before heading down to the coffeehouse, I stopped to give my sleeping fiancé a quick good-morning kiss.

Mike's sandy hair was mussed, his angular jawline was dark with stubble, and his nose flared with a slight snore. Sleeping beauty he wasn't. But I couldn't have loved him more.

Bending over the mound of his big, snoozing form, I pressed my lips to his cactus cheek.

"Mmm . . . that's nice," Mike murmured, his deep voice still raspy from sleep.

"Sorry," I said. "I didn't mean to wake you."

"Come here . . ."

Mike's strong arms pulled me closer, and when he deepened our kiss, it went completely through me. I could tell he felt that, too. With a moan of regret, I broke it off—

"I have to go," I whispered.

"I know." He touched my cheek. "You need help with your bandages?"

"No, I've already cleaned and redressed my arm, and my long sleeves will cover it for the day."

"You can't take the day off?"

"Because of a few scrapes and scratches? Oh, please. Go back to sleep, Lieutenant. I'll be up later with some fresh, hot coffee—and something sweet."

Mike lifted an eyebrow. "That sounds promising."

"You know I'm talking about *pastries*."

"We'll see." Mike began to smile, until he caught my shift in mood. "What's wrong?"

"I have to tell Esther. You know, about what happened last night to Mr. Scrib—that is, Mr. Van Dyne."

Mike propped himself up. "Why?"

"What do you mean why? She cares about him, and I don't want to keep the truth from her."

"I know you don't, but . . . you might consider delaying it."

"What do you mean?"

Mike rubbed his eyes. "Van Dyne's vitals were strong when they took him to the hospital. He may have recovered overnight. And you'll have worried Esther for no reason."

"I'll consider it."

"Whatever you think, Clare. But I'll be down later with news, good or bad. If you like, we can speak with her together. Okay?"

Feeling relieved, at least for the moment, I nodded—

"Okay."

Twenty-one

～～～～～～～～～～～～～～～～～～～～～～～～～

WHEN I entered the coffeehouse, I was surprised by a text message from Dante Silva, asking me to unlock the front door. I raised the door shade and found my barista waving at me, his breath clouding the glass.

Standing beside him was a compact young man wearing a cobalt blue hoodie under a gray vest that looked like a patchwork of pockets sewn together, each one holding something different—pens, pads, a flashlight, an iPod, and three different phones.

"Come on in before you freeze." I waved them inside and relocked the door. "Why are you here, Dante? Your shift doesn't start until this afternoon."

Dante pointed to his companion. "Tony just got off work and I wanted to introduce him. He drives for Uber by night, and he's been struggling with writing his graphic novel by day. His roommates are always bugging him, which is why he'd like to try our new Writer's Block Lounge."

The young man tugged off his hood to reveal short black hair, spiked on the top and buzz-cut on the sides into an expert fade. His deep dark eyes were smiling behind wire-rimmed glasses.

"Tony Tanaka," he said, extending one chilly bare hand—the other remained in his blue hoodie's snug pocket.

"Happy you're joining us, Tony," I said. "I've seen you here before, haven't I?"

As Tony rubbed his cold hands together, Dante replied for him—

"Tony usually drops in on my night shift, whenever he's taking a break from driving."

"I drove by late last night," Tony said. "I saw the lights in the alley, and an ambulance. Was someone hurt?"

"There was an assault after we closed," I said. "A man was taken to the hospital. Why do you ask? Did you see anything that could help the police?"

For a second, I was hopeful, but Tony quickly shook his head.

"No, Ms. Cosi. It was over by the time I got there."

"Oh, I see." I checked my watch. "So why are you gentlemen here this early?"

Once again, Dante answered. "Tony would like to take a picture of that print you took down when you decorated the second floor."

"The Lynn Bogue Hunt?"

"No, Boss. Not the bird print. The one with all the flags."

"Childe Hassam's *The Avenue in the Rain*."

"That's the one," Tony said. "I should have shot it before now, but I didn't know you were going to take it down."

"You must admire Hassam's work."

"Sure, that's why I'm going to crib his style for a splash page in the graphic novel I'm working on." Tony shrugged. "Storytelling is a struggle for me, but the illustration, *that's* my favorite part of the process, creating the artwork. When I saw that giant print of Hassam's on your wall, a light bulb went on. Unfortunately, the images I found online of his work aren't detailed enough."

"You want to examine his brushstrokes," I assumed.

"Exactly. You're a painter, too?"

"Once upon a time—and a fine arts major."

"Then you know how seminal that work is, Ms. Cosi, and why I'd like to see a large print for inspiration. The original is at the White House, so your large print is the next best thing."

"No problem," I said. "A local artist donated it to us years ago. She was inspired by Hassam's work. If the print can now inspire you, that's a nice bit of kismet."

Dante spoke up. "The only problem is where to find it. Did you move the pictures to the attic? It's pretty cluttered up there. We may need your help locating it."

"You're in luck," I said. "All the artwork I took down from the lounge yesterday morning is still locked away in the upstairs hall. You both would do me a huge favor if you carted everything up to the attic for me after you're done snapping your close-ups. I'll show my appreciation with an hour's pay for Dante, and Mr. Tanaka gets free coffee and pastry."

The boys were enthusiastic, so I handed over the keys and cautioned them to "please be careful."

The value of those works ranged from negligible to sky-high, but all were irreplaceable mementos of this landmark shop. On a down night, when I discussed the shop's reduced foot traffic with Mike, he suggested selling some of the art to pay the bills. But that was an unsustainable solution.

Sure, we would have money in the short term, but eventually we would run out of works to sell—and it wasn't my call to sell them anyway. Madame was still the majority owner of this shop, and almost every piece in our collection had special meaning for her. I doubted she'd agree to part with even one.

Moments later the bakery delivery arrived. After scraping my hair into a kitchen-ready ponytail, I washed up, and started filling the pastry case. I was almost finished when I heard a tapping at the locked front door.

My favorite bickering barista roommates were reporting for duty.

Twenty-two

ရာ ၀ ၀ ၀ ၀ ၀ ၀ ၀ ၀ ၀ ၀ ၀ ၀ ၀ ၀ ၀ ၀ ၀ ၀ ၀

"It's mighty cold out there," Nancy declared, stamping her boots.

Esther tugged the wool hat off her crushed bouffant and removed her mittens. "My nose feels like a specimen in a cryo-lab." As she tugged the black frames off her face and cleaned her fogged-up lenses, Nancy hugged herself.

"My nose isn't the only part of me that's cold! My poor—"

Esther raised a hand. "Please, spare me the *titular* details. I'm *abreast* of the situation!"

"I need more layers!" Nancy complained.

"You're too skinny. What you need is more carbs . . ."

Esther put away her coat and messenger bag, tied on her apron, washed up, and joined me behind the pastry case.

"Wow, these look amazing. Hey, Nancy, why don't you eat a few of our new Twinkie Tribute Cupcakes for breakfast? It might solve your padding problem!"

"Tempting," Nancy said, stifling a yawn at the espresso machine. "For now, I'm sticking to my morning double and buying a hoodie to wear under my coat."

Esther shrugged. "Suit yourself. But little golden cakes with gooey marshmallow filling are a much tastier solution."

I waved Esther closer. "How did it go last night? Were you able to get the word out on our new project?"

"Absolutely. Remember that really cool pic of the shop that Dante painted? I posted a photo of it in all my social media groups with text describing our new Writer's Block Lounge. My slam poetry community has an Events page, and I posted it there, too, along with a teaser for a future poetry slam, staged right here, featuring Writer's Block patrons."

"Great idea. Do you think they'll bite?"

"When I checked this morning, we already had more than a dozen people interested in stopping by to check things out, and four solid bookings for tomorrow."

"Five," I said. "Dante will introduce you to Tony Tanaka when they're finished in the attic."

"Not bad for the first day, Boss Lady, don't you think?"

"It's a start," I said, finally feeling pretty good. That is, until Esther shifted topics to her favorite customer.

"So what's the word on Mr. Scrib's condition?" Behind her glasses, her dark eyes stared at me with a cross between hope and dread. "If he's still stuck in the hospital, I'm going to visit him when my shift is over. I'm sure I can cheer him up with our poetry game."

"That's very nice of you," I said carefully. "I mean about visiting him."

"So he *is* still in the hospital?"

"Yes, and we'll know more soon."

"Soon?" She planted a hand on her hip. "Is something going on that you're not telling me? I mean, can't we just call the hospital right now and find out how he's doing?"

"Since we're not family, I doubt they'll update us," I said, which was all too true.

Esther frowned. "Then how do we find out—"

"Mike promised to track down more information this morning," I said quickly. "He's asleep upstairs. When he wakes up, we'll know more . . ."

As my voice trailed off, I considered confessing the whole truth about last night's assault on her elderly friend. But seeing Esther's distressed face froze my tongue. Instead, I forced a smile.

"Let's hope for the best and be patient, okay?"

Behind her glasses, Esther's worried eyes squinted slightly. For a moment, I expected her to grill me on why Mike Quinn was suddenly involved. Instead, she pursed her lips and (in her own Esther way) expressed her trust in me with an aggrieved yet accepting—

"I *guess* . . ."

"Good. Now let's get the coffee started."

Fifteen minutes later, I signaled Nancy to flip our CLOSED sign to OPEN, unlock the door, and let our first customers in.

Twenty-three

~~~~~~

For two hours, the welcome bell got a fairly good workout, ringing steadily as early-morning regulars flowed in and out, and my baristas and I served a continuous stream of caffeine-deprived customers.

And then, as it always did these days, the crowd thinned, and the Village Blend became a ghost shop. While Nancy staffed the espresso machines in the unlikely event that a new patron might arrive, Esther took a break at the coffee bar with an item she'd retrieved from her messenger bag.

"That's Mr. Scrib's notebook, isn't it?"

Esther nodded. "I didn't have time to look through it much yesterday. But I'm keeping it safe for him. And I'm still wondering if he's composed anything coherent in all these scribblings . . ."

Given what had happened last night, I was just as curious and was about to join her at the bar when a surprise customer came down our spiral staircase.

Mike's short sandy hair was still damp from the shower. He kept a change of clothes upstairs, and his new dress shirt looked freshly pressed. The jacket of his gray suit, now out of its dry-cleaning bag, was stretched across his broad shoulders, and the morning sun glinted off the gold shield that he'd tucked into his breast pocket.

I moved to speak privately with him. "I can't believe you're up already. I planned to make a breakfast-in-bed delivery, but not for another hour."

"Sorry I missed *that*," he said, descending the last few steps. "How about we reschedule for tonight?"

"Breakfast in bed? For tonight?"

"Absolutely." He leaned down to convince me. It wasn't difficult. His lips were warm, and the kiss was sweet. Considering our location, I kept it short.

"If you'd waited upstairs, that could have gone on much longer," I whispered as we parted.

"Not my fault. Java and Frothy woke me. They were acting pretty feisty, but they calmed down after I fed them. Did you forget?"

"No, Lieutenant. I did not forget. What you described are two clever cats who successfully conned a second breakfast out of a supposedly smart cop."

"Hey, they were meowing at me like crazy, acting like they were famished. I couldn't take it."

"Excuse me? You run stakeouts on the most dangerous drug dealers in the five boroughs, but you fold under feline pressure?"

"Guilty."

"And it's not the first time," I reminded him. "If my clever kitties keep this up, I'm going to have to buy them tiny Peloton machines."

Mike smiled, but I didn't return it. Instead, I tilted my head in Esther's direction and quietly asked—

"Since you're up now, can you make some calls about Mr. Van Dyne's status?"

"Already did. While your conniving cats ate, I spoke with—"

"Hey, you two!" Esther shouted from the coffee bar. "I found something in Mr. Scrib's notebook. Something important! So when you're done with the kissy-face, I'd like to show you!"

I met Mike's gaze. "She still doesn't know about the assault."

"Like I promised, Clare, we'll tell her together."

Twenty-Four

〜◎〜◎〜◎〜◎〜◎〜◎〜◎〜◎〜◎〜◎〜◎〜◎〜◎〜◎〜◎〜◎

Esther listened quietly, her eyes welling, as we told her about the vicious attack on her friend in our back alley. I could feel the emotions rising in me again as I recounted the terrible state in which I'd found the poor man. Alarm, horror, anger—

"If only I'd gone outside sooner," I said. "I could have stopped it."

"Or *you* could have ended up in the hospital with him." Esther shook her head. "You can't blame yourself, Boss Lady. And it's awesome that you tried to chase down the jerk. But why was Mr. Scrib in the back alley in the first place?"

I was about to suggest my theory when Mike spoke up—

"It appears he was confused. After Mr. Van Dyne's mental health episode in your lounge yesterday morning, he was taken to the hospital, but he signed himself out. The EMTs said he was still wearing his hospital wristband. Obviously, he shouldn't have left so soon. He needed care."

Esther had more questions. I did, too. Lots of them.

With patience, Mike did his best to answer.

"I spoke with Detective Russell, out of the Sixth. He caught the assault investigation, and he told me Mr. Van Dyne is now in the ICU at Bellevue Hospital. He hasn't regained consciousness."

"Can I visit Mr. Scrib anyway?" Esther asked. "And I know you said his real name is Van Dyne, but he told me to call him by his nickname, and I can't think of him as anything but Mr. Scrib."

"I understand," Mike said. "And if and when he regains consciousness, I'm sure you can visit him. As of now, in the ICU, the rule is verified family only."

"Does he *have* family?" I asked.

"Detective Russell accessed his New York identification card info, and it lists an address here in the Village. He's already sent officers to the building. The residents they were able to reach provided little information about him, except that he lived alone. Russell also turned up a history of mental illness. Van Dyne was released a year ago from a facility in Connecticut, and Russell is trying to access more information up there."

"What's he looking for?" I asked.

"Next of kin, emergency contacts, more background on his illness."

"What about the *here and now*?" I said, echoing Mike's own words last night.

"What do you mean?"

"If Mr. Van Dyne is still unconscious, then he's not able to name or describe who assaulted him. So what is Detective Russell going to do about that? About finding and arresting his attacker or his—" I caught Mike's gaze with a look that added *murderer*, a dreadful result that we both knew was possible but neither wanted to say in front of Esther.

Mike shifted on his feet. "Well, your eyewitness description of the perp and the direction the suspect fled is in the file, so Russell will put in a request for camera tracking. Officers will be canvassing, as well, and visiting that nightclub where you were hit, to find out if someone remembers a person wearing the coat you described and recover said coat if it was ditched."

"But are they likely to catch this person?"

"Possibly," Mike said. "There are cameras all over the streets. Unless he's a river rat, that perp had to double back at some point. If our camera crew gets lucky, they'll track the suspect right up to their doorstep and arrest them at home."

"Okay." I glanced at Esther. "Sounds like the NYPD is on top of it."

Mike assured me and Esther that Detective Russell would keep him in the loop.

"Listen," Esther said, "I still need to tell you both what I found in Mr. Scrib's notebook." She tapped the stained brown cover. "Now that I know how bad his condition is, I think what I found is even more important."

Twenty-Five

෮෮෮෮෮෮෮෮෮෮෮෮෮෮෮෮෮෮෮෮෮෮෮෮

Suddenly, Esther found herself in the center of a huddle at the coffee bar with me, Mike, and Nancy hanging over her.

"Did you find something we can understand?" I asked. "Something that makes sense?"

Esther shook her head. "I found some coherent phrases, but most of the handwritten pages are gibberish, at least to me."

"So what *did* you find?" Nancy asked.

"Well, this is a five-subject notebook," Esther said, "which means the pages are divided into sections. See these color-coded cardboard pockets separating each subject? Four of the pockets are empty. But look at this."

Esther probed a yellow cardboard pocket and produced a plain steel ring with two keys and a paper tag attached. Cramped handwriting on the tag read:

If I am incapacitated, please take care of Wacker.

"Wacker!" Nancy giggled. "That sounds kind of obscene."

Esther sighed. "Let's not dive into the gutter."

"Hey, I'm just being honest!!" Nancy said. "Could Wacker be a person? Like a roommate?"

"Roommates can usually take care of themselves," I said. "And Lieutenant Quinn just told us that Mr. Scrib lives alone. So he must be talking about something more vulnerable, like a pet."

"Aha!" Nancy cried. "Then I'll bet it's a monkey."

"Now why would you say that?" Esther asked.

"You've seen monkeys at the zoo. They do that 'whacker' thing a lot."

Esther gawked at her roommate. "Do you have a one-track mind or what?"

"Hey, I'm just trying to be helpful—"

As the pair bickered, Mike leafed through the notebook without comment while I considered Esther's discovery. The thought of some poor pet locked in a cramped New York City apartment, alone, hungry, thirsty, and scared, tore at the heart of the animal lover in me until I couldn't hold back.

"We've got to do something. A little life could be in danger. Where does Mr. Scrib live?"

Esther flipped to the pocket where she found the two keys. "The address is written right here on the cardboard. It's not far."

"Maybe Mr. Scrib's building will have a super that you can ask for help," Nancy suggested.

"I think we just enter ourselves," I said.

My baristas both stared at me.

"Why not?" I asked. "Esther has keys. We can perform two good deeds at the same time—"

"You can save the monkey!" Nancy exclaimed.

"*And* maybe find some clues to help Detective Russell with Mr. Scrib's background or his next-of-kin contacts." I glanced at Mike. He nodded his approval.

Esther chewed her lower lip. "But going in with his keys, wouldn't that be breaking and entering?"

"Not at all," Mike said. "You possess the keys, so there's no breaking—"

"What about the entering part?" Esther asked.

"This man is your friend," Mike pointed out. "And your friend is incapacitated. The note attached to those keys can be construed as written permission to enter his premises and take care of his . . . pet, or plant, or whatever *Wacker* is."

"Could you go with us, Lieutenant?"

"That's where things get thorny, Esther. I'm not a friend. You are. As an officer of the law, I should have a warrant to enter anyone's home or place of business. There are also statutes that—"

"Okay, okay," Esther griped and faced me. "It looks like we're in this alone, Boss Lady. When do we leave?"

"As soon as I can get another barista to fill in while we're—"

"Hey, guys!" Dante called.

We all jumped at the sudden sound of Dante Silva's voice, followed by the loud clang of fast footsteps on our spiral staircase. I turned to see Dante and his friend descending to the main floor. I'd completely forgotten about those two. They'd been exploring the attic for almost three hours!

Nancy gave a little wave to her coworker, but her gaze quickly shifted. "Who's your cute friend?"

"This is Tony," he said as they approached the coffee bar. "Tony Tanaka . . ."

Clutching his notebook in one hand, Tony tucked his phone into one of his dozen or more vest pockets, waved back at Nancy, and smiled a greeting to the rest of us. That's when he spotted Mike's detective badge.

"Hey, Officer . . ." Tony paused a moment. His mind seemed to be working. "Are you here to investigate the assault last night? Do you have any suspects? Or witnesses?"

If Mike was surprised by the questions, he didn't show it. Instead, he offered a friendly cop smile, though it didn't reach his arctic blue eyes.

"Why do you ask, Mr. Tanaka? Do you *know* something I should be made aware of?"

"Me? Oh, no. No, no, no. I drive at night, you see? And I'm in this neighborhood a lot. I don't want to get assaulted myself, and I'd like to know the score, that's all."

There was an awkward pause while Mike put the young artist under an icy spotlight (a look I knew well). Finally, Mike said—

"If you do remember seeing anything suspicious, be sure to let us know."

"Oh, sure, will do," Tony said, then glanced uneasily at Dante, who turned to me and said—

"We moved everything to the attic, Boss. Do you need help with anything else?"

"Now that you mention it . . ."

Twenty-six

◎◎◎◎◎◎◎◎◎◎◎◎◎◎◎◎◎◎◎◎◎◎◎

After thanking Dante for covering part of Esther's shift, wishing Mike a good day at work, and waving at Nancy (who couldn't resist flirting with Tony Tanaka), we climbed into our Uber.

During our short ride, Esther kept her eyes on her phone while I wondered what surprises we might find at Scrib's apartment. Unfortunately, my first surprise (more of a *shock*, really) came while I was still in the car's back seat.

We detoured for another rideshare customer and were stopped at a traffic light when I spotted my ex-husband loitering in front of a trendy bistro and wine bar. Twice he glanced at his watch, as if he was waiting for someone.

His hair and beard were freshly trimmed, and his slick attire (pressed chinos, black turtleneck, and a brushed cashmere blazer with a matching scarf, no less) had me reaching an obvious conclusion.

Less than twenty-four hours after crash-landing from a transatlantic trip, Matt was already diving into the dating pool—though, when it came to my ex, jumping into a hot tub would be more accurate.

Curious about his latest swipe-to-meet hookup, I continued spying with amused attention, expecting to tease him later about my Matt-in-the-Wild sighting. Then his "date" arrived, and I was no longer laughing. In fact, the sight of the tanned blond shaking Matt's hand felt like a gut punch.

All my life I've tried to treat everyone fairly, to always provide service with a smile, and to constantly strive to improve my game. These virtues, first instilled in me by my hardworking grandmother, who ran a small

Italian grocery store in a little Pennsylvania town, were even more important if your work involved serving the public every day. My credo has always been to welcome everyone to my table.

However—

If I had *one* enemy in this world, it was the blue-eyed Adonis with the golden locks now shaking my business partner's hand: Cody "Drifter" Wood, former champion surfer, current CEO of Driftwood Coffee, and the Village Blend's chief cheating, scheming competitor.

All style and zero substance, Cody Wood and his national chain of Driftwood coffee stores served subpar beans with gimmicky commercials along with drinks filled with corn syrup and imitation flavorings. The only constant they appeared to strive for was to cheapen their products and expand their bank account.

Okay, maybe I was being overly judgmental, but I wasn't imagining the way Driftwood not only continually "borrowed" ideas that we worked hard to develop for our customers, but also fully trashed them.

Take last year's Village Blend Valentine's Day specials, praised by New York foodies, written up in the local press, and subsequently stolen by Driftwood. It started with our Vanilla-Cinnamon Caress, our award-winning latte flavored with beautifully infused milk using Grade A Madagascar bourbon vanilla beans and fresh Ceylon cinnamon sticks. Shortly after we began serving ours, Driftwood's national chain introduced their "Creamy Orgasm," a monstrosity of artificial vanilla, cheap cinnamon syrup, and more grams of sugar than any human should ingest in a day, let alone in one drink.

Our popular Cherry Kiss, a whimsical mix of espresso, artisan dark chocolate, and natural fruit syrup, designed to mimic a chocolate-covered cherry, was reverse engineered by "Drifter" Cody, who swapped in junk ingredients, and renamed it "The Cherry Hooter."

He even degraded our Lavender Chocolate Truffle recipe, a drink praised by *New York* magazine for the way we infused artisan white chocolate with real lavender and colored the drink naturally with ube powder. After that write-up, the Driftwood chain stores were suddenly dumping violet food coloring into a standard vanilla latte and calling it "The Purple Haze."

Their actions were as insufferable as they were unethical. My baristas and I had worked hard on our specialty drinks, only to have them filched, debased, and peddled with marketing techniques better suited for a marijuana dispensary.

And then there were the personal attacks. More than once, Cody Wood had publicly insulted the Village Blend's baristas, our coffee, even our beloved owner. He referred to me (an accomplished master roaster) as a "coffee bimbo ex-wife," and his attack on Matt was quite literally below the belt.

So why was I now watching my business partner greet Cody Wood, the so-called Blond Adonis of Caffeine, as some kind of lunch buddy? What possible reason could Matt Allegro have to meet with the jerk that called him a fading playboy who should be sourcing Viagra instead of coffee?

What was going on here?

Was Matt that worried about our financial future? Was he contemplating a—heaven forbid—merger? Was he sniffing around for investment money? Or was it even worse than that?

A nightmarish vision of our historic Village Blend with a *DRIFT-WOOD* sign above its French doors exploded in my head, a name that was the antithesis of the sterling reputation of excellence, integrity, and service that Matt and I had strived to uphold in our constant quest to make a consistently perfect cup.

Speechless, I continued watching as the two men turned toward the bistro's entrance. Smiling, Cody Wood opened the door for Matt as if they were a couple of buds meeting for brunch.

I reached for the car door handle just as the driver hit the gas. Trapped and frustrated, I finally found my voice—

"Esther, did you see that? Did you see what I saw?"

"Sorry, I was texting." She looked up from her phone. "What did I miss?"

By then it was too late to see anything. The men were inside, and the car had turned the corner.

"Never mind," I replied, deciding to spare Esther the pain.

Why torture her with the horror of what I'd witnessed, or the ugly implications swirling in my mind? Until I spoke with Matt and heard a satisfying explanation for this inexplicable development, I decided to keep what I saw to myself.

While I stewed silently, Esther went back to her thumb dance, and the car drove on.

Twenty-seven

〜〜〜〜〜〜〜〜〜〜〜〜〜〜〜〜〜〜〜〜

We exited on West 10th, not far from Madame's penthouse on Fifth Avenue.

"Look at this," I said, astonished. "Mr. Scrib lives on the same street as the Emma Lazarus House . . ."

Lazarus was a poet who loomed large among Greenwich Village's literary legends. I couldn't quote any of her other works, but one sonnet was destined to live forever. "The New Colossus," which she'd penned in 1883, was cast in bronze and set in the pedestal of the Statue of Liberty.

"I memorized that poem in third grade," Esther said. "But I don't see too many tired and poor on this block . . ."

Esther was right. We were standing amid what Realtors called the "Gold Coast" of Greenwich Village. Rows of nineteenth-century brownstones with wrought iron work, arched windows, and Juliet balconies stood together like elegant ladies in perfectly preserved vintage finery. Leafy trees lined wide sidewalks dappled with amber light, while a stroll away, residents would find some of the city's most charming bars and restaurants.

This block boasted not only the Italianate home of Emma Lazarus and the former residence of author Mark Twain, but also the famous Astor "farmhouse," a redbrick Federal-style structure built on farmland once owned by John Jacob Astor.

At one point the Astor home was separated into ten different apartments until an anonymous buyer paid $31 million for it and even more to convert it back into a single-family mega mansion, continuing a trend of rich and famous folk snapping up properties in this area and then converting them, including a Hollywood actress who'd fused two town houses into one Frankenmansion; a telecom exec who invested millions in transforming a garage; and the founder of a notorious music-sharing app who recently snapped up three "Gold Coast" buildings when they hit the market.

While I gawked at the Astor house, Esther elbowed me.

"What is it?" I asked.

She pointed to her phone screen. A Realtor's website displayed images of a luxury apartment for rent a few doors down, describing it as "a multi-room suite with garden access, parquet floors, and a working fireplace." The rent for a few months was more than many people earned in a year—and the address was the one Mr. Scrib scribbled on his notebook pocket with the two keys.

Esther and I stared at each other for a few seconds with amazed expressions. Clearly, we were thinking the same thing—

How could Mr. Scrib, a gentleman who appeared to be mentally unstable and borderline homeless, possess the financial power to live on this block?

"Do you think he wrote down the wrong address?" Esther whispered.

"Maybe. Or maybe he knows someone who lives here?"

"Or *used* to know them. Either way, these keys might not work, and we're on a wild-goose chase."

I faced her. "We both know there's only one way to find out."

"We better be careful," she said, chewing her bottom lip. "We don't want anyone to think we're trying to break in and rob the building."

"Let's stay calm and try these keys, okay? What could possibly go wrong?"

Esther blinked. "You want a list?"

Twenty-Eight

⊚⌒⊚⌒⊚⌒⊚⌒⊚⌒⊚⌒⊚⌒⊚⌒⊚⌒⊚⌒⊚⌒⊚⌒⊚⌒⊚⌒⊚⌒⊚⌒⊚⌒⊚

DESPITE her misgivings, Esther's raven bouffant and zaftig hips followed me to the entrance of the building. The front door was below street level, so we descended a short flight of stone stairs before entering the narrow vestibule.

Polished brass mailboxes lined one wall, and I counted them up. "Looks like this brownstone's been divided into six apartments."

Esther nodded. "If Mr. Scrib's scribblings can be believed, he lives in apartment 3B."

"Okay," I said softly. "Let's try to get in."

The interior security door was locked, of course. Esther inserted one of the two keys she'd found. It didn't fit.

"Try the other," I whispered.

The second one slipped right into the lock. When she turned it, I heard a click. "We're in!" she cried.

I shushed her. "We're only halfway there. Come on . . ."

Muted gold wallpaper dominated the little lobby. We saw a door to a stairway and a small, wood-paneled elevator standing open. We stepped inside.

The elevator was slow, but nonstop. We found the third floor as quiet and seemingly deserted as the rest of the building. There were two apartments on this floor, A and B.

Apartment B was our destination, but there were no markings on the front door, just a peephole, a doorbell, and a brass nameplate with no name listed.

"I think we better try the doorbell," I whispered.

We heard the muted ringing, a sound that easily reached us in the silent hallway. I rang two more times with no response.

"There's nobody home, Boss."

"Okay, Esther, you're on."

Her hand was shaky as she slipped the second key into the lock. She took a deep breath and turned the knob. The door opened.

"It worked," she whispered. "Now we're *really* in."

No snarling dog or hungry cat greeted us. The apartment was as soundless as the hall. The air felt stale and smelled odd. It was an unpleasant odor, and one I couldn't identify.

I half expected to find a hoarder's nest inside with old newspapers scattered about and gibberish-filled notebooks piled to the ceiling. Instead, we entered a cozy luxury apartment with a living room that was clutter-free, almost Spartan.

A French Provincial sofa sat next to an end table that held a stack of books and a brass lamp. The polished hardwood floor shone dully in what little sunlight filtered through a tall, dark-curtained window. There were no cabinets, and the off-white walls were naked except for a series of framed nature prints.

As I opened the curtain for more light, Esther pointed to one of them. "Didn't I just see that bird art hanging in our second-floor lounge?"

"Good eye, Esther. That's one of Lynn Bogue Hunt's pieces. He was a New York artist and, according to Madame, a customer of the Village Blend back when he was creating illustrations for *Field and Stream*. That's just a print, like ours. The original would be extremely valuable."

I continued scanning the room and saw no television, no computer— not even a telephone. I ducked into the adjoining room, a small kitchen, and came back.

"I don't see or hear any sign of a dog or cat," I said. "Or *monkey* behaving badly for that matter, which means Nancy will be disappointed."

Esther groaned. "Don't remind me."

"I don't even see a fish tank or birdcage," I said. "We'll need to check the bedroom, too."

"I'll do it." She turned to go but stopped when I reminded her—

"We're not *just* looking for a pet named Wacker to save."

"I know," she said, "but I feel weird about snooping through Mr. Scrib's stuff."

"I understand, but we're trying to help him. Look for anything that might indicate a family member, maybe a sibling or a child, someone whose name we can pass on to Detective Russell."

"Do you think that's who's paying for him to live at this address? A wealthy relative?"

"Good question. Maybe we can find a rental agreement. The name on it might give us a clue."

"Hey, what if Mr. Scrib is secretly rich? Lots of really rich people have spent time in psychiatric facilities."

"That's true."

"Or maybe he's a famous author. Lots of them go crazy, too."

"Also true. But I don't recognize the name Jensen Van Dyne as being a famous author, do you?"

"Van Dyne doesn't ring any literary bells, but there are plenty of authors who hit bestseller lists whose names I wouldn't recognize. Maybe years ago he was a one-hit wonder. He could have banked big royalties and made some good investments. We should search online. Give me a second—"

Esther pulled out her phone and resumed her thumb dancing, but the only published work she found under Van Dyne's name was an obscure short story published in *Wordsmyth* magazine around the time of the original Writer's Block Lounge. After that, there was (in Esther's words) "nothing, nada, zip!"

Unwilling to abandon her theory, Esther tapped her chin. "Maybe he wrote under a pseudonym?"

"That's possible. While I look for next-of-kin info, see what clues you can find."

"What sort of clues? Give *me* a clue."

"An author is likely to keep his own works where he lives, right? If you find a collection of books in this apartment by the same author, it could be his pen name."

"Unless the author is Stephen King."

"Right. I doubt he's James Patterson, either."

"Speaking of Patterson, Mr. Scrib could be the ghostwriter for a bigger writer. Maybe we'll find an old contract. Should we look in his desk?"

I followed her pointing finger to the mahogany antique dominating a small nook adjacent to the main room. Next to the desk was a tall bookshelf packed with books.

"You check that bookshelf," I told her. "I'll check the desk. There might be a clue to his relatives in here, too."

"Aye, aye, captain."

Mr. Scrib's desk had not been gently used. No blotter covered the top, and the wooden surface was scratched and stained with ink. A coffee mug filled with pencils and pens sat on top, next to a sharpener and a huge dictionary, but that was it.

The side drawers were unlocked, and there was nothing in them but more pencils and pens, and lots of blank notebooks. In the top drawer, however, just under the desk surface I hit pay dirt.

Inside was a business letter from a New York publisher with a recent date. Right beneath it sat papers that looked like a legal document with a revealing header—

Author: Jensen Van Dyne

Project: Untitled True Crime

Twenty-nine

"**Esther**, look at this."

Esther stopped her own search, glanced at the cover letter, and quickly focused on the contract.

"This contract was signed six months ago. Mr. Scrib was hired to write a book based on a submitted proposal, and the full manuscript is due in two weeks."

I stared Esther down. "After Mr. Scrib's mental health episode yesterday morning, didn't you tell me he was working on a book, something about a crime story?"

"That's what he told me when I asked what he was working on so diligently. He said, and these were his exact words—" She lowered her voice to mimic Scrib. *"My dear Esther, I'm writing a true story that will shake up the whole city. A tale of crime and no punishment."*

"Oh, no," I whispered.

"What is it, Boss?"

"Two and two is four," I said.

Esther blinked. "Are we doing math now?"

"I'm adding up some things, and it's an ugly equation."

"Enlighten me."

"There *was* a crime years ago. A major, unsolved crime. A member of the original Writer's Block Lounge was murdered. Madame told me about it."

"And you think that's what Mr. Scrib is writing about?"

"Yes! According to Madame, your Mr. Scrib was a member of the original Writer's Block group. One of the men in the group, a young actor, was killed and his body was dumped in Brooklyn. The case was never solved."

As Esther's eyes widened with this bit of news, I started to pace.

"Now it's starting to make sense," I said. "I mean, it's one thing to brag to a barista that you're writing some bombshell book while being unstable enough to think your notebook full of gibberish is a masterpiece. It's quite another to secure a contract for that book from a legitimate publisher."

"I don't follow."

"Don't you see? Your eccentric old friend wasn't bluffing about that book." I pointed to the contract. "*This* must be it!"

"I hate to break it to you, Boss, but that's not a book. It's a *contract* commissioning a book. And judging from Mr. Scrib's gibberish-filled notebook, I have to wonder whether his mind is capable of fulfilling that contract."

"You're right. Let's look for his manuscript—if it even exists. Did you find anything in the bookshelf?"

She shook her head. "The books are just volumes of poetry arranged in an alphabetical row. Most of them are dead poets, and all are major ones I recognize, but I'm not finished yet."

"Keep looking."

While Esther continued looking through Scrib's library, I laid the letter and document on the parquet floor and used my phone to snap pictures of every page.

"Hey, Boss, check this out!"

Esther showed me what she found: several notebooks, like the one filled with gibberish, only these were filled with handwritten poetry. Original poems, all in the same handwriting as the Mr. Scrib scribbles.

They were all dated, and they weren't from the distant past. He wrote these perfectly understandable verses over the past year. Many of them were love poems—sad, sweet verses of unrequited love.

"This is clearly proof he can write," I said. "I mean something other than gibberish. These poems are perfectly coherent and beautifully written."

"I know!" Esther said. "He writes a lot about a woman named Juliet,

but I assume that's just a Shakespeare reference. And I found this, too."
She handed me a slim hardcover that she'd plucked from the collection. "I
was curious because there was no title on the spine. Go on, open it."

"Oh, wow, this is a photo album."

"And the pictures are prehistoric."

While I examined the album, Esther wandered down a dark hallway
in search of the elusive Wacker, and any other clues she could find.

Most of the album was blank except for the first few pages, which
contained about a dozen photos. The pictures featured a group of young
people, and the background was clearly the Village Blend's second floor.
On the wall, I saw the telltale sign, and I knew for sure—

These were the faces of the original Writer's Block Lounge!

I didn't quite strike gold. I only had their faces. There were no names,
no captions, a dead end. But maybe not. If I showed these pictures to Madame, they might shake loose more memories.

With that goal in mind, I opened the photo album on the desk and once
again used my phone camera. As I snapped my pictures, a chill took hold.

One of these carefree-looking kids would soon be a murder victim, his
body dumped in a Columbia Street lot. Was someone else in this group
the killer? Or did Jensen Van Dyne's true crime story involve outsiders?

I considered what Mike told me about that part of Brooklyn, how it
was a dumping ground for murdered victims of the mob. An icier chill
gripped me at that thought, especially when I noticed something else.

The photos always featured the same people, but in one of the pictures, I glimpsed a big, middle-aged Italian-looking man with a walrus
mustache standing in the background. I released a nervous breath, hoping
Madame's memory wouldn't fail me on this one.

As I finished and closed the album, I heard Esther's urgent call—

"Hey, Boss, come here quick!"

I tucked my phone away and hurried down the shadowy hall, passing
the apartment's only bedroom. Esther lingered in front of a closed door,
which I assumed was the bathroom. The sour smell that tainted the entire
place was more pronounced here.

"I checked the bedroom already," Esther said, "even under the bed
and the closet, but I didn't find anything. No clues to his next of kin, just
a few more books of poetry collections on his nightstand."

"You didn't find a manuscript?"

"Sorry, but it's a mystery where Mr. Scrib is hiding his true crime manuscript. There was no mobile phone, no computer laptop, not even a typewriter. I did find an empty cage—"

"A cage? What do you mean? A birdcage?"

"No. A square cage, a pretty big one. Then I came to this closed door. I think it's his bathroom—"

I was about to speak, but a fluttering sound from the other side of the door silenced me.

"Did you hear that?" Esther whispered.

"It sounds like a bird's wings."

"Big wings," Esther said. "Maybe it's a parrot. If it is, I hope it's friendly."

"Whatever it is, I doubt it's going to attack," I said. "Unless it's a hunting hawk or an illegal fighting cock."

Esther's eyes went wide. "A fighting cock!"

Her loud cry provoked the creature on the other side of the door.

QUACK, QUACK . . . QUACK, QUACK, QUACK.

"It's a duck," Esther said, relieved. "Nothing to fear from a cute little—"

She opened the door and a virgin white whirlwind of fluttering feathers exploded out of the room. Esther screamed, reared back, and tripped over her own combat boots.

She hit the floor butt first and the mad flapping thing was on her!

Thirty

◎◎◎◎◎◎◎◎◎◎◎◎◎◎◎◎◎◎◎◎◎◎◎◎

"Help! Get this vulture off me!"

Esther was sprawled on the hardwood floor, her body blanketed by wide flapping wings. Though she shielded her face, the bird's orange beak kept slipping under her hands.

"It's not a vulture, Esther. It's a duck!"

"I don't want to go like Tippi Hedren," she whined.

But instead of grabbing her exposed throat, the duck folded its huge wings and settled down on Esther's chest like a hen warming an egg. Bowing its downy white head, it rubbed against Esther's cheek.

"Scat! Scoot! Get off me," Esther pleaded with closed eyes. The duck quacked contentedly but refused to budge.

"It's a pet, Esther. Maybe it's trained."

"It's not a dog, Boss Lady!"

"It's still a pet. You should try using its name."

She opened her eyes. "Wacker, go to your room!"

At the sound of its name, the duck lifted its head, stuck out its feathery chest, and hopped to the floor. Esther sat up on her elbows.

"I thought that thing was going to eat my liver."

"Relax, Prometheus, I think Wacker is calm now—"

The duck shook its white feathered rear and, with an abrupt squirting noise . . . evacuated. Esther climbed to her feet, gingerly avoiding the green spew on the hardwood floor.

"I can see why that beast was locked up."

Wacker cocked its head to gaze at us with one strangely contemplative eye. Then the duck waddled back into its lair. Esther quickly closed the door and pushed me down the hall to the living room.

"That was intense." Esther shook her disheveled raven bouffant. "Did you see that bathroom? There's duck guano everywhere."

"That explains the smell."

"I might need a mask to go back in there," Esther continued. "Poor Wacker needs care—"

The angry, booming voice startled us both.

"WHAT THE HELL IS GOING ON HERE?"

A raging man swathed in terrycloth burst into the living room. He wasn't old, but he wasn't young, either, maybe late thirties. And if his boyish features hadn't been twisted up with outraged fury, he might have been considered handsome.

The whites of his wide, angry eyes matched the robe, which barely reached his knees. His legs were covered with dark hair. His feet were bare, his face unshaven, and this was no five-o'clock shadow. The cactus growth looked several days old, and his dark, longish hair was Einstein wild, as if he'd just rolled out of bed.

As he strode into the room, his hastily tied robe came undone, exposing a hairy chest to go with the hairy legs and a pair of tighty-whities with a visible bulge.

Esther hid her eyes. "Unsee, unsee!" she chanted.

But I was less concerned with propriety and more worried about the large mallet the man was waving around in one white-knuckled hand.

THIRTY-ONE

"**W**HO are you people?" the Terror in Terrycloth demanded. "What's all the screaming about? Where is Mr. Van Dyne?"

That was my opening. "He's in the hospital."

The man's voice dropped a few decibels, but his aggressive stance remained. "That doesn't explain who you are or why you're here."

He took two steps forward. Esther took a step back. I stood my ground. Planting my hands on my hips, I demanded, "Who are you to ask?"

Baffled for a second, he blinked, and was now close enough that I could tell he'd been smoking—and *not* tobacco.

"I'm . . . I'm Mr. Van Dyne's neighbor," the man said, lowering the mallet. "I live across the hall. I heard a woman screaming—"

"That was my friend Esther." I gestured to her. "She's Mr. Van Dyne's friend, as well. He left her the keys to his apartment. While he's in the hospital, he requested that she take care of his duck."

"Duck?"

Esther spoke up. "His name is Wacker. The little guy got feisty and gave me a scare, that's all."

"We're sorry for the noise," I added.

The neighbor blinked again. "Van Dyne is in the hospital, you say?"

Wow, this one's quick, I thought.

"Yes, he had an accident last night. We're going to take care of his pet duck until he's out of the hospital."

"This is a no-pet building," he replied. "If the owner finds out Van Dyne was hiding a pet, he could lose his lease."

"But—"

He cut Esther off. "You're going to have to take that duck with you unless you want the building manager to call animal control."

"Don't do that," Esther said.

"Are you going to take it?" he demanded.

"Yes!" Esther suddenly decided, glancing anxiously my way. "But we need a little time to pack up and call for a ride."

"How much time?" He glanced at his naked wrist, realized he wasn't wearing a watch, and scowled. That's when I heard voices in the hall and saw an elderly couple peek through the wide-open door.

"I'd better let my neighbors know what's going on," he said, heading for the exit.

"You might consider putting on pants while you're at it," I called.

Annoyed, he shook the mallet until his bathrobe flared like terrycloth wings. "I'm not going *anywhere* until you and that duck are gone!"

Esther smirked. "Back to flashing us, are we?"

Scowling again, he retied his robe. Then he wheeled on us, marched to the door, and addressed the couple in the hall.

"Everything is under control," he said. "And if not, I'm calling *animal control!*"

Esther gripped my arm. "I can't let Wacker end up served with orange sauce at some shady restaurant."

"I agree," I said. "He's a pet. We have to take care of him."

As Madame had done for me more times than I could count, I patted Esther's hand, and was touched by the grateful look I glimpsed behind her black-framed glasses.

"Okay, let's work fast," I whispered.

"We better," Esther returned. "Or else King Killjoy is liable to flash us with his scepter—and I would pay good money *never* to see that again!"

In a kitchen cabinet I found a bag of duck chow (who knew?), and we quickly fed the hungry bird. Then Esther put the duck in the cage she'd found in the bedroom while I sent a text to Nancy at the Village Blend, asking her to send our van to this address.

ASAP, I typed.

When she sent back three thumbs-up emojis with five exclamation points, we headed out.

Thirty-two

꩜꩜꩜꩜꩜꩜꩜꩜꩜꩜꩜꩜꩜꩜꩜꩜꩜꩜꩜꩜꩜꩜

"I couldn't leave Wacker to his fate." Esther's voice echoed inside the empty back of the Village Blend van.

"Sure you could," Tucker replied, eyes on the road.

I was surprised to see Tuck pick us up since his shift didn't start for several hours, but I was so grateful to get away from the Terrycloth Terror that I didn't question it. Neither did Esther. Perched on a sack of duck food, one arm resting on the oversized cage covered with a beach towel, she shook her head.

"No way was I abandoning Wacker back there. I'm friends with Mr. Scrib. I found his keys. I found his note. And while he's in the hospital recovering, I'm going to take care of his duck."

"We could call animal control," Tucker countered. "They'll probably figure out a humane solution. Maybe take him to a sanctuary on Long Island."

"I'm not risking it. Given the state of the overworked bureaucracy in this burg, it's more likely Wacker will end up in an East Hampton confit."

"You have a point," Tucker replied. "Though I wonder how you're so certain of that bird's pronoun."

Esther shrugged. "I just know."

Tucker swerved to avoid a stalled taxi. From inside the covered cage, Wacker let out a string of outraged quacks.

Tucker frowned. "I hope that duck doesn't get carsick."

"Ducks can fly, so they're *probably* immune," Esther said hopefully.

"Will you two stop arguing about the duck!" I cried, loud enough to make Tucker wince. "Sorry for shouting, but I'm still processing everything I discovered back there, and I'm more than a little freaked out."

"You're right beside me," Tucker reminded me. "So, no need to shout. I can hear every word you say. Now what's freaking you out?"

"You want a list? It's a long one," I said.

"Then you better save it."

"Why?"

"'Because we've got trouble,'" Tuck chanted in singsong verse. "'Right here in River City.'"

"What?" I turned in my seat, suddenly alarmed. "What kind of trouble?"

"Yes, enlighten us, Music Man," Esther cracked from the back.

Tucker grinned. "'It's trouble with a capital *T* and that rhymes with *P* and that stands for—'"

"Pool!" Esther finished.

"No, not pool," Tucker said.

"But that's how the song goes," Esther insisted. "The Music Man warns everyone in River City about the evils of the pool hall."

"I know how the song goes," Tucker said. "I once played the title role in an off-off-Broadway cabaret tribute. We got raves! And if you remember the libretto, then you'll recall the 'problem' of River City, Iowa, wasn't really a problem. It was invented by the con artist who wanted to bilk the people of the town by convincing them to purchase musical instruments to keep their kids away from the so-called bad influences of the pool hall. But in reality, the con man is scheming to abscond with their money. Anyway, pool is not our problem—"

"Then what is?!" Esther and I demanded in duet.

"We're packed," Tucker said. "With a capital *P*."

"Packed?" I echoed in confusion.

"Yes!" His head bobbed again. "And that 'starts with *P* and that rhymes with *T* and that stands for—'"

"Stop with the lyrics!" I shouted.

Tucker frowned. "I told you already. You're *right beside* me. You don't have to shout."

"Sorry. Just tell me, okay? No more lyrics. What exactly is going on?"

"I told you. The Village Blend is swamped with customers."

I checked my watch, incredulous. "But we're always a ghost shop at this time of day."

Esther squealed. "It worked! My social outreach worked!" Dancing in her seat, she began to chant. "'Come, and trip it as ye go. On the light fantastic toe!' John Milton, natch!"

QUACK! QUACK!

"Hey, look at that!" Esther clapped her hands. "Wacker knows Milton! All that poetry reading by Mr. Scrib must have rubbed off."

"I posted, too," Tucker said. "Dozens of places that might catch the eye of local playwrights and authors. Oh, and I advertised a contest for black box one-acts, exclusive to members of our Writer's Block Lounge. I said we'd stage it upstairs, invite indie producers and critics, and the winners will get free coffee and pastries for a month. Great idea, right?"

"Stellar," Esther said, pushing up her glasses. "Just don't schedule it on the night of my Writer's Block poetry slam, or else—"

"Stop!" I cried. "Tucker, tell me more. When exactly did these new customers appear?"

"Nancy said they started trickling in after you two went on your Wack hunt—"

"Wacker!" Esther called from the back. "His name is—"

"Whatever!" Tuck cut in. "The trickle of curious writers turned into a flood, and Dante called me in early to help serve. Now everyone is sucking down espresso drinks, eating up our pastry case, and milling around, wondering what to do."

"Well, what *do* we do?" I demanded. "We better figure it out fast."

"I'm on it," Esther said. "Give me two hours to get Wacker settled in my place, and I'll be ready to help."

"Oh, no, you don't," I said, turning to face her. "You got us into this. We need a plan *now*."

"All right, all right, cool your cucumbers. I'll tell you both what to do . . ."

Esther gave us a quick plan of action. Tuck said he was fine with getting things started. After pulling up to the Village Blend curb, he popped his door, and bailed out of the driver's seat.

I exited the van, too, but held my door open—

"Thirty minutes and not a second more," I warned Esther as she slipped behind the wheel. "I want this van and your butt back here ASAP. We're going to need all hands on deck."

Esther rolled her eyes as she released the parking brake.

"Aye, aye, Captain Bligh."

Thirty-three

∿∿∿∿∿∿∿∿∿∿∿∿∿∿∿∿∿∿∿∿∿∿∿∿

Aᴘᴛᴇʀ pushing through the coffeehouse door, I froze.

I wasn't cold. I was in shock.

Tucker had warned me the place was packed with a capital *P*, but he'd failed to mention the C word: CHAOS. Our charming Village Blend looked and sounded like my old high school cafeteria on the day the lunch monitors failed to show.

Our café tables had been dragged into group gatherings, creating a lab-rat maze that customers had to navigate just to reach the restrooms. Those without seats were forced to mill about with coffee in one hand and pastry in the other, resulting in collisions, spillage, shouting, and arguments. No food fights yet, but it was only a matter of time.

The coffee bar was jammed with the line for service doubling back on itself and reaching nearly out the door. Behind the counter, poor Dante was frantically pulling espressos while Nancy filled food orders and rang up sales faster than Ticketmaster for a Taylor Swift tour. No extra hands were on duty to clean up the floor spills or bus tables, which were horribly strewn with debris.

If ever there was a "be careful what you wish for" moment, this was it.

Sure, I was grateful for the business. But, like any sane shop owner, I was horrified by the mayhem. I was also instantly skeptical.

Would these rowdy drop-in drinkers stick with us? Or were they one-day wonders?

Beyond the cackling laughter and angry arguments, somewhere in this crazy crowd a wannabe Broadway star felt the need to croon a number from the show *Wicked*.

Tuck appeared at my side, shaking his head. "Why that woman is attempting one of the most difficult pieces in modern musical theater is beyond me. 'Defying Gravity' calls for a tempo change, which she just blew, not to mention one of the high Fs."

"Forget *Wicked* woman. It's time to restore order."

"Huh?"

"You're a part-time theater director. *There* is your potential cast. How would you handle this anarchy on audition day?"

"Got it!"

With a clearly defined role to play, Tucker squared his narrow shoulders and squeezed his lanky form into the center of the room. Stepping onto a chair, he rose above the highly caffeinated crowd and commanded—

"Okay, people! Listen up!"

They didn't.

The mob chattered on, the wannabe Broadway star continued her caterwauling, and customers kept on milling and spilling.

Tuck clapped his hands and tried again, louder this time. "People, work with me! We are ready to start our program!"

The room didn't appear to care. If anything, the crowd noise grew to an almost deafening level, until a knife-sharp voice cut loose with—

"EVERYONE, SHUT UP!"

Unbelievably, they did.

"CAN'T YOU SEE THIS MAN IS TRYING TO SPEAK!"

The girl-power roar erupted from a statuesque young woman wrapped in colorfully patterned kente cloth. A full head taller than the people around her, she stood up near the hearth and faced the crowd.

When complete silence descended, the young woman waved a relaxed arm at Tuck, and said—

"Go on, string bean, tell them what's what."

"Thanks!" Tucker said, eyes wide. After taking a moment to clear his throat, he began again. "First question. Who is here for the Writer's Block Lounge?"

The woman in African print tossed her long ebony braids and told him: "That's why we're all here." She pointed to a crowded table in the corner. "I kept asking the Voice over there to lower her decibels, but it's clear the drunks I serve as a bartender are easier to manage than folks jacked on coffee."

"Ain't it the truth," Tuck muttered before he addressed the crowd again. "Writers! Where are you? Come on! I want a show of hands!"

More than a dozen men and women raised their arms. I spotted Dante's friend Tony Tanaka among them in his cobalt blue hoodie. Our show tune crooner was another.

Tuck pointed at her.

"You! Name, please?"

"Dina. I'm Dina Nardini."

"Well, Ms. Nardini, if you're here to *write* music, welcome to the group. But if you plan on *singing*, from now on please do it with a tin cup in Times Square!"

As Tucker continued to address the crowd, I ducked behind the counter and grabbed a stack of saucer doilies. Esther had suggested Post-it notes, but I had no time to run up to my office to fetch them.

These little rounds of paper would have to work double duty as both place settings and guest checks.

After moving aside enough tables to clear a path (and slamming my poor, pathetic bandaged arm in the process), I positioned myself at the base of our spiral staircase. Unhooking the velvet rope that stretched across the wrought iron rails, I officially opened our upstairs Writer's Block Lounge.

"Okay, you scribblers!" Tucker cried as he herded them. "Stage left and up those steps."

As Tony Tanaka led the stampede, I stood ready to greet each guest. Forcing a smile through throbbing limb pain, I slipped him two doilies, each marked with the number one in bold ink. I continued to hand out a pair of numbered doilies to each patron, while Tucker issued instructions—

"Place one of those cute little paper circles in plain sight and write your beverage and pastry orders on the other. I'll be up to collect your orders once you're all settled, and you'll be served as soon as possible."

Then Tuck continued to circle the room, rounding up more writers and placing each of them on our "conga line to caffeine-fueled creativity!"

Thirty-Four

"Pretty impressive the way you two righted the ship," said the statuesque woman with the ebony braids.

"Thank you for lending a hand with that," I replied as I numbered her doilies.

Her bright brown eyes scanned the coffeehouse. "Where is Esther Best? I thought she would be running this show."

"Esther had to *duck out* for a bit, but she'll be right back," I promised. "I gather you're a friend?"

"When we're not competing. But, even then, I consider us Spoken Word sisters." She flashed me a smile and extended her hand. "I'm Lachelle LaLande."

"Oh, yes! Esther mentioned that you work in hospitality, too."

"I've been tending bar for five years," she said with a shrug. "I started out in some real dives, you know? I'm talking spit-and-sawdust places. But that's in my rearview. These days I work at an exclusive speakeasy. It's a good gig. We serve creative cocktails, and the tips are great, but . . ."

"You aren't happy?" I guessed.

"Mixing drinks for upscale drunks who make cringeworthy passes? That is *not* my destiny." She shook her head. "The truth is most of my customers are all right. Some of the guys, though, they get handsy, and one is nearly at stalker level."

"That sounds dangerous, Lachelle. Have you considered a restraining order?"

"Not my style. I don't like dealing with the police. And I don't intend to be at that job much longer."

"Following your bliss?" I asked.

"'Reality is wrong,'" she recited. "'Dreams are for real.'"

"That's a beautiful thought," I said. "Did you write that?"

"No, that was Tupac. Tupac Shakur."

"I get it," I said. "And I hope it gets you where you want to go."

"Thanks."

As she headed upstairs I greeted the next young woman in line.

Her pale features were partially obscured by flyaway brown hair with bold blue highlights. An oversized black tee hung on her boyish frame. The shirt, emblazoned with a large tombstone and the epitaph *INSERT NAME HERE*, was long enough for the hem to drape over the thighs of her black jeans.

Secured tightly under her armpit was a slim black laptop adorned with bright white skulls. A bag in the oblong shape of a coffin hung from a shoulder strap.

She offered Tuck and me a lopsided grin.

"Interesting shirt," Tuck said, pointing to the gravestone. "And whose name belongs there?"

"Everyone's," she said brightly. "Eventually."

"And what is your name?"

"Mason. Mason Dunn."

"What brings you to the Writer's Block Lounge, Mason? An assignment penning obituaries, perhaps?"

"Funny," she said. "Actually, I'm trying to finish the script for my second film."

"Second?" Tuck said. "Was your first ever made?"

"Hell, yeah. I gave up my day job to make it, and all the film festival crowds gave it high marks."

"Sundance and Tribeca?"

"Oh, no!" She counted off fingers. "Toronto After Dark, Buried Alive in Atlanta, Dead by Dawn in Scotland, Celluloid Screams in Sheffield, and NYC's Horror Film Fest, among others."

"What's the name of your picture? Maybe I've seen it."

"*Cannibal Honeymoon.*"

"Ah, romantic comedy."

Mason Dunn's eyes widened. "You have seen it? Then you know.

Everybody thinks it's pure horror, but it's really a genre-bender with rom-com at its heart."

"What's the premise?" I asked, genuinely interested to hear how anything with *cannibal* in the title could possibly be described as part romance.

"Well," she said, "Maxwell is a burned-out New York top chef who's gone over the edge. He's already married several socialites, then killed, cooked, and consumed them on their honeymoons. But there's a problem with his new bride. Turns out Shelly is the editor in chief of a national gourmet magazine and a cannibal, too. After battling to see who would end up as the main course, the couple finds true love, opens a restaurant in the Hamptons, and dines on their neighbors happily ever after."

"Wow, that story is really out there," Tuck said.

"The audience at San Francisco's Another Hole in the Head fest thought so. They gave it a Warped Dimension Award."

"Impressive. What was the day job you quit?"

"I filmed cookery videos for *Good Housekeeping*."

As Tuck and I exchanged holy-cow glances, Mason moved on and a new writer—that overly enthusiastic show tune singer—stepped up for her doilies.

For such a big voice, she was a petite little thing with plaid leggings, a fuzzy sweater, and a cute, chopped-off mop of blond hair. She held a silver laptop (adorned with Disney character stickers) in her tiny arms, and I prayed that she planned to use it for writing and not live streaming her next musical number. I was about to bring up that very subject when she did it for me—

"I apologize for the singing," she said with a sheepish look on her heart-shaped face. "I didn't mean to be disruptive. But one of my coworkers is here, too, and he bet me that I couldn't do it."

"Do what?" Tuck asked after overhearing us.

"Belt out Idina Menzel's big number in *Wicked*." With a sweep of her arm, she brushed back her choppy blond bangs. "See, where I work, they want me to stick to Disney Princess stuff." She planted her small hand on one hip. "I may *look* like Glinda the Good Witch, but I'm perfectly capable of slapping on a black wig and green face paint, and playing the Wicked Witch of the West."

"So, you're a Broadway actress?" Tuck assumed.

"I wish!" Dina cried. "I've been to every open audition for the last eighteen months without one callback."

"Then where exactly do you work?" Tuck asked.

"At the Broadway Spotlight Diner on 42nd Street. I'm one of their singing waitstaff."

"Oh!" Tuck nodded in recognition. "My partner used to work there. Punch does excellent drag tributes to stage and screen legends, and they adored him. He said the customers were glorious, the tips were fantastic, but the drama behind the kitchen door was intense."

"Intense? It's insane! We all battle over who can perform which show tunes—and the best times to perform them. Everyone wants the prime-time spotlight. That's when the most customers will broadcast you live on their social feeds, and you're more likely to go viral and be discovered, which is why—if you're doing really well—you've always got to be on the lookout for sabotage."

"Sabotage," I said, astonished. "What kind of sabotage?"

"One girl had a costume 'malfunction' that left her topless while she was belting out 'Take Me or Leave Me.'"

"How mortifying," I said.

Dina's head bobbed. "There were like twenty mobile phone cameras broadcasting the whole thing. She was so caught up in singing her *Rent* showstopper that she didn't even notice she was half-naked until she took her bow. That's when she turned red, ran out the door, and never came back. *No one* believed it was an accident. And then there was the chorus boy who slipped on a patch of chicken schmaltz. *Someone* placed it strategically on the counter that he always leaped onto during his 'My Shot' rap from *Hamilton*."

"Did he slip?" I asked.

"Does Niagara fall? Sprained ankle and a broken wrist. We never found out who did the dirty deed."

Tucker raised an eyebrow. "Must have been Aaron Burr."

"Honestly, everyone suspected the new kid, a wannabe rapper from Scarsdale who desperately wanted to do that crowd-pleaser, which he *did* after Jimmy was carted away in an ambulance and never came back."

"Wow," I said. "Sounds like songbird-eat-songbird."

"Hey, that's funny!" Dina laughed. "Mind if I use it?"

"For what?" I asked.

Dina grinned wide. "I'm writing my own musical. It's based on my memoir."

Tucker looked skeptical. "Aren't you a little young to be publishing a memoir?"

"Kenneth Branagh published his when he was twenty-nine. I'm only twenty-four. I've still got five years on Ken to find a publisher."

Tuck blinked. "I guess you do. Have you decided on a title?"

"I'm still waffling. But I'm partial to *Service with a Song: A Broadway Tragedy*. What do you think?"

I could tell Tuck was doing his best not to cringe. Then he tapped his chin in thought.

"You know what, Dina? I believe you'll have better luck finding a producer if you lighten things up and maybe give it a hooky backbone."

"What do you mean by backbone?"

"I mean use your memoir-based material, sure, but shape the story structure around an accessible genre, like a romance plot or maybe a murder mystery."

Dina's baby blues lit up. "Oh, I love the idea of a murder mystery! I can think of several coworkers who I wouldn't mind killing—fictionally, of course."

"Sweetie, I know what you mean."

"Thanks for the input. I knew this was the place for me!"

"Nice job," I whispered to Tuck.

"No sweat," he said. "And who knows. You might have just witnessed the birth of a future off-Broadway smash—or a roman à clef of a latent serial killer."

"Let's stay positive, shall we? And hope for the former."

Feeling better, I took a deep breath. Diva Dina was the last writer in line. As she headed up the stairs, a text message rattled my phone. Joy was contacting me from our shop in Washington, DC—and it was a joy to hear from her, even if it was a business call.

Hi, Mom. No time for a chat, but we'll FaceTime soon, and I can't wait to catch up. In the meantime, a quick reminder that we urgently need your special Fireside blend for a Georgetown party this weekend. As of this AM, we're completely out. Happy roasting! Love you!

I checked the time and realized that I'd never get those beans to the shipper today. Tomorrow was fine, but in order to get this consignment down to DC, first thing in the morning, I had to start roasting.

But how?

My staff was near their breaking point. Tuck was in charge of servicing the upstairs lounge—at least until Esther arrived. Dante and Nancy were working the line, and I had to get to my roasting room. But the shop was a mess and there was no one to clean it.

Or was there?

Faster than a dating app swipe, I speed-dialed my ex-husband. I knew Matt was already in Manhattan. I saw him a short time ago, dining with the Village Blend's chief competitor (and my mortal enemy), Cody "Drifter" Wood—an unfortunate fact that I was dying to grill him about.

But I didn't get the chance. My call went directly to voicemail. I left an urgent message and hoped he'd respond in time to bail us out.

In the meantime, *someone* had to bus these tables and clean the puddles off our restored plank floor before one of these new customers slipped and fell—and hired a slip-and-fall lawyer to sue us. So, unless I found a solution fast, that unlucky someone would have to be—

"Howard Johnson!" Tuck suddenly cried. "What are you doing here?"

THIRTY-FIVE

LUCK waved over a gangly, denim-clad kid in his late twenties. As soon as I laid eyes on his flattop head, I thought "Howard Johnson" had to be a nickname. His hair was the same orange shade as the roof of that classic hotel and restaurant chain.

"Clare Cosi, I want you to meet Howie Miller, the budding playwright I told you about."

"Howard Johnson Miller, Ms. Cosi." His handshake was firm, his wide, crooked grin almost comic in his freckled face.

"Mr. *Miller*, is that right?" I said. "I'm guessing Howard Johnson is a nickname?"

"No, that's my given name. One hundred percent authentic," he replied with a note of zany pride. "My grandfather was born in a booth at a Howard Johnson's restaurant."

"You're serious?"

His orange head bobbed. "My very pregnant great-grandmother had this craving for tender sweet fried clams and orange sherbet, but her timing was a little off."

"And they named *you* after the restaurant, too?"

"You have to understand, Ms. Cosi. That was about the most exciting thing to happen to my family in three generations. They've been running the same hardware store in the same little town of Hickory Hill for years. So, Howard Johnson Miller named his son Howard Johnson Miller, Junior. Then I came along. I'm officially Howard Johnson Miller the Third, if anyone is counting."

Tuck spoke up. "I didn't expect to see you at our Writer's Block Lounge until tomorrow."

Howie sighed. "Yeah, well . . . I *was* scheduled to work a couple of blocks from here, helping a guy move to a new apartment. Unfortunately for my bank account, that side hustle fell through—"

"Still working the side hustles?" Tuck said. "You already work two jobs as it is." Tuck turned to me. "Howie works nights as an usher at the Minskoff Theatre. And in the daytime, he works at the Library for the Performing Arts at Lincoln Center—"

"Only two days a week," Howie corrected. "Thus, the dire need for another side hustle."

He abruptly peeled off his backpack, pulled a folder from a compartment, and passed it to Tuck.

"That's the stuff you asked me to research at the library."

"It's for Punch," Tuck told me. "He's recreating Carol Channing's Dolly and wants to get the costuming right." Tuck thanked Howie with a twenty-dollar bill and a pat on the back. "I owe you one."

Those words sealed the deal on what I was considering. "Howie, what sort of side jobs are you willing to do?"

"Pretty much any—"

"Tell Clare what you did for the Steinway Street Players," Tuck cut in.

"The Steinway Street Players?" I said. "Sorry, I never heard of that theater group."

"And you never will," Howie said with a laugh, "because there was only one—and he really was a player."

"I don't understand," I said.

"It's the subject of his current dramatic project," Tuck informed me, "though I think songs would blast it off. With the right lyricist and composer, it could be another *Music Man*."

"I don't know about that," Howie said. "But the story is true. When I first landed in the city, I hooked up with this guy who bought an old movie theater in Queens. He announced it would soon be the home of a brand-new drama school and theatrical troupe. He had an impressive résumé, too—worked in Hollywood for major film companies and said he was now a part-time casting director for productions at the Kaufman Astoria Studios, which was less than a mile from his theater. So you can imagine how excited I was when he hired me. I'd applied for a part-time gig, but he offered me a full-time job as the theater manager."

Howie threw up his palms. "I'd never been a theater manager, but the thousand-dollar-a-week salary was too good to pass up. So I spent two weeks painting the lobby, fixing broken seats, hanging signs, and helping with community outreach. Right on time, I got my paycheck.

"Meanwhile the boss announces open auditions for his first production and launches a website for his acting school with classes like How to Impress a Casting Director and Acing Auditions for Stage and Screen. I help him post notices on college and high school campuses, mostly in affluent areas of Westchester and Long Island.

"During his week of open auditions, he asks all the young actors who show—and there are hundreds of them—to sign up for his classes as a commitment to the troupe's vision. He collects their tuition in advance, handing every one of them a *Steinway Street Players* T-shirt to make them feel like they made his team. He was a real charmer and even got donations from local businesses for future ads in his theater programs.

"Two more weeks go by, and I expect my second paycheck. He asks me to defer my salary until his classes officially start. I agree, only there's never another paycheck because the guy disappears, and the sheriff's office shows up to padlock the theater."

"Oh, no," I said. "Don't tell me . . ."

"Yeah." Howie nodded. "He was a total fraud. He didn't buy the place. He was renting it and paid for only one month. There was no drama school, no theatrical troupe, and all the money he raised for tuition and program ads, more than fifty thousand dollars, was gone with the wind."

Tucker shook his head. "The guy made the whole thing up, including his background and identity."

"Did they catch him?" I asked.

"Nope," Howie said. "Maybe someday they will, and I'll get the money I'm owed, but I doubt it. The worst part is I can't show my face in that part of the city. People believed I was involved in the scam, but it was me who went to the authorities and alerted them about the con job. The police thanked me for my help—but some of those people who lost money were really pissed about being taken. A few actually threatened me with bodily harm. It's a raw deal . . ."

A flash of all-too-human anger lit his eyes and I sympathized. Cons and con artists thrived in New York City. They could always spot a mark, and young people with big dreams were often the most vulnerable. It was easy to see how a naive kid from Hickory Hill got played.

"It's terrible what happened," I said. "And I'm sorry you lost your job today, too. But I think I can help you out."

His face brightened. "Free coffee?"

"Better than that. How would you like to work here for a few hours?"

Howie hesitated. "I don't know how to work an espresso machine."

"I don't need another barista. I need a dedicated busser. You'll clean off tables, mop the floor, take out the garbage, and help our baristas with restocking. You'll get minimum wage, all the free coffee you can drink, and free food on your breaks. We don't serve tender sweet fried clams or orange sherbet, but I'll make sure you don't go hungry."

Howie's wide smile stretched across his freckled face. "Where can I find an apron, Ms. Cosi?"

"Tuck will get you one. If you need me, I'll be downstairs in the roasting room."

Thirty-six

∿∿∿∿∿∿∿∿∿∿∿∿∿∿∿∿∿∿∿∿∿

Hours later, when I finally flipped the *OPEN* sign to *CLOSED*, I felt like I was sealing the hatch of a war-ravaged vessel. This day had been one of the longest of my life, right up there with going into labor—and almost as painful.

The moment I locked the shop's front door, visions of sitting in a candlelit bath and sipping a glass of mulled cider while a shirtless Mike massaged my tense shoulders floated through my head like puffs of perfumed foam. That happy image calmed me considerably, along with the realization that, in the end, my shop had a good day . . .

Though Esther had been late coming back, she'd been fully successful on her duck rescue mission and worked hard to help Tuck manage the upstairs lounge.

I gave even more kudos to Tuck. Not only had he handled the writers' lounge like a pro, but he also introduced me to Howie. The orange-roofed powerhouse proved so invaluable that I asked him to stay until closing.

I had no choice, because Matt never responded to my voicemail.

My ex was ghosting me, and I could guess why. Something was brewing with Cody Wood. Something that Matt didn't want to discuss. Not yet anyway.

Fortunately, we managed without him.

As for Mr. Scrib, I had no updates on his condition or the NYPD's progress on arresting his attacker, but I planned on grilling Mike tonight. And I was glad we saved the poor man's pet, at least according to Esther—

"Wacker is one happy duck," she'd assured me after returning to the shop. "I left him plenty of feed, turned my bathtub into a play pond, and dialed the radio to a classical music station. I figured if Wacker knows Milton, he probably likes Bach."

Bird psychology was beyond me, but I did know a thing or two about roommates, and I feared what Nancy's reaction would be upon learning that her living space had been invaded by a guest who flapped and quacked.

To keep the coffeehouse drama to a minimum, I'd asked Esther to refrain from informing Nancy at work. My blond, braided barista would discover the truth soon enough, at the very least when she used her bathroom.

And speaking of bathrooms . . .

That image of a candlelit bath with a sweet glass of cider and Mike massaging my shoulders drifted back to my head like a buoyant bubble. Considering all the insanity I'd gone through today—from the Terrycloth Terror with his King Killjoy scepter to the wacky quacker and bewildering torrent of uber-caffeinated creatives—I was relieved the sun had set without a new crisis.

Leaning back against the door, I closed my eyes . . . and then, like all floaty dreams, my perfect bubble was burst by the harsh prick of reality. In this case, the pin jab of my vibrating phone.

I was ready to ignore the blasted buzzing, until I saw who was calling.

"Madame?" I checked my watch, frowning at the late hour. "Is everything all right?"

"No, Clare. I need your help."

"Now?"

"Yes!"

"Are you in trouble?"

"Not me. You said you wanted to meet a member of the original Writer's Block group. Now is your chance, but you must come quickly!"

"Where?"

"The Grande Maison on Fifth. The Wordsmyth Awards Dinner is about to end, and it may be a disaster for one of the guests of honor. I'll explain the rest when you get here."

I considered my wrinkled sweater, disheveled ponytail, and imminent threat of body odor.

"Be warned," I told her, "I'm not dressed for uptown. I doubt I'll get past the valet—"

"There's an employee entrance left of the main door and down a flight of stairs. If I'm not there, someone else will be, and they'll tell you where to go."

"What if the door is locked? Do I have to use a special knock?"

"Text me when you arrive, and please hurry!"

With that, Madame ended the call.

Although her request was beyond obscure, and I was yearning to re-inflate the dreamy bubble of my candlelit bathroom, I couldn't leave her hanging. It was Madame, after all—and she did dangle the chance to meet a member of the original Writer's Block crew.

Would it be the famous author she'd mentioned, A. F. Babcock? Or someone else? I had to admit, curiosity revved my tired engine. Grabbing my coat, keys, phone, and wallet, I felt my energy rise as I ran for the door.

No rest for the weary. As usual!

Thirty-seven

With Madame stressing urgency, I wasn't about to waste time with ride-share detours and multiple stops. After locking up the shop, I raced to the street, threw my arm in the air, and bellowed—

"Taxi!"

Diving into the back of the first cab that stopped, I declared my destination, promising a generous tip for speed. Then I sat back to catch my breath and watch the quiet city race by. Of course, "quiet" was a relative term in New York. Blaring horns and meandering mobs were reduced at this late hour, but never completely eliminated, and the howl of *some* siren *somewhere* was ever-present.

After rolling up Hudson, veering onto Eighth Avenue, and stalling at an accident scene, my driver shot east and headed north on Sixth. Moving uptown, the buildings rose in height and retreated in age. As the structures grew higher, so did my anxiety level—

What possible catastrophe could strike a literary awards dinner at a posh hotel? And why would Madame believe I could resolve it?

A coffee emergency?

Under-extracted espresso was a crime in my book, but I couldn't imagine bad coffee being a major concern to a gathering of literary lights.

As we blew by Macy's flagship store, prewar granite and brick gave way to cloud-kissing skyscrapers of glass and steel, and I decided that, whatever the problem, if my mentor needed me, I wasn't about to let her down. That thought lifted my confidence again, even if I looked a fright with the stained shop apron under my coat, thick-soled kitchen shoes, and ratty hair.

When traffic slowed in front of the neon lights of Radio City, I re-scraped my espresso brown locks into a tightly bound ponytail, applied the lip gloss I found in my coat pocket, and felt better. Eventually, we made our way to Fifth, veered toward the curb of the Grande Maison, and my heart started pounding again.

The restored Beaux-Arts façade of this majestic building always wowed me. Once upon a time, this place was a robber baron's sprawling manor, gracefully situated across from the sculpted serenity of Central Park. Then, sometime in the 1930s, after the owner's vast fortune went down with the crashing market, the great home was sold and eventually expanded and transformed into this grand hotel. Bathed in a golden glow, it practically illuminated the entire block. But tonight, the wide marble stairs, gilded entranceway, and valets in their crisp uniforms couldn't out-shine the celebrity authors I spotted out front.

There was the great Stephen King, in evening clothes and bright white Nikes, talking with the extraordinary Alice Walker, fittingly dressed in the color purple. Mega bestseller John Grisham, quite the distinguished legal eagle in navy blue, was conversing with the incomparable Margaret Atwood, resplendent in *Handmaid's Tale* red. And George R. R. Martin, dressed like a gray-bearded version of Johnny Cash's Man in Black, was laughing with Lin-Manuel Miranda, handsomely clad in a *Hamilton*-style tailcoat. Other attendees in formal garb were also wandering about, waiting for limos or valet-fetched cars.

In a fangirl moment—after paying my cabbie and bailing onto the sidewalk—I nearly whipped out my phone camera and started snapping. But I didn't want to risk being ejected by hotel security for harassing liter-ary royalty.

So, instead of snapping photos, I used my phone to text my mentor. Two simple words—

I'm here.

With one final glance at the star-studded activity on the hotel's red carpet, I headed left, away from the lights, to descend a dark flight of un-obtrusive stairs. At the bottom, I faced a door that still bore a plaque stat-ing its original purpose:

SERVANTS' ENTRANCE

Having dedicated my life to an industry of service, the plaque didn't bother me. In fact, I was relieved to be heading toward familiar territory, though before reaching for the handle, I did hesitate. What if a security guard stopped me? What would I say?

As it turned out, I didn't have to worry. The door swung open, and there was Madame.

"Thank goodness you're here!" she cried. Then she seized my hand and took off like a determined locomotive pulling a confused caboose.

"Where are we going?"

"You'll see, my dear. Don't lollygag. Move your feet and follow me!"

Thirty-Eight

ᘒᘓᘒᘓᘒᘓᘒᘓᘒᘓᘒᘓᘒᘓᘒᘓᘒᘓᘒᘓᘒᘓᘒᘓᘒᘓᘒᘓᘒᘓ

THE low heels of Madame's evening slingbacks clickety-clacked on a single-minded track as she pulled me along a utilitarian hallway.

The end of the line was the hotel's busy restaurant kitchen. When we pushed through the double doors, I expected the clang of pots and pans, shouted commands answered by "yes, Chef," and white-clad figures laboring over countless culinary tasks.

The kitchen staff was indeed present, but they weren't cooking. Every one of them was transfixed by the drama unfolding in a private dining room, walled off by a thick glass partition that allowed views of the kitchen.

The room was empty, except for two women of a certain age, their couture as elegant as Madame's, who were locked in a bitter argument. A slender bottle-redhead in an emerald green sheath raged at a more full-figured woman in a smartly tailored Tom Wolfe–white pantsuit, her severe pixie cut dyed a stark white blond.

The fire versus ice battle was surreal because the glass cut off all sound—warfare in mime. But there was nothing amusing about this silent movie.

As the redhead raged, her porcelain face flushed almost the same bright color as her elaborate French twist. Meanwhile, the cool blonde, hands on hips, smirked with ice pick–hard defiance before replying with a verbal punch so cutting that the redhead dropped her flailing hands and stepped back.

That's when I noticed the only other person in that empty room, a young man with a prematurely receding hairline standing right behind the cool blonde. He wore an ill-fitting gray suit, little round Harry Potter glasses, and a tense expression on his pointy face.

The timid manner in which the pointy-faced Potter stepped up to the cool blonde made me think that he was an assistant of some sort. As he whispered in the woman's ear, he showed her something on his phone screen. The icy blonde nodded, grabbed the phone from him, and shoved the screen at the redhead, who gawked at it and then began raging again.

Madame tsk-tsked.

"They're still going at it. But we have no time to meet Addy now. She's the cultured, sophisticated woman in green, the one screaming like a banshee at another guest. I'll introduce you after this whole affair is settled."

I resisted Madame's tugging and took a second look.

"The redhead—*that's* your friend Addy? *That's* Addison Ford Babcock?"

"Yes, dear," Madame said patiently. "I mentioned last evening that I was acquainted with A. F. Babcock, didn't I?"

"I remember. I'm just a little starstruck—and still trying to catch up. The only photos I ever saw of her were on her book jackets when she was much younger, wore tortoiseshell glasses, and had short brown hair. Why is she arguing? And who is she arguing with?"

"I don't know the other woman. As far as what they're arguing about, all I could pick up before they went private was something about 'old scores.' Now come along." Madame tugged harder. "We've got a serious situation to deal with."

"You mean this isn't it? They look like they're about to kill each other."

Madame waved her manicured hand. "This is a sideshow. The real drama is upstairs."

She tugged me across the idled kitchen and through another door that led to a bank of elevators. She released my hand and hit the call button. As we waited for one to descend, I faced her.

"Now can you please explain why I'm here?"

"My friend Addy—"

"Yes, I saw her in the kitchen."

"—she's one of tonight's honorees," Madame continued. "The Wordsmyths presented her with an award for supporting literacy programs nationwide. The press is here. In fact, the *New York Post*'s Page

Six reporter is still at the bar, trying to dig up gossip." She paused. "Unfortunately, Addy's young nephew is also here, and he is the problem."

"Oh, no. Is he a teenager in some kind of crisis?"

"It's a crisis, all right. But he's hardly a teenager. Ethan Humphrey is an adjunct professor at New York University, and unless we do something to extricate him from his current situation, the professor will end up in prison, lose his position, and poor Addy will be humiliated on what should be a night of triumph and celebration."

"What on earth did this man do that's worse than the silent catfight we just witnessed?"

"Well . . . quite a few things, actually. It started in the middle of the dinner when Professor Humphrey, who'd already had a few too many vodka martinis, began flirting with a young woman."

"How young?"

"*Very* young. She drifted over from a Sweet Sixteen party in the hotel's restaurant."

"Yikes."

"It was a natural mistake. She looked and acted a lot more mature than sixteen, and outright lied that she was celebrating her twenty-first birthday. Even the bartender was fooled."

"Then the professor's troubles don't seem all that dire."

"If only it ended there."

"There's more?"

"After the professor put away more cocktails, he became visibly inebriated and the bartender cut him off. That's when Professor Humphrey and the young lady began sniffing lines of cocaine off the bar top."

"Good grief."

"When the bartender spotted the cocaine, she alerted hotel security. They arrived and escorted the young lady back to her Sweet Sixteen party."

"And the professor?"

"At that point, Addy's nephew became quite belligerent. Fortunately, the security here is efficient and discreet. They escorted him out of the dinner and back to the courtesy suite that the hotel provided for Addy and her guests."

"That's good," I said. "I assume Humphrey has had a chance to simmer down and sober up."

Madame rolled her violet eyes. "If only."

The elevator finally arrived. Its doors opened, and we stepped inside. Madame pressed 9 and the doors closed.

"Okay, I'll bite. What happened after the professor got to the suite?"

"The security guard discovered a plethora of illegal substances scattered about. Professor Humphrey saw the guard's reaction. And then . . ." Madame sighed.

"And then *what?*"

"The professor tricked the guard into stepping outside the suite and barricaded himself inside."

"You've got to be kidding."

"He's there now, taking drugs and taunting the staff. The night manager is up there, too, and his patience is wearing thin. He's threatening to summon the police."

"And you want me to help you fix this?"

"You're a miracle worker, Clare. I've seen it countless times, and I have every faith you'll think of a way out of this." Madame patted my hand. "If you do, Addy is sure to be grateful—and you're eager to gain her confidence, aren't you?"

"Of course, but the situation you described is a nightmare, a train wreck, an absolute toxic mess."

"It is. But don't worry. You have until we reach the ninth floor to decide how to clean it up."

As the floors creeped by, my mind raced. Then the bell dinged, and the elevator doors opened.

Time was up.

Thirty-nine

◎◎◎◎◎◎◎◎◎◎◎◎◎◎◎◎◎◎◎◎◎◎◎◎

The ninth-floor hallway looked like the hotel was conducting a fire drill.

Straight-backed, stern-faced men in suits mixed with baffled guests in a variety of dress and undress. Above the confused chatter of the milling mob, I heard a loud animalistic cry—and I mean literally.

The man inside the locked suite was doing a spot-on imitation of a wolf baying at the moon. As the howl faded, I heard one of the men in the hallway exclaim—

"That's it! I'm making the call!"

"Please, give me another minute," a young woman said, her tone more demanding than pleading.

"You've had your minute, Ms. Woodbridge. By my watch, you've had thirty minutes, and you still haven't been able to coax him out of there. Tell your boss I won't risk a lawsuit against our own security. That's why I'm having her nephew and his drugs removed by the authorities."

"Please make way," I said, gently pushing through the hallway crowd. As the bodies parted, Madame followed me forward.

The last guest stepped aside, and I saw the man who had spoken. Small of stature, with beady eyes and thin lips, he wore a *Manager* badge on his black jacket, and his mustache—as dark as his funereal suit— twitched like a caterpillar in its death throes.

He was forcefully arguing with a model-tall young woman in a Versace split-thigh gown of a silvery aqua. Though slender, she looked like she could hold her own with her tanned, toned arms and a stiff spine to match.

"A. F. Babcock is a guest at your hotel, a *guest* who has agreed to financially compensate the hotel for any inconvenience," she declared with a toss of her loose brunette curls. "The least your hotel can do is extend your guest the courtesy of—"

Another animal howl interrupted her, this one accompanied by shattering glass.

"Uh-oh!" called the voice inside the suite. "I guess that's seven years' bad luck!"

The young woman opened her red lips to speak again, but the manager shut her down with a wave of his open palm.

"No more talk, Ms. Woodbridge! It's past time I call the police—"

"Excuse me!" I stepped forward, my mind working fast. "I can help with that. Calling the police, I mean."

They both stared.

"And who are *you*?" the scowling manager demanded.

"Someone who's concerned about this situation," I declared, channeling the haughty confidence of Sherlock Holmes.

The manager was not impressed. "That's not an answer."

"What do you mean?" I asked.

"I mean, Ms. Woodbridge here is Ms. Babcock's assistant. The crazy man inside that suite is Ms. Babcock's guest. Why in the world should this matter concern *you*?"

"Because I can get one of the top narcotics officers in the NYPD here in minutes. He'll bring his whole squad. They'll be happy to canvass the floor. That is, bang on the doors of every room and interview each guest about what they may have witnessed in connection to the drug crimes you'll be reporting."

The manager opened his mouth. I closed it again, this time by channeling good old Perry Mason—

"This incident began at the Wordsmyth Awards Dinner, correct?"

"Yes," he said.

"Then the narcotics detectives will want to clear all the guests who attended as well."

The manager blinked. "Clear?"

"Apologies for the police jargon. In plain language I meant *interview*. You see, if another guest or a member of your staff sold drugs to the professor, the detectives will want to find out. Oh, and I understand that an underage female from a Sweet Sixteen party was involved. She'll have to be interviewed, too. And since she's a minor, I believe the law requires that her parents be notified, which presents another problem. For the hotel, I mean. You see, this underage girl consumed narcotics right under the nose of your staff. It was your bartender who served her alcohol. That is a serious offense, sir, which could lose this entire establishment its liquor license."

The glamorous assistant in Versace turned to Madame. "Who is this, Mrs. Dubois? A lawyer friend? If she is, please inform her that she is not helping!"

"I agree," the manager said. "I think we'd all be better off with a hostage negotiator."

Madame gave them a wily smile. "Clare is much better than a lawyer. Or a negotiator. She runs my downtown coffeehouse."

The caterpillar on the manager's lip was really twitching now. His beady eyes glared at me. "Is this some kind of joke?"

"It's no joke," I assured him. "The head of the NYPD's OD Squad is my fiancé." I leaned closer. "And he's *very* zealous."

The manager's already pale skin blanched even whiter. "All right, miss. What exactly do you want?"

"I want to solve your problem for you, but *discreetly*. I plan to remove the professor and any drugs in that suite from these premises as soon— and as quietly—as possible. Or we can handle this another way—" I tipped my head toward Madame. "I can escort *this* eyewitness to the whole embarrassing affair back down to the ballroom's bar, where she can relate the entire sordid story to her reporter friend from Page Six." I shrugged. "I'm sure the newspaper account will be fair and not show the Grande Maison in too bad a light."

The manager was now fuming, but I could see in his knitted brow and shifting eyes that he was also worried. "Fine!" he said at last. "If you've got a plan, we'll try it your way."

"I assume the front door to Professor Humphrey's suite—"

"It's locked, chained, and barricaded with furniture," the manager said.

"Is there a door to a connecting suite?"

"Yes. I was going to let the police in that way."

"Give me the key and I'll deal with the professor," I said, sounding far more confident than I felt.

"If I do," said the manager, "how soon can you get that crazy man out of here?"

I didn't have a clue, and unfortunately that fact *might* have been written on my face. When I didn't answer right away, the manager called my bluff. Tapping the stopwatch app on his phone screen, he warned—

"I'll give you fifteen minutes to remove that animal, or I'll call your boyfriend myself!"

As I took a deep breath, the irony struck me. This wouldn't be the first time I herded a beast from a room—and twice in one day had to be a record for someone not working for animal control.

Meanwhile, the manager waved over someone in the crowd. One of the security men, a giant in dark slacks and a gray blazer, stepped up.

"Take her to the door of the adjoining suite," the manager told the guard. "Let her in, but do not follow. This is her plan; let her execute it."

The guard nodded and led the way. Madame caught up with us and took hold of my arm.

"Clare, stop. I appreciate what you've done thus far to help, but I never meant to put you in harm's way."

"You're not. I want to do this. And you know I can take care of myself. I've handled drunken frat boys, drug addicts, and Village eccentrics for years. You managed the Blend. You've done it yourself."

"That's true enough. But I'll feel better if you put this in your pocket."

Madame reached into her beaded evening bag, pulled out a small, black rectangular item, and pressed it into my hand.

"What is this?"

She leaned close. "Pepper spray. It's quite effective, and I'll feel better knowing you have it."

"All right." I slipped it into my pants pocket. "Now go back to the group, and I'll see you in a few minutes."

As the guard continued to lead me down the hall, I spotted a room service tray that had been left outside a door for the staff to collect. The food was picked over, the coffeepot empty, but that didn't matter because I had a plan.

"Wait just a minute!" I called out to the guard.

I peeled off my coat, revealing the Village Blend apron that I still wore underneath. Working quickly, I did what I could to make the used room service tray look new. Finally, I said—

"Okay, I'm ready."

The guard unlocked the main door to the suite and handed me a key card for the connecting door inside.

"Good luck, ma'am, and stay safe."

His ominous tone on those last two words gave me pause. Clearly, he was convinced I'd be leaving the hotel on a stretcher.

"Don't worry," I said, tray in hand. "I can handle this."

And if I couldn't? At least I'd finally get some rest.

Forty

꩜◌꩜◌꩜◌꩜◌꩜◌꩜◌꩜◌꩜◌꩜◌꩜◌꩜◌꩜◌꩜◌꩜◌꩜◌꩜

Stepping through the hotel room's door, I found myself in a lushly furnished space with a spectacular view of Central Park. I crossed a rug thicker than the city's annual snowfall and approached the suite's connecting door on the opposite side of the room.

While balancing the tray in one hand, I inserted the key card and opened the door a crack.

"Room service!" I called as brightly as I could manage, given my state of trepidation.

In response, the American werewolf let loose with a howl that startled me enough to drop the tray.

With his back to me, Professor Humphrey stood looming over a potted plant. Though he was decked out in evening clothes, his belt was undone, and his pants dangled halfway down his hairy legs.

When he heard the tray crash to the floor, he whirled, though he was not finished "watering" the plant. Closing my eyes, I channeled Esther—

"Unsee, unsee . . ."

"Hey!" he cried in excited recognition. "You're the duck lady from this morning!"

I opened my eyes to a confounding shock. Standing before me was Mr. Scrib's neighbor. Yes, the obnoxious Terror in Terrycloth. And he wasn't just standing. The man was presenting me with an awfully familiar (and truly awful) spectacle—

King Killjoy was tucking away his "scepter."

"*You're* Professor Ethan Humphrey?!"

The Terror (no longer in Terrycloth) attempted to bow but ruined the gallant gesture with a clumsy stumble.

"At your service . . ."

"You'd better be," I said, summoning my sternest *you're grounded* mom voice. "Now please do me the 'service' of zipping your zipper and buckling your belt because we're leaving."

Seemingly baffled by my command, Professor Humphrey scratched his head at the base of his unraveling man-bun and stared at me in a haze of narcotics and alcohol.

"What about the room service?" he asked.

"Sorry, I lied. I don't work for the hotel." Stepping around shards from a broken mirror, I quickly scanned the area for evidence of narcotics or drug paraphernalia. I found an empty champagne bottle, a hash pipe, and a bag of pot with the logo of a marijuana dispensary.

"Listen to me, okay? I'm here as your friend to help you avoid a mug shot and criminal arraignment, but we've got to move fast before the police arrive."

The word *police* worked better than a glass of ice water in the face. A spark of intelligence actually appeared in Ethan Humphrey's glazed eyes. He stared at me for a moment, scowled, and finally checked his zipper, notched his belt, and clumsily fumbled with his protruding collar.

"May I help?" I asked.

"Leave me alone, lady."

I kept my physical distance, but continued conversing. "We haven't been properly introduced. My name is Clare Cosi. I'm the manager of the Village Blend coffeehouse."

Another flicker of recognition lit his eyes before it faded once more. As he continued putting himself together, I noticed the professor had taken his shoes off, and one foot was completely bare. I located the shoes, but there was no sign of the wayward sock. I placed the footwear in front of him and stepped back.

With a grunt he sat down on a footrest and put them on.

I spotted a pitcher of ice water, poured a glass, and—though I was seriously tempted to dash it in his face—simply handed it to him. Humphrey drank deeply until the glass was empty, tiny droplets running down his cleft chin. And just like that, the American werewolf was tamed.

"Thanks," he grunted.

As disturbing as Ethan Humphrey's behavior was, he'd never become violent. And it hit me why he'd barricaded himself in here. It was his way of hiding from his troubles. Just like the drugs. *Same reason,* I thought. It was just another version of running away.

From that moment on, I saw Ethan Humphrey for what he was. Not a howling-mad beast or a dangerous drunk, but a scared little boy in a university professor's body.

I grabbed the hash pipe and pot and tucked them into Ethan's lapel pocket.

"What about my Dupont?" he asked.

"Dupont?"

"There it is." Ethan pointed at a gleaming silver rectangle on the rug. I scooped it up. The "Dupont" turned out to be a high-end lighter. I noticed a personal engraving on the side and read the quotation:

Nobody realizes that some people expend tremendous energy merely to be normal

"Are these your words?" I asked.

"Me?" Ethan shook his head and wobbled a little as his slurred reply informed me, "Albert Camus gets the credit because after his death they found the quotation in one of his handwritten notebooks. But he was just transcribing a quote from a French actress and poet named Blanche Balain." He waved his arm as if he were instructing a class. "Of course, she said it in French. And being a poet, she said it with more flare. Not 'tremendous energy' but *'une force herculéenne!'*"

"Herculean strength?"

"Yes."

I read the quote again. "A lot of drug users feel this way, Ethan. Is that why you do what you do?"

He stared at me. "What do you think?"

Suddenly, all the air seemed to whoosh out of him. His shoulders slumped, his chin dropped to his chest, and he let out a low moan. I feared he was going to pass out.

"Do you need an ambulance?" I asked.

"Hell, no!" He waved his arm. "I'm fine. I'm fine."

"I'm sorry I didn't bring you coffee," I said sincerely. "You could use it."

He looked up, pointed to the phone. "We can call for room service—"

"I'm afraid our welcome has worn out," I warned. "And, anyway, I think they serve Driftwood."

He stared blankly.

"Sorry, private joke."

But it wasn't my humor that dazed him. The seriousness of the situation appeared to dawn on the professor, and he felt an immediate need to escape. He rose, swaying unsteadily—and then bolted for the barricaded door.

I grabbed his arm as he stumbled by.

"Whoa, slow down. Let's go out the other way. It's easier."

When he nodded in agreement, I tucked his engraved sliver lighter into his lapel pocket. Then I led him through the connecting suite and toward the promised land of the hotel hallway.

Forty-one

~~~~~~

I COULDN'T believe it, but I had managed to extract the howling-mad professor from a barricaded room without a SWAT team for him—or a stretcher for me.

When we reached the hall, I was surprised to find it nearly deserted. On the other hand, given the scenario that I threatened with Mike's OD Squad, I shouldn't have been. The night manager obviously instructed his hotel staff to coax the guests back to their rooms and return to their posts.

Nothing to see here!

Now only the mustachioed manager, Addy's elegant young assistant, and my security guard escort remained. Madame was there, too, lurking behind them.

While the nice guard gave me back my coat, along with an impressed thumbs-up, the arrogant manager merely sneered and bolted down the hall to call the elevator.

Addy's assistant, Blair Woodbridge, was more civil. After a quick nod of thanks to me, she focused on her boss's nephew. Moving swiftly to the professor's side, she wrapped her arm around his waist to help me steady him.

"Are you okay, Ethan?" she asked.

He met the woman's long-lashed green eyes and grinned foolishly.

"Hiya, Blair. Where have you been? I could have used your help a little while ago."

"I was here the whole time," she said with a hint of impatience. "Didn't you hear me calling you through the door?"

"I thought you were a little bird." He pointed to me. "Like she has."

Professor Humphrey then let loose with a stream of loud quacks.

Horrified, Ms. Woodbridge shushed him. "Please, Ethan, quiet down. You'll disturb the guests."

"Okay." He put his index finger to his lips. "Shhhhh. But you know what, Blair?" he whispered. "You missed all the fun. Aunt Addy's event had an open bar."

"And clearly you took advantage of it."

He frowned. "Don't be miffed."

Blair Woodbridge rolled her eyes.

The manager waited at the elevator, holding the door. The guard was already inside, and he helped Blair Woodbridge move Professor Humphrey into the car. But when I tried to enter, Mr. Mustache barred my way.

"*You* can wait for the next one," he snapped and let the doors close in my face.

Forty-two

~~~~~~

"Now there's a candidate for charm school."

I turned to find Madame standing behind me in the hallway, arms crossed. "Shall we sign him up for Miss Mimi's?" she asked. "Or the Plaza's Finishing School?"

"Both, I think."

Stepping up, she gave me a hug. "I knew you could do it."

"I'm glad one of us did."

Madame smiled. "*And* I understand you had quite a busy day downtown."

"We all did. Did you stop by the shop while I was roasting in the basement?"

"No. But my date did."

"Oh, right. The former astronaut. Did he come with his Golden Ticket?"

"Indeed, he did. But he said the Village Blend looked busier than Grand Central Station with a line out the front door, so he opted to stop by another day."

"I'd love to meet him. Is he still here?"

"No. When the unfortunate Professor Humphrey problem arose, I sent him home with a promise to get together again."

"Well, given his Golden Ticket, I'm sure I'll be meeting him soon enough. I only hope the paying customers keep returning."

"Stay positive, dear. And . . ." She stepped toward the opening doors of a newly arrived elevator. "Stay up on this floor for a few minutes, will you?"

"Why?"

"Because I want to speak privately with Addy about what you did to help her—by helping her nephew, of course. I believe she'll be much more inclined to give you her time once she's made aware of the debt she owes you."

"Will that work?"

"It's worth a try," Madame said, and once again the doors closed in my face.

Suddenly exhausted, I collapsed onto the plush couch across from the elevator bank. Closing my tired eyes, I could have fallen asleep then and there, but after a few brief seconds of bliss my phone buzzed. Answering showed me a surprise: Mike Quinn's face on my phone screen.

"You're using FaceTime?" I was surprised because he hardly ever did.

"I don't know where you disappeared to," he said, "but I'm hoping to lure you back home by showing off my spread—"

"Spread?"

"We agreed to breakfast in bed tonight, remember?"

"I . . . didn't forget," I fibbed.

"I bought a basket at Murray's Cheese. Just look at this feast." Mike turned the camera on the food laid out on my kitchen table. "We've got aged Asiago, crusty Italian bread, cured olives, and all kinds of Italian delicacies that taste great but I can't pronounce. I've got wine chilling, and we have chocolate-covered strawberries and imported nut candy for dessert."

"That's some breakfast," I marveled, feeling the sweetness of his gesture tug at my heart.

"I *could* share this romantic meal with Java and Frothy, but they've already enjoyed their favorite cat food—and as cute as your feline friends are, I'd prefer the company of my fiancée. So, where are you?" Mike asked.

And there's the rub, I thought.

"Madame needed me uptown. She had a problem—"

"How serious?" Mike's buoyant expression instantly turned to iron. "Is there anything I can do to help?"

"You already have."

"How?"

"By being who you are."

"I don't get it."

"You don't have to," I said. "I'll explain everything when I get there."

"Then the problem is solved?"

"I'm heading home to you and my well-fed cats," I assured him. "And I can't wait to see you." (At least that was the truth.)

Feeling much better, I grabbed the next elevator. When I reached the lobby, I found Madame waiting for me. As she promised, beside my mentor stood the writer I'd admired for years, internationally bestselling author, philanthropist, multi-award winner, and the scarlet-headed opponent in that bizarre fire-and-ice struggle that I'd witnessed in the hotel basement—

A. F. Babcock.

FORTY-THREE

⠿⠿⠿⠿⠿⠿⠿⠿⠿⠿⠿⠿⠿⠿⠿⠿⠿⠿⠿⠿⠿⠿⠿⠿

"CLARE Cosi," Madame said. "This is Addy—"

The woman didn't wait for a formal introduction. She practically lunged forward, extending her two hands to capture mine.

"Ms. Cosi, I want to thank you. Both Blair and Madame told me how you helped with . . ."

As her voice trailed off, she shook her head in obvious mortification. But Addison Ford Babcock looked none the worse for wear. Her emerald gown was unblemished, her makeup looked perfect, and every red hair of her French twist was still in place.

"It's okay," I said. "Your nephew had a bad night. It happens to all of us."

Addy visibly relaxed. "Well, he's in the hands of my chauffeur now and on his way home. I'm sure Ethan will feel quite ashamed of himself in the morning."

"Perhaps he will."

With thoughts of Professor Humphrey dismissed, I pressed on.

"It's a thrill to meet you, Ms. Babcock. I absolutely adored your *New Amsterdam* novels, and I was excited to learn that you were a member of the Village Blend's original Writer's Block Lounge—"

"Oh, that old group?" She waved a bejeweled hand. "Ancient history. Just like me." She laughed. "Though Madame tells me you're starting the whole thing up again. Good for you."

Her smile, so natural a moment ago, now seemed a little forced.

"I do realize it was many years ago," I pressed, "but I have a favor to ask. Would you mind speaking with me about the people in the original group? One of them came back to our shop recently. His name is Jensen Van Dyne. Do you remember him?"

Her reaction surprised me. Instead of putting me off, Addy's green eyes suddenly seemed to sharpen. "How about we talk over a nightcap?"

Before I could answer, she shook her head.

"Oh, no. I'm sorry—" She tapped a tiny, diamond-encrusted watch on her porcelain wrist. "I didn't realize the time. It's getting late, and you must be exhausted. Let's meet tomorrow. Come to my place for brunch. You enjoy a good brunch, don't you, Ms. Cosi?"

"Doesn't everyone? And, please, call me Clare."

"Let's say eleven AM. My cook will do it up right."

"Thank you. That sounds lovely."

"Here's my address." She thrust a business card into my hand. "Feel free to bring a date, or someone from your new writers' lounge. I'll be glad to answer any of your questions, Clare. I'm an open book!"

Addy flashed a final smile before she and Blair Woodbridge headed for the doors. After they departed, Madame gave me a sly look.

"What do you think?"

"About the brunch?" I asked. "Or the promise to be an open book?"

"Both."

"I'm sure the brunch will be delicious. As for the open book, I guess we'll see. You're coming with me, aren't you?"

"Heavens, no." Madame shook her head. "I tried to question Addy earlier in the evening about the original Writer's Block group and that young actor who was killed, but I got nowhere. I believe you may have more luck persuading her to open up without me there."

"You mean she'll feel less guarded because I'm so far below her social station, and she'll assume there's little chance of me gossiping to anyone in her circle—besides you, of course."

"I'm not in her circle, per se, just passing through. But you're not wrong about Addy. She's a snob." Madame thought for a moment. "Bring someone from your staff. Someone not easily impressed. Someone who'll put Addy off-balance and give you a better chance at excavating pieces of that ancient history."

"I know just the person."

"Good. Because I know you, Clare. If Addy's book doesn't open, I'm sure you'll find some way to pry the cover loose."

"I'll do my best."

"You always do." Once again Madame gave me a tight hug. Then she tugged my hand.

"Come, dear. My driver will take us home."

Forty-Four

~~~~~~

I DIDN'T get my dream bubble bath or even that back rub from Mike. But at some point during my overwrought evening, that threat of body odor became a reality.

After greeting my disappointed fiancé with a blown kiss from five feet away and giving Java and Frothy a quick hello-cuddle, I hurried to the bathroom, stripped off my sweaty clothes, and stepped under a stream of warm water.

Since my early days of single motherhood, a long shower was a little vacation. Like waves tumbling a rough shell, the flowing rain would blunt the sharp edges of my rocky day, polishing it into a smoother, more manageable thing. The cleansing cascade almost always calmed my clanging nerves, relaxed my tense muscles, and washed away my cares (at least until the hot water ran out).

Now, as I lathered my sweaty skin with a suitably fragrant coconut-and-orchid soap, I tried to picture myself bathing under a tropical waterfall, beside an azure blue ocean, with a tall, fruity cocktail (and bare-chested Mike) waiting for me at the imaginary open-air bar when I finished.

But it didn't work. Not tonight.

So much had happened in the past two days that my anxious thoughts wouldn't stop churning. I rinsed off, toweled off, and squeezed the water out of my freshly shampooed hair, but I hadn't been able to wash away my worries.

The least of them involved my ex-husband, who had yet to return my text messages. Given Matt's secret lunch meeting with Cody "Drifter"

Wood, the prolonged silence didn't help my state of mind, which wasn't in a good place to begin with.

Despite my success at helping Madame impress her friend and the glimmer of hope that our Writer's Block Lounge relaunch would save our shop, I couldn't shake the disturbing sense of futility over helping a crime victim who'd been attacked, right in our back alley.

I could still see the sparkle in Mr. Scrib's eyes as he played his poetry game with Esther. The terror in his face when he'd lapsed into that disturbing episode in our lounge. And the horrible sight of his slight body slumped next to our dumpster, head bleeding.

Someone had hurt that poor old man so badly that he might not live to see another day, drink another cup of coffee, play another round with his young barista friend.

Many years ago, that alley had seen another crime, one that my mentor still believed she could have prevented.

I knew how she felt.

I'd been close to the attack on Mr. Scrib, yet I couldn't stop it.

I'd chased his attacker, but I'd been unable to catch up.

I was an eyewitness, yet I was unable to provide a proper ID.

And while I'd taken in a lot of information about our sweet elderly customer, I didn't know what—if anything—to make of it.

Fortunately, there was a seasoned detective waiting for me in the kitchen, a professional, albeit skeptical, listener. And while I didn't always share Mike's viewpoints, I did value his counsel.

After blow-drying my hair on autopilot, I wrapped a thick terry robe around me, stuffed my feet into slippers, and descended my duplex apartment's short flight of steps.

The prince of patience, Mike was still calmly waiting for me in the kitchen. No, he wasn't shirtless. But he had changed out of his work clothes and into a soft gray *Police Athletic League* T-shirt and sweatpants.

He had shaved and showered, too. I could see his sandy hair was still damp. But though his suit, gun, and gold shield were put away, his job was still clearly on his mind—and in his hands.

His brow was furrowed in concentration (or was it concern?) as he finished a text.

When he realized I was standing in the doorway, watching him, he set his phone aside, and we finally shared a proper kiss hello.

"You smell nice," he whispered. "Hard day?"

"Yeah, which was why I needed the shower. To improve my mood and—shall we say—*fragrance*."

Mike's serious face cracked at that. "So it was a good shower?"

"I was doing my best to picture you on a white sand beach, half-naked."

"Which half?"

"I'll tell you later."

"Promise?"

"I do."

The strong embrace of my fiancé's arms made me feel less alone in my troubles, and I hugged him in return. Then he sat me down in front of a picnic spread worthy of a Tuscan villa, poured me a glass of Chianti, and got right to the point—

"Now *what* exactly was Madame's problem and *why* did she need your help?"

Answering Mike's questions would require so much explanation that I couldn't help reprising my three-fingered Girl Scout salute.

"On pain of losing my merit badges, Lieutenant, I promise to submit to your interrogation. But first, I have some questions for you. And I'm starving, so let's eat."

Forty-Five

⁂⁂⁂⁂⁂⁂⁂⁂⁂⁂⁂⁂⁂⁂⁂⁂⁂⁂⁂⁂⁂⁂⁂

Mike agreed to my "feast first" proposal, and I quickly inhaled a plate of buttery Prosciutto di Parma, aged Asiago, and slices of crusty semolina.

Java and Frothy watched my carnivore consumption with no more than mild interest, which told me Mike had not only fed them dinner but likely plied them with tasty treats.

By now, Mike had sampled the spread for himself, and he took pleasure in pointing out items for me to try—the oil-cured olives, eggplant caponata, garlicky Genoa salami, and marinated artichoke hearts.

I ate them all in a foodie fugue state, along with the out-of-this-world combination of Pecorino Calabrese drizzled with sweet and smoky Italian chestnut honey.

"I'm not sure what this one is called," Mike said, slipping a slice of cured meat into my mouth, "but it's delicious."

As the flavorful morsel caressed my taste buds, I informed my fiancé that he'd just fed me finocchiona, a delightful Tuscan salami named after its star ingredient, fennel—*finocchio* in Italian. The delicacy dated back to the Renaissance era when country people began using fennel in their cured meat instead of pepper since pepper was prohibitively expensive at that time while fennel grew freely across the countryside.

"Culinary creativity out of adversity," I concluded.

"Or inflation as the mother of invention," Mike said.

"That too."

Next came the caprese salad platter, which Mike said he'd left intact because "it looked so pretty, I wanted you to see it."

I was touched by his thoughtfulness, and together we tucked into the edible Italian flag with its bright red slices of tomato, fresh white buffalo mozzarella, and sweet green basil. The drizzle of fruity olive oil and sprinkle of coarsely ground Mediterranean sea salt completed the mouthwatering joy, and I licked my lips as I dipped a fresh hunk of crusty bread into the extra-virgin olive oil.

As I continued stuffing my cheeks like a crazed lady going for chipmunk chic, Mike watched me with a sweet smile in his blue gaze. It cheered me to see him taking pleasure from my pleasure at his surprise picnic.

I knew how he felt.

Cooking up special dishes for family and friends gave me joy for the same reason. When you loved someone, making them happy made you happy. And I needed that tonight . . .

In a span of twenty-four hours, I'd felt many things—anger, despair, betrayal, confusion—but of all the emotions I'd felt, *surprise* wasn't one of them. I'd been through too many hard times and seen enough dark acts to be shocked when new ones presented themselves.

Maybe that was why Mike's little picnic moved me so much.

As complicated and challenging as our modern world was, as trying and complex as our relationships seemed, I found it deeply nourishing to know how a simple act of caring could boil it all down and make life feel good again—at least for a little while.

Forty-six

~~~~~~

Of course, our "little while" bubble didn't last, though we did make it through dessert . . .

After gorging myself on specialty meats and cheeses, I managed to find room for several mouthwatering pieces of imported Almond Brittle— a glorious candy that reminded me of the homemade kind my *nonna* and I used to make around the holidays for the customers of our family's little Italian grocery.

Unfortunately, the name proved to be prophetic. *Brittle* was exactly the feeling that settled over us after I swallowed that final bit of crunchy sweet goodness and asked—

"So what's the latest on Mr. Scrib? I mean Jensen Van Dyne."

"I know who you mean," Mike said. "I haven't forgotten Esther's favorite customer."

"Great! Then you have news?"

"I have news. But it isn't great."

Seeing the downcast look on Mike's face sent my high spirits into a nosedive. Our kitchen picnic had put me in such a nice mood that I'd naively assumed my simple question would yield a reassuring answer. Now all the anxieties that I'd felt before our happy meal came crashing back.

"I heard from Detective Russell when you were in the shower," Mike said.

"What is it?" I whispered, remembering the sight of his furrowed brow before we started our meal. "Is Mr. Scrib . . . is he—"

"No, he's not dead. And he's not brain-dead, either, but he still hasn't regained consciousness."

"And was Detective Russell counting on that to solve his case?" I asked and immediately regretted the tone of it. "I'm sorry," I quickly added. "That question sounded more like an accusation. I didn't mean anything by it. I'm just—"

"Tired, I know."

"I'm more frustrated than tired, Mike."

"Then let's keep talking . . ." He reached for the bottle of Chianti, but refilling my glass couldn't reinflate our bubble of bliss. Neither could changing the subject.

"So," he said, "are you going to tell me what happened with Madame tonight, and why she needed you uptown?"

"I have more questions for you first."

"All right. Shoot." Mike showed me his palms. "Not literally."

"You're the one with the gun."

"Not at the moment. I left it in the bedroom, along with my handcuffs." He arched an eyebrow. "Not that I'm trying to give you any kinky ideas."

"Don't even try to make me laugh. None of this is a laughing matter."

"Gallows humor," he said with a shrug, and I couldn't blame him.

Countless acts of violence and cruelty happened every hour in this city, and first responders needed ways to release the dark and disheartening tensions of what they dealt with daily. *Quips won't help you solve a crime*, Mike once told me, *but they will keep you sane.*

Wine didn't hurt, either. And on that thought, I took a long sip of the fruity, spicy Chianti that Mike had poured.

"Go on," he prompted, filling his own glass. "What else do you want to know?"

"I want to know what the NYPD is doing with the case. Given the fact that Mr. Scrib is still unconscious—and obviously can't provide an ID on his attacker—is Detective Russell making any progress?"

"Russell didn't solely rely on a victim statement, if that's what you're worried about. He followed through with an aggressive investigation."

"And?"

Mike's blue gaze turned steely. "I'm sorry to report that he's reached a dead end."

I couldn't believe my ears. "With all the cameras on these streets, how is that possible?"

"Our eyes in the sky have better luck with vehicles than perps on foot. And when your perp—the one you chased last night—fled the crime scene and slipped into the crowd in front of that nightclub, our camera squad lost the trail."

"Did they get any kind of ID?"

"Not much. The images were blurry, and the hood was up on the perp's coat, hiding the hair and face. That black hooded puffer coat, a pair of blue jeans, and black gloves were the best markers for tracking. After they lost the trail within the crowd outside the club, they believe the perp ducked inside the club, ditched the coat somehow, and slipped out undetected, because no one wearing that same black hooded puffer coat showed up on camera again that entire night or the next day."

"Did Detective Russell check inside the club?"

"Of course. He and his people canvassed the entire area. The only security cameras inside were focused on a small section of the bar where cash registers could be monitored. Russell and his team checked that footage with no luck. They also talked to the club owner, the bartenders, and the bouncers. Nobody recalled seeing anything that could help. They remembered plenty of people in blue jeans, but none in a black hooded coat. And there was no sign of the coat discarded on the premises, in the restrooms, out the windows, or in their club's garbage."

I gritted my teeth, trying to control my frustration. "So what did this person do with the coat? Eat it?"

"Even with a little salt and Tabasco sauce, I doubt a puffer jacket would have been digestible."

"Okay, then what do you think happened?"

"I think this person was clever enough to roll up the coat into a tight little package, hide it under their arm, and take it out with them at the center of a group of people leaving the club at the same time, so it wouldn't be picked up by detectives monitoring a traffic or security camera. That's what I think."

I sat back. "Is that all the news you have?"

"No. Like I said, the detectives in our camera squad have always had better luck with vehicles, and they did track your hit-and-run scooter into a blacked-out area—a place with no cameras. A bike patrol searched the general location and found it abandoned near the Hudson River. The scooter had been stolen."

"And the driver who left the scene?"

Mike shook his head. "Locating the scooter was the best they could do."

"Great. Zero for two."

"Yeah. Not a good average for our Finest Eyes team."

"No," I said, "but what you just told me about the nightclub does make me more certain of one thing."

"What's that?"

"The responding officers last night were wrong. I don't believe the attack on Mr. Scrib was a random act of street violence. That vanishing act by the perpetrator was too calculated. I doubt a street person would have gone to such lengths to avoid being tracked—or been able to melt so easily into a trendy, young nightclub crowd. Given those assumptions and what I learned today, I have another theory that you and Detective Russell ought to hear."

"Okay. I'm listening."

"Then settle back for a strange story, because Mr. Scrib isn't what he seems."

"Now I'm intrigued."

"You should be, though let me say up front that this man's life is a puzzle that I haven't entirely solved. I'll do my best to lay out the pieces I've discovered so far, but plenty are still missing, which is highly frustrating."

Mike gave me a little smile.

"Something funny?" I asked.

"No. It's just that . . . your description sounds familiar."

"Which part? The missing pieces or the feeling of frustration?"

"Both," Mike said. "Welcome to my world, Detective."

Forty-seven

〰〰〰〰〰〰〰〰〰〰〰〰〰〰〰〰

WHILE Mike sat back and sipped his wine, my cats curled up at his feet (because, after all, he was the man with the treats) and I shared everything I'd discovered, including the "Gold Coast" location where Mr. Scrib lived, the tidy apartment with the sky-high market value, Esther's rescue of Wacker the duck, and the bizarre confrontation with Mr. Scrib's half-dressed, mallet-wielding neighbor.

"I wish you would have called me," Mike said when I got to that point in my story. "Things could have gotten ugly."

"They could have," I conceded. "But they didn't. Like I told Madame this evening, I've had plenty of experience handling unpredictable coffeehouse customers."

"Unpredictable is one thing," Mike said. "The guy you described sounds a bit unbalanced."

"Oh, I'd say Professor Ethan Humphrey is more than *a bit* unbalanced."

Mike blinked. "He's a professor?"

"Yes, but I didn't discover that until this evening, when I went uptown and found myself coping with the Terror in Terrycloth for the second time in twelve hours."

Mike stared in disbelief. "Don't tell me."

I nodded. "Professor Humphrey was the reason that Madame needed my help . . ."

I recounted the hotel mini drama with King Killjoy and his unsheathed scepter, then finished the story of this never-ending day.

Mike rubbed the back of his neck. "So . . . this professor was drinking with an underage female. And snorting lines of cocaine in public. Then he barricaded himself inside a hotel room—and Madame called you *why*?"

"You know why, Mike. I've helped her friends out of tight spots before. And she had faith that I could do it again, which I did."

"Is there something you're not telling me?"

"If you're looking for motivation, that's easy to explain. Madame knew how much I wanted to meet a member of the original Writer's Block group. And when I said 'meet,' she knew what I really meant was—"

"Interview at length," Mike said.

I nodded again. "The most famous member of that original group appears to be bestselling author A. F. Babcock, and Madame knew if I could be of service to Addy tonight, then the woman would be grateful, and I would earn her trust."

"But why would helping this crazy professor neighbor of Mr. Scrib's earn you A. F. Babcock's trust?"

"Oh, that's right. I forgot to mention. A. F. Babcock is Professor Humphrey's Aunt Addy."

Mike sat with that for a moment. "That's quite a coincidence."

"Yes, and I know how you feel about those."

"You remember?"

"How could I forget? You've said it plenty of times, and in quite the Mike Quinn serious tone. 'In a criminal investigation, there are no coincidences.'"

"I stand by it," Mike said. "But in this case, it's not so much a coincidence as a connection."

"Yes, and I admit that I don't know what—if anything—to make of it. But it's too strange a coincidence not to mean something."

Once again, Mike fell silent. "Clare, I'm trying to give you some latitude here, but I just don't see a theory. How does any of this tie into the crime that took place in your alley?"

"Not crime singular, Mike. *Crimes plural*. Remember that young actor who was murdered years ago? The one who was a member of our original Writer's Block Lounge?"

"Of course. His homicide was never solved."

"Well, Mr. Scrib was a member of that same writers' group, and he told Esther that he was writing a book about *a crime with no punishment.*

I believe he was writing a true crime tell-all about that young actor's unsolved murder, and that's why he was attacked last night."

"But, Clare, there's one big problem with what you're proposing. You saw the man's notebook. It's full of nonsense and doodles. Why do you think a mentally unstable man like Jensen Van Dyne is capable of writing a publishable book?"

"Because Esther and I found many more notebooks in his apartment, full of lucid writing and beautiful poetry. The poems were dated and many of them were written recently. I also found a contract with a New York publisher. Hold on—"

I retrieved my phone and showed Mike the photos I took of the cover letter and contract.

"See what it says there? The contract is with Jensen Van Dyne for an untitled work of—"

"True crime," Mike finished for me with an expression he rarely showed: genuine surprise.

Forty-eight

❧❧❧❧❧❧❧❧❧❧❧❧❧❧❧❧❧❧

THE astonishment on the lieutenant's face slowly turned into another expression, one that he usually reserved for members of his squad when they produced a solid lead.

"This is interesting, Clare, what you've found . . ."

"His manuscript is due in a few weeks, so it's probably almost finished. At the very least, a written proposal exists. See the cover letter to the contract signed by an executive named Joan Gibson? She must have *something* in writing about the project. Esther tells me that publishers don't offer contracts without seeing written proposals."

"Did you locate the manuscript?"

"No, and that's why I think Mr. Scrib came to the coffeehouse last night in such a distressed state. I overheard his part of a conversation with his attacker. And I remember every word."

Mike leaned forward. "Tell me again. Everything you remember."

I closed my eyes to replay it all for Mike, the darkness of the alley and the sound of Mr. Scrib's loud, frantic voice, declaring—

"I don't have it! That's why I'm here. That's what I'm looking for!"

I explained to Mike how I'd strained to listen for a reply, but he or she was speaking or whispering at a level too quiet for me to hear. "Then Mr. Scrib cried out again—"

"It must be here. I've got to find it."

"Another pause came, and then I heard—"

"NO! It's mine. I would never give it to you! Never!"

"His words ended in a terrible choked scream. That's when I found his unconscious body slumped against the dumpster, saw his attacker fleeing, and gave chase."

With a deep breath, I gave Mike my conclusion.

"Yesterday, the police assumed what I'd heard were pointless rantings, part of another mental health episode, and the alley attack was the result of a random street crime. And you and I assumed the notebook he'd come back for was the one Esther was keeping for him. But after everything that I discovered today, I believe it's more likely that Mr. Scrib knew his attacker."

"I agree," Mike said. "You convinced me."

"I also believe Mr. Scrib could have been searching for another notebook, the one he was using to write his true crime book. I think he left it—or at least believed he left it—somewhere in our shop, and that's why he came back."

Mike frowned. "Have you found another notebook in the shop?"

"No. Not yet anyway."

"And you really think he was writing an entire book in longhand?"

"He wrote everything else that way. And the practice isn't as far-fetched as you'd think. Esther mentioned that C. S. Lewis composed his manuscripts in longhand and had his brother type them up for his publisher."

"Does Van Dyne have a typist?"

"He doesn't need one. Look—" I pointed to my phone. "There's a paragraph in the cover letter assuring him that they have someone ready to turn his handwriting into digital text."

Mike nodded as he reviewed the letter. "Forward whatever you have to me. I'll talk to Detective Russell tomorrow. I'm sure he'll want to speak with Ms. Gibson for any more background she can provide."

"See if she'll confirm my theory. Has Mr. Scrib turned in his book yet? I'll bet he hasn't. And what 'true crime' is he revealing? I assume it's the actor's murder, but I don't know for certain."

"I'll see what I can do."

"Good," I said. "And tomorrow I'll do some questioning of my own. I have a brunch invitation from A. F. Babcock."

"You do?" He looked astonished again.

"She wanted to thank me for helping her nephew out of his, uh, *predicament* at the hotel."

"When are you going?"

"Eleven. The shop should be under control enough at that time of day for me to take a long lunch break."

"And what do you hope to discover?"

"More background on Mr. Scrib and anything she can remember about the rest of the group members, including and especially that young actor who was murdered. She told me to bring a date."

Mike raised an eyebrow. "You mean me?"

"Sorry, Mike, but after that embarrassing scene tonight with her nephew, a police lieutenant would just make her clam up. I'm bringing Esther. The girl has no filter, and I'm banking on that to give me an edge."

"Good luck with that."

"I'm not sure what I'll find out. It could be a waste of my time to even question her."

"Like I said. Welcome to my world."

"Okay. When you put it that way . . ."

"Look, the case is in a holding pattern. Either Van Dyne will wake up and help identify who attacked him. Or . . ."

"Or that poor old man will die of his injuries."

"If that happens, we'll be looking for a murderer."

"And not likely to catch them, right?"

Mike took a breath. "Let's just say what you're doing could be very helpful."

"Thanks, I appreciate hearing that."

"I mean it, Clare. You're like those Tuscan farmers who found a way to make their salami using fennel when they couldn't afford pepper. It reminds me of a saying we had back when I was doing tours in squad cars. If you hit a light, make a right."

"I get it," I said. "Sometimes, to move forward you have to move sideways."

"Find a way to make progress. That's what I remind the detectives on my squad, and you've done that here. You've discovered a remarkable amount of information about a man who's basically a recluse. More than that, the kind of person who society looks down on—and too often abandons. The fact that you want to help him, that's one of the reasons I love you. One of the many reasons . . ."

"It's why I love you, too," I whispered. "One of the many reasons."

In the silence that followed, the gaze we shared buoyed my spirit. I could tell Mike felt the same.

"So . . ." he said, voice soft. "I have an idea."

"What's that?"

"Even police detectives know when to give their heads a rest. In fact, it's required."

"What do you suggest?"

Mike's powerful body rose from his chair. "Let's start by clearing the table."

"And then what?"

"And then we can head upstairs and discuss what you promised to tell me."

"What's that?"

His blue eyes smiled. "Which half of me you imagined naked."

"With luck, I won't have to imagine it."

Forty-nine

֎֎֎֎֎֎֎֎֎֎֎֎֎֎֎֎֎֎֎֎

Together we climbed the short flight of steps to the apartment's second floor. There was no white sandy beach up here, no tropical waterfall, or azure blue ocean, but the quiet bedroom and crackling fireplace were all Mike and I needed to give our minds (and bodies) a break from the impossible stresses of our lives.

I agreed with Mike about a sense of humor keeping you sane. But so did sharing a meal with someone you loved, and feeling their embrace on a cold, dark night.

Like that aged Pecorino drizzled with chestnut honey, Mike's lovemaking was a delicious combination of sharp and sweet. Tender caresses gave way to urgent needs. I needed him just as much, and my passion easily matched his.

When our lovemaking was over, the release was luxurious. Hours of tension melted away and a tranquil blanket settled over us. As Mike tucked me close against his strong form, I settled my head into the crook of his shoulder and rested my hand on his warm skin.

Mike's chest was solid, and his muscles well-defined. There were scars here, lots of them, including an angry-looking slash from a knife wound, healed incisions from emergency surgeries, entry points from multiple gunshot wounds.

"So, Cosi," he said, "I'm not half-naked anymore."

"No, you certainly aren't."

"You said you pictured me that way during your shower, but imagination is a tricky thing. Reality can be a letdown. It doesn't always measure up."

"*Measure* up? That's a daring choice of words for a naked guy."

Mike laughed. He knew I was kidding. And he was well aware that I knew his scarred body almost as well as my own. Not only could I trace every wound, but I could also appreciate the courage and costs involved in their making.

"Given the choice, Mike, I'll always prefer the real you—fully clothed or not—any hour of the day, any day of the week."

"Good to know," he said, "because I feel the same about you. In fact, I have an idea. Why don't we get married?"

"You already asked."

"And what did you say?"

"Yes."

"Oh, that's right. I remember. Just checking."

"Well, you can keep on checking if you need to, but I'm not changing my mind. You and I are officially headed for wedded bliss."

"Lucky me," he said.

"See that? And you didn't even have to use handcuffs."

"Hey, the night is young."

"I hope you're still teasing," I said on a yawn. "Because this night is now morning."

"Good morning, then, sweetheart. And sweet dreams."

A SHARP sound woke me.

The loud noise came from somewhere outside. I couldn't tell if it was an engine backfiring, an exploding firework, or (God forbid) a gunshot, since this was New York and anything was possible.

The room was darker now, the logs in the hearth had burned down to red embers, and I stared drowsily into the chilly gloom, but I didn't hear anything new, only the distant drone of the city. I was nearly lulled back to sleep when I heard the noise again, louder this time—

BANG!

I could swear the explosive sound came from right below my bedroom windows.

"Mike?" I called. "Did you hear that?"

Reaching over, I expected to shake the mound of his big body, but all I felt were flat bedcovers.

He's gone, I realized. *But where did he go? Was he called away on some police emergency?*

I threw off the rest of the bedcovers and pulled on my robe. That's when I heard shouting in the street.

I hurried to the window. The glass pane was white with frost. Only a small, rough circle in the center was clear. Peering through the lopsided porthole, I saw a figure in an overcoat standing on the sidewalk. The man was tall and broad shouldered with short sandy hair.

That's Mike! I realized. *But what is he doing down there? Was that the bang I heard? Was he shooting off his gun?*

I didn't see a weapon in his hand, but I noticed he was staring at something. I followed his gaze directly across the intersection and spotted a figure in jeans and a black puffer coat with the hood up—just like the attacker who'd left Mr. Scrib to die!

Once again, I only caught a glimpse before the figure became a blur, darting down the cross street and vanishing in the shadows beneath the sidewalk scaffolding.

That's when Mike took off running. And so did I.

I raced down the back stairs, unbolted our alley door, and threw it open. The alley was completely black. I was barefoot and still in my robe. I hurried outside anyway. Shattered glass from the broken light littered the ground. The sharp shards tore up my feet, but I kept going.

When I reached the sidewalk, I saw the Village Blend's windows were dark and the whole area was deserted, including Hudson Street, which stood eerily empty. I was about to cross when a yellow cab suddenly pulled up right in front of me.

"Taxi!" I called, deciding to use it to catch up to Mike.

But the door was locked. I couldn't get in!

I moved to shout at the driver to unlock the doors and saw Dante's friend Tony Tanaka behind the wheel. Tony shook his head and took off. That's when I noticed the two passengers riding in the back: Mr. Scrib and his pet duck!

"Stop!" I cried, stepping into the bike lane. I waved my arms and shouted after the departing cab. "Mr. Scrib, I need to speak with you! Where is your notebook?! Where did you put it?!"

But the only answer I got came from Wacker, who stuck his head out the window with a—

QUACK, QUACK, QUACK!

I wheeled around and found the lights were now brightly glowing inside the Village Blend, and it was packed with customers. But it wasn't the Village Blend anymore. To my absolute horror, a sign in the window read *DRIFTWOOD COFFEE*.

Peering through the windows, I saw Matt sharing a café table with Cody "Drifter" Wood.

Cody poured a cup of coffee for Matt, who drank it down. I could see Matt didn't like it. He even made a face, but he swallowed it anyway. Then the two of them laughed and shook hands.

That's when I noticed Tucker standing there, still in his Village Blend apron. He approached a table where two women were arguing. One of the women had red hair, the other white blond. Fire and ice.

Tucker tried to speak with the two women, but they were too busy arguing. Their vicious verbal sparring quickly turned physical, and they began to punch and kick each other. Tucker clapped his hand and shouted at them, trying to restore order. But when he attempted to pull them apart, the women began to punch and kick him!

"No!" I cried. "Don't hurt Tucker!"

That's when I heard a loud revving engine behind me. I wheeled around to find a scooter with no driver racing toward me. I tried to leap out of the way, but I couldn't. I was frozen in place!

The scooter hit me dead-on. I flew into the air, all the way up above the rooftops.

Floating like a feather, I drifted back to the ground and landed on my feet, but I was no longer in front of my coffeehouse. I was now in a vacant lot somewhere in Brooklyn. The area was run-down, with cracked concrete, rusted chain-link fencing, and trash littering the dirt.

The sound of someone shoveling echoed behind me. When I turned to look, no one was there. Just a shallow grave, already dug. I moved closer to the coffin-sized rectangle and looked down.

"No!" I cried. "It can't be!"

But there he was, my dear friend Tucker, lying dead in the dirt.

I wailed and screamed but no one came to help—

"Clare!"

I heard my name. Someone was calling me. A hand on my shoulder was gently shaking my body.

"Clare, wake up! You're dreaming. Wake up!"

I opened my eyes.

Fifty

~~~~~~~~~~~~~~~~~~~~~~~~~~~~~~

"That must have been some nightmare," Mike said softly.

"It was, and I'm glad it's over."

But though the nightmare images were gone, my breathing was still labored, my skin felt clammy, and my heart was galloping like a Triple Crown contender.

"Maybe I should get up," I said. "I need to sleep but I don't want to close my eyes again. I don't want to go back there—"

"Then just hold on to me until you feel better. I'm not going anywhere."

Under the bedcovers, Mike pulled me close. With his arms around me, my heart rate began to slow and my breathing gradually returned to normal. As they did, Mike reminded me how he'd suffered nightmares about the darker cases he'd worked.

Sometimes his dreams painted images that were bloody and violent, other times minute and mundane. He said it was his mind attempting to process all the little details—the people and evidence—as a way of trying to make sense out of things that made no sense.

"Dreams are like that," he said. "Puzzles with pieces missing. Somewhere there's a complete picture, but you can't make it out."

"Not yet, anyway," I said.

"Do you remember the details of your dream?"

"Some of them," I said and told him. "So, what do you think?"

"Well, I can't explain what the duck was trying to tell you," Mike said, "or why your Fire and Ice ladies were fighting, but I'm pretty sure I know why you saw Tucker in that shallow grave."

"Why? Is he in danger?"

"No, Clare. I doubt that he is."

"Then why did I see Tucker lying dead in a vacant lot?"

"Because he's an actor."

"An actor," I whispered. "Of course. My mind substituted him for the young actor who was killed all those years ago."

"And discovered buried under debris in a vacant lot in Brooklyn. Obviously, your head won't let that cold case rest."

I pulled away from Mike's arms and propped myself up to meet his eyes. "That unsolved case is the key to the attack on Mr. Scrib. I'm sure of it. If we could find out more about what really happened all those years ago, I'll bet it will shed light on who attacked Mr. Scrib and why."

"You know what? That's something I can help you with."

"You can?"

"I can request the file. Because it's an older case, it will take a few days to get my hands on it; but, like you said, it's unsolved, and I can certainly review it."

"That would be a huge help."

"All right, then. How's this? You tell me what you discover at brunch today, and when I obtain the cold case file on the actor's death, I'll share what I learn. Deal?"

"Deal. Thank you, Mike. I could kiss you."

"You *could*—" he began to reply, but I didn't give him the chance to finish his quip. My lips were already covering his.

Fifty-one

I HAD high hopes for the next morning, but the start of the day only fueled my fears.

The weather was overcast and business was slow. Even our early-morning rush wasn't as rushed as usual, and I wondered if our Writer's Block Lounge was already a bust. My baristas remained true believers, however, and continued to tell me that business would pick up after lunch.

On the positive side, Esther and I were easily able to head out for our brunch meeting—and we were leaving the shop in good hands.

Tuck and Nancy were all set behind the counter, and in case our sluggish business did pick up, Dante was scheduled to come in at noon, along with Howie Johnson, who was happy to support my baristas by bussing tables, hauling garbage, and restocking.

By now, I'd brought Esther up to speed on Addy's invitation, and she was excited about it. Who wouldn't be? We were about to share a meal with an internationally famous author, which made me a little self-conscious. But this was supposed to be a casual meeting at her home, so neither of us wasted time dressing up.

We were both presentable in black slacks and clean sweaters. And when the time came, we simply took off our aprons, threw on coats, and ordered a rideshare.

While I watched for the car's arrival, Esther ducked into the restroom, and Tucker sidled up to me.

"I'm so jealous of you two, getting to dine with Addy Babcock. Promise to dish when you come back."

"Sure," I said. "But I didn't know you were a fan of her *New Amsterdam* books."

"Actually, I'm not. I'm a fan of her old TV show."

"Her TV show?"

"Yes, Clare, her groundbreaking, *Emmy-winning* network television show, *She Slays Me*. You know it, don't you?"

"I know the show. It was a big hit back in its day. To be honest, it looked too violent for my taste. Not my kind of entertainment. And you say Addy had something to do with it?"

"She only created it—and wrote nearly every episode. It may have first aired decades ago, but it's been in syndication for years. That's where I saw it. And one of my old drama teachers was actually in the pilot, which was set during a production of Shakespeare in the Park, even though they filmed it on a Hollywood back lot."

"Is that unusual?" I asked.

"What? The back lot set?"

"No, that a writer would move from working in show business to writing novels?"

"Not really." Tuck shrugged. "Before James Clavell wrote *Shōgun*, he worked on a bunch of screenplays and directed *To Sir, with Love*. Robert Ludlum was a theatrical producer before he wrote the Jason Bourne novels. And Sidney Sheldon went from creating *The Patty Duke Show*, *I Dream of Jeannie*, and *Hart to Hart* to becoming one of the biggest best-selling authors ever."

A few minutes later, our car arrived. Esther joined me. Then Tucker sang, "Have fun, you two!" And we were on our way.

As we settled into the back seat, I silently digested what Tuck had told me about Addy's work in Hollywood . . .

She Slays Me followed the harrowing assignments of a young female intelligence agency operative. It featured elaborate fight scenes and clandestine assassinations. Nothing like Addy's *New Amsterdam* novels, which were basically time travel historical adventures with some soft romance thrown in. The switch in tone seemed odd, and because Addy would have conceived her award-winning TV show close to the time she'd been a member of the Writer's Block group, I wondered if she'd worked with others in the group on the idea for *She Slays Me*.

Given that her show's pilot episode involved a Shakespeare in the Park production, I couldn't help wondering if she'd been influenced by the young actor who'd been murdered.

As we headed downtown, even Esther admitted her excitement about meeting Addy wasn't because of her fame as a novelist.

"I never read any of A. F. Babcock's books," she confessed.

Esther was giddy because Addy had known Mr. Scrib all those years ago.

"I can't wait to hear what he was like when he was a young writer," she said before turning her attention to her phone screen.

I did, too, but not to check my social media or play *Candy Crush*.

This morning's lackluster customer traffic had revived my worries about our shop's financial health, which is why I made my *third* attempt to reach Matt in the past twenty-four hours.

Did he return my brief text, asking him to get back to me?

No. He did not.

Despite my nightmare image of Matt choking down the juice of Cody Wood's *over-roasted* beans (a classic masking technique for subpar cherries), I forced myself to breathe through my nose and put thoughts of that awful Driftwood franchise out of my mind.

Fifteen minutes later, however, Matt's ghosting would not stop grating, and I realized what bothered me most about his secret lunch with Cody was the silent treatment that followed.

Given our history, I couldn't help feeling (in a word) *triggered*.

During our marriage, I had tolerated Matt's silences and his secrets—until I couldn't.

Rising above those years had been a hard climb, but I'd done it. I was no longer Matt's young, gullible wife, so infatuated with him that I was willing to pretend that everything was fine (*just fine!*) when I suspected it wasn't.

Although Matt and I were no longer married, we still had an important relationship, a *working* one, and the best thing I could do for the health of our partnership was be honest with him about my state of mind.

So, as we rolled across the Brooklyn Bridge, I ignored the magnificent view of Upper New York Bay in favor of my phone screen, where I pounded out a new text message—

> Okay, Matt. Enough with the ghosting. When are you going to tell me about that lunch you had yesterday? I saw you both. The cat is out of the bag. Or should I say rat? (I'm talking about Cody, not you.) So please get back to me!

Yes, the note's tone was emotional, and I considered deleting it. But in the face of Matt's silence, I had to be blunt. In utter exasperation, I pressed *SEND*.

For long-suffering minutes, I watched the screen for a reply, but nothing came, and I finally tucked away the phone, along with my frustrations with Matt.

By now, our driver had reached the far side of the bridge and was soon sailing through Brooklyn Heights, an upscale historic neighborhood with national landmark status, a majestic canopy of trees, and a bumper crop of meticulously maintained brownstones.

Many of these town houses had been built in the robber baron era as grand single-family "country retreats" for the wealthy. By now, most had been subdivided into separate apartments. But the multimillion-dollar address where we were heading had only one tenant, renowned author Addison Ford Babcock.

Fifty-two

∽∿∽∿∽∿∽∿∽∿∽∿∽∿∽∿∽∿∽∿∽∿∽∿∽∿

ADDY'S home was an imposing three-story structure that crowned the crest of a gentle hill overlooking the Brooklyn Heights Promenade. The exclusive location gave her rear windows a view of the East River and the towering skyline of Lower Manhattan.

Esther and I stood a moment, gawking up at the urban mansion. Then together we climbed the steep flight of stone stairs to the main door.

A maid greeted us and led us into a pristine white foyer with a ceiling high enough to create an echo all the way up to the skylight three floors above. There were French Provincial chairs flanking a console table, towering potted palms, ornate vases, and a wide curved staircase with gilded rails that I whispered looked worthy of Versailles—

"Or Trump Tower," Esther cracked. "And I thought Mr. Scrib was living high. Sheesh!"

The young maid took our coats, and we were left alone. Minutes passed in stillness. Not even the potted palms swayed. Esther looked at me questioningly.

"Are we plebeians awaiting royalty?"

"Maybe Ms. Babcock is busy on a phone call."

"Or maybe she likes to make people wait, so she can make a grand entrance down those Mall of America stairs. Do you think we should curtsy?"

"A polite smile should suffice. Though she is *literary* royalty, so do what you feel."

After another minute ticked by, Esther gazed at the soaring ceiling with a jaundiced eye. "I wonder if clouds form up there."

"I don't see an umbrella stand, so let's hope not."

Just then, a door opened somewhere high above us, and we heard an enthusiastic cry. "Ah, there you are!"

Addison Ford Babcock glided down the stairs like a swan approaching shore. Her slender body was wrapped in a silky chartreuse sheath, and her long neck and porcelain wrists glittered with a Tiffany showroom's worth of jewelry. With her upswept red hair, perfectly applied makeup, and designer heels, she appeared ready for a Michelin-starred fine dining experience.

"I think we're underdressed," I whispered in Esther's ear.

"For a casual brunch at home? Naw, this is classic intimidation by affluence."

When Addy reached the bottom of the staircase, she clasped my hands (as best as she could with an emerald the size of a walnut on one finger and a ring of solid jade on another).

"So glad you've come, Clare, and you *did* bring a guest!"

Esther nodded. "Nice to meet you, Ms. Babcock—"

"Call me Addy, please. All my friends do, and I certainly hope you'll think of me as a friend."

I introduced Esther as the young force behind resurrecting our Village Blend's Writer's Block Lounge. Addy began to gush, telling Esther how important her task was and the hope she gave to aspiring writers.

"And you can count my granddaughter among them," Addy revealed. "She's a serious writer herself, and just before you arrived, she left for the Village Blend to try out your relaunched Writer's Block Lounge."

That news surprised us, but Addy hardly let us absorb it before issuing a gentle command. "Come along now. We'll dine in the parlor."

Fifty-three

༄྾ༀ྾ༀ྾ༀ྾ༀ྾ༀ྾ༀ྾ༀ྾ༀ྾ༀ྾ༀ྾ༀ྾ༀ྾ༀ྾ༀ྾ༀ

We followed Addy's clicking designer heels along a museum-like, marble-floored corridor where first edition copies of her six *New Amsterdam* novels were mounted like old masters, each in its own illuminated glass case.

Now it was my turn to gush. "I devoured every one of these books. The way you brought New York's history to life deepened my love affair with this city."

"Thank you, Clare. You're very kind."

We soon discovered the "parlor" was actually an extension constructed at the back of the mansion. The space was Gothic Revival by design, with an elaborately carved stone hearth, tiny gargoyles in each corner of the ceiling, and heavy mahogany furniture.

The room was intense, daunting, maybe even a little scary.

"How cathedral-esque," Esther whispered in my ear. "Will the Hunch-back of Notre Dame be joining us?"

I bit my tongue to keep from laughing—or shushing her, because I realized that Madame, in all her octogenarian wisdom, was absolutely right about bringing Esther with me.

Madame knew that I idolized this author, and that Addy was a formi-dable presence. Add them up and Esther was doing precisely what Ma-dame hoped she would. Esther's prickly cracks couldn't help but release some of the air from Addy's inflated world. And what a world it was.

The massive round dining table at the center of the room looked as if it could seat all of King Arthur's knights. For today, however, I saw only three place settings, and at the center of the spotless white tablecloth was a sizable antique vase displaying an arrangement of lovely blush-peach roses, their riot of petals opening in unique cup shapes.

Addy noticed where my gaze had strayed.

"It took the breeder fifteen years and three million British pounds to create these floral works of art. What I love most about these exquisite blossoms is their literary connection. They're named after the most memorable of Shakespeare's heroines."

Esther nodded knowingly. "Lady Macbeth."

"Goodness no!" Addy looked appalled. "These are *Sweet Juliet* roses. I have a fresh bouquet placed in this room every morning." She sighed, gazing at them. "They're my only weakness."

Addy gestured for us to sit, and we found ourselves facing a line of massive arched windows, framed in stone with a clear view of neatly cut hedges and beyond them, the Brooklyn Heights Promenade and its awe-inspiring view.

By now the cloudy morning had given way to a crisp, sunny day. From our high vantage, we could easily watch the public strolling along the esplanade; barges moving up and down the sparkling, choppy waters of the East River; and in the distance, sight-seeing helicopters buzzing around the Financial District's skyscrapers—all under a brilliant blue late-morning sky.

The young woman who took our coats reappeared in an apron and set down plates. "For your brunch service today, Ms. Babcock's chef has prepared appetizers of semi-cured goat cheese with sweet paprika. One is topped with a freshly blended fig paste and the other with *boquerón*, a Spanish-style, vinegar-macerated anchovy. The vinegar mellows the fish. Both are served on crostini toasted with duck fat."

Esther winced at me and silently mouthed, "Duck fat? I love Wacker! I can't eat this!"

"Just eat the cheese and toppings," I mouthed back.

She frowned at the plate and leaned close to whisper, "I thought brunch meant Belgian waffles and fruity pancakes topped with ice cream."

"Apparently not in Brooklyn Heights," I whispered back.

Thankfully, Addy was too busy discussing our beverage service to notice our miming.

"No wine, Elena. Bring us a liter of the Vichy Catalan. Chilled, but no ice . . ."

Meanwhile, I amused myself with bites of the chef's amuse-bouche.

Crostini meant "little crusts" in Italian, and that perfectly described this slice of freshly baked semolina baguette gently browned in duck fat with a dash of salt and white pepper. The goat cheese, creamy and delicious with a subtle hint of sweet paprika, mitigated the unctuousness of the duck fat and paired well with both the tangy anchovy and sweet fig paste.

Esther unceremoniously licked off the cheese and toppings and slapped the duck-fat toasted bread back on her plate. Then she pushed up her black-framed glasses and got down to business.

"So, Ms. Babcock—"

"Please, call me Addy! We're all friends here."

"Okay, Addy," Esther said. "Let's make like girlfriends and dish. We're dying to know everything you remember about the Writer's Block Lounge."

Fifty-four

"Oh, my goodness, ancient history," Addy said, suddenly interested in the view. "I wouldn't know where to start."

I quickly solved that dilemma. "How about we narrow the scope of the question? You must recall why you joined in the first place."

Addy paused, could see I wasn't going to back down, and finally replied.

"Well, I suppose, all those years ago when I first went to your charming Village Blend, I thought I was emulating the famous authors who recorded their own thoughts inside coffeehouses. Who wouldn't want to write like Voltaire, Dostoevsky, Albert Camus—or even Jack Kerouac? But in human terms, these authors also engaged in discussions with other patrons as much as they actually sat and wrote. They went to coffeehouses for intellectual stimulation, for inspiration, for fellowship, as well as a place to write . . ."

Elena reappeared to clear our plates and pour the (very expensive) mineral water. Addy took a sip.

"Ah, this Vichy Catalan is my only weakness. I've had it imported from Spain for years, ever since I first tasted the healing thermal waters of Caldes de Malavella. Enjoy it, ladies!"

Esther sipped and shrugged. "I guess it's as good as San Pellegrino. Have you tasted their flavors? Dark morello cherry's pretty awesome, and you're in luck. It's on sale right now at Key Food and ShopRite."

Addy gave her a tight smile. "Getting back to your question, Clare. If there is a one-word answer to *why* I joined the Village Blend writers' group, besides inspiration, it was simply this: *loneliness*. I came to New

York fresh out of school and moved in with a college friend who ulti-mately couldn't cope with the many challenges of this city. She went home after six months, which left me with no friends, a squalid apartment I could barely afford, and a dead-end job at a Midtown law firm."

"Were you a paralegal?" I asked.

"I wish. No, I was a lowly clerical worker. In those days, law books were in binders and updated pages were issued as the laws changed. My job was to swap out the old pages for the new. Tedious work done in a tiny, window-less library where I was pretty much ignored by the rest of the staff."

"Sounds like one of Dante's Circles of Hell," Esther said.

"The First Circle, I'd say. *Limbo*. I was so miserable I started writing alone in my apartment at night. That's when I began working on what would become the launch book in my *New Amsterdam* series."

"Really? That long ago?" I asked, calculating the publication date. "But you didn't publish it until decades later."

"I didn't *finish* the novel until decades later, after my writing career took off with another project." Addy reached for her glass and her enor-mous ring dinged the crystal. "You see, while I was a member of the Writer's Block Lounge I dreamed up the concept that eventually became the television series *She Slays Me*."

Esther's jaw dropped. "You worked on that show?"

"I *created* and wrote nearly every episode, Esther. But you're far too young to have watched its original run. Am I right?"

"You're right. I watched it in syndication—"

Just then, Elena was back. "For your main dish, we have a duo of Pennsylvania game: Roasted Saddle of Rabbit and Paccheri Pasta Stuffed with Venison."

"Delightful!" Addy exclaimed, and as she asked Elena to compliment the chef, Esther leaned close again to whisper—

"I can't eat Bambi and Thumper!"

"Is anything wrong?" Addy asked.

I spoke up. "Would you have a vegetarian plate for Esther?"

"Oh, my goodness, yes! Elena, would you—"

"Be right back," she said and in a flash presented Esther with "*Aigre-Doux* Beets, Asparagus Roasted with Lemon and Garlic, and a Horse-radish Tartelette with Sauce Roquefort."

"Thank you, Elena," Addy said and turned to us. "Many of these delightful offerings were featured on Daniel Boulud's Mother's Day menu last year. I hired away one of his chefs de partie on the spot. The fine dining at Daniel's is my only weakness. Enjoy!"

We did, and as Esther happily tucked into her lemon and garlic asparagus, she continued to chatter about Addy's hit TV show. "My older sister was an even bigger fan of *She Slays Me* than I was."

"How nice," Addy replied absently.

"Sis was the kind of teenager who read textbooks for entertainment. Her idea of a hot Saturday night was spotting a meteor while stargazing with her science club girlfriends. They were all fascinated by the ingenious ways people were offed by the girl assassin on your show."

Addy's polite smile grew bigger. "Yes, those plot devices were ingenious, if I do say so myself."

"My sister was absolutely inspired," Esther said. "One of her science club projects was engineering a tiny balloon hidden behind her ring that dispensed a few drips of liquid saccharin for her tea."

Addy laughed. "She took that from 'The Ricin Ring.' One of my favorite episodes . . ."

Seeing Addy more relaxed, I tried to steer the conversation back to her personal memories. "If you enjoyed working on the show so much, why did you leave it for novel writing?"

"Oh, after a few years, our star was getting major motion picture offers and held the production up for ransom. The novelty of the show had worn off by then and the ratings were down. So we all agreed to do one final season. Then I pitched my *New Amsterdam* idea, but I was told the production would be too costly. They didn't have the vision that I did, and I was desperate to write the story, so I left Hollywood, and the rest— as you know—is literary history."

"Then you were happier writing novels?" I asked.

"Absolutely. It's a singular vision. That's the beauty of being a novelist. You don't have to limit your cast or locations, or worry about costuming and above the line casting costs." She sighed. "I still remember the headaches with the *She Slays Me* production: the star constantly complaining about her skimpy costumes; the struggles to get the stunt double looking believable in the fight scenes; and the network exec who would not stop griping that a female assassin would create a backlash for the show."

"I don't remember any backlash," Esther replied. "And didn't the show win an Emmy?"

"Three Emmys. But despite the overall acclaim, some critics—older male critics, by the way—did find it disturbing to watch a sweet, innocent-looking young woman commit cold-blooded murder in every episode, never mind that the villains were evil incarnate and *certainly* had it coming."

"Not everyone embraces the new," Esther said. "*She Slays Me* was one of the earliest shows to shake up the male-dominated action category. It came before *La Femme Nikita, Buffy, Alias, Dark Angel*—the whole kick-ass girl revolution."

"Yes, and the groundbreaking nature of *She Slays Me* was why I received an Emmy for writing, the show won best drama, and the lead actress took home a statuette for her work as Stephanie Slay. I remember the *New York Times* glowingly describing my protagonist as *Jane* Bond and the show as *That Girl* with a license to kill."

"Kill is right!" Esther replied. "And so ingeniously. I'll never forget the tube of body lotion that fired a bullet. After I watched that episode, a woman beside me on the bus pulled out a tube of hand cream and I almost lost it."

"Ah, yes, 'Beauty Creamed,'" Addy said wistfully. "I enjoyed writing that episode, but I hated the title. What can I say? Sometimes the producers win."

"Deadly body lotion is a pretty outré idea," Esther said. "Is that even real?"

"Yes, I fear that it is."

"What about the others?" Esther asked. "Let me see . . . there was a plastic explosive-stuffed cigar, a radioactive teapot laced with polonium, a pen filled with poison instead of ink, a stiletto umbrella, anesthetic toothpaste—"

"Yes," Addy cut in. "Every one of those methods of kidnapping and assassination that I used in *She Slays Me* was researched."

"Researched how?" I asked, taking a thousand mental notes.

"All sorts of ways," Addy said, waving her rings dismissively. "I made sure things were accurate from the very first episode."

"That first episode was my favorite," Esther said. "Talk about memorable Shakespearean heroines. You certainly created one."

"How did she do that?" I asked.

"In the pilot episode, Stephanie Slay poses as an actress in *A Midsummer Night's Dream*. Between acts she kills a terrorist in the audience of the Delacorte Theater with a poison dart fired from a blowgun—"

"That's right," Addy said. "She was playing a fairy and the blowgun was disguised as a wooden flute."

"It blew *me* away," Esther cracked. "Pardon the pun."

"I'm flattered to know you enjoyed it."

I was now on the edge of my seat. "Addy, you said you came to the coffeehouse for inspiration. Did the group help you hone your idea? Did you incorporate any feedback?"

"Who can remember that far back?" Addy said, this time with a forced laugh. "And, really, if I did incorporate any suggestions I received, they were quickly rendered irrelevant."

"What do you mean?" Esther couldn't mask her skepticism. "That's not my experience with writing groups. Didn't you keep a notebook?"

"You misunderstand, Esther. The moment I signed my Hollywood contract, *everyone* wanted to jump in with suggestions. The network executives, the producer, the director, even the actors had their own ideas about what the show should be. By the time *She Slays Me* debuted, dozens of cooks had contributed to my soup."

"Speaking of literary soups," I cut in, "I'd like to hear more about the members of the original Writer's Block Lounge."

"It was so long ago, Clare, I can't recall them all by name."

"I'm sure you can remember *some* of them."

She paused to sip her mineral water, but I got the distinct impression her writer's mind was working up another evasive answer.

I took a breath for patience, thinking Madame was right.

Despite Addy's claim last evening that she was an "open book," when it came to the history of the Writer's Block Lounge, that book remained frustratingly closed.

Fifty-Five

∽ ∽ ∽ ∽ ∽ ∽ ∽ ∽ ∽ ∽ ∽ ∽ ∽ ∽ ∽ ∽ ∽ ∽ ∽ ∽

It was Esther who found the lever to pry open Addy's tight lips.

"Didn't you say that your granddaughter is a writer?" she asked. "And that she's checking out our new Writer's Block Lounge this very day?"

"That's right, Esther."

"Well, for her sake, you should share whatever you remember about that first group." Esther glanced at me. "We want to make it a success, right, Boss?"

"Yes, we do," I said. "And knowing what worked and what didn't all those years ago will be a big help to us."

Addy hemmed and hawed a moment, refilled her glass, and finally said, "To be honest, ladies, only the *serious* writers made an impression on me, and less than half were truly dedicated to the craft of writing. The rest struck me as, I'm sorry to say, dilettantes. They didn't do the work required, though they enjoyed the *idea* of being a writer; of making a living or even a fortune on flights of creative fancy; of being admired, gaining prestige; or maybe simply finding an escape from the daily grind of conventional life."

"Well, I understand the need to escape the confinement of the conventional," Esther said. "Ray Bradbury once wrote that 'you must stay drunk on writing so reality cannot destroy you.'"

"Apropos, since some of those members were simply *drunk*," Addy added flatly. "As far as the functioning of the group, there were no set rules. We took turns reading our work and everyone offered their suggestions, but mostly it was a social gathering. We traded opinions on books we read, on films we saw, and the news of the day. At most get-togethers, the coffee turned Irish the moment it was served. Someone even concocted a signature spiked coffee for the group. We had a name for it, but I can't quite remember . . . It began with a *K*, I think."

I sat up a little straighter. "Was the drink, by any chance, *Kismet*?"

"That's it!" Addy blinked. "Goodness, Clare, how could you know?"

"Jensen Van Dyne mentioned it."

Addy's face blanched. Was it my reference to Mr. Scrib? Or the connection of the man with the Kismet drink?

In the throes of his breakdown at our shop, he had shouted a frantic and cryptic warning never to touch the stuff. I'd dismissed his ravings as part of his mental instability, but after seeing Addy's reaction, I didn't hesitate to press forward.

"Speaking of Jensen Van Dyne, would you share what you remember about him? Did you think he was a 'serious' writer, as you put it?"

Addy's frozen expression melted a little. "Yes. Jensen was serious and quite dedicated to his work. Every writing group has their star, and Jensen was ours. He was a sweet, unassuming young man who was always quoting the great poets."

Esther leaned forward. "Why was he a star?"

"Jensen's first fiction was published in *Wordsmyth*, which was prestigious enough. But then his story was selected for its annual *Best Short Stories* anthology. We all admired Jensen's talent, his success, too—some to the point of jealousy."

"Jealousy? Who was jealous of him?"

Addy shook her head. "We were all a little jealous of each other—for various reasons. Human nature, dear."

"More like the nature of high school," Esther said. "If you're evolving as a human being, you outgrow that kind of thing."

"Exactly," Addy shot back. "Maybe you ought to remember that for your new writers' lounge. Ambitious people can be jealous. And the young are the most ambitious of all because they haven't had time to accomplish much. Watch out for their jealousy. It can be dangerous."

"Dangerous?" I sat up a little straighter. "Addy, did you know that Mr. Van Dyne is in the hospital because someone attacked him in our alley?"

Addy looked taken aback. "My goodness, no, I didn't, Clare. Is he all right?"

"We don't know yet, but we're trying to find out who attacked him."

"That's very distressing news. Please let me know if I can help in any way."

"You can," I said, "by answering more questions."

"I don't understand. How will that help you find his attacker?"

"I think it may have had something to do with the original Writer's Block Lounge."

"That's quite a leap. I don't see it."

"Did you know that Mr. Van Dyne has an apartment in the same building, and on the same floor, as your nephew Ethan Humphrey?"

That also appeared to catch Addy by surprise. "That's quite a coincidence, Clare. Are you certain?"

"We visited Jensen's apartment ourselves," Esther said. "I found the keys in the notebook he left at the Village Blend. He wrote in it every day, and I'm keeping it safe for him—until he gets out of the hospital."

"A notebook?" Addy frowned. "How very interesting."

I pushed again. "So, Addy, have you had any contact with Mr. Van Dyne recently?"

"No, Clare. I didn't even know he was out of the . . . *facility*."

"Then you knew about his condition?"

"That Jensen was institutionalized for a number of years? Yes, I knew. The poor man always had emotional issues. When I first met him, he was mourning an unrequited love."

Esther leaned forward. "Was her name Juliet, by any chance?"

"Juliet?" Addy echoed, looking surprised again. "Where did you come up with that name?"

"In Mr. Scrib's poetry. When we visited his apartment, we found notebooks filled with beautiful handwritten poems. Many of them were either about, or dedicated to, someone named Juliet."

Addy waved a dismissive hand. "I can't help you."

"Are you sure?" Esther pressed. "What about the other women in the group? Were any of them named Juliet?"

"No," Addy said. "And none of those frivolous girls would have made a lasting impression on him."

"Well, this girl, whoever she was, must have had something going for her, if Mr. Scrib—I mean Jensen—loved her."

Addy shook her head, focusing on her food. "Jensen is a romantic, Esther. He always was. If you want my opinion, Juliet is nothing more than a fantasy, like Dante's Beatrice. A relic of courtly love delusions. A metaphor for Shakespeare, poetry, and the arts he loves so much . . ."

We were on a roll now, and I didn't want to lose momentum. "Addy, I took some screenshots of pictures in Mr. Van Dyne's photo album. Would you mind looking at them? They might jog your memory."

Addy didn't move a muscle, but I did.

Reaching for my phone, I hoped for the best.

Fifty-six

〜〜〜〜〜〜〜〜〜〜〜〜〜〜〜〜〜〜〜〜〜

I SHOWED Addy several group photos. She shook her head at the larger gatherings of twenty-plus people, claiming it was hard to make out their faces.

I swiped my phone screen. "How about this one? There are only four men and two women—" I pointed at a strikingly handsome young man with golden hair and a cleft chin who occupied center stage. "You must remember him, right?"

"That's Ace," Addy said, expression guarded. "I don't recall his last name. He was an actor, quite good-looking, as you can see. Also very full of himself. He was always dreaming up projects that he could star in— plays, television shows, movies. I admit the man was charismatic."

"And popular with the ladies?"

Addy's brow furrowed. "A little too popular, Clare, if you take my meaning. Thankfully, I was immune to his charm offensive."

"So, Ace was the one who was murdered?"

Addy didn't even blink. "That's what I heard. I was gone by then, of course, living in Los Angeles. *She Slays Me* was in development."

"How did you find out about the death? Did someone from the group tell you?"

"I can't actually remember how I found out. Probably a newspaper report."

"The LA papers?" I said. "Why would they bother with what would have essentially been a local New York police blotter report?"

"Well, I know I didn't hear it from anyone in the group. I didn't keep in touch with anyone—including Ace's young friend."

I perked up. "Young friend?"

"Or maybe he was a relative? Ace and this young man were close. His name was Bobby . . . something. He was tall, and a bit rough around the edges. Long hair. Generally scruffy. A little too bohemian for my taste."

"How do you define *too bohemian*?" Esther asked.

"A hippie throwback. The boy wore shirts with holes in the armpits and he didn't bathe enough."

I went back to a larger group photo. "Can you see Bobby in this crowd?"

"There he is. The skinny young kid with the long, stringy hair. And that man on the right is . . . *was* Peter."

"Was?" I said.

"Yes, Peter and I dated very briefly. He had a day job at a Wall Street firm where his father was a partner. He was quite romantic about the bohemian history of Greenwich Village, but he was writing an odd sort of novel. I didn't get it. A philosophical book about golf. Can you imagine?"

"Sure," Esther said. "Like *The Legend of Bagger Vance*."

"I suppose," Addy said. "I read his obituary in the *Times* two years ago. He made it to the board of directors of his father's company." She shook her head. "He never did finish that book about golf."

"Are you in this picture?" I asked, swiping back to the smaller group with the actor Ace at center stage.

Addy pointed to a slender young woman with high cheekbones and a light brown ponytail. "That's me—goodness, I was so young."

"And who is this?" I asked, pointing to the second woman in the photo, a little heavier with frizzy dark hair. It was hard to see her face. She was half turned from the camera, putting up a hand, as if she didn't want to have her picture taken.

Addy shrugged and shook her head. "I don't recall."

"Do you remember *any* of the women?" I asked.

"No one stands out."

"Madame mentioned one young woman who left the group in tears, never to return."

She looked away a moment, toward the cathedral windows with the panoramic view. "That must have been after I left."

"Do you see Mr. Van Dyne?" Esther asked.

"Jensen was always behind the camera," Addy replied. "He was the only one of us who owned one."

I showed her more photos but got nowhere. Addy said she didn't even remember the big, middle-aged Italian-looking man with the walrus mustache who was lurking in the background.

"I'm sorry there are no photos of Jensen," Esther lamented. "I would love to see what he looked like in his prime."

Esther's tone was affectionate, which is why Addy's harsh reply felt almost hurtful—

"I wouldn't foster too many romantic notions about the man, if I were you, Esther. Despite his initial success, Jensen Van Dyne was, in the end, just a cup of coffee."

Esther blinked. "Excuse me?"

"It's a baseball term. I learned it while doing research for the 'Seventh Inning Stretcher' episode of *She Slays Me*. 'A cup of coffee' refers to a player who was in the major leagues only for as long as it took to drink a cup of the beverage you peddle. My agent would call someone like that a one-hit wonder. It's a tragedy, but after the success of his first short story, Jensen never published again."

I could see that Addy's comment, along with her tone, infuriated Esther. I didn't know how much until her next words.

"Well, that's about to change," she said sharply. "Jensen Van Dyne has a brand-new contract with a very enthusiastic publisher!"

Fifty-seven

〰〰〰〰〰〰〰〰〰〰〰〰〰〰〰〰〰〰

FOR a few seconds, silence descended. With all the stone and dark wood around us, it felt like we actually were in a cathedral. At last, Addy flatly said—

"Oh, my, that is exciting news. You must be quite close to Jensen to know about it, Esther."

"I certainly care about him, and I think—"

I bumped Esther's foot under the table. "Mr. Van Dyne hasn't told us much—"

"Yes, he has!" Esther declared. "He says his book is going to make news. He told me his story will shake up the whole city!"

I finally stomped on Esther's Doc Martens hard enough for her to get the message.

"Perhaps I can help," Addy said. "Can you get me the manuscript to read?"

"Isn't that something you should get from his publisher?" I quickly replied, remembering his contract. "Do you know his editor, Joan Gibson?"

"Joan Gibson, you say?" She shook her head. "I never heard of her . . ."

Addy pushed her plate aside. "But if and when Jensen recovers from his unfortunate injuries, I hope he'll be up to the task. Publishing is a very different business than it was when he wrote his short story all those years ago. Success is much more difficult to attain these days."

"A good book is a good book," Esther countered. "And a good book will always find an audience."

Addy scoffed. "If only it were that simple. Sales require promotion, and the publisher can only do so much. For any hope of success, Jensen will be asked to give interviews, make appearances, and have a vibrant social media presence. I'm not sure he has the emotional stamina to withstand the attention or meet the demands of the publisher and the public. Those demands are why I have an entire publicity team in place and ready to go for next summer."

Once again, Addy had managed to derail the subject of our conversation.

"What's happening next summer?" Esther asked.

"Two things." Addy turned to me. "As a fan of my novels, Clare, you should be especially excited to learn that my *New Amsterdam* series is being adapted—all six of them—into a Netflix streaming event."

"That is exciting," I said (even though I didn't have Netflix).

Addy signaled for the server to clear the table. "With this streaming series, my *New Amsterdam* novels will find a whole new audience."

"I haven't read your novels yet," Esther confessed. "What's the premise?"

Seeing Addy's grimacing reaction to *that* request, I jumped in.

"They're excellent reads, Esther. Addy's heroine is Tabitha Sloan, a young engineering student who falls into a pit at a Lower Manhattan construction site. Ancient forces in an underground stream pull her into the ocean and she washes ashore in another time, when New York was called New Amsterdam and ruled by the Dutch. But though she's stuck in the seventeenth century, she still has her modern knowledge and uses it to help the community that becomes her new home."

Esther nodded. "Like Mark Twain's *Connecticut Yankee in King Arthur's Court*."

"Exactly," Addy said. "Twain's time travel story was one of my early inspirations. But my heroine rescues her newfound community from the scourge of cholera. She finds romance with a dashing sea captain, battles pirates, and with her engineering knowledge outmaneuvers the king of England."

Esther looked impressed. "Sounds like a strong STEMinist character." She tapped her chin. "Did someone make a movie out of your book at one time? I ask because I think I saw it."

"Oh, that was a dreadful film." Addy shuddered. "I never got over the trauma. The one consolation is that they didn't call it *New Amsterdam* and sully the brand forever."

"*Time After Time*, right?" Esther said.

"That's what they wanted to call it, until I reminded the studio executives that my colleague Nicholas Meyer had already made a movie called *Time After Time*."

"Oh, right. Was it *Time and Time Again*?"

"Close." Addy grimaced. "You're missing a third *Time*."

Esther winced. "Really?"

"Yes. Some genius executive decided the title should be *Time and Time and Time Again*. He said the third *Time* was the charm. At that point I washed my hands of the project and walked away."

Elena was back to serve dessert. This time Addy introduced the dish herself.

"I rode the *Venice Simplon-Orient-Express* three times before I wrangled this recipe out of Executive Chef Christian Bodiguel. He's passed on now, but his superb cuisine lives on in my memory. This delectable little Cherry Clafoutis is my only weakness."

"You have a lot of weaknesses," Esther cracked. "At least four by my count."

"Aren't you an observant one," Addy said. "You'd be quite good as a kick-ass girl assassin, wouldn't you, Esther?"

"Nah, I'd rather save people than off them."

"Well, as far as enjoying the good life, I'm guilty as charged. I paid my dues to get here, and I intend to enjoy every fringe benefit—*la dolce vita!* Sample your desserts, ladies, and see if you don't agree."

I had to admit, these cute little ramekins offered a nice taste of Addy's sweet life. The unique treat—part custard, part cake—blended perfectly with the fresh cherries, splash of kirsch, and scoop of vanilla bean gelato on top.

For the first time, Esther didn't whisper a complaint. In fact, this classic French indulgence was based on a crepe batter, which is why I pointed to her ramekin and mouthed—

"See that? You got your fruity pancake with ice cream topping!"

After we all took a few silent, blissful bites, Addy picked up the conversation where she left off.

"You know that first adaptation of *New Amsterdam* was not at all faithful. The budget was miniscule, and it lacked an epic feel. The whole thing looked cheap, which is why I'm thrilled about the Netflix production . . ."

Addy set down her spoon and licked her lips.

"This time, I'll be consulting, and with the latest developments in special effects, we're going to do it right. This series will be on the scale of *Outlander*, *Shōgun*, and *The Crown*. Its launch will coincide with the publication of my seventh *New Amsterdam* novel, which will start a whole new cycle in Tabitha's saga."

"A new *New Amsterdam* book?" I honestly gushed. "That's even more exciting than the streaming series. I'll be first in line to buy it."

"It's tough to give up writing, isn't it?" Esther said. "There are always new stories to tell."

"Yes, Esther, and more ways to tell them. One simple tweak can turn an old idea into something fresh and new."

"What do you mean?" Esther asked.

"Decades ago, when I first conceived my *New Amsterdam* series, I made my protagonist a man, like the engineer Hank Morgan in Twain's *Connecticut Yankee*. But after my Hollywood success, I changed my mind. Flipping the genders had worked for *She Slays Me* when I thought, *Who needs another James Bond?* So I decided to try the same gender switch for *New Amsterdam*, and look what it's got me . . ."

She gestured to the room with the view—and when she did, my attention was drawn to the activity outside.

During the meal, we were able to watch through the arched windows as people strolled the promenade. Now, as Addy continued to talk, I spotted a familiar-looking young man on an electric scooter. He had a receding hairline and wore round Harry Potter glasses, and he was slowly cruising down the walkway in a clear violation of park rules about motorized vehicles.

As he passed Addy's brownstone, he stared right at us from over the hedges. Though he was thirty feet away, I was sure I'd seen this young man before—and recently.

I kept watching, and a few moments later he rolled by in the opposite direction. Once again he stared directly at us. This time he slowed down enough for me to get a long look at him.

That's when I knew where I'd first seen him. He was that timid young man in the basement of the Grand Maison hotel, standing deferentially behind the white blond Ice Woman while a furious Addison Ford Babcock lashed out at her.

"Look!" I cried.

Addy stopped talking mid-sentence. "Look at what, Clare?"

"Outside!" I pointed.

Abby turned her head—the wrong way.

"No, over there!"

Addy turned again, and this time she seemed to look right at the man as he raced out of sight.

"Don't you recognize him?" I asked.

"Goodness, Clare. Who?"

For a moment I did not reply, my mind working. Did the Ice Woman send her assistant to spy on Addy? If she did, then why? What did he, and presumably the Ice Woman, expect to see by watching Addy's home?

"Clare, do you feel all right?" Addy asked.

The answer was no. The man's appearance was disturbing enough to prompt me into asking an uncomfortable question:

"I wonder if you could shed some light on the argument you had last evening at the Grand Maison."

"Argument?"

"I was moving through the kitchen and saw you speaking to a woman with white blond hair. She had a young man with her—he might have been her assistant. The reason I'm bringing it up is because I just saw that same man riding a scooter on the promenade, peering through your windows. Do you have any idea why?"

"My goodness, Clare, what you witnessed last evening was simply a discussion between two old acquaintances. I don't know the man whom you're describing, and I saw no one when you pointed."

"I saw him," Esther cut in. "Harry Potter glasses and a prematurely receding hairline—"

Addy was now clearly annoyed. "Frankly, Clare, you sound a little paranoid, and I don't appreciate hearing that *you* were spying on me."

"I wasn't spying. I just happened to see—"

"Oh, no!" Addy said, suddenly checking her watch. "Where did the time go? I'm sorry, ladies, but I have a scheduled call with my West Coast agent, and I'm afraid it cannot wait."

With crisp steps, Addy escorted us to the front door.

"Thank you for lunch," I said sincerely.

"You're more than welcome, Clare. This was my small way of thanking you for your help with my nephew's awkward situation last evening—"

I was about to give Addy a polite reply when she aggressively added, "—and I *do* hope, since we're *friends* now, that I can rely on you to keep the particulars of that incident *private*?"

"Of course."

"Oh, you're a treasure!"

As Elena handed us our coats, Addy asked me for a final favor, one that left me mildly stunned.

"Now if you don't mind, Clare, I'd like to have a little private chat—"

"With me?"

"No. With Esther."

Fifty-Eight

﴾✿﴿﴾✿﴿﴾✿﴿﴾✿﴿﴾✿﴿﴾✿﴿﴾✿﴿﴾✿﴿﴾✿﴿﴾✿﴿

With clicking heels, Addy escorted Esther to an anteroom and firmly shut the door.

I tried to be patient, but after pacing under Addy's potted palms, wondering what she could be discussing with Esther, I decided to put on my coat and step outside to clear my head.

On the chilly stone portico, I breathed in the late autumn air. The sun had warmed the ground enough to melt much of the freakishly early snow, and I watched locals stroll toward the promenade—dog walkers, nannies with young children, and joggers in running shoes.

While the brunch was delicious, and the news Addy shared about her new Netflix series would surely excite Tucker, I was disappointed that I didn't have more to tell Mike.

As much as I admired Addy as an author, I couldn't help being disappointed by her evasiveness and her condescending view of poor Mr. Scrib. I was ready for a certain amount of arrogance on her part, but not for the level she displayed, and I couldn't help feeling skeptical about many of her replies.

Did her memory about the writers' group really fail? Or was she being cagey because she was guilty of more than having weaknesses for imported mineral water, Juliet roses, Cherry Clafoutis, and Daniel Boulud's kitchen help?

Just then, I heard the sound of an electric scooter hurtling down the street. It was the Ice Woman's associate, buzzing by Addy's house again!

The scooter spy had swapped his Harry Potter spectacles for aviator sunglasses and kept his head down, but his receding hairline was hard to miss. I hurried down the stone steps, but he zoomed past before I could reach the sidewalk.

"Hey, YOU!"

Yelling was a futile gesture, and an embarrassing one in this uber chic neighborhood. A flock of pigeons under a tall oak tree took flight, and across the street a woman walking her Pekingese gave me a nasty stare.

As I shrugged an apology, I felt my mobile phone vibrating and was relieved to see who it was.

"Hi, sweetheart, are you still brunching?"

"We just finished, and we're heading back to the shop."

"I can't talk long," Mike said. "Miami PD has picked up a dealer we've been after for months. I'll be heading down there for a few days to meet with my counterparts and assist in the questioning. If we can flip him, we're closer to bringing down a major tranq distributor."

"That's good news, but I'll miss you."

"I'll miss you, too. Before I go, I have some feedback from Detective Russell. First thing this morning, he followed the lead you found with that publishing executive."

"Joan Gibson?"

"That's right. Ms. Gibson confirmed the book contract with Jensen Van Dyne for a true crime memoir, but she said he only submitted a general outline. He promised to reveal the specifics in his first draft, including why and how actor Ace Archer, a member of Mr. Van Dyne's writing group, ended up dead in a vacant lot—"

"So it *is* about the actor's murder! And the actor's name is definitely Ace Archer?"

"That's what Russell conveyed."

"Did Van Dyne deliver his manuscript?"

"No, he hasn't turned in the book yet. And Ms. Gibson told Russell that she has no idea who might have attacked him in your alley."

"Anything else?"

"That's all I have. Did you learn anything new from Ms. Babcock?"

"Not much. Addy identified the actor from an old photo. She said his name was Ace—and you just confirmed his last name is Archer."

Just then, I heard a door slam and saw Esther on the porch, pulling on her coat. She looked upset.

"Mike, I'll talk with you later, okay? Have a safe trip."

"I'll stay in touch," he promised.

As I tucked away my phone, Esther descended from the porch and joined me on the sidewalk. Her face was flushed and twisted into an angry scowl.

"What is it, Esther? What happened?"

She shook her head and refused to talk until our car arrived. After we settled into the back seat and Addy's brownstone receded from view, Esther finally let loose.

"'You do for me, and I'll do for you,'" she quoted with bitterness.

"What are you talking about?"

"Addy propositioned me! She started the conversation by telling me she could help my career as a writer. She claimed she could open doors to editors, publishers, literary agents. All I had to do was one little favor for her."

"What favor?"

"She wanted me to hand over Mr. Scrib's notebook, the one he left behind at the Village Blend."

"What did you say?"

"Are you kidding? I wouldn't betray Mr. Scrib! Not to her, not to anyone. I told her that I loathe transactional relationships. I want nothing to do with them. Not in my life or my art. And I would never sell out a friend!"

"What did Addy say to that?"

"It was weird. I expected her to lash out or try to persuade me. But she just turned her back and walked away." Esther moaned. "What is going on?"

"What's going on isn't a big leap. I'm guessing Addy thinks *you* have the notebook that Mr. Scrib was using to write his true crime exposé."

"But why would she want it?"

"I can think of two reasons. Either Addy wants to know what really happened to Ace all those years ago because she wasn't there. Or she's lying and she *was* there. And if Addy was there, then she could have been involved in the actor's murder or the cover-up of moving his body."

"Do you think Addy killed him? Do you think that's what Mr. Scrib is going to reveal? And is that why he was attacked in our alley? Did Addy send someone to do her dirty work?"

"I don't know, Esther. Let's not get ahead of ourselves."

"You have to admit, it seems likely."

"Maybe. But even if it is, we have no proof."

"Well, I'm going to take a closer look at the notebook we do have," Esther said. "Given the info Addy *did* reveal, maybe I can put together clues buried in all those doodles and gibberish."

"That's a good idea," I said, remembering Mike Quinn's patrol car philosophy. "'If you hit a light, make a right.'"

"I don't get it," Esther said. "Right on red is illegal here. Do you want our driver to get a ticket?"

"No. I want us to continue moving forward, despite our setbacks. You want to help Mr. Scrib, don't you?"

"Yes!"

"Then keep looking for answers. And I'll do the same."

Fifty-nine

~~~~~~

Ten minutes later, even right turns wouldn't have helped us.

Our driver was planted in the middle of standstill traffic, waiting for entry to the Brooklyn Bridge. I was about to call Tucker and check in when my phone dinged with a text message.

After all my attempts to raise my ex-husband's ghost on the distressing subject of Cody Wood, Matt spooked me with exactly three words:

WE'LL TALK SOON.

That was it. That was all the answer my business partner saw fit to give me: We'll talk soon.

No, Matt. We'll talk now!

"Stay in the car and get back to the Blend," I told Esther, popping the door.

"Where are you going?"

"To pick a fight."

After zigzagging my way through the de facto parking lot, I ordered another rideshare and headed in the opposite direction—literally and figuratively.

Matt's warehouse was located in Red Hook. Though geographically only a few miles from Brooklyn Heights and its affluent residents, culturally and economically the two neighborhoods could not have been further apart.

Matt's converted warehouse sat at the water's edge, next to one of Red

Hook's defunct docks. In its heyday, this area had been a thriving seaport community. While working piers still peppered the peninsula, the nautical activity was nothing compared to what it once was. And while some gentrification had taken place with the opening of a few hipster eateries and the conversion of old factories into offices for start-ups, Red Hook was still primarily "residustrial"—part residential and part industrial— with its gritty roots still evident as my car passed rusty fencing, ramshackle row houses, and a run-down auto repair shop.

After exiting the car, I crossed the cracked concrete of the narrow sidewalk and stepped onto the newly paved driveway of Matt's property. The gate in his shiny silver chain-link fencing was open and I strode through it.

Here the view across New York Bay was very different from Addy's. No glittering Wall Street skyscrapers, just the industrial ports of Bayonne, New Jersey, and (admittedly) a nice view of Miss Liberty, the statue where the poetry of Emma Lazarus had lifted up the poor, the wretched, the homeless, and tempest-tossed, who'd risked their lives with dreams of opening the well-heeled young poet's "golden door."

There were no golden doors in neighborhoods like this one, with public housing, pockmarked streets, random graffiti, and the ghosts of shantytowns past. Here is where dreamers landed and sometimes perished.

My visits to Red Hook were always reminders of the countless hard lives that ended too soon in this city, and some not far from here. Columbia Street was where they found Ace Archer's decomposing body.

Despite the deceptively sunny sky, a salt-tinged wind whipping off the water set my skin shivering. Or maybe it was the thought of a golden-haired boy left in a vacant lot.

With a deep breath, I cleared my head, pulled out my phone, and finally replied to Matt's text.

TWO MINUTE WARNING.
I'M OUTSIDE AND COMING IN!

Even though I had a key and the code for the security system, my warning was necessary . . .

After the failure of Matt's second marriage to a powerful corporate queen bee, he made a firm decision to set up his new life not with a romantic partner but with the coffee cherries that he'd sourced around the world and stored in climate-controlled purity.

Consequently, my globe-trotting ex-husband's NYC base camp was now the wide balcony that ran the length of his coffee warehouse, which he'd converted into an open loft apartment, complete with bedroom, bath, office, and kitchen, all of which overlooked his precious coffee beans. On the roof was a large wooden deck with a grill and lounge chairs, where he sometimes slept on a bedroll, under the stars.

None of this surprised me.

Matt would always prefer pitching a tent among the shade-grown cherries of Peru's northern highlands or bunking with the smallholder coffee farmers of Yandaro than checking into a five-star hotel in Paris, Rome, or his New York home.

After the bitter betrayal of his status-conscious second wife, who'd dumped him when he no longer served her purposes, Matt was content to resume his confirmed bachelor status, free to hook up with whomever he wanted and "swipe right" whenever he liked, which meant he might not be alone at the moment.

Another frigid gust off the bay increased my shivering, but I was determined to give Matt the full one hundred twenty seconds to warn me off.

When time was up with no reply, I unlocked the door and pushed it open. Piercing alarm bells went off throughout the warehouse. They only fell silent after I shut the door and typed the code into the keypad.

Relieved to be inside, I began rubbing my freezing hands together in the glorious warmth when a voice startled me.

"Clare?"

I turned to find myself facing the coffee hunter who ruled this castle of caffeination—my ex-husband, dripping wet and half-naked.

Sixty

～～～～～～～～～～～～～～～～～～～～～

"What are you doing here, Clare?"

Clearly surprised by the security alarm, Matteo Allegro had wrapped a white bath towel around his hips and hurried to investigate. He smelled of soap, and a little lather still clung to the dark curls on his chest.

"You said we'd talk soon," I said. "Now is soon enough for me."

"I might not have been alone."

"That's why I sent a text warning. Didn't you see it?"

"I'm not in the habit of taking my phone into the shower."

As Matt secured his slipping towel with his muscular forearms, I turned my gaze away, staring hard at the shiny concrete floor, the spacious loading zone, the utilitarian metal stairs, the running loft that oversaw the whole complex, and the hundreds of airtight barrels of raw coffee cherries inside the glassed-in, climate-controlled storage area.

I looked at pretty much everything but my inadequately clad ex, whose deep tan from his last sourcing trip extended across his hard shoulders and all the way down to his still-firm abs—which gave me a clue how much time he'd spent with his shirt off under the Central Africa sun (likely playing soccer with the locals or relaxing by a pool with a special lady; probably both).

"You *are* alone, aren't you?" I said.

"Yes, and you can stop averting your eyes. I'll put something on."

I gave Matt a head start, then I followed him up the staircase, the low heels of my ankle boots clanking on the metal steps. Matt disappeared into his balcony bedroom, where he'd drawn drapes for privacy.

"I'll make coffee," I loudly called, and heard my voice echo from the cozy loft space into the cavernous warehouse.

Matt's kitchen was an efficient setup. A fridge, microwave, deep stainless steel sink, and two high-end hot plates—one of which was set on low with a pot gently simmering. I recognized the savory aroma and sighed. It smelled amazing.

While I loaded a French press and boiled water on the second hot plate, Matt reappeared in sweatpants and a tight black tee with *Volcano Surfing! Black Hill, Nicaragua!* written in Spanish—a reminder that Matt's extreme sports–junkie addiction was still alive and well. I could still see the drone footage of his hike up the side of that live Nicaraguan volcano along with his death-defying descent, sliding down the ash on a thin board.

Gritting my teeth against that worrying memory, I forced myself to say something positive—

"Your beef stew smells heavenly."

"It's your recipe," he said.

"I can tell, but I adapted it from yours . . ."

Early in our marriage, Matt made an excellent beef stew for me, using coffee as a marinade. When I tried the recipe, however, I found the large portion time-consuming to cook, so I shrunk the yield for a quicker and easier dinner and made a few tweaks, including replacing the coffee with red wine for a lovely beef bourguignon flare.

My "Cozy Beef Stew for Two" (as I called it) was a far cry from Addy's brunch of fine dining delicacies. But while her dainty gourmet bites worked great for someone who sat at a laptop all day, they left me fairly famished. In my defense, most of us in the service industry (on our feet from sunrise until *way* past sunset) knew cuisine-that-sustained was the name of the game.

Matt seemed to read my mind. He pulled two bowls off a shelf, dished up the cozy stew, and sliced up a crusty loaf of sourdough. We sat at his kitchen table and feasted in silence. Finally, as we sopped up the last of the stew with thick hunks of bread, he tried to make small talk. But I was too bantered out after Addy's brunch to beat around the bush—

"So, are you going to source coffee for Driftwood's master roaster? Is that what the meeting with Cody was about?"

"If you think I'm going to source beans for the Driftwood label, then you don't have a clue what's going on—"

"By all means, Matt, clue me in."

"Cody Wood wants to buy the Village Blend—"

I dropped my spoon. "YOU HAVE GOT TO BE KIDDING!"

"Calm down and listen—"

"To what?! Matt, *please* tell me that you are not for a blessed second considering selling our business and your family's legacy brand to that purveyor of industrial waste—"

"He doesn't want our business, Clare. We can still call ourselves the Village Blend, even though . . ."

"Even though *what*?!"

"Even though we won't be in Greenwich Village anymore."

Suddenly, I found it very hard to breathe. *Is this what a panic attack feels like?* "Jump right into my nightmare," I rasped. "The water's so cold it's paralyzing."

"Take it easy, honey. Breathe, okay? In through the nose, out through the mouth."

I did. But my nightmare didn't end because Matt kept talking—

"Look," he said in a soothing tone, "it's not as bad as it sounds. Cody simply wants to buy our landmark building and turn it into a Driftwood coffeehouse."

"Oh, is that all?!"

"He's put together some investors, and he's offering more than double the market value for it. He's sweetening the deal by adding a long-term contract that would triple our revenue."

"Why would he do this?" I gasped. "We've been adversaries for so long!"

"He wants to put all that animosity behind us. He said times are tough for a lot of retail businesses, and we'd have a better chance at financial success if we worked together. He seemed perfectly sincere about it, Clare. 'Money is money and success is success.' That's how he put it. And we should partner up for those ends."

"Okay, Matt, let's say I would consider the lunacy of trusting that shark enough to go into business with him. Out of sheer curiosity, how does Cody the Drifter propose to triple our business? With a force multiplier of AI baristas?"

"No. Driftwood would sell our beans—the cherries that I source and you roast—as a special Village Blend label in select Driftwood stores across the country. It would be a partnership of sorts, given the national business Cody would open up for us. But the whole deal hinges on, well, you know . . ."

"On selling him our landmark coffeehouse?"

"That's right."

"No, Matt, it's wrong—as wrong as it gets."

Sixty-one

~~~~~~

Matt didn't seem surprised by my words, but I was outraged by his un-ruffled reply. Sitting back in his kitchen chair, he sipped his coffee and said—

"It's just a building, Clare."

"I can't believe you think that! Why would he even want the building? What good would it do him?"

"He says it's the start of a strategy to lift the Driftwood image in the bigger cities, one community at a time. He says his franchise shops are all too slick and modern. He wants to improve the optics of his brand by opening next-level shops in older historic structures to make them look as though they've been part of those neighborhoods for years."

"He wants to buy our legacy? Like we're a sepia filter he can slap on a photo that he took an hour ago to make people think it has historic value?"

"Regardless of the reason," Matt said, "he knows we need the money. He's aware of the recent dramatic drop in our foot traffic—"

"He knows that, does he? Well, no surprise there! He's been using spies for years to rip off our seasonal menus!"

Matt reached across the table and touched my hand. "Listen to me—"

"No." I pulled away. "You listen to me. You're talking about selling my home. Our daughter's inheritance. Why? Cody doesn't want to buy a legacy. I don't believe what he told you. The man is doing what all big fish companies do. Eat up their competition. Our roastery is going to compete with him in an even bigger way, and he wants to nip that coffee bloom in the bud. He's threatened by our plans, so he came up with his own—an offer to cut our own throats."

"You're overreacting. You don't know all the particulars of the deal—"

"I know Cody Wood! And this isn't about business. It's about his giant ego. He wants to erase the identity of the quality competitor who shows him up. The one he can't hope to compete with. Don't you see? If we make this deal with him, instead of staying independent, most of our income will come through Driftwood, and Cody will control us—and he can finish us off and shut us down anytime he likes."

"It doesn't have to be like that. We can put protections in our contract. And he's offering us the kind of money some corporations pay to buy an entire brand and all its assets. All Cody wants is to go into partnership to nationally distribute our Village Blend beans and buy our landmark building . . ."

My nightmare vision was actually coming true: our Village Blend with a *DRIFTWOOD* sign flashing in big, bold, Las Vegas neon!

Meanwhile, Matt kept droning on. "We'll still be the Village Blend. We can set up shop anywhere we want. There are so many hot neighborhoods in this city. What about a modern shop in Hudson Yards? Or the Financial District? Or Williamsburg, Brooklyn? There are some amazing real estate opportunities in Long Island City—"

"Why not Boise, Idaho?" I said. "Or Tokyo? How about Barcelona? Or Bavaria? We can serve Octoberfest beer and outfit Tuck and Dante in lederhosen!"

"Stop it, Clare—"

"Does the century-old history of the Village Blend mean nothing to you? The bohemian legacy, the artists and creators who embraced our shop like a second home, the roots your own mother and father planted in a rich, vibrant community. It's not the Village Blend if it isn't in Greenwich Village!"

Matt sighed. "Fine. We'll find a vacant storefront somewhere else in the Village. It will be a smaller footprint because you won't need a roasting room when our new roastery is up and running. You can design the space from the ground up, in any style that suits your fancy, any décor you want—"

I furiously shook my head. "I don't understand what brought this on!"

"You brought it on yourself, when you told me about the drastic decline in foot traffic. That's when I finally agreed to the meeting."

"What do you mean finally?"

"I never told you, but Cody has been pestering me for a deal for some time—"

"We don't need him, Matt. We can pull out of this slump ourselves. The Writer's Block Lounge might be the thing that turns it all around for our retail business."

"Or it might not."

"I only told you about our troubles to be up front and honest with my business partner. I think I deserve the same consideration. You had no intention of telling me about Cody's offer, did you?"

"Not true. Eventually—"

"Eventually, I would have found out. But that's not how a partnership should function, is it? You kept secrets from me when we were married partners, and it was devastating. Now we're business partners, and you're doing the same thing—"

"Don't do that. Leave our past in the past—"

"How can I, when you're acting like the old Matt *from* our past? Keeping secrets, going behind my back, ghosting me. You need to respect me as your partner!"

Matt fell silent after that. Finally, he shifted in his seat and admitted—

"You're not wrong. I was avoiding you. I'm sorry, okay? But I needed time to think things through."

"What things? The deal?"

Matt sighed. "This roastery I'm building is a financial risk. Remember the coffee rust in Central America? In Guatemala, in Honduras, and even in Costa Rica—all those farmers I'd bought from lost their livelihood, their land—and that was in the last ten years."

"I remember."

"My mother still talks about the 1975 frost that killed two-thirds of the coffee crop in Brazil. Half the world's crop was destroyed, and prices skyrocketed. If something like that happens again, we could go bankrupt. And the worst part is that I have absolutely no control over it."

I stared him down. "Is that really your biggest worry? The uncertainties of coffee agribiz?"

"It's more than that. I mean, yeah, you told me about your financial troubles three hours before Cody called me again. I might not have listened otherwise; in fact, I probably would have hung up on the SOB. But between your bad news about the shop's foot traffic and the bloating construction costs for the roastery . . ."

"We both understand the risks."

"I don't think you do, and it's a subject that's been torturing me lately."

"Torturing?" I sat back. "Why? You haven't shared anything like this with me."

"No, I haven't."

"Well, I'm your business partner, pal. If something about the business is bothering you, I'm the one to tell."

Matt took a breath. "I guess it would be a relief to get it off my chest."

"Okay, then. Start talking."

Sixty-two

~~~~~~~~~~~~~~~~~~~~~~~~~~~~~~~~~~~~~

"You oversee the two shops and the roasting," Matt said, "but I run the import business. I do the sourcing. I attend the auctions, and I have the connections."

"So?"

"Well, what if something happens to me on one of these sourcing trips? Our whole business goes down the drain, that's what. I leave you and my mother ruined. When I listened to Cody Wood's pitch, I thought about my mother's future, Joy's future, and your future, too."

"What brought on this sudden outbreak of responsibility? Did you find a new volcano to surf in Burundi?"

"No," he said. "I'm just realizing that I'm, you know, getting older, and if anything were to happen to me—"

"Stop! If the worst happens, I can take care of myself, so can Joy, and your mother is already taken care of."

"I wish."

"What does that mean?"

"When Pierre died, he left my mother the Fifth Avenue apartment and a generous annuity. But the property taxes and monthly maintenance fee on her place have gone up every year. She won't admit it, but it's becoming a real strain on her finances."

"What are you saying?"

"I'm saying don't be surprised if she welcomes a generous financial offer that all of us can benefit from."

"You're wrong," I said.

"We'll see. It's possible she'll feel the way I do. The money Cody is offering would provide a cushion, some security—"

"There's no such thing as *security*, Matt. It's an illusion. We could walk out of here and be struck by lightning. A nor'easter could wreck your warehouse and blow us all away."

I paused to let that sink in before telling him something I believed from the heart—

"After just one day with those determined young writers who showed up at our shop, I learned something. If you want to feel *alive*, you don't give up your dreams. You accept the risks. You fly across oceans, hike up mountains, surf volcanos, and you *don't trade away what you love* for so-called security."

Matt's brown gaze softened at my words and a slight smile lifted his face. "Given the potential hazards ahead, those words are pretty ballsy. But I have to admit, they're nice to hear."

"All your life, you've embraced risk," I said. "Don't stop now. Keep doing what you're doing, and I'll keep doing my job. We'll get through this. All we have to do is reject Cody's offer."

"It's not for us to say. While my mother is alive, she's the controlling party when it comes to the Village Blend."

"Your mother is going to say *no* to selling to Cody in four of the dozen languages you speak—with a few choice expletives to boot. And I insist on being there when she does. I don't want you talking her into something she'll regret."

Matt snorted. "I can't talk my mother into anything. I never could. Just don't jump to any conclusions."

"What do you mean?"

"Don't be so sure she'll reject Cody's offer. Her main concern is going to be what's best for your future, my future, and the future of her granddaughter. I'm betting she'll welcome the chance to cash in our chips, leave the table with millions, and free you, me, and Joy from a struggling business."

I tried to push Matt's view aside, but he was persuasive enough to plant a seed of doubt.

"She'll say no," I insisted again, though it came out less strongly this time.

"Even if she does, that might not be the end of it."

"Of course it will."

"I told you Cody has been working on this for some time. He's already approached your new city councilwoman with his proposal. She's all in—"

"What?! The Village Blend hosted her nomination party! So much for loyalty."

"I warned you," Matt said. "Cody has a silver tongue and a determined plan. He cited improvements he'd make to the neighborhood, an increase in employment. He even promised more security after a spike in crime around the Village Blend—"

"Spike in crime?"

Matt nodded. "Are you ready for this? When we sat down for lunch, Cody informed me that there was an assault in an alley behind our shop the night before—"

"That was Mr. Scrib," I said. "But how could he know?"

"He claimed he's been keeping tabs on crime in the area."

"Right. I'd love to know how Cody Wood is 'keeping tabs.' A creep like him would resort to any number of nasty tactics to get what he wants. And don't forget, he has a vendetta against us. We have a history of bad blood."

"What's your point?"

"My point is that a man who resorts to spying and stealing might have been sick enough to hire a thug to assault someone on our property. It would certainly reinforce his 'spike in crime' theory. And now I've got to wonder: Is he willing to go further than that to get what he wants? Are my baristas and customers at risk?"

"Don't be paranoid. I know you dislike Cody, but you're reaching with that theory."

"Just the same, I'd like this drifter's offer off our plates. Let's tell your mother tonight."

"No." He shook his head and sat back. "In the next few days, Cody and his people are going to provide a written proposal. When I have it, we'll go to my mother and review the whole offer."

"As long as we do it *together*," I insisted. "And when she says no—"

"*If* she says no."

"*When* she says no, I'm going to tell Cody where he can stick his invitation to put our neck in his noose."

Just then my phone buzzed. I checked the screen.

"Speaking of your mother," I said, waving my mobile, "it's a text from her. She's coming by the Blend this afternoon with her new beau."

"Another one?"

"Like mother, like son."

"Low-hanging fruit, Clare."

"Well, you're both social butterflies—though your style is more buzzard."

"Hey, I get no complaints," Matt said. "So, what is he like?"

"I haven't met him yet, but from her description he's out of this world."

"What's that supposed to mean?"

"He's a former astronaut."

Just then, another text came through, this one from my youngest barista.

"Hey, good news! Nancy says we're packed, and they need hands!"

"For now," Matt said.

"Don't be a killjoy."

"I'm not. It's nice to know there's a temporary boom, but if you can't sustain it, Cody's offer might be our only hope."

"Stop already. I can't argue anymore. I won't change how I feel, and your mother and her astronaut are expecting me."

"Then I guess you better blast off."

Sixty-three

⌇⌇⌇⌇⌇⌇⌇⌇⌇⌇⌇⌇⌇⌇⌇⌇⌇⌇⌇⌇⌇⌇⌇⌇⌇⌇⌇⌇⌇⌇

Nancy's text warned me that our coffeehouse was busy, but when I saw a small crowd blocking the entrance, I felt a pang of panic.

Was this a sign of more chaos with a capital C?

While we certainly wanted retail traffic, chaotic disorder wouldn't serve us for long. Customers came to our shop expecting a coffeehouse, not a madhouse, and if we couldn't provide quality service in a pleasant atmosphere, any new business we attracted would soon melt away.

With rising trepidation, I approached our front door and realized (with great relief) that the logjam was only temporary. A quartet of university students, bearing overstuffed backpacks, were competing to get through our entrance. Once they did, I heard the cheerful greeting of Nancy Kelly from inside the shop—

"Welcome to the Village Blend! If you're here to join the Writer's Block Lounge, we've got a full house upstairs, but you'll find one table still empty on our ground floor, over there. We have a free proctor service to help you meet your deadlines; just sign in with me. Our Village Blend Wi-Fi is free, too. You'll get the password with your first beverage order."

I stood for a moment, processing Nancy's words. *Did she say full house? Upstairs and down?*

I followed the throng inside, where I found a very different scene than the appalling frenzy that had greeted me yesterday. Through eyes tearing with gratitude, I scanned our busy but relaxed and organized shop.

I hadn't seen the Village Blend this packed since . . . I couldn't remember when. And despite the crowd, everyone was being served quickly, the floor was tidy, the tables were bussed—and judging from the line at the coffee bar, business was booming.

I made a beeline for Esther.

"Did I hear Nancy correctly? Do we actually have a full house upstairs?"

"Can you believe it?" she said. "Our outreach worked for a second day, and better than I ever expected. As soon as I arrived, Nancy told me we'd run out of seats in our lounge. So I set up this area for new Writer's Block members, and people have been showing up ever since."

"Who's covering upstairs?"

"Tucker. Nancy is steering traffic and finding seats for the latecomers. Dante is pulling espressos faster than Banksy sprays street art. And Howie Johnson is bussing tables on both floors."

"That's amazing," I said, "and a monumental relief to see everything under control, because I'm running late on my roasting schedule. I've got to get down to the basement—"

"One more thing before you do. We have a VIP guest visiting our upstairs lounge—"

"Madame and her astronaut friend are here already?"

"No," Esther said. "It's an editor. An actual New York book editor dropped by and she's doing one-on-one meetings with the writers in our upstairs lounge."

That shocked the heck out of me. "It's only our second day. How could she know?"

Esther shrugged. "Maybe a writer here is a friend or relative of hers. Or maybe she saw our notices on social media."

"Do you know when this editor arrived?"

"Nancy said she showed up a couple of hours ago, while we were still at brunch."

"Have you spoken with her?"

"Not yet. Tuck's been managing upstairs, and I've been too busy relieving Dante and Nancy for their breaks."

"Well, this visit is odd, but it does sound promising, doesn't it? Like we're already on the literary map."

"I wouldn't put it that way," Esther said, pushing up her glasses.

"You sound annoyed. What's the matter?"

"I just hope people don't get the wrong idea. I mean, I don't know this editor's name or what publishing house she represents, but I wouldn't want people to think we're going to have a book editor drop in to hear pitches *every* week."

Just then, Dante frantically signaled Esther from behind the counter. "Sorry, got to go. My orders are up!"

As Esther hurried to the coffee bar, I decided to put off the roasting for a few more minutes to check on things upstairs—and check out this VIP editor.

But my steps were halted when I saw an even bigger VIP coming through our front door.

Sixty-Four

~ ~

MADAME had arrived.

Matt's mother was seasonably wrapped for a fall afternoon in fawn brown cashmere. Sweetly, she waved a single red rose in greeting. A token, no doubt, from the striking figure following her through our front door.

A minute later I was shaking hands with the first and only holder of the Village Blend's Golden Ticket and the first genuine astronaut I'd ever met.

Captain Richard Siebold, USN, retired, was out of uniform but hardly informal in a dark suit, a starched white shirt, and a silver tie under a long navy blue overcoat.

The captain greeted us warmly. Though his deep voice instantly commanded respect, the artist in me was drawn to his face, a weathered map etched from years of experiences. In profile, his hawkish nose and close-cropped white hair reminded me of a bald eagle.

Nancy, who regarded New York City's annual Fleet Week as the official start of her summer dating season, followed her natural inclination and gave the officer a grinning salute.

Why not? Saluting the man seemed like the natural thing to do. Well into his seventh decade, he had shoulders that were still square and his spine was as straight as a frigate's main mast. With his sharp blue eyes under a furrowed brow, I could easily imagine him on a ship's deck, peering hard at the horizon.

"I've brought us a new member," Madame informed me. "Captain Siebold would like to join our Writer's Block Lounge."

The captain nodded. "I'm working on a piece for the *Annual Review of Earth and Planetary Sciences*, but my skills aren't up to the task—"

"Oh, pooh," Madame said, playfully swatting his chest with the rose. "I read your article in *National Geographic*. You're a fine writer."

"I meant my coffee-making skills, Blanche. I reasoned that if I wrote at the Village Blend, that all-important issue would be resolved."

"Would you like to attend a session today?" I asked.

"Thank you, ma'am, but I'll have to belay that action for the present, though I'm postponing for a fine reason—"

"Yes," Madame said. "The captain and I are winging our way to Florida for a week."

"Ah, snowbirds out for some fun in the sun?" I assumed.

"It's much more exciting than that," Madame said, her violet eyes brightening. "We're going to watch the launch of a weather satellite at Cape Canaveral."

Blast off, indeed! I thought.

Though I was happy for them both, inside I felt a tightening tension. Madame's trip would delay more than the captain's writing schedule. It would also postpone any discussion of the offer from Driftwood's CEO.

On the other hand, I thought, *this could be a good thing for my purposes.* This space launch trip would buy me some time to look for cracks in Cody Wood's mask. There had to be a way to expose him, get him to admit his real intentions, show his true hand.

"If it's not too much trouble," Captain Siebold said, "I'd enjoy a tour of your coffeehouse, the roasting room, and the upstairs lounge."

"Of course," I said. "You couldn't get a better tour guide than my dear mentor here. And please do put your Golden Ticket to use. Try our freshly roasted single-origin Rwandan. I think you'll be impressed. After your coffee and Madame's tour, I'll introduce you to Esther Best and she can answer any questions you might have about joining our Writer's Block Lounge . . ."

With Madame and the captain happily settled at the coffee bar, I decided to head upstairs to check on Tucker and finally satisfy my curiosity about this New York editor who was already in our midst.

So, as Dante prepared drinks for our golden couple, I excused myself and quickly climbed our spiral staircase.

Sixty-Five

~~~~~~

TRUE to Esther's word, the second floor was nearly full enough to reach the fire marshal's maximum occupancy. Every spot was taken, and customers were using their time to do serious work. Even better, a coffee drink and snack sat within everyone's reach.

The barista responsible for this efficient service greeted me with a grin.

"Pretty exciting, right?" Tucker whispered. "A full house on the second day, and a visit from a New York publishing executive."

"How did it go down?"

"Well, when she first got here, she gave a pep talk, telling everyone that decades ago, she'd been a member of the first writers' group that met here—"

"Wait, stop—" I needed a second to process that. "She said she was an *original* member of the Writer's Block Lounge?"

"That's right. Then she announced that she would be happy to listen to a five-minute pitch from anybody who wanted to give one. She warned them that she wouldn't be asking for written proposals from everyone, but she would do her best to provide suggestions and advice. You should have seen the stampede!"

Tuck sounded like a proud parent. "Tony Tanaka moved like blue lightning to be the first in line, and I noticed the editor gave extra time to his pitch, along with the one by our horror rom-com filmmaker, Mason Dunn."

"I've got to meet this editor. Where is she?"

"Over there at the corner table. Right now she's meeting with Howie."

I followed Tuck's gaze and quickly spotted Howard Johnson's orange roof. Then I saw the mysterious editor. The woman's short white blond hair and tailored Tom Wolfe suit blew me backward two steps.

Just last night I had watched this same woman remain as cool as an arctic cucumber while facing down the fury of a fiery Addy Babcock in the basement of the Grand Maison Hotel. Their verbal war had been disturbing enough to enter my nightmare as a violent Fire and Ice brawl.

"What is this editor's *name*, Tucker?"

"It's Joan something. I have her business card—" He reached into his apron pocket. "Yes, her name is Joan Gibson."

I gaped at Tuck. "Are you *sure*?"

He showed me the card.

JOAN GIBSON

VP and Publisher, Gibson Books

Plenary Partners Book Group, Inc.

This was no coincidence. Our visiting editor, a former member of the original Writer's Block group, was the very same Joan Gibson who'd signed Mr. Scrib to publish the truth about the unsolved murder of Ace Archer.

Joan Gibson, who Addy Babcock *claimed* she'd never heard of, was a woman she'd known for decades!

Addy lied to me. But why?

My blood turned to ice when I remembered something else. Detective Russell had interviewed Ms. Gibson this very morning.

Is that why she's here? Is she looking for answers, too?

The timing of this woman's visit was clearly suspicious, but also auspicious, because I had questions, and plenty of them.

I couldn't be sure of much when it came to the attack on Mr. Scrib, or Addy's lies, or Ace Archer's murder. But I was certain of one thing: Joan Gibson wasn't leaving here until I got some answers.

Sixty-six

For several minutes, I stood there, arms folded, closely watching the Ice Woman's huddle with Howie Johnson. They sat with heads so close together the editor's white blond hair almost merged with Howie's bright orange flattop.

I tried to discern the gist of their conversation—aka lip-read—but soon gave up and turned to Tuck.

"Do you know what Howie is pitching?"

"Sure do. It's that story of the con man who bilked him in Queens, written as a novel." Tuck sighed. "I told Howie the story would be better as a modern musical: you know, *The Music Man* with a Sondheim edge? But the second Ms. Gibson dangled this opportunity, he suddenly decided it should be a novel first."

"I don't blame him, do you? And she does seem interested."

"I know. It's great, right? But then Joan looked interested in almost everyone's pitch. See, I took lots of pictures for our social media." He pulled out his phone. "I know she's not likely to buy many—if any—of these writers' projects, but this is a fantastic boon for our shop. And who knows? I may have captured the photo of a future bestselling author in their very first pitch meeting. Wouldn't it be amazing to frame these pictures for our wall? And maybe show the moment something really big began?"

Tuck opened his phone and scrolled through dozens of images. I bided my time, glancing at the screen until *finally* Howie and Joan rose and shook hands.

As soon as they parted, I moved in.

"Excuse me, Ms. Gibson. I'm the manager here, Clare Cosi, and I'm thrilled to meet an original member of the Writer's Block Lounge."

"Nice to meet you, too."

"I wonder if we might talk."

"You have a book idea, do you?"

"Oh, no. Nothing like that. You see, I brunched today with another member of that original Village Blend writers' group, but when your name was mentioned she claimed that she had never heard of you."

The Ice Woman studied me a moment, then offered a half smile.

"A shame," she said, her voice a little colder. "But I'm not surprised Addison Ford Babcock pretended that I didn't exist, since she always preferred I didn't."

"I'm surprised you mentioned Ms. Babcock," I said.

"Why is that?"

"Because I didn't name her. How did you know? Did your assistant phone in a report?"

"Excuse me?"

"While I was visiting Addy Babcock, I noticed a young man scootering back and forth on the Brooklyn Heights Promenade, peering into the windows of her brownstone, and I'm pretty sure he works for you. Or was it this morning's conversation with Detective Russell that prompted this visit?"

Despite my blunt words, Joan never lost her aloof smile.

"Kenny lives in an apartment on Montague Street, Ms. Cosi, just a few blocks from Casa Babcock. I only guessed it was her because other than me and Jensen Van Dyne, there's no one left around here from those days. But since we're asking pointed questions, how did *you* wrangle an invitation to Dame Addy's Gothic dungeon of a dining room?"

"My employer knows Ms. Babcock socially. She knew I was an admirer of her work and that I would be thrilled to meet her, so she set up the brunch."

"Okay, I get it. You're a little fangirl. Well, A. F. Babcock has plenty of them—and few are admitted into her royal red-haired presence. Do you feel blessed?"

I noticed our (rather acid) conversation had drawn the unwanted attention of some of my customers.

"Come into my office, Ms. Gibson. I'll have coffee brought up for us. I'd like to show you something."

"Are you sure it's not a book proposal?" she asked with a laugh, letting her voice carry over the room.

"I'm sure," I said.

"A memoir, perhaps? *Coffee and Me: My Love Affair with the Bean*?"

Snickers came from the crowd.

"I know! A self-help book! *How to Improve Your Latte in Life: Dreams and Schemes from a Coffee Shop Queen*."

"Very funny," I said, expecting her to stop. But she didn't—or couldn't. The Ice Woman appeared to need that show-you-up spotlight as much as Addy Babcock. And both women were clearly formidable forces.

"*Eat, Pray, Grind*?" she announced, thinking I had no game.

But she was wrong.

"Okay, Dorothy Parker," I said, raising my voice above the level of hers. "Your Algonquin Round Table is ready."

The writers in the room not only laughed; they clapped.

I deadpanned the woman. "Can we talk now?"

With a smirk, she replied, "Lay on, Macduff."

Sixty-seven

My roasting room was in the basement, but as I led the prickly publishing VIP into my tiny second-floor office, I was wholly determined to apply the heat up here.

After Tuck brought us both coffees, I closed the door and pulled out my phone. "This is what I wanted to show you, Ms. Gibson."

I called up the photos that I'd taken at Mr. Scrib's apartment. "Since you were a member of the original Writer's Block group, I'm hoping you'll help me identify some of these other members. Do you recall any of them?"

Joan plopped her monogrammed leather handbag on my desk and took the phone. This time she didn't smirk. A genuine smile crossed her face.

"That tall drink of water is Bobby Briscoe. Well, that's what he called himself, anyway. Bobby was quite sexy, in his own scruffy way. He was funny, too, and so were his short stories. He worked as a bartender and lived in Alphabet City. He was also our candy man—"

"Candy man?"

"Weed, cocaine, LSD, mushrooms, uppers, downers. If you wanted it, Bobby could get it."

"Who wanted it?"

She laughed. "You're asking me to narc on these people?"

"It's for my own curiosity. I promise I won't tell anyone."

Joan shrugged. "Ah, what the hell. I'll dish. These people are mostly gone anyway." She scrolled back and forth on the photos. "Most of the members of our group were casual users of some sort of drug, but all of us were really big drinkers. Bobby could brew up a mean cocktail, too—"

"Like a Kismet?"

Joan let my question slide as if she hadn't heard it. "I don't know what ever happened to Bobby. But if I was to speculate, I'd say he's serving a twenty-year stint in Sing Sing on a narcotics rap."

She blinked, then smiled again. "Oh, here's a picture of Peter. He was a broker on Wall Street, so he preferred the real thing." Joan touched her nose.

"Cocaine?"

She nodded. "Peter wasn't a very good writer. But he had money, nice clothes, a Corvette. That's why Addy was attracted to him—"

"Did they have a love affair?"

"Oh, Addy wanted to—" She smirked again. "Pete wasn't interested. He was smitten with a long-legged dancer named Lola who was into the New Age movement. She would drop by the group occasionally, mostly to read her truly awful poems: 'Come Cha-Cha with my Chakras,' that sort of thing."

"Did you, by any chance, know a *Juliet*?"

The name wiped the smirk from Joan's face. She sat back. "What makes you ask about her?"

"I had a chance to read some of Mr. Van Dyne's poetry. His love poems were beautiful and often dedicated to a woman named Juliet. Do you know anything about that?"

"About Juliet?"

"Yes."

She looked away and shook her head. "Jensen Van Dyne was madly in love with her back then. Poor bastard. He probably still is."

"So Juliet was real. Was she part of the Writer's Block group?"

Joan met my gaze. "Yes, she was."

"And is she still alive?"

"No, Ms. Cosi. Many years ago Juliet decided to put an end to Juliet."

"Suicide?"

"In a manner of speaking."

"That's so sad for Mr. Van Dyne," I said, feeling my heart ache for him. It was awful enough to lose a romantic love so young—but to lose her to suicide was almost too horrible to endure. And now I wondered . . .

Was Juliet's death the event that pushed Mr. Scrib into a psychiatric facility?

Suddenly, Joan Gibson had questions for me. "What exactly is *your* relationship with Jensen, Ms. Cosi? What's the purpose behind all this curiosity? Are you on Addy's payroll?"

"No, of course not. I consider Mr. Van Dyne a friend. He came to our coffeehouse every day to write—he even asked us to call him by his nickname, Mr. Scrib. And he became quite close to one of my baristas."

"How close?"

"Very close. Esther is a writer and poet herself. After Mr. Scrib had a mental health episode in our shop, she volunteered to hold the notebook that he'd left here until he returned. She found a pair of keys to his apartment in that notebook, too. After the poor man was attacked—you *do* know he was attacked?"

"Detective Russell told me about it."

"Well, after that awful event, Esther went to his place and retrieved his pet to care for it."

"And where is that notebook now?"

"Esther is keeping it safe. It's Mr. Van Dyne's property, and she intends to return it to him."

"I'm looking for a notebook, Ms. Cosi. Jensen Van Dyne's notebook. He wrote in longhand, you know? He went into the hospital before he turned in his manuscript. I wonder—"

"It's not your true crime memoir," I said, cutting her off. "It's . . . something else."

I expected her to press me on this, but she suddenly seemed indifferent.

Then she began scrolling again, only to pause on a photo of Ace Archer beside a young woman with dark, frizzy hair. This woman seemed shy of the camera, and she partially hid her face behind one hand.

"There I am," Joan said, surprising me. "Many decades, another hair color, and too many pounds ago."

"That's odd," I said. "Addy pretended not to know that girl."

"Oh, she knows that girl. Too well. That's why she pretended not to."

I pushed a little more on that but got nowhere. Worried her patience was running out, I turned down the heat and switched to another subject.

"Were you friendly with Ace Archer?"

"We all were." She stared at the screen. "I forgot how handsome that boy was. Too pretty for his own good."

"Addy told me he was popular with the girls in the group—"

"She would know. She was his choice."

"So you're saying Addy and Ace were hooking up?"

"I'm saying she was Ace's *choice*. I'm not talking about who slept with whom—you'd need a scorecard to track the way some of the group changed partners. It was about who Ace *chose*. And he picked Addy."

"I'm not sure I understand—"

"I've said enough about that, Ms. Cosi." She set the phone on my desk. "I'm sorry. I don't remember anyone else."

"Not even the dark-haired man with the mustache?"

Joan just shook her head.

"Do you know what happened to Ace Archer, Ms. Gibson?"

"His murder, you mean? I'd left the group at that point, so I wasn't there that night."

"Why did you quit?"

"Because it was time to bow out. There's no reason for an also-ran to stick around—"

"Then you quit because—as you put it—Ace Archer made his choice, and that choice was Addy. So, again, I'm a little confused. Are we talking about a romantic triangle? You see, my employer managed this coffeehouse back then, and she always wondered how Ace Archer's life ended the way it did. She doesn't remember much about those days, but she does recall that a young woman left the group in tears one night and never returned."

"I hope my exit wasn't *that* dramatic," Joan said with a harsh laugh. "But I suppose that could have been me. In any case, I was long gone when whatever terrible thing that happened to Ace happened."

"Addy says she was in LA by then—"

"If she said that, she's lying," Joan said coolly. "I know for a fact that Addy was here, along with Peter, Bobby, Jensen Van Dyne, and someone else."

"Who else?"

"That has yet to be revealed. When I get Jensen's finished manuscript and publish it, I'll send you a first edition, gratis. Then you can read all about it."

"Why exactly did you buy Mr. Van Dyne's book? A decades-old unsolved murder, even one involving a bestselling author, doesn't sound like a sure winner."

"Let's say I'm as curious as you are about what happened. Presumably, all will be revealed."

"Presumably? You don't know?"

Joan slipped me an icy smile. "I know Addy was there that night, though she claims she wasn't. But Bobby was there, too, and we were still friends back then. He didn't tell me everything, but he told me enough to know there are more secrets to be revealed."

"In a manuscript you don't have."

"It's not due for another ten days."

"But Mr. Van Dyne is in the hospital. He's unconscious, and he may not live."

"Jensen more than anyone wants this story to get out—he made that clear. I think we'll find a way."

"What does that mean?"

"Just what I said." Joan Gibson checked her watch. "It's getting late, Ms. Cosi—"

"Only a few more questions. I happened to be at the Grand Maison Hotel last evening. Is Mr. Van Dyne's true crime memoir the reason you and Addy were arguing?"

"I'll tell you the truth, Ms. Cosi, in the hopes that this will get back to that Scarlett O'Harridan. What we were arguing about is bigger than Jensen's memoir, which might amount to nothing. Our fight was about the future. Addy is concerned about her reputation, for whatever that's worth. But my stakes are higher. I want to save my imprint and my career."

"How could Addy save your career?"

"My imprint has been operating in the red for two years. And Addison Ford Babcock is the only person standing in the way of a multimillion-dollar multimedia project that I put together and that everyone involved wants to happen. Everyone but Addy."

"And that is?"

"A reboot of her old TV series, *She Slays Me*."

I could hear the sharp determination in Joan's voice. "I've invested a lot of time and a hell of a lot of money in this project. I have two best-selling thriller authors lined up to develop and write a series of novels featuring the female assassin Stephanie Slay, to be published in the run-up to the debut of the *She Slays Me* streaming reboot, and many more novels will follow—not to mention comic books, video games, merchandising . . ."

Joan took a breath and drained her coffee cup.

"This is a big deal," she said. "There's already a top director attached. The actress who's dying to play assassin Stephanie Slay—if you'll pardon the pun—was up for an Oscar last year. All the ducks are in a row and ready to fly."

"And Addy is stopping this how?"

"As the original creator and executive producer of *She Slays Me*, she secured an unusual contract term that gives her the right of refusal over any spin-off or licensed projects. The studio moved forward on development without realizing this, and now she won't approve the *She Slays Me* reboot or my deal to publish new Stephanie Slay novels and graphic novels."

"Why not?" I asked. "At our brunch today she shared how excited she was about her *New Amsterdam* books being adapted into a big new streaming series. I would think she'd be thrilled to have the same thing happen with her old TV show. Why wouldn't she want *She Slays Me* to have the chance to become a big moneymaking franchise, too?"

"She won't admit why she's killing my deal, but for some reason she wants to bury Stephanie Slay. I told her she shouldn't. These are savage times. Today's audience wants a hard-hitting, fantasy-game-level heroine who gets the job done."

"Is Addy holding out for more money?" I asked.

Joan shook her head. "She's not. She made that clear, which is why I believe this is about the past. Well, in my opinion Addy should let go of the past. I'm willing to do that if she is. I mean, success is success, and money is money . . ."

I suppressed a shiver at those words and suddenly realized why. They sounded exactly like Cody Wood's.

"Anyway, Ms. Cosi, for her own reasons, Addy isn't willing to see things my way. But that's all right—" She flashed a sly grin. "I still have an ace in the hole. And I'm certain it will persuade Addy to see reason."

On that triumphant note, Joan Gibson rose.

"Thanks for the coffee. It's quite good, by the way. My compliments.

But a stack of work is waiting uptown, and Kenny's taken a personal day, so I'm off."

As I watched the Ice Woman leave my office, I sat back in my creaky desk chair and considered what she'd revealed. Like Addy, she made a show of acting frank but stopped short of providing clarity.

I needed more answers, and it occurred to me where I might get them.

At brunch, Addy mentioned that her granddaughter had come to the Village Blend to work in our Writer's Block Lounge. For all I knew, the girl was a sweet young thing just naive enough to tell all. Or she could be as crusty as Grandma. So I decided to enlist Esther in the hunt to find and question her.

I was about to rise from my chair when my eardrums were pierced by a bloodcurdling siren-like noise. Then someone let loose with a shattering scream. Next came angry shouts.

Fearing the worst, I did exactly what Matt had suggested and *blasted off*—straight into the chaos.

Sixty-eight

~~~~~~

Racing out of my office, I entered our second-floor lounge at the same moment Howie, Esther, and Captain Siebold reached the top of the spiral staircase. Nancy followed, her yellow braids flying.

The cause of the commotion wasn't hard to find. In the center of the room, the customer who'd screamed jumped to her feet.

"Turn it off!" she shouted.

Dark hair tumbling loose, the young woman's demand was directed at a tattooed guy with an overgrown beard and dirty blond hair. Lazily sprawled in one of our overstuffed lounge chairs, the dude rolled his eyes at the woman, which made her even angrier.

"I had the perfect words to end my essay. *Perfect!*" She swiped back her dark bangs. "And your obnoxious ringtone blasted them right out of my head. What kind of a selfish jerk puts an *air raid siren* ringtone on his phone and lets it scream away while others are trying to work?!"

The bearded, tattooed dude held up his mobile phone, which suddenly began re-blasting the siren at top volume. "My calls are important and your brain dysfunction is *not*," he shouted over the obnoxious siren. "So take your lousy essay and shove it right up your—"

His reply was cut off by shouted complaints from the other writers. Then something was thrown—a hurtling ball of golden cake and marshmallow frosting (a tragic waste of our new Twinkie Tribute Cupcake).

The perfectly pitched pastry smacked the sneering dude right in his nose. The move was pure elementary school cafeteria. Half the room stared in shock. The other half dived for cover when the splattered dude, scowling under a mask of gooey marshmallow deliciousness, scooped the mashed cupcake off his bearded face and shot it back at his attacker. The scrumptious cake snowball disintegrated mid-flight and the pieces went wide!

Dante's friend Tony Tanaka ducked just in time, and a woman behind him took the brunt of the cake-plosion. Sputtering with outrage, she sent her container of mixed-berry yogurt flying.

Dina Nardini, the singing waitress, shrieked a high C note and took cover behind her laptop screen while Mason Dunn—with a calculating filmmaker's gaze—aimed the business end of her phone's camera at the action.

Refusing to be distracted, Lachelle LaLande glanced up once from her keyboard, rolled her expressive brown eyes, and resumed typing.

In the meantime, Dante—who'd replaced Tucker as proctor—tried to force a cease-fire by jumping between the main combatants. His reward was a face full of Ethiopian with double almond milk, fortunately tepid (as he told me later). When the cup bounced off his razored scalp, Nancy yelped and ran protectively to his side.

At that point, all the customers began to shout at one another with some joining in the food fight as they threw pastry and coffee cups!

I leaped into the fray, trying to help restore order. Esther gamely joined in. But it was the deep, loud command from six-foot-something Captain Siebold to "CEASE AND DESIST OR I'LL HAVE YOU ALL KEEL-HAULED!" that finally did the trick.

The authoritative voice from the giant man in a federal agent–sharp suit snapped everyone back to their adult senses.

Since the three-hour writing session was minutes away from ending anyway, Esther announced: "Take a break, everyone! Clean yourselves up! We'll start a new session in thirty minutes."

Tony Tanaka was the first to hit the spiral stairs, and many others followed. As food-splattered customers either headed for the restroom or packed up and left in disgust, Howie grabbed a mop and Dante and Nancy helped him clean up the lounge.

To say I was mortified would be an understatement. I had wanted us to make a good impression on Madame's new beau. Having the captain witness this *Titanic* of a shop-wreck felt like a disaster in itself.

Even worse, if we couldn't control this kind of acrimonious anarchy inside our Writer's Block Lounge, it was destined for failure—which would give Cody Wood the edge he needed to push us over a cliff.

Esther looked even more upset than I was. As she watched a parade of writers move downstairs and out the door, she placed her hands on her ample hips and groaned.

"How did this happen?"

"I think I know," Captain Siebold said. "If you'd like some advice to avoid scenes like this in the future, I'd be happy to give it."

"Please do!" Esther said, and we all gathered around.

Sixty-nine

~~~~~~

"Let me start with a story," the captain began, settling into a café chair. "Some years ago, I was part of a think tank—heliophysics space weather research, but that's beside the point. What you need to know is that our project team members were all rational, intelligent people with advanced degrees. Yet three hours into a work session, we became impatient with each other. One day, a shouting match broke out between two visiting British researchers. They even came to blows."

"Clashing theories?" Esther asked.

"Clashing ringtones and sports teams," the captain said. "One fellow's phone played Manchester United's chant—quite loudly, I'm afraid. The man who attacked him was from Liverpool."

Dante snorted. "Those guys shouldn't have been in the same room."

"After that incident, we collected the phones."

Esther frowned. "You're saying we should collect everyone's phones? No one will agree to that!"

"Of course they won't," the captain said. "But if you don't want more disruptions like the last one, you should enforce the muting of their devices, and forbid phone use in the writers' lounge."

"It's not just the phones," Dante said. "People were already restless when I got here. During the last half hour, I saw two people spill coffee, a guy began to talk to himself, and several people looked fidgety and distracted. Meanwhile, Tony Tanaka is chomping on marijuana gummies, and then he gets chatty and starts passing them around. Finally, just before the food fight started, a woman slammed her laptop shut and clomped down the stairs like she'd lost the will to go on."

"It's not a problem of will," the captain said. "It's a problem of *rhythm*."

"Rhythm?" Esther said. "What are you suggesting? That everyone claps their hands and taps their feet?"

"I'm talking about *ultradian* rhythm."

"Is that like finding your zodiac sign?" Nancy asked. "Or that third eye thing?"

"It's not magic," the captain said. "It's biology."

Nancy cringed. "I never liked biology. If what you're about to suggest involves dissecting a frog, I'm out of here."

The captain smiled. "No frogs are involved, I promise. However, understanding ultradian cycles is the key to better productivity."

"I'm down with that," Dante said.

"When you begin a sustained activity involving mental focus—creative writing in this case—your body and brain start burning through oxygen, glucose, and other vital fuels. You can go like the Energizer Bunny for a while, but there is a time limit."

"Then what?" Dante asked. "You run out of juice?"

"Precisely. After approximately ninety minutes of focus, most people have passed their peak performance. At that point, the by-products of all that mental activity have accumulated in the body. Toxic buildup is felt physically and emotionally. We call it *stress*. And when we are stressed, irritability increases along with cravings for food, for sugar, tobacco, caffeine, alcohol, or even narcotics."

"That's Tony and his loaded gummies," Dante cracked.

"I hope he isn't driving his rideshare under the influence," Lachelle LaLande declared from behind her laptop. She'd remained sitting at Tony's table, along with Dina Nardini and Mason Dunn. All of them had become friendly, and since they'd already signed up for the next proctor session, they stayed put.

It was Nancy who came to Tony's defense. "He never drives under the influence," she insisted. "That's a firm rule. Tony only chews bubble gum when he's on duty. And he has a secret spot in Manhattan where he parks his car and takes catnaps when he's tired."

"And you know about this secret spot how?" Dante asked.

"Tony and I . . ." Nancy blushed. "Well, we got super friendly last night."

"Forget about Tony's work habits and Nancy's love life!" Esther cried. "I'm more worried about our writers hitting this ultradian rhythm wall. There's got to be a solution."

"There is," the captain said. "It's called a work break. As soon as we step away from external demands, detoxification, maintenance, refueling, and repair can begin to take place inside our minds and bodies."

"All this from one break?" Dante looked skeptical.

"During a twenty- to thirty-minute break, your body recalibrates and once again the brain functions to its fullest capacity."

"But only for another ninety minutes, right?" Esther said, frowning.

"Approximately. However, the word *ultradian* means 'many times a day' because this cycle repeats itself over and over again during our waking hours."

Esther sighed. "If all that's true, then our three-hour Writer's Block Lounge sessions are—"

"Too long," the captain finished for her. "During my time at the institute, we not only curtailed phone use, but we also shortened each work session to ninety minutes."

"We could do that here without much impact," Esther reasoned.

"And if the response continues to be this good, we should add evening sessions," Dante said. "It will improve the bottom line and give us more work hours."

Captain Siebold offered another idea. "The breaks between your sessions can be put to good use. At the think tank, many of us would venture outside for brisk walks. Breakthrough solutions would often strike us during those walks . . ."

Esther pulled a pen and small notebook out of her apron pocket. I'd seen her use it to jot down creative ideas for her spoken-word performances. Now she began recording the captain's suggestions.

"What else would you do?" Esther asked.

"Well, I hesitate to say, since it's rather unorthodox—"

"Please tell us!" Nancy urged.

"All right," the captain said. "Have you ever seen what children do when they're finally let out of confining classrooms and allowed to hit the playground?"

"They run around, shouting and yelling," Dante said.

"Yes. It's quite natural. And at the institute, a group of us sometimes employed that stress reliever during our work breaks."

"Employed *what* exactly?" I asked.

"Scream therapy. Of course, our facility was on private property with nothing but grass and trees around. It isn't feasible in a public place like your coffeehouse."

"You're right," Esther said, "but it's such a good idea! We should find a way to do it."

"How?" Nancy asked. "Screaming in the alley would only bring the police."

"Let me think." Esther tapped her chin. "We're only three blocks from the Hudson River. We could take turns leading groups over to the Greenway."

Dante nodded. "That strip of riverside park is separated from everything by the West Side Highway, so we'd be soundproofed."

"That's it!" Esther grinned wide. "Every ninety minutes, we'll lead our writers to the water for de-stressing."

Mason Dunn spoke up. "That's genius. I'd join you for that. And so would a lot of others. Do you know how many people in this city need to yell into the void?!"

"It's not a void. It's a river," Lachelle countered. "I like the idea, too. You should call it River Scream."

"Like *Riverdance*!" Nancy said. "Only we can move our arms!"

Everyone stared at my youngest barista.

"I'm not kidding," she said. "After six months of Irish Dance lessons, I learned two things. Clogging is hard. And keeping your arms from flapping around is even harder."

"Any movement is beneficial for refreshing the mind," Captain Siebold noted.

"Can I *sing* instead of scream?" Dina Nardini asked.

"I don't see why not," Esther said.

"The walk to the river and back should reinvigorate your writers, as well," the captain said. "And not everyone needs to scream. A few minutes of simple deep breathing would be beneficial . . ."

I agreed and voiced my approval.

Though the River Scream project sounded eccentric, I loved the idea. I could just picture the writers chatting with one another on the way to the Hudson Greenway, making new friends, laughing as they let off steam and breathed in fresh air. Then they'd all come back to the Village Blend to warm up with fresh cups of coffee.

"I'm going to film it!" Mason Dunn declared. "I have a huge social media following. I'm sure River Scream will go viral!"

We all applauded that.

"Wow, Captain Siebold, you're awesome," Nancy gushed. "Do you have any more ideas to help unblock our writers?"

"Writer's block is really just a productivity slump, and there are many ways to address it. For example, a brainstorming notebook . . ."

As the captain continued his suggestions, Esther scribbled in her own little notebook. And that's where I left them.

It was getting late, and green beans were waiting in my roasting room, so I gave a little wave and headed downstairs.

Seventy

≈≈≈≈≈≈≈≈≈≈≈≈≈≈≈≈≈≈≈≈

Before descending to the basement, I made a pit stop at our coffee bar, where I told Madame how much her dashing astronaut was appreciated upstairs.

"Looks like your Golden Ticket holder is worth his weight in gold."

Madame smiled big, pleased to hear that her charity auction prize had turned into a benefit for us all.

In that moment, I nearly spilled the beans on Cody Wood's offer. I opened my mouth, ready to let off steam, but instead I bit my tongue.

Yes, I'd promised Matt that we'd discuss the offer together. But there was another reason I was willing to delay my primal screaming. Given the disastrous food fight upstairs, I couldn't help worrying (once again) about our financial future. Matt was clearly skeptical. But with Madame blasting off for the Space Coast, I would have a little more time to prove my case of a retail turnaround before Cody's offer landed. I just hoped there was smooth sailing ahead—and not just on getting our shop back into shipshape.

"Before you go, Madame, would you mind taking a look at a few photos?"

With Joan and Addy giving me conflicting feedback on the photos from the original Writer's Block group, I asked Madame if her memory might shed some light . . .

"Let me see," she said, taking my phone.

She nodded as she scrolled through the images. "They do look familiar, but I couldn't tell you their names . . ."

She handed back the phone. "I'm sorry, dear."

"Wait. What about this middle-aged guy with a walrus mustache?" I flipped to the group photo that included that big, Italian-looking man standing in the background. "Do you recognize him?"

"Yes, of course. But he wasn't a member of the group. He was the one who served them. That's a picture of my dear barista Nero."

"Nero? That's Nero?"

"You didn't recognize him?"

"The only picture I ever saw of Nero was when Matt's father was young. The two were laughing together. And Nero was just a skinny kid, late teens, early twenties, clean-shaven."

Madame smiled, a faraway look in her eyes. "I remember that photo. I framed it for Matt."

"He still has it . . ." I thought for a moment. "Is Nero still with us?"

"If that's a polite way of asking has he kicked the bucket, the answer is no. He's still around and enjoying his life. He retired to Sicily."

"Do you have a phone number?"

"Only an address. I don't think he owns a phone, Clare. He's living with family. Spends quite a bit of time on his nephew's fishing boat. What are you thinking?"

"I'd like to write to him, ask him if he'll speak with me. I'll give him my phone number and tell him to call collect."

Madame fell silent. "You want to question him about what happened that night in the alley, don't you?"

"I do."

Madame sighed. "I didn't have reason to doubt him back then. Not at first. But after the police visited us, after they told us about that poor dead boy in the vacant lot, I had a gut feeling Nero was holding back the truth."

"To protect you and the shop," I said.

Madame nodded. "I pressed him privately, but he was a stubborn man, and he stuck by his story: a juvenile fight that ended in a bloody nose."

As she shook her head with regret, I touched her hand, and softly said, "Maybe he'll talk to me. I can assure him that, after all these years, he no longer has to worry about you and the shop. That you're both perfectly safe. But Jensen Van Dyne's life may be on the line, so if there's more to the story, it's time for him to tell it."

Madame closed her eyes when I mentioned Jensen. Then she squeezed my fingers. "It's a good idea, Clare, and it's certainly worth a try . . ."

She promised to text me Nero's address, then she headed for the stairs to join her date, and I pulled an espresso for a quick pick-me-up.

I needed it.

While I was feeling hopeful about the captain's suggestions for righting our caffeinated ship, I felt completely defeated in my mission to question Addy's granddaughter.

I shuddered to think of the young woman returning to her elegant grandmother (who was still one of my favorite authors) with dried frosting on her clothes and pastry crumbs in her hair.

For solace, I took a rich, warm sip from my demitasse and was about to take another when I froze at the sight of a familiar face—though I almost didn't recognize her.

Across the room, quietly laughing with Tony Tanaka at an intimate café table, was Blair Woodbridge, the glamorous assistant to Addison Ford Babcock.

Last night, at the Grand Maison Hotel, the tanned, toned, model-tall Blair was decked out in a glitzy designer split-thigh gown, her brunette hair styled in loose curls, makeup perfect.

Today in our coffeehouse, the glam was gone. Blair's hair was tied back in a sloppy ponytail. She wore baggy jeans, an oversized hoodie, and no makeup on her face, just a large pair of horn-rimmed glasses.

After knocking back the rest of my espresso in a single gulp, I moved toward Blair's table. Suddenly, she and Tony weren't laughing anymore. They seemed more serious, almost secretive, their heads close together.

I was curious about what they were discussing, but Tony seemed to have radar. As soon as I stepped close, he pulled away from Addy's beautiful assistant.

"Hey, Ms. Cosi!" he said, with an awkward smile. "Would you like some gummies? I call them *happy* gummies." He winked. "They're the low-THC kind. Great for relaxing."

"No thanks, Tony. Would you mind if I had a private word with Blair?"

"Oh, sure. I've got to get back to work upstairs, anyway. See you later, Blair."

"Bye, Tony, thanks for the gummies," she said and turned to me with a smile. "Nice to see you, Ms. Cosi. Hey, thanks again—I mean it—for helping us out with Ethan last night. He said you were very kind to him."

"He's a bit of a lost soul, isn't he?"

"I guess you could put it that way. He's unhappy. He's admitted as much to me, and he's been in that state for some time . . ."

It was sad to hear that. And I couldn't help seeing Professor Ethan Humphrey as a young Mr. Scrib. The two men were clearly intelligent, sensitive, and (for whatever reasons) tragically disturbed.

"Anyway, Ms. Cosi, your coffee is superb. I truly appreciate a good cup, so I thank you for that, too."

"You're welcome. Listen, would you mind doing me a small favor?"

"Sure. How can I help?"

I took Tony's seat and lowered my voice. "I had brunch with your boss today, and Addy mentioned that her granddaughter was coming to my shop. If she's still here, would you mind pointing her out? I'd like to say hello."

The request seemed to catch Blair off guard, and she shifted uncomfortably.

"What is it?" I asked. "I hope she wasn't a victim of that horrible food fight upstairs. I'm so sorry about that."

"What happened upstairs wasn't your fault," Blair said with conviction. "If anyone is to blame it's that jerk with the air raid siren ringtone. I can't believe how awful he was. He just kept it blasting, and instead of apologizing, he insulted that girl."

I tensed. "That girl wasn't Addy's granddaughter, was it?"

"No. She wasn't."

"That's a relief," I said. "So, where is she? Or did she leave already?"

Blair took a breath. "To be perfectly honest, Ms. Cosi, she's here."

"Where?"

"Here." Blair pointed to herself.

I was tired and a little fuzzy, and I wanted to make sure. "Do you mean to say that *you're* Addy's assistant and also her—"

"Granddaughter, yes. You have to understand, in professional situations, like the event last evening, I never identify myself as a relative. When some people hear 'granddaughter' instead of 'assistant,' they stop taking you seriously. And I'm very serious about my writing career."

I thought about that for a moment, and I couldn't help but ask, "Do you live with your grandmother?"

"Yes. I do."

"Then I'm going to be frank. What are you *really* doing here?"

"I'm sorry? I don't understand the question."

As Blair blinked at me with her long-lashed eyes, I couldn't tell if she was truly clueless or pretending to be.

"Look, I had brunch with your grandmother today and I saw her big, beautiful home, where a writer could sit all day, be waited on by staff, and type with a stunning view of the Manhattan skyline. With all your grandmother's experience, you also have the best writing advice and publishing connections at your fingertips. The writers who are coming to our coffeehouse don't have those advantages. They're looking for feedback and support while sharing living spaces with roommates and working gig-economy jobs. With all the advantages you have in Brooklyn Heights, what are you *really* doing here?"

Blair's skin flushed red. She fell silent, and I thought she might be angry. But when she spoke again, her voice was pleading and so quiet it was almost a whisper.

"I'll be honest with you, Ms. Cosi, because I'd like to continue coming here. I'm here to work on my own writing. Something that I find *impossible* to do at my grandmother's place."

"I don't understand."

"My grandmother and I are completing a project together—I'm her cowriter for the new cycle of *New Amsterdam* novels. It's not a secret. She's crediting me in the acknowledgments, not as her granddaughter, but as Blair Woodbridge, and I'm being compensated quite well, but . . ."

"But it's not what you want to write?"

"I didn't say that. I'm enjoying the process, and I love her *New Amsterdam* world and characters. I just don't want to obsess over it twenty-four hours a day. I have my own ideas for creative projects. But, as I'm sure you noticed, my grandmother is rather—"

"Overbearing?"

"Strong-minded. She likes things her way. My mother moved to Europe to get away from her. And I admit my grandmother isn't easy to put up with, but I do, because . . ."

"She holds the purse strings?" I said, finishing for her. "Or should I say puppet strings?"

Blair sighed. "I'd like to come here a few times a week to be free of those strings. Hear my own voice in my head, you know? Anyway, I should get going—"

"Before you do, I'd like to ask you about this feud between your grandmother and Joan Gibson."

"I can't help you there. Or maybe I can . . ."

"Go on."

"It's my turn to be frank with you, okay? My grandmother texted me to be careful of you."

"Excuse me?"

"She said you were asking prying questions at brunch today, and if you started grilling me, I should tell you something."

"What's that?"

"For all our sakes, stop asking questions."

"Well, I can't. I consider Jensen Van Dyne a friend, and all of us here are concerned about his well-being."

"We are, too," Blair insisted. "My grandmother has known Mr. Van Dyne for decades. She's always been a dear friend to him, but Joan Gibson, for her own purposes, has twisted that relationship. She turned Mr. Van Dyne against my grandmother, misled him."

"How, exactly? By convincing him to tell the truth about Ace Archer's murder?"

Blair's eyes widened. "I've said too much. I have to go!"

Not yet, I thought. I knew from Mike that sometimes interviews had to get heated. With Blair about to run back to her grandmother, it was time to turn up the heat and watch her reaction.

"Tell me the truth," I pressed. "Do you know who attacked Mr. Van Dyne in my alley? Was it you? Or someone that you or your grandmother sent?"

Instead of denying it, Blair's eyes went wide and she rasped, "Why would we do that?"

"To get the notebook Van Dyne was using to write his true crime memoir—and maybe, in the process, shut him up for good about the past by putting an end to his life."

"That's ridiculous!" she cried, but the uncertain look on her face told me she was either guilty or suspected her grandmother was. Suddenly, she shook her head. "I don't know anything about what happened in your alley."

"I don't believe you."

"It doesn't matter what you believe. What matters is that you can trust *us*. Not Joan."

"Trust you? Do you realize that you've contradicted what your grandmother told me? She pretended she hardly knew Mr. Van Dyne and didn't know Joan at all."

"If she lied to you, then she had good reasons. And you need to butt out, Ms. Cosi. This isn't your business. We're going to take care of everything, including Mr. Van Dyne."

"What does that mean? Is that a threat?"

Instead of answering, she jumped to her feet. "My grandmother is expecting me. Thanks again for the coffee, and for helping my cousin Ethan, but I've got to go!"

And just like that, she was gone.

Seventy-one

~~~~~~

HOURS later, I ascended from the hot roasting room, feeling like a refugee from Dante's Inferno, sweaty, tired, and defeated. I longed for a soothing shower and dreamless sleep. But more than that, I wanted answers.

Although I'd learned a lot today, it wasn't nearly enough.

Mike agreed.

He was already in Miami and busy with his own work, but he continued to relay text message updates from Detective Russell, which is why I knew Mr. Scrib was stable but still unconscious in the ICU.

I also knew Russell was making even less progress than I was in finding Mr. Scrib's attacker. Sure, I had my guesses. I even had possible motives. But I had no definitive answers, no confessions, and no proof.

After my meeting with Matt today, I felt just as frustrated with the precarious state of my own future.

What if I misjudged Madame? What if she ends up agreeing with her son and decides to sell this landmark shop to Cody Wood? The very idea struck at my heart.

I loved this old coffeehouse. I loved opening the shop in the early morning. I loved serving its customers. And I loved this time of the evening, too. Outside our wall of French doors, the lights of the city sparkled in the chilly darkness. We'd just locked up for the night, and the whole place was serenely quiet.

By now, Dante had left for a friend's gallery show, and Howie Johnson was giving our plank floor one last mopping.

I noticed Esther and Tucker sitting at a table near the flickering hearth, and I joined them with a freshly roasted and brewed mug of Matt's latest shipment of diligently sourced beans.

The high-grown Rwandan made an outstanding cup. Its bright note of citrus and its crisp, clean finish lifted my flagging energy, and I began to share everything I'd learned today with my two most trusted baristas.

When I finished spilling all I knew, I sadly told them that we'd hit a wall.

Esther didn't agree. In fact, she surprised me with the announcement that she'd made a potential breakthrough.

"Earlier today, when Captain Siebold ran down his list of suggestions to combat productivity slumps, he mentioned brainstorming journals. He said lots of professionals use them—researchers, mathematicians, artists. As a writer myself, I use an idea notebook, and the captain reminded me of Beatrix Potter. Before she wrote her *Peter Rabbit* tales, she filled her teenage journals with thoughts and observations, all of them written in a code that only she could understand because she feared prying eyes."

Esther tapped the notebook on the table in front of her.

"After speaking with the captain, I'm sure of something. *This* is Mr. Scrib's brainstorming journal."

"Is it written in code?" I asked.

"Not a coherent one like Beatrix's. But I believe Mr. Scrib used these pages as a tool to help him call up memories and free-associate related words and phrases. There are hundreds of pages in this book. It's a thought playground for his poetry as well as his true crime memoir. To all of us, it reads like gibberish. But for him, even the doodling would have helped his mind relax, create, and think about—among other things—people from his past."

"His past?" I said. "Does that include the Writer's Block group?"

Esther nodded. "Until our brunch with Addy this morning, I didn't know who or what to look for. But I do now, so I can show you this . . ."

Esther flipped through dozens of pages filled with seemingly disconnected phrases and scribblings. On one page at the center of the chaos, Mr. Scrib wrote BB in big block letters, followed by the doodle of a cocktail glass.

"This must be Bobby Briscoe," I realized. "Joan said he was a bartender as well as the group's drug dealer."

Around Bobby's initials were scrawled words: *walking pharmacy, Rx to order, class clown, loved by all, scruffy puppy.*

"And see this?" Esther flipped to another page and pointed to one corner. "An elaborate letter *J* with flowers around it."

"That must be Juliet," I said and read the nearby words: *class by herself, creative soul, sparkling prose, starlight laugh, want the world for her . . .*

She turned more pages and showed us an ace of spades, with a doodle of a bow and arrow beside it.

"Ace Archer," she and I said in unison.

Tuck leaned in, and we all read the scrawled writing around Ace:

Hack + Actor = Hacktor

dumb blond

pecs who needs Rx

"Wow," Tuck said, "Mr. Scrib sure wasn't a fan of this guy."

"Clearly not," Esther said.

When she turned to the next page, we saw the picture of flying birds, and the keys to Mr. Scrib's apartment fell out of the notebook pocket. Tucker picked them off the floor and scanned the plea Mr. Scrib had written on the tab:

If I am incapacitated, please take care of Wacker.

"It's a good thing he didn't write *this* in code," Tuck said. "You never would have gotten into his apartment and Wacker would be one dead duck."

"That's *so* not funny." Esther snatched the dangling keys from Tuck and stuffed them back into the notebook.

"I wanted to show you this, too." Esther pointed. "It's another doodle representing Ace Archer. But this time, there's a second arrow pointing directly to a huge picture of a top hat. A rabbit is popping out of the hat and a magic wand is waving over its head."

"That's the universal symbol for a magician," Tuck said.

"Thanks, Sherlock. I guessed that already. What I don't know is why a magician is important to Ace Archer. The stuff around it doesn't make sense, either . . ."

We all fell silent, staring at the scribbled words:

tricky ideas, into his lap

cheap treasure alchemized into golden opportunity

inherited secrets, adapt ability, triggered it all

"*Triggered it all* must mean something," Esther said.

"Except no one mentioned anything about a magician being part of the Writer's Block group," I pointed out. "Unless Ace was a magician, too, although he was never described as anything more than a handsome young actor."

"A very obscure one," Tuck said.

"Did I hear the words *obscure* and *actor*?" Mop in hand, Howie Johnson moved closer. "Because if you want info, I can dig up pretty much anything written about any actor alive or dead at the Performing Arts Library."

"Could you look up Ace Archer?" Tuck asked. "We'll pay you for your time, as always."

"Sure. I've got a shift there in the morning." Howie checked his watch. "Which means I better call it a night."

As Howie headed out the door, Nancy appeared with newly applied makeup and styled and sprayed hair.

"I have a date in an hour," she announced as she bundled up for the cold. "Don't wait up for me, Esther, and don't forget to stop by the grocery store. You told me to remind you!"

After Nancy left, I locked the door again.

Esther and I continued to page through the notebook, this time looking for any reference to Addy—a word, an initial, a hieroglyphic, anything!—but nothing popped out. Twenty minutes later, Tucker departed, and still Esther lingered, riveted by the notebook.

"I wonder if the true crime manuscript everyone is looking for will be in an elaborate code," I said. "Like Beatrix Potter's teenage journals."

"Definitely not," Esther said. "Like that note about Wacker attached to his apartment keys, Mr. Scrib wants his memoir to be read. This notebook, not so much."

With that, she thrust the notebook inside her messenger bag.

"I better head home. I'll read more in the morning."

"You should call for a car," I said. "It's cold and you don't have Nancy with you."

Esther scoffed. "It's only a fifteen-minute walk, and I need to pick up peas at the grocery store. Wacker gobbles them up like bonbons."

After we said good night, I stepped behind the coffee bar. Glancing out the front window, I noticed Esther hadn't left. She was still standing on the chilly sidewalk, and I assumed she'd forgotten something and would need to get back in.

I was about to head to the door when I realized she was simply checking her phone. As she did, I spotted something disturbing. An ominous figure appeared to be speeding right toward her on a blue Citi Bike. The fast-moving cyclist wore a black ski mask and long black coat and was flying at her from behind, so she couldn't see!

Before I could move or even cry out, the thief attacked. With one gloved hand, the cyclist grabbed the long strap of Esther's messenger bag and zoomed forward.

The violent pull of her shoulder strap yanked her sideways. She lost her balance, and for a horrified moment I feared she might be dragged. Instead, the strap broke, and my barista tumbled to the concrete!

Seventy-two

~~~~~~

"ESTHER! Esther! Are you all right?!"

Yelling, I burst through the door, baseball bat in hand, but the thief was gone, barreling down Hudson. I dropped to one knee beside her. She was already sitting up and favoring one arm.

"Are you hurt?"

"Not much," Esther said, frowning over a rip in her coat. "But I'm *really* pissed at that stupid-ass thief!"

"What did they get?" I asked. "Your wallet? Your phone? As long as you're not hurt, that's what matters—"

"I've got my phone!" Esther cried. "And my wallet's in my pocket. But that creep stole Mr. Scrib's notebook! I was supposed to take care of it and now it's gone!"

Esther teared up. I didn't know whether it was because she was in physical pain or mental anguish over the loss of Mr. Scrib's property. I suspected it was both.

I put down the baseball bat and hugged her tightly. After a minute, I helped her to her feet.

As I gave Esther the once-over, I heard a car door slam. I turned at the sound and noticed a flashy sports car parked across Hudson. Its sleek red finish gleamed under a streetlight. With air scoops on the side, it looked like a rocket, or maybe a UFO. The windows were tinted so dark it was impossible to see inside.

I never saw a car like it, but I instantly recognized the blond Adonis who exited the vehicle.

"Cody Wood," I spat with a visceral sense of purpose. "Call the police," I told Esther.

Traffic was light on Hudson Street, and I stepped off the curb, twirling the bat like a designated hitter warming up.

"Hey, Wood!" I shouted, moving straight for him. "Did you have something to do with this?"

The former champion surfer turned coffee chain CEO stopped dead. "What? You mean the purse snatching? I don't know a thing—"

"Then what are you doing here?"

"Whoa, Cosi, whoa!" Jumping between me and his sports car, Cody spread his arms wide. "Hit me if you want to, but don't touch my baby!" His panicked voice was reaching Bee Gees–level octaves, rising higher and higher with each new syllable. "This is a quarter-million-dollar McLaren GT Coupe!"

"I don't care what it is! I repeat: *What are you doing here?*"

"I came to see you. I figured by now Allegro would have told you about the deal I proposed."

"He told me," I said through gritted teeth.

"Listen, Clare, I come in peace. And I don't blame you for being upset. It's understandable after all the years you wasted on an antiquated business model."

"Keep flapping your gums, Wood, but I'm not buying what you're selling. Actually, I couldn't *choke down* what you're selling."

"I'm sure you could, if I added enough sweetener. And that's why I'm here. To give you something to consider. Something that will change your life."

"And what could that be?"

"First think about this. We both know Allegro is good at what he does. But do you honestly believe traipsing around the world's coffee belt, visiting smallholder farms, and befriending community co-ops is the future of this business?"

"Get to your point."

"You're the talent and the brains behind the Village Blend, I know that. Your drinks are phenomenal, and you're an exemplary roaster; even my own research team says so."

"Where is all this flattery going?"

"To an inescapable place, Clare. Come work for me at Driftwood."

For a moment I was dumbstruck by the man's casual tone. I could hardly believe it. He was trying to lure me away, and he was betraying Matt in the process with disturbing ease.

"Aren't you sick of sweating in front of a Probat in the basement of an ancient building? Don't you want to stop slaving over a balance sheet, just to keep an old shop on track like some dollar-store manager? You're better than that."

"What about everything you promised Matt?" I shot back. "Was that all baloney?"

"No, I fully intend to honor the offer I made. I just think *you* would be better off joining my Driftwood team. Sure, I realize you're used to roasting premium small-batch beans sourced by the father of your child. But Matt's whole approach—" He shook his blond head. "It's fine dining when you and I both know that the vast majority of people are perfectly content to consume fast food—"

"So now you're serving hamburgers?"

"No. But I'm a realist about large markets. And I know you care about quality, which means you can help us at Driftwood bring our less-than-perfect beans to another level."

"You want me to help you serve better burgers?"

"Exactly! Who needs small indigenous farmers when we can cut costs with mass production? See what I mean? And you can do your job nine to five, in a clean lab, with a whole team at your beck and call."

"And it's more efficient for you, right? You won't have to hire spies to come to my shop and steal my seasonal menus."

"And *you* can contribute your ideas without the troubles of a dollar-store manager!" Cody's temper was showing, and he knew it. After taking a breath, he tried again with a more conciliatory tone.

"Look, Clare, I know you're emotional now. Change is always hard to swallow—"

"Like your Driftwood coffee?"

"Just think about my offer. I'll start you off with a salary in the low six figures. Within a year you'll be a VP earning half a million—"

"And by the third year, I'll be fired. Because I'll insist on doing away with high-fructose corn syrup and artificial flavorings, and your 'team' will tell me those choices won't work with the bottom-line numbers for your national chain."

"Hey, I know you don't trust me. I know you think I'm some sort of rat who's trying to sabotage your business, but nothing could be further from the truth." He flashed his Vegas neon Driftwood smile. "You can trust me, Clare—"

At that moment, the shameless CEO popped his driver's side door. The car's ceiling light went on and showed me Cody's dark interior, in more ways than one. The bright illumination unmasked a shockingly familiar face.

Lazily sprawled in the passenger seat was the very same tattooed guy with the overgrown beard and dirty blond hair who'd started the food fight in our packed Writer's Block Lounge.

"You're the jerk with the air raid siren ringtone!" I cried, pointing. "You're a hired gun! Cody's plant! A saboteur!"

Suddenly, a camera flash went off, and I realized Esther had been lurking behind me in the shadows. And when she saw who was sitting in Cody's car, she swooped in, aimed her camera, and snapped a picture.

"Thank you, Esther!" I cried. "You see that, Wood? I've got wanted posters now, and you're both on them. The two of you are hereby banned from the Village Blend for life!"

Cody rolled his eyes. "Calm down, Cosi. Get over yourself. And get some rest. When you wake up, you'll realize the two deals I'm offering are too good to pass up. I advise you and your ex-husband to take them. If you don't, you could both end up with *nothing*."

Before I could shout back, he was already jumping into his four-wheel rocket. As the engine roared, and he hit the gas, I was ready to hurl my bat at his precious sports car, but Esther stopped me.

"Don't waste a good slugger," she said. "He's not worth it."

Then together we watched the ex-surfer ride a wave of darkness into the New York night.

Seventy-three

M**inutes** after Cody took off, two NYPD officers arrived in response to Esther's call. They came with no siren, no drama, and (in the end) left us with almost no hope of catching the criminal.

As we quickly learned, Esther's cycling mugger was a literal bicycle thief.

Fifteen minutes before Esther was mowed down, a woman reported that her Citi Bike was stolen by a person who matched the description of Esther's attacker.

One of the responding officers told us that many street thieves used this method of operation. Since Citi Bikes could be traced to an ID through a payment method, these perps would steal the bikes, use them to commit their drive-by crimes, and then ditch the stolen vehicles.

"Same thing happens with cars," the officer said. "A stolen car becomes a getaway car and is dumped right after the crime . . ."

I couldn't argue with that since I'd been a victim myself when a thief slammed me with a stolen scooter and sped off, leaving me in the street before ditching his hot wheels near the river.

According to the officer, such tactics made it more difficult to track down these thieves, and in the end I was left with little hope that Esther would get her messenger bag back or anything inside it, including Mr. Scrib's notebook.

"Random crimes" like these, he said, were all too common.

When the police business was finished, I put Esther in a taxi. And I didn't stop fretting until she called to say she was safe at home, defrosting the last of her frozen peas for Wacker's midnight snack.

After that, I fed my own pampered pets, took a long, hot shower, and crawled into bed.

LYING alone in the big four-poster, I stared at the ceiling missing Mike. With all the excitement, I'd even missed his good night call. He'd left a sweet message and invited me to call him back, but I was too exhausted to talk.

Java and Frothy seemed to sense my sadness and cuddled up close. I was glad for their purring company; and as I rubbed their soft chins and scratched their little ears, I thought about that responding officer's words.

He'd described Esther's mugging as a "random crime."

I wasn't so sure.

I had no proof, of course, but Addison Ford Babcock had tried to bribe Esther out of that notebook earlier today. So now I wondered: Did Addy hire someone to steal it? Or did her granddaughter Blair arrange the theft? She'd been hanging out in the Village Blend for hours, snooping around in her baggy jeans and oversized hoodie. Was it Blair who'd pulled on a big black coat and ski mask? Or did she hire someone to do it?

And then there was Joan Gibson. The icy publishing exec was equally desperate to get her hands on Mr. Scrib's notebook. I told her that Esther didn't have the material she was looking for, but did she believe me? Or did she send her assistant Kenny in a ski mask to grab it?

Who *really* robbed Esther?

Lying there in the dark, I couldn't say. But the timing seemed far too suspicious to be mere coincidence.

In the morning, I fully intended to tell Detective Russell about the mugging, though I doubted his response would be much different than the equivalent of the cop shrug we'd gotten tonight.

When I finally slipped into slumber, my sleep was fitful. I tossed and turned so much that even Java and Frothy complained. As the sun came up, my girls issued even louder meows.

I didn't blame them for the feline reveille. My little beasties were bellowing for breakfast because I was usually rising and shining by now. *This* morning, however, was one that came too soon.

Dragging myself out of bed, I felt like a drooling zombie, arms outstretched, desperate not for human flesh but that first cup of coffee.

Why is that first sip of the day always the most amazing?

I had my theories, but my favorite boiled down to my own poetic thought (one even Mr. Scrib might like):

A lover denied in the night is fulfilled in the morning.

As I stood in my cozy little kitchen, watching Java and Frothy happily devour their favorite fishy cat food, I consumed my effervescent Breakfast blend (voted best in the city) with equal purity of pleasure. This rich, warm, freshly roasted joy was an energizing embrace.

Maybe that's why Cody and his Driftwood dreck were so unspeakably distressing to me. A rocket-ship sports car was more important to that golden-haired gangster than serving his customers a quality product.

If there was one thing I could not stand, one thing I could never tolerate, one thing that drove me absolutely bat-guano crazy, it was this: A *BAD* CUP OF COFFEE.

And that was why I could never, ever, *ever* work for Cody Wood.

Cody's visit had been disturbing on many levels—the least of which was his shameless job offer. Even worse was the hard evidence (thanks to Esther's camera flash) of Cody's underhanded attempt to sabotage the budding success of our Writer's Block Lounge.

These were serious revelations, and I did not want to convey them to Matt in a phone call or text message. So, with my second cup of the day, I sent him a quick request.

We need to talk about Cody.
Come by the shop today.

Matt needed to hear what had happened last night, but I was also looking for advice. People like Cody Wood could be dangerous. They would do almost anything to get what they wanted. And this man wanted to buy me and erase the Village Blend. How far would he go to achieve those ends?

The idea unnerved me, and Matt's reply to my request for a meeting didn't help. *Sorry,* he texted. *No can do . . .*

On my way to Baltimore to pick up a diverted shipment. We'll talk about Cody when Mother flies back from FLA. Unless she and her astronaut elope to the International Space Station. CU soon. Matt

*   *   *

A FEW hours later, I was on the job again, resigned to waiting out a meeting with Matt and his mother, which (since I had no choice in the matter) I concluded was for the best.

The week ahead would give me the chance to prove our retail business could be profitable again. And (so far) today was looking good.

Our ground-floor tables were full, and the upstairs lounge was functioning even better, thanks to the permanent ejection of Cody's hired henchman and the helpful suggestions from Madame's gallant captain.

I was just finishing up a morning session in the roasting room when I heard from *my* favorite officer—a lieutenant, not a captain, but gallant just the same.

Mike had phoned me from Miami during breakfast, but this time it wasn't sweet talk. He'd stepped out of a meeting to relay some urgent news—

"Mr. Van Dyne is conscious," he said. "Detective Russell tried to interview him but didn't get far. He'd like you and Esther to meet him at the hospital. He's hoping the man will respond to questioning better if Esther is present."

I didn't hesitate. Tearing off my apron, I raced upstairs.

After Dante and Nancy agreed to cover for Esther, I bundled her up, grabbed her hand, and pulled my duck-rescuing barista out the front door.

Seventy-Four

❧❧❧❧❧❧❧❧❧❧❧❧❧❧❧❧❧❧❧❧❧❧

Esther and I met up with Detective Russell at the intensive care unit. An affable heavyset man close to retirement age, he joined us as we followed an RN across the busy ICU.

Human sounds were fleeting. Whispered words and muffled moans mingled with the incessant beeps and pings of machines and monitors. There were no rooms, not even partitions, only curtained beds arranged in a wide circle around the nurses' station.

Esther gasped when we got our first glimpse of poor Mr. Scrib in his hospital bed. He appeared to be sleeping, and I feared he would be unresponsive. But when she whispered his name, one eye opened, and a smile lifted his lips—

"Esther . . ." he rasped. "Hello. I don't have a poem for you. I'm sorry."

"We don't have to play the game today," Esther said as she brushed a tear from her cheek.

The sight of him choked me up, too. Dwarfed by the massive bed and humming medical devices, he looked as colorless as the sheets around him. His head was encased in bandages that covered one eye. An IV was plugged into one arm, and a tube was taped to his nose.

At the foot of the bed, Detective Russell stood listening with a recorder going and a notebook ready.

"I'm glad to see you," Esther told the poor man. "How are you feeling? You look like you could use some Village Blend coffee."

Mr. Scrib tried to laugh, but his mirth ended with a weak cough.

"Do you remember what happened to you?" Esther asked. "You were attacked in the alley behind the Village Blend."

He shook his head weakly. "Not me . . . That happened to Ace."

"Yes, we know about Ace Archer," Esther said. "But you were attacked in the alley, too."

"Not me," he repeated weakly.

"You don't remember?"

Mr. Scrib seemed baffled by the question. I could see the disappointment in Detective Russell's expression.

"We'd better forget our first question and move to the second," I whispered.

Esther began with a gentle prodding. "Hey, I heard you're going to get a book published."

"That's what Joan said . . ."

"Do you mean Joan Gibson?"

Under the bandages, he nodded. "It's almost finished."

"I'd love to read it, if you'll let me."

"It's not poetry."

"I'll read anything you write, Mr. Scrib. But the problem is, we can't find the manuscript."

"The duck," he gasped, weakly raising his arm. Esther took his hand, and he gripped it.

"Don't worry about Wacker. He's staying at my place until you get home. Wacker is doing fine."

With that, he closed his one visible eye.

"Mr. Scrib? Mr. Scrib?"

This time not even Esther could awaken him. He'd slipped back into unconsciousness. After a moment, Detective Russell gestured for us to leave.

"I'm going to stay and hold his hand a little longer," Esther whispered.

The detective and I quietly left together. In the waiting room, we found a private corner, and I told him about Esther's mugging the night before, including my suspicions.

"Thanks for this information, Ms. Cosi," the detective said when I was done. "I agree with you. Like the attack on Mr. Van Dyne, what happened last evening to Esther could very well be more than a random crime, given the connections to an unsolved murder."

"What do you know about that cold case?"

"Not much. I'm still waiting to see the file."

You and me both, I thought.

"Did you search Mr. Van Dyne's apartment?"

"I contacted the building manager," he said. "Turns out the man lives on the same floor as Van Dyne. I sent a couple of detectives over. They turned up nothing."

"Wait a minute. You said the building manager lives on the same floor as Mr. Van Dyne?"

"Yeah, a guy named Humphrey—"

"Ethan Humphrey?"

"That's him."

Seventy-Five

The news about Ethan Humphrey surprised me.

"If you don't mind, Detective, what else can you tell me about Mr. Humphrey?"

"Not much. He teaches part-time at NYU. Told my guys he gets a rent break for doing the side hustle of managing the building."

Wow, I thought, *Ethan must have some great connections to get that job.* It was either that or the building's owner had shockingly low standards, given the man's penchant for drug-induced disorderly conduct.

Just then, Detective Russell's phone dinged. He checked the text and apologized. "I've got to run. There's a break on another case. If you find out anything more from Van Dyne, please pass it on."

I'd just watched the detective scramble for the elevator when Esther reappeared. She tried to speak, but when her chin quivered and she broke down in tears, I took her in my arms.

After a few moments, Esther pulled away and looked around. "Where is Detective Russell?"

"He had to leave on another case."

"Then we should call him," Esther said. "Mr. Scrib woke up after you guys left. He told me where to find the manuscript."

"What? Where?"

"He said he hid it 'behind the duck where no one can find it.' Those were his exact words. He repeated it three times."

"Behind the duck?" I was baffled. "What could that mean?"

"No clue, and there's one more thing. He said he also told Joan

Gibson where the notebook was hidden. He claims she visited him this morning."

Esther took off her glasses and swiped at her eyes. "Behind the duck must mean something. I found Wacker in Mr. Scrib's bathroom. Maybe there's a hidden compartment in there. Or maybe he hid it behind a heating grille or something. You can't *literally* hide something behind a duck; it would be dripping with guano—oh, no. No!"

"Esther, what's wrong?"

"What if the manuscript was thrown away? That bathroom was a real mess. If someone thoroughly cleaned the place, then they might have found it."

"Someone like the building manager?" I thought of Ethan Humphrey, who also happened to be Addy's nephew. "Esther, do you have the keys to Mr. Scrib's apartment?"

"No. They were stolen last night, remember? When that bicycle thief grabbed my bag, the jerk got the notebook with the keys inside."

"Okay, don't panic. All is not lost. I know the building manager personally. He likely has the keys to all the apartments, and he owes me . . ."

We flagged a taxi for a speedy trip back to the Gold Coast of Greenwich Village. As soon as we arrived, we entered the small lobby and hit the buzzer marked *Building Manager* multiple times. Ethan Humphrey did not respond. Fortunately, an Instacart delivery woman exited through the interior security door, and we slipped in.

The elevator was waiting, but we had no clue how to get inside Mr. Scrib's apartment without keys. The question turned out to be moot when we found his front door ajar.

Esther and I exchanged uneasy glances and pushed through anyway.

Entering the living room, we both instantly realized that the unpleasant odor that had permeated the air on our first visit was gone, replaced with the strong smell of lemony soap. Someone had cleaned up. But the new smell was not the only thing we noticed.

"Look at those brown spots on the floor," Esther said.

The spots left a trail through the living room, right up to the front door.

"Whoever cleaned this place should have sealed the trash bags before dragging wet guano to the dumpster," Esther said.

Though it was possibly unfair, I thought that was just the sort of shoddy work Ethan might have done if he'd cleaned the place under the influence of whatever drug he decided to indulge in that day.

"Is there no respect?" Esther cried. "That's a parquet floor!"

She was about to check the bathroom when I called her back. "Esther, look at that picture. Do you remember it from the last time we were here?"

Hanging on the wall was a print copy of the classic Lynn Bogue Hunt painting of ducks flying over a pond.

"Behind the duck," I said. "Maybe he was talking about that framed duck print."

I took off my shoes and stood on the French Provincial sofa to examine the print. I noticed scrapes on the wall paint around the bottom left side of the frame. Holding out hope, I slipped one hand behind the painting to probe around and felt something sticky.

"I'm going to pass this picture down to you, okay?"

Though not heavy, the print was large. Esther carefully set the picture face down on the floor, and that's when we knew.

Attached to the cardboard backing were four strips of double-sided tape. They formed a rectangle the size of a notebook. If we had any doubts that this tape was used to hide a spiral-bound notebook, the bits of white paper chaff clinging to the adhesive convinced us.

"It looks like Mr. Scrib's notebook *was* here," Esther said, "but now it's gone!"

To get so close, only to have our hopes dashed, made me want to scream. Esther couldn't hide her disappointment, either.

"Do you think Joan Gibson got here first?" she asked.

"Probably. And the door was unlocked, which tells me she had a key. I doubt Ethan would have helped Joan get into this apartment since he's Addy's nephew. Blair knew all about the animosity between Addy and Joan. No doubt Ethan did, too."

"But where would Joan Gibson get a key to Mr. Scrib's apartment?"

Even as she asked the question, Esther's eyes narrowed, and I knew what she was thinking.

"If you're wondering whether Ms. Gibson had something to do with your mugging last night, I can't argue."

"But what can we do?!"

"Not much, Esther. If Mr. Scrib's editor found his manuscript, then she's holding all the cards. She can argue that it's hers by contract. Or even lie and say she doesn't have it. The most we can do is inform Detective Russell what we discovered here."

"Well, I'm going to check the bathroom anyway!" Turning on her Doc Martens, Esther moved to explore her desperate last hope of a secret compartment.

I stayed behind to rehang the nature print. That's when I noticed something shiny on the floor. As I bent down to examine it, I realized it was a high-end lighter with a quotation inscribed on its surface.

Nobody realizes that some people expend tremendous energy merely to be normal

This lighter belonged to Ethan Humphrey. I remembered it from the night I'd helped him out of trouble at the Grand Maison.

But what was it doing here?

I was about to pick it up when I heard Esther's horrified scream.

Seventy-six

~~~~~~

I RUSHED into the hallway and nearly collided with my panicked barista.

"What happened, Esther?"

Face pale, hands partially covering her eyes, she just shook her head. I tried to step around her, but she gripped my arm to stop me.

"Don't go in there. Don't look!"

I couldn't *not* look, so I broke away and approached the open bathroom door.

I quickly realized that the spotty stains we'd noticed in the living room weren't duck guano. I knew it when I saw the crumpled form on the bathroom floor and the same dark splatters on the tile walls, the mirror, and the sink.

I stepped back and took several deep breaths, steeling myself for a closer look. This time I focused on the corpse. She was clad head to heels in a Tom Wolfe–white pantsuit, now bloodstained red. Her face was turned away, but I knew who it was. A familiar handbag had been dropped right inside the bathroom door. I wasn't stupid enough to touch it, but I did see the monogrammed *J.G.* carved into the exquisite leather.

"Clare?"

I jumped, startled. Esther was standing at the far end of the hall, still in fight-or-flight mode from the look of her. "Is that person . . . Are they . . . ?"

"She's dead."

I peeked around the door again. Despite the nausea that threatened to overwhelm me, I took another look at the bashed-in head. The hair that wasn't stained with blood was as white as an icy snowstorm.

"Do you know who it is?"

"Joan Gibson."

I retraced my steps, this time following the blood splatters dotting the hardwood.

"Shouldn't we call 911?" Esther asked.

"Yes, of course, and I want to see where these drops lead."

Esther looked down, realized she was standing on some of the stains, and quickly stepped aside.

"You won't need a yellow brick road to follow this trail."

The dried bloodstains led all the way to the front door, and there were more in the hall that we hadn't noticed when we'd first arrived. The brown drops didn't lead to the garbage chute or the elevator, which would have made sense. Instead, the dark trail took me to another apartment, its door slightly ajar.

"What do you see?"

I jumped again. Esther had followed me.

"Do you think someone is dead in there, too?" she whispered, eyes the size of tennis balls behind her glasses.

"We're about to find out," I said.

There was no name above the doorbell, just:

BUILDING MANAGER

I carefully nudged the door with my elbow and it opened wider.

The dark trail led into the room, and I spied a disturbingly familiar mallet lying on the floor, now splattered with blood.

A low coffee table was covered with beer bottles, half-squeezed tubes of oil paint, and paintbrushes. By the window I saw an easel holding a partially completed oil painting—a striking image in swirling purple and magenta. Other paintings were scattered around the room. Unframed, they leaned against the walls and the furniture.

I heard a grunt.

The sound came from the couch, where a man in a spotless gray tracksuit was stretched out on saggy cushions, arms akimbo. A familiar face peeked out from behind a dirty bong that lay across the sleeper's chest. Ethan Humphrey appeared to have passed out after a booze- and drug-fueled binge.

Baffled, filled with pity and horror, but resigned to the tragic truth, I stepped away from the door, pulled Esther down the hall, and called 911.

The police response was immediate. Two uniformed officers pulled Esther and me apart to question us separately. Esther was led around the corner while I was taken to a spot near the fire door and grilled by a detective.

She asked me why I was there, what I was looking for, how I got in. I answered all her questions and explained that Detective Russell from the Sixth could verify my story.

Our talk took place close to Ethan's apartment, which gave me a front-row seat to the professor's arrest. It did not go well.

The police had to wake him, and once they explained why they were there, what charges he faced, and the reason he was being taken into custody, Ethan grew combative.

"No!" he protested. "I didn't do anything! I don't understand!"

I pushed past the detective and watched officers wrestle him to the ground, knocking his easel to the floor in their efforts to restrain him. As they cuffed him, Ethan continued to thrash about, his own kicks and struggles destroying his beautiful unfinished canvas.

Detective Russell made an appearance minutes later, and after speaking with the responding detectives and the crime scene unit, he told us we were free to go.

I rejoined Esther in the hallway, and together we watched a phalanx of police officers bring out the still-struggling Ethan.

He pleaded his innocence every step of the way.

Seventy-seven

In the two days that followed Ethan Humphrey's arrest, I couldn't sleep. When I wasn't pacing the kitchen and opening the fridge every fifteen minutes, I was tossing and turning alone in bed.

My workdays were fueled by caffeine, and while my body stayed robotically busy, my mind was so distracted that I'd heard my staff say, "Earth to Clare!" more times than I could count.

Part of it was post-traumatic stress. Finding Joan Gibson's bloody body would have given anyone nightmares. But the troubling sight of Ethan's arrest also haunted me. I couldn't stop seeing the childlike confusion on his face and hearing that pitiful little-boy cry—"*I didn't do anything! I don't understand!*"—as they hauled him away.

The police had more than enough evidence to charge Ethan with murder. I saw it with my own eyes. The trouble was—

I didn't know if I believed it.

Yes, his inscribed lighter was found at the crime scene. Yes, there were bloodstains leading to his apartment and on his mallet. But when I closed my eyes and visualized Ethan lying on his couch, I saw a gray tracksuit with absolutely no blood on it. In fact, his clothes were spotless until they became stained with his paints during his struggle with the police.

As criminal behavior went, that didn't make sense.

A murderer was either crazy enough to leave a Hansel and Gretel trail of blood right to his couch, or careful enough to shower and change into clean clothes. But then that careful killer wouldn't get high, pass out, leave the murder weapon on the floor and the door ajar.

Yet, according to Detective Russell, who kept me abreast of the investigation, homicide detectives believed Ethan did all those things. They found no traces of blood in his bathroom or kitchen. None on his towels or soiled laundry. And nothing in his apartment garbage or the building's dumpster.

Nevertheless, the police sent his towels and clothes to the crime lab hoping to find at least traces of Joan's blood to prove their theory.

Results were still pending.

As for the autopsy, the cause of death was not blunt force trauma to the head but *strangulation*. While the blows to Joan's head came from the bloody mallet found in Ethan's apartment, those blows came *post-mortem*, which seemed odd to me.

Another question was motive. *Why would Ethan want to kill Joan?*

Yes, Joan Gibson was at war with his aunt over the approval of a business deal and publication of a true crime memoir (that I could only suppose revealed Addy to be guilty of some kind of criminal behavior), but would Ethan care enough about that to commit murder?

Was he trying to help his aunt? Or had he been high as a kite, assumed Joan broke into Mr. Scrib's apartment, and attacked her as some kind of intruder? If he had, why would he strangle her first and then—after she was dead—beat her head bloody with his mallet?

And where was Mr. Scrib's notebook?

The missing notebook was *still missing*.

The police hadn't found it in Ethan's apartment, Joan's handbag, or in a third search of Jensen Van Dyne's place. Detective Russell told me the investigators were hot to get it, too, since it would bolster their case of premeditated murder.

That very question of Ethan's mental state—argued by his high-priced attorney—is what got him remanded to a drug rehab facility for treatment and a psych evaluation rather than a jail cell.

Despite the brutality of the crime, Ethan's lawyer convinced the judge that the adjunct professor (*former*, since he was fired the day after his arrest) was no danger to the public, and that his drug addiction issues required humane treatment.

The plea was "not guilty" by reason of "settled insanity," a legal term for a mind addled by long-standing drug use. Mike Quinn believed that defense was weak. In his calls to me from Miami, he voiced the opinion that the evidence against Ethan was strong enough for a conviction of premeditated murder.

If Ethan was guilty, I agreed he should be punished. But was he guilty?

These were the things that troubled me over the past two days and long, lonely nights. This evening, however, despite the fact that it was close to midnight, I was glad to be awake.

Earlier today, Mike texted me from Florida that he'd be catching a flight this evening and arriving in Manhattan around twelve AM.

Should I come to you? he asked.

My reply was an all-caps *ABSOLUTELY*.

After that exchange, waiting was difficult. I distracted myself with roasting work in the basement and a dinner break upstairs—for me and my feisty felines.

Cooking always calmed my nerves, and I took pleasure in preparing my Sautéed Pork Chops with Caramelized Onions and a side of Pan-Roasted Baby Yukon Potatoes crisped golden in beef tallow. It was one of Mike's favorite suppers, and I'd made extra in case he was hungry for a midnight meal.

As I sopped up the mouthwatering juices on my plate with a hunk of crusty bread, I shared a few small morsels with my purring roommates. Then I placed a catch-up call to my daughter in DC, gave Java and Frothy a loving brushing, and returned to the shop to help with closing. After my baristas said good night, I worked on staff schedules and inventory lists while waiting for Mike to arrive.

I'd set up a table for two by our flickering fireplace with a French press and a plate of Baileys Irish Cream and Caramel Nut Fudge saved from today's pastry case. Then I settled in, doing my best to focus on my laptop screen (instead of that fudge). Before long, the shrill buzz of the night bell startled me.

I assumed it was Mike and hurried through the pantry to the back door. Eagerly, I turned the locks and unhooked the security chain. When I threw open the steel door, I saw a man waiting for me under the stark glare of our repaired LED light, but that man was *not* my fiancé.

It was Ethan Humphrey.

"Good evening, Clare."

For a moment, I stood stiller than stone, as if Ethan were Medusa and I'd been caught in his mythic spell. Then I moved to slam the door in his face.

"No! Wait! Listen to me. I'm here to tell you the truth—"

His pleading words made me pause, but only for another second. I was a witness against an accused murderer who was now confronting me in an alley at midnight. The most likely reason banged through my brain—

He's here to kill me!

I swung the heavy door. Ethan lunged forward to hold it open, and I screamed. That's when a deep voice shouted from the darkness.

"Police! Freeze or I'll blow your head off!"

Mike was finally home.

Seventy-eight

࿂࿂࿂࿂࿂࿂࿂࿂࿂࿂࿂࿂࿂࿂࿂࿂࿂࿂࿂

"PLEASE don't shoot!"

As Ethan threw up his hands, Mike closed in fast, leveling the barrel of his gun at Ethan's head. The look on Mike's face was ferocious.

"Who are you and why are you here?"

"My name is Ethan Humphrey, and I came to talk to Clare. She needs to hear what's happening to me. I'm being set up!"

Ethan's longish hair had been cut short, and he was obviously exhausted. His boyish features showed new lines etched into his face, as if he'd aged years in just a few days, and with his trembling lower lip, he looked as if he was about to cry.

"Don't hurt him, Mike."

"That is going to depend entirely on him," Mike said, his gaze and gun remaining fixed on Ethan. "Dial 911."

"No. Not yet. I think we should let Ethan talk."

"Be reasonable, Clare. This man is accused of—"

"I *know* what he's accused of. But with you here, he poses no threat. And if he actually risked breaking out of custody to speak with me, then I'd like to give him that chance."

"It won't take long," Ethan promised. "I'm not a violent person. I have no intention of harming Clare. Or you. Or anyone. I didn't *kill* anyone, either. What's happening to me is completely absurd, Kafkaesque. It's *wrong*. That's what I'm trying to say."

"Mike, let him come inside. It's cold. The man is shivering . . ."

I wasn't surprised. All he was wearing on this freezing fall night was a set of thin gray pajamas, sneakers without socks, and (for some reason) a long white lab coat.

"Please," Ethan begged.

"All right," Mike said, not happy about it. "Step inside *slowly*. Keep your hands where I can see them. And don't make a single move in her direction, or I'm shooting to kill."

"I promise, you won't have to," Ethan meekly replied.

Once inside, Ethan did exactly as Mike asked and placed his hands behind his back. Mike cuffed him, sat him down on a stool at the coffee bar, and insisted I stand on the other side of the counter several feet away while he stood behind Ethan with his weapon drawn.

"The man who handcuffed you is my fiancé," I told our unexpected guest. "His name is Mike Quinn, and he's a detective lieutenant with the NYPD."

"Pleased to meet you, Lieutenant," Ethan said.

"How did you get out?" Mike asked.

Ethan shrugged. "I faked abdominal pain at the rehab facility. They took me to an ER, which was very busy. While I was waiting for some test, I stole a doctor's coat and slipped away."

Mike grunted. "Not again."

"Does that happen often?" I asked.

"A few times a year," Mike said. "Now why are you here, Mr. Humphrey? Get to the point."

"I'm here because Clare treated me like a human being."

"What are you talking about?" Mike demanded.

"Clare knows." Ethan held my gaze. "Do you remember the hotel suite at the Grand Maison? I was in horrible shape that night. They sent you in to evict me, but you were kind about it. You even said you were sorry that you couldn't give me coffee."

"I remember."

"I'm relying on that sense of decency now, Clare. I know you're a witness for the prosecution, but I'm here to ask you to be a witness for my defense."

"Why would I do that?"

"Because you care about Jensen Van Dyne, and so do I. To be honest, I have great affection for the old poet. If you want to save Jensen's life, then you need to listen to everything I have to say."

Mike and I exchanged glances, and he lowered his weapon.

"Go on," I said. "I'm listening."

"I was arrested for Joan Gibson's murder, but I *did not* do it. That's the absolute truth, and I'll prove it to you. When you found me sleeping on the couch in my apartment, was there any blood on me?"

"No. None."

"Was my door wide open?"

"No, it was only slightly ajar. I used my elbow to push it open."

"Well, I painted all night, and I kept my door *wide open* to clear away the smell of the linseed oil. I smoked some weed around seven AM and fell asleep—next thing I know a cop is waking me and charging me with murder."

"Okay," I said. "Now I have some questions for you. Why was your inscribed lighter in Mr. Van Dyne's apartment?"

"I left that lighter on my coffee table. That's also where I left the mallet I use to align my canvas frames. The killer must have seen me passed out, took my lighter and mallet to link me to the crime scene, left a trail of blood, and closed my door nearly all the way to make the scene more plausible."

"And who is this clever killer?" Mike asked.

He shook his head with sadness. "It's someone Clare knows. Someone she met the same night that she helped me at the hotel."

My mind raced back to that night. Ethan had left the hotel by the time I'd met his aunt Addy, which left only one other person. "Do you mean Blair?"

Ethan nodded. "It was my own cousin, Blair Woodbridge, who killed Joan Gibson and framed me for the murder. I'm sure of it."

Seventy-nine

❀❀❀❀❀❀❀❀❀❀❀❀❀❀❀❀❀❀❀❀❀❀

Ethan seemed convinced of his cousin's guilt, but I found it difficult to believe.

"I know what you're thinking," Ethan said. "I can see it in your face. You're wondering if Blair is capable of killing a woman so brutally and framing me for it."

"Did Blair confess to you?" I asked.

"No, but it's the only explanation that makes sense because I *know* I didn't do it. And you have to understand, Blair wouldn't have done it of her own volition. My aunt Addy would have put her up to it."

"And Blair would do whatever your aunt asked?" I pressed. "Even murder?"

"She's been financially dependent on my aunt for much of her life. Just as I have. Don't you see, by framing me, my cousin and aunt not only erase the threat of Joan Gibson but also rid themselves of me and my problems. Two troublesome birds taken out with one stone."

"When you say your 'problems,' are you talking about your drug use?"

"I'm an embarrassment to them. The night of Addy's award dinner was the last straw. They were both livid. But my substance abuse issues aren't the only reason I'm a liability. I've been a financial drain on Addy for years. I'm not proud of it, but my aunt paid for everything—my boarding school, my college and graduate degrees—though there were always strings attached. She insisted I take the adjunct professor position at NYU, which she arranged, but it's never been my passion. I wanted to pursue my painting, to live and study in Paris, not lecture students who'd rather be scrolling their social media. But Addy wouldn't support that. She insisted ours was a literary family and she wanted to polish me up for presentation to her circle of friends."

Ethan sighed. "It was easier to do what she wanted, so I painted on the side. She gave me a generous monthly stipend to remedy my impecunious state, given my meager part-time income, and she let me live rent-free, as long as I served as her building manager—"

"Wait. Did you say *her* building manager?"

"Yes, Addy Babcock owns the Gold Coast building where I live. And for all her financial support, she demanded one more thing of me."

"What was that?"

"To look after Jensen Van Dyne. Last year, when Jensen was released from the psychiatric facility, my aunt told me that he was an old friend, and she gave him that apartment you visited. Like me, he lives there rent-free."

Hearing that astonished me. "Ethan, if your aunt has been sheltering Jensen, and you've been looking after him, then tell me this. Do you know who confronted him in our shop's alley? Did Blair do it?"

Ethan shifted in his seat. "To be honest with you, I did—"

"You?! You said you were looking after him, yet you attacked him?"

"It *wasn't* an attack. Please, don't jump to conclusions—"

"Then you better explain."

"Believe me, I *want* to explain because it's all connected. On the same day that Jensen Van Dyne suffered a mental breakdown in your shop, my aunt learned about Joan Gibson's contract with him to publish and publicize the truth of what happened in that old writers' group. Aunt Addy was outraged. She said if the truth got out, it could ruin her career."

"And what is the truth?" I pressed. "Was she involved in the murder of Ace Archer?"

"I have no idea. She refused to discuss the details. She simply told me to find Jensen's true crime manuscript and destroy it. As the building manager, I had a key to his place. I knew he wrote everything longhand in notebooks, and I searched and searched, but I couldn't find it."

"Wait," I said. "If you searched his apartment, then you had to know about the man's pet duck."

"Sure, I knew about Wacker," Ethan said. "And I'm sorry that I lied to you and your friend, but I was never a fan of the mess it made. So, when you said you wanted to take care of it—" He shrugged. "I lied to get the duck out of there."

"Forget the duck!" Mike said. "What happened after you told your aunt that you couldn't find the notebook?"

"She was furious. She *demanded* that I convince Jensen to hand it over. He signed himself out of the hospital that evening and came back to the apartment. He said he had lost his keys, so I let him in. But when I tried to speak to him about the book he was writing, he became angry."

"Why?" I asked.

"Joan convinced him that his book would not only help Addy's career but also make him rich. Jensen felt that he was a financial burden on my aunt, and he wanted to repay her with the so-called *fortune* that he was going to make from his memoir. Clearly, he was deluded."

Ethan shook his head. "I tried to tell him that his memoir would *hurt* Addy rather than help her, and it wasn't likely to make much money. But he refused to believe me and stormed away. I was worried about him, and I followed him to your alley. He was in a state of panic. He said that he had left the notebook in your shop, and he started looking for it in the dumpster. I tried to help, but he was acting irrationally. He began to fight. During our struggle, he fell and hit his head. Then you came out and I ran . . ."

As Ethan spoke, I couldn't help remembering how violently Jensen had thrashed about when Matt tried to help him in our shop. But still, I told him—

"You shouldn't have run away."

"I *never* meant to hurt him. I didn't think he was injured that badly, and I assumed the people rushing into the alley would help him. Then I heard someone chasing me. I ran, ducked into a nightclub, took off my coat, rolled it up, and left with a group of people exiting the club to make sure no one noticed me."

"I knew it," Mike muttered.

"You have to understand," Ethan said. "I couldn't get caught or I'd risk losing everything."

"But you've lost everything now," I pointed out.

"And my aunt is *still* pulling the strings. She hired a top attorney to represent me, but he told me that the 'settled insanity' defense won't hold up at a jury trial, that it was just a bargaining strategy. Now he's pressuring me to accept a deal from the DA's office. He wants me to plead guilty to murder, show remorse, and use my history of drug abuse to get a lesser sentence. My aunt and her attorney are just fine with sending me to prison for five to seven years, but *I didn't do anything.* I didn't kill Joan. And beyond my own ruined life, you have to understand that this *isn't over.*"

"Why not?"

"Because my aunt and cousin still do not have Jensen's notebook. They told me so. They're still searching for it, and they're absolutely terrified that it will fall into the wrong hands. If it does, Addy will be ruined—and so will Blair."

"Because Blair is cowriting the new *New Amsterdam* novel," I assumed.

Ethan nodded. "That whole reboot with the streaming series is set to revitalize Addy's career and make her millions in international book sales. But if Addy is charged with a terrible crime, then she'll be canceled, and Blair knows her future is tied to Addy. That's how much is at stake for them both, and that's why I believe they'll be ruthless. If I'm right, they won't stop with the murder of Joan. They'll try to silence Jensen Van Dyne permanently—and anyone else who reads that notebook."

EIGHTY

～～～～～～～～～～～～～～～～～～～～～

I SPOKE with Ethan a little while longer. Finally, Mike shut us down.

"I'm sorry, but I have to take Ethan back into custody now. If we wait much longer, we'll risk a BOLO being issued. Then Ethan will be the star of a Citizen app alert and a citywide manhunt."

"I don't want that," Ethan said, resigned. "You better take me in."

I PACED the shop until Mike returned. When he did, our embrace was long overdue.

"You must be tired," I said, although he didn't look it.

"I napped on the plane," he said, "and now I've got so much adrenaline going, I won't be able to sleep."

"Then let's sit down and decompress. I have coffee and your favorite Irish Cream Fudge waiting, unless you'd like pork chops and pan-roasted potatoes. I can warm a plate upstairs."

"I'll eat the chops for breakfast," he said. "Right now, hot coffee and Baileys Fudge sounds like heaven to me."

I showed him the café table that I'd set up by the hearth, and Mike gave me an appreciative smile. The change in climate from sunny Miami day to freezing New York night had him rubbing his hands near the flames.

"This is nice," he said, sitting back in his chair.

I poured him a hot cup of my Fireside blend, appropriate enough for our table's location, but also for the time of evening. The rich, dark roast with its flavor notes of milk chocolate, cinnamon, and smoke was also low in caffeine, and designed for after-dinner service or (in our case) late-night talks.

"I feel sad for Ethan," I said, filling my own cup. "Did he say anything more to you after you two left?"

"Yes, he did. Enough to make me warn you not to get your hopes up." Mike took a long sip of the dark roast. "Your professor friend is going down hard."

"What do you mean? Ethan said he wants to fight the murder charge."

"Yes, but his aunt is the one paying for that top attorney, and she won't shoulder the substantial cost of a jury trial. She and the attorney want Ethan to take the plea bargain—plead guilty and serve a reduced prison sentence. Ethan won't do that, which means he'll have to rely on a public defender for his jury trial."

"He has a right to a trial, Mike."

"Of course, he does. But Ethan intends to present a case of being framed by his cousin and aunt. That's why he wants your testimony about Van Dyne's memoir and Joan Gibson's publishing scheme. Apparently, his aunt told him all about your 'prying into her affairs,' as she put it. But his case is weak. He has zero evidence that his cousin—or anyone else—killed Joan Gibson, apart from a paranoid theory."

"Paranoid? Then you don't believe any part of his story?"

"The question isn't whether I believe him, but whether a jury will."

"You don't think a public defender will be able to handle the case?"

"It's David and Goliath, Clare."

"Are you sure you want to use that metaphor? You know who won that particular battle, don't you?"

"Come on, you know what I mean. The DA's office will paint Ethan as a troubled and paranoid drug addict with a record of disorderly conduct and physical evidence that ties him to the murder." Mike blew out air. "That poor, pathetic guy. He'll be doing twenty to twenty-five years if he doesn't take that plea."

"But if he doesn't fight the murder charge, he'll still be slapped in a prison cell for five to seven years."

"He can make the most of his time," Mike said gently. "Maybe teach other prisoners. Pursue his art studies. Get clean."

"Don't make prison sound like a trip to Paris. You know it's not, and if he's distraught and depressed, Ethan's the kind of lost soul who might take his own life."

"I can't argue with that possibility, but the evidence is damning—"

"Not all of it is. What if Ethan is right? What if he's being framed?"

"Okay." Mike leaned forward, blue eyes sharp. "Let's say the man *is* having a 'Kafkaesque' experience, and he's been made a patsy for some elaborate revenge scheme. Then how did his cousin Blair know that Joan Gibson would be at Van Dyne's apartment? Answer me that."

I stared down the lieutenant. "If the plan was to end Joan's life, then Blair—or someone she or her aunt hired—could have been shadowing Joan, looking for a chance to kill her. They found it when she entered Van Dyne's place."

"And where did Joan get the key?"

"If her assistant Kenny put on a ski mask and mugged Esther the night before, then Joan had the keys from Mr. Scrib's brainstorming notebook."

"Good answers, counselor, but where is your evidence for any of this? Beyond conjecture, hearsay, and a drug addict's imagination?"

"I have none." I sat back. "But I'm not going to dismiss Ethan's warnings. If he is right, there could be more deaths to come. And Mr. Van Dyne may be in mortal danger."

"Not as long as he's in the hospital. He's under safe watch."

"What happens when he gets out of the hospital and returns to Addy's building?"

"If and when Van Dyne is well enough, let's assume he can tell you where his potentially incriminating notebook is, or give a coherent deposition on its contents. Until then—"

"Until then," I cut in, "Mr. Scrib's notebook is the key. Once it's in the hands of the police, this whole thing is over. There won't be anything more Addy can do. Now I just have to find it . . ."

Mike drained his cup. "If Ethan's warnings have validity, then whoever gets that notebook could be in grave danger. So, if you're going to keep looking, Clare, do me one favor. No, *two*. And the first one is vital."

"What is it?"

"Be careful."

"I can do that. What's the second?"

"If you do find anything, call me."

Eighty-one

~~~~~~

In the days that followed, my worries continued about the sad fate of Ethan Humphrey, the vulnerability of Mr. Scrib, and the ongoing threat of sabotage by Cody Wood, but my work kept me busy, and the Village Blend's financial turnaround became the silver lining to those dark clouds.

The Writer's Block Lounge quickly grew into a normal aspect of our coffeehouse life, and we attracted new sign-ups with every gathering. Esther's trips to Hudson River Park for "River Scream" became as popular as the writers' lounge itself. Some folks wanted to join up just for the screaming sessions.

More work meant more hours, and I added them to everyone's schedule. The only one to complain was Nancy, who believed her overtime was why Tony Tanaka "dumped" her—although his excuse for continually canceling their late-night dates was supposedly a "secret project" involving other lounge writers.

I didn't want to burst my barista's romantic bubble, but the way Blair Woodbridge had cozied up to Tony on her visit the previous week, I thought that "secret project" might be a hot date or two with her.

As for Blair, given Ethan's belief in her duplicity, I kept watch for her reappearance at our shop. But (so far) she hadn't returned.

Meanwhile, our newest staff member, Howie Johnson, came through with a file of photocopies from the Performing Arts Library on the deceased actor Ace Archer.

Tuck, Esther, and I got together after closing time and pored over it.

There wasn't much in the file: some old Playbills and clippings with reviews of Ace's performances. Few of those reviews were kind, and one—from an off-Broadway production of Shakespeare's *A Midsummer Night's Dream*—was downright scathing. We didn't learn much more about the murdered member of the old Writer's Block group, with one exception.

"This must be the magician connection," Tucker said, reading another newspaper clipping. "It's an obituary for Ezra Stephano, an old stage magician who performed under the name 'The Amazing Stephano, Sleight of Hand Master.' The obit reads that he is 'survived by his son, Elmer Archibald Stephano, a New York actor who performs under the name Ace Archer.'"

"So Ace wasn't his real name," Esther said.

Tuck shrugged. "I'm not surprised. Stage names are de rigueur when it comes to Actors' Equity. And look at this swoon-worthy headshot of the boy. Under the name Ace, he's got a chance at leading man roles. Under the name Elmer, not so much."

Later that same evening, Mike shared his notes on the NYPD's cold case file, which was finally delivered to his office.

"The deceased actor's legal name was—"

"Elmer Archibald Stephano," I said. "He performed under the name Ace Archer."

"How did you know?" Mike asked, surprised.

I told him my source and asked him to go on.

"Are you sure you need me to?" he said with a half smile. "Or do you have more sources I should know about?"

"No, Lieutenant, I'm all ears. Please continue . . ."

Mike did, but there was nothing in the police file that could tell me very much.

"What was the *cause* of death?" I asked.

"Blunt force trauma to the head."

"What about Madame's memory of blood in the alley? She said Nero, the barista who served them, told her there was a fistfight in the alley between two men from the writers' group. More of the group went into that alley before it was over."

Mike shook his head. "Everyone's statements, including Nero's, amounted to Ace Archer leaving the coffeehouse alone one night and never coming back."

"Then there was a group cover-up?"

"Looks that way, unless Madame's memory was faulty."

"I don't believe that," I said. "And I've already written to Nero in Sicily, asking him to contact me. Was there anything else?"

"The investigators found that drug dealing was going on behind the Village Blend at that time. Witnesses said Ace Archer was a user. Given the Brooklyn location of his remains, the detectives pursued a line of investigation that suggested Archer was involved in a drug deal that went bad. The case was left open and, in my opinion, the detectives expected that a mobster or drug dealer could be linked to the crime down the line."

"Except that didn't happen, did it?" I asked.

"No," Mike said. "The murder of Ace Archer remains unsolved."

A**FTER** that disappointing evening, work and life continued without incident.

Although I kept watching for Blair Woodbridge to return, and I knew that Driftwood could drop another saboteur's shoe on us at any time, several consecutive days of peace lulled me into cautious complacency.

That is, until one chilly morning.

Mike and his most senior officer, Sergeant Franco, headed up to Albany for a meeting on diversion control, and I caught up on my roasting schedule. Then I helped out my baristas in the shop.

As I climbed the spiral staircase that day, serving tray in hand, I looked down on the busy coffee bar and crowded tables and couldn't help feeling a sense of pride. By pulling together, my baristas and I had resuscitated our dying retail business. We were thriving, and I was feeling happy about that.

As I delivered coffee and pastries to the second floor, I noticed a familiar figure in cobalt blue at a corner table. Tony Tanaka had fallen asleep, doubtless after a long night of Uber driving. He slumped over his work, head completely covered by his hoodie.

No rest for the weary, I thought.

But as I approached, something seemed wrong. Another few steps and I nearly dropped my tray.

"Hey, are you okay?"

I shook Tony's shoulder and one limp arm slipped off the table. I shook him again and his whole body toppled to the floor. That's when I realized what I was looking at—or rather *who*.

The body on the floor wasn't Tony Tanaka's.

The sight of the corpse chilled me to the bone. The glassy eyes were open but unfocused. The mouth was gaping wide, and I spied a half-chewed red gummy on the lolling tongue. More gummies were clutched in one waxy dead hand.

That hand belonged to our fledgling filmmaker, the Goth girl who'd shot the viral video of our River Scream.

I bit back my own scream at that moment. Choking back tears, I realized the eerie blank spaces on her black tombstone T-shirt could finally be filled. Death had found another victim to *INSERT NAME HERE*, and today that name was Mason Dunn.

Eighty-two

Once again, chaos swept through my coffeehouse. The call to 911 brought paramedics and the police. Poor Mason Dunn was officially pronounced dead, and the second-floor lounge was declared a crime scene.

The NYPD field-tested the gummies that Mason had been eating. Though they were branded as marijuana treats, the candy had been tainted with tranq and fentanyl—a deadly combination.

After that, the police confiscated every bit of food in our shop. Then they shut the Village Blend down until we passed a Health Department inspection, which would take a week or more.

Late that night, my baristas and I met in our closed shop. The second floor was off-limits, so we gathered at the coffee bar. Our situation had never been more dire. My beloved Village Blend was once again teetering on the edge of an existential cliff.

"Even a few days without business will hurt us," I said. "And there's no guarantee the Health Department will clear us in a week. We need to find out *how* the drugs got here. We need *solid evidence*, and we need to find it as fast as possible."

Tuck was livid. "If Cody Wood did this, he may have planted even more drugs somewhere in this shop!"

"If they find more tranq here, it's game over," Dante said.

"And Driftwood wins," Esther said, throwing up her hands.

"We can't let that happen!" Nancy cried.

"Calm down, everyone," I said. "Let's use our heads and reason this out. I'm no fan of Cody, but we don't know that he was behind poisoning

Mason. Cold-blooded murder of a young, innocent woman is an extreme stunt, even for him. This could be something else entirely."

"What else?" Nancy asked.

I told my baristas about Ethan Humphrey's shocking late-night visit to lay out his theory that his cousin Blair was helping his aunt Addy protect her reputation and fortune.

"Ethan has no hard evidence," I warned. "But he believes they were behind the brutal murder of Joan Gibson and framed him for it."

"How could killing Mason Dunn be connected to that?" Dante asked.

"Ethan warned me that because Mr. Scrib's notebook was such a threat to Addy and Blair, they would do anything to get it back—and permanently silence anyone who learned about its contents. He said there could be more deaths to come."

"I actually agree with our Boss Lady on that theory," Esther said. "While I loathe Cody Wood, I don't think poisoned gummies are his style. If the Driftwood CEO wanted to sink us, wouldn't he have poisoned our *coffee*?"

"You're probably right," Dante said. "An annoying ringtone is one thing. Murder is something else."

Tuck turned to me. "Do you know *how* that deadly cocktail of drugs got into those gummies?"

I nodded. "Mike is in Albany today, but Detective DeMarco from his squad told me that a hypodermic needle was most likely used to inject the gummies with the fatal cocktail."

"A syringe injection of gummy candy," Esther said. "That's right out of Addy's show, *She Slays Me!*"

"Second-season opener," Tuck declared. "'Snake in the Big Apple.' A villain is killed when he samples a box of Jujyfruits injected with cobra venom."

"That's a curious connection, but it's not proof," I pointed out.

Nancy scratched her head. "I still don't get it. *Why* would Addison Babcock and her granddaughter want to poison poor Mason Dunn?"

Dante spoke up. "I don't think they were trying to poison Mason, because I'm pretty sure that hoodie belonged to Tony Tanaka. It looks just like the one he wears. And those gummy candies in the pocket looked like the kind he always carries around."

"I thought that hoodie looked like Tony's, too," I said. "But why would Mason be wearing it?"

"I think Tony may have left it here," Dante said. "He stopped by late last night. I remember he was working by the fireplace upstairs and his hoodie was draped over a chair—"

"He *did* leave it behind," Tuck said. "When I went up to light the hearth this morning, Mason was already working up there. The second floor is always chilly until that hearth is lit—and I saw her take the hoodie off the back of the chair and put it on."

"That's it," Dante said. "She put on Tony's hoodie. Then she found the plastic bag filled with gummies that he always carries in his pocket, and she snacked on the candy."

"So, we're back to asking the same question," I said, "but for a different member of our writers' group. Why would Addy and Blair want to kill Tony Tanaka?"

"The only way that makes sense is if they believe Tony has Mr. Scrib's notebook," Esther said.

"But where would he have gotten it?" Dante asked.

"I don't know, Picasso."

"Well, please catch me up," Dante said, "because I can't see why Tony would have that old poet's notebook."

Esther shrugged. "Neither can I. All I can tell you is that we searched Mr. Scrib's apartment, and all we found was his pet duck. Then Mr. Scrib briefly regained consciousness in the ICU, and the only clue he gave us about the location of his notebook was to look *behind the duck*—and I thought he meant Wacker."

"But we figured out that Mr. Scrib was referring to a Lynn Bogue Hunt duck print," I explained. "I found double-sided tape outlining the shape of a notebook on the backing behind the framed print. Unfortunately, the notebook was gone."

"Wait," Dante said. "Are you talking about the Lynn Bogue Hunt duck print that was hanging in our upstairs lounge?"

I stared at Dante for a long moment. Then Esther and I exchanged glances.

"Son of a bunny!" I cried. "Mr. Scrib wasn't *only* using the duck print in his apartment to hide his notebook; he was doing the same thing here at the Village Blend!"

Esther grabbed Dante's arm. "Where is that duck print now?"

"Tony and I hauled all that old lounge art up to the attic," he said. "Remember, Boss? Tony wanted to check out the brushstrokes on the Childe Hassam print, and you asked us to help move everything from the hallway to the attic."

"I remember that day," Nancy chimed in. "That's when I first met Tony."

I closed my eyes. "Behind the duck! That's got to be the answer. Everyone, follow me to the attic!"

"Wait!" Dante cried.

I didn't. Instead, I took off like a Space Coast rocket and shot up the back service staircase.

Eighty-three

~~~~~~

On the highest floor, I pulled down the ladder, climbed into the attic, and quickly located the Lynn Bogue Hunt print, right beside the Childe Hassam art that Tony had wanted to photograph that day.

As Dante, Esther, Tuck, and Nancy caught up to me, I turned the framed duck print around, and we all saw the same kind of double-sided tape in the shape of a notebook that I'd found at Mr. Scrib's place.

"He hid it here, too!" I cried. "No wonder he had a breakdown that morning in our shop. If the picture was gone, so was his notebook—"

"Worse than that," Esther said, "you replaced it with the Writer's Block Lounge plaque and all the artwork from his era. He must have thought a ghost from his past was terrorizing him."

"The shock must have been what pushed him over the edge." I felt terrible. "It was my fault."

"No, it wasn't," Esther said. "How could you have known?"

"The least I can do now is recover the man's notebook. But it isn't here, either—"

"That's what I tried to tell you when you ran off," Dante said. "On the day that Tony and I moved the art, I saw a spiral-bound notebook on the floor of the attic. I thought it belonged to Tony because he picked it right up. I figured he must have dropped it."

"You're telling us Tony *took* the notebook?" Esther moaned in frustration.

"If he did, I'm sure it was out of innocent curiosity," Dante said defensively. "Look at all the vintage stuff up here. I'll bet Tony thought it was some odd piece of Village Blend memorabilia that nobody cared about."

"Sure, maybe he was curious about checking it out," Esther said. "But why did he *keep* it?"

"I think I know why," Nancy said in a sheepish voice.

We all stared and waited.

"I told you that Tony dumped me for a 'secret project,'" she said. "He swore me to secrecy, but I don't think I should keep it secret anymore . . ."

Nancy went on to explain that on one of their hot dates, Tony got "real relaxed" and bragged to her that he was working on a vintage Greenwich Village murder mystery, which he claimed "fell into his lap."

"He was super excited," Nancy said, "because the story was completely formed."

"What kind of story did he describe?" I pressed.

"He said it's about bohemian writers embroiled in romantic triangles, drug and alcohol abuse, plagiarism, double crosses, and outright betrayals. One of the members ends up dead and a cover-up goes on for years. With all the intrigue, Tony thought the story could be turned into a streaming series, a manga, and a bunch of novels. That's why he decided to collaborate to create a multimedia pitch."

"With other graphic artists," Dante assumed.

Nancy shook her head. "Tony wanted to collaborate with people who didn't work in his medium so there wouldn't be any jealousy. If they all contributed ideas from different media, they could work together as a team and still be individual stars. Smart, right?"

"Except the material isn't *his* to exploit!" Esther cried.

"Who are these other creators?" I asked, my worries starting to mount.

"They all belong to the Writer's Block Lounge," she said. "Esther's friend Lachelle LaLande is writing the first novel. Mason Dunn *was* writing the pilot script, and she was also working with that singing waitress Dina Nardini to turn it into a musical. Tony swore them all to secrecy. He wouldn't let anyone copy the pages or even read the notebook openly in the shop. They took turns lending Tony's notebook around."

Esther smacked her forehead. "I'll say it again. It isn't *Tony's* notebook!"

"How could I know that?" Nancy cried. "The whole lounge is filled with writers working on stuff!"

"Let's get back to Tony's so-called 'secret project,'" I said. "Was Blair Woodbridge part of his writing group? Did Tony mention her?"

Nancy made a face. "She got awfully close to Tony. She may have tried to slink her way in. I wouldn't have put it past that snooty preppie."

I stared at Nancy. She soon realized we were all staring at her.

"Call Tony right now," I told her. "Warn him he's in danger. Tell him to bring that notebook back ASAP!"

"Okay, okay," said Nancy, stepping away for privacy.

"And he'd better do it," Esther shouted after her. "Or I'll see him arrested for theft!"

I pulled Dante, Tuck, and Esther into a huddle. "If all of those writers read Mr. Scrib's notebook, they could be in as much danger as Tony. We need to get that notebook *tonight* and deliver it to the police!"

"Don't worry," Dante said. "Once Nancy contacts Tony, I'm sure he'll bring it straight to us."

Just then, Nancy rushed back. "Tony's not answering! I called his personal number and his work number, and he didn't pick up."

"Could we be too late?" Dante asked.

"Maybe not," Nancy said. "Around this time of night, Tony takes a break. He likes to park his car at an out-of-the-way spot and grab a catnap. It's a spooky area, but kind of romantic, too. You can see the lighted boats going up and down the Hudson."

"Gee, I wonder how you know all that," Esther said flatly.

"Never mind how!" I cried. "Can you take me there, Nancy?"

"Sure, it's not far."

"Wait," Dante said. "Tony might be taking the night off. If he is, then he's in his bedroom working at his drawing board with a silenced phone and earphones on. I'll go to his place to warn him."

"But *everyone* in his writing group is in danger," Tuck insisted. "What about Lachelle and Dina?"

"We have to call them and warn them, too," Esther said.

Tuck shook his head. "You won't be able to reach Dina by phone. She's singing her little heart out at the Broadway Spotlight Diner, and she won't have her phone. Management locks them up until quitting time."

Esther groaned. "Then we have to go up there and warn her, too?"

"If *you* go, Esther, you won't get in for an hour. That place is an international tourist trap. There's always a line around the block. But—" Tucker flashed a grin. "I can get right in."

"You can't be *that* famous," Esther cracked.

"It's not fame. Punch used to work there, so I know about the secret employee entrance."

"Good," I said. "Tucker, you go to the Spotlight and warn Dina. Esther, you call Lachelle and warn her."

"Sorry, Boss," Esther said. "Lachelle works at the First Class Club, and they don't allow mobile phone use. Their whole gimmick is 'airplane mode,' so people will engage in conversation instead of doomscrolling. They don't even have Wi-Fi—"

"That's the stupidest idea I ever heard," Nancy said.

"Lachelle says they're always packed with VIPs networking. Anyway, there's a bouncer at the door who enforces the rules. Phone use is verboten."

"That's it, then," I said. "The only way we can warn everyone is to split up. Let's go!"

Eighty-Four

〜〜〜〜〜〜〜〜〜〜〜〜〜〜〜〜〜〜〜〜

Esther was familiar with Lachelle's bar. Show business was Tucker's element. And Dante was fine checking on a friend. None of them required a backup. Nancy Kelly, however, was a different story.

The girl needed an escort, especially since she "didn't remember the name of the street" where Tony parked for his catnaps, but she could "lead me there," which meant we had to make the trip on foot, at night, to what Nancy described as an "out-of-the-way" spot.

"Don't worry," she assured me. "It's just a quick walk."

I had another motive for traveling with Nancy—expedience.

Tony Tanaka either had the notebook with him, or he knew who had it. Either way, finding Tony was sure to be the fastest way to get my hands on Mr. Scrib's magnum opus.

Nancy and I were the last to depart the coffeehouse. Before we left, I pounded out a text to Mike Quinn—

We may have located the notebook. Following up now.

Mike's response from Albany was immediate. *Do you need backup?*

Don't worry, I told him. *911 is only three digits away . . .*

After adding that I'd keep in touch, Nancy and I hurried across Hudson Street. As we headed down Leroy in the direction of the river, I felt a chill that had nothing to do with the freezing cold night. Not long ago, I'd chased a fleeing figure through this same jungle of scaffolding, until a stolen scooter slammed into me.

I didn't relish another midnight stroll through this barren part of our neighborhood where the glow from streetlights was blotted out by the scaffolding's rough wooden planks and no light shined through the shuttered windows.

Few pedestrians were out at this hour; even the entrance of that newly opened nightclub was quiet as we moved through the hazy shadows. Suddenly, a scooter whizzed by and made me flinch.

"Are you sure you know where you're going, Nancy?"

"Sure, I'm sure," she brightly replied, as if we were strolling through Central Park on a sunny morning.

It took several more minutes on our feet before Nancy spotted a powder blue graffiti-covered one-story building that was her landmark.

"Look, there's the street!"

Weehawken Street was deserted except for a few parked cars. With a single streetlight in the middle of the short block, it was dim, too.

"Keep moving," I said, clutching the pepper spray in my pocket. Madame had never asked for it back, and I was glad to have it now.

"There's a construction site at the other end of the block," Nancy said. "Tony moves a wooden barricade and backs his car into a loading area. It's dark and private because it's under—"

"Let me guess. More scaffolding."

Nancy nodded. "It's surrounded on three sides by plywood, too, but you can see the river if you sit in the front seat."

As we approached Tony's secret spot, Nancy pointed to a couple of long wooden planks leaning against the plywood fence.

"Look, he's moved the barricade. Tony must be here."

Nancy picked up her pace, and we reached Tony's car. The doors were locked, the interior so black that I had to pull out the key chain flashlight in my coat pocket to see inside.

In the focused beam of the LED, I saw Tony sprawled across the front seat. He didn't respond to the light, so I knocked on the windshield and called his name. When there was no reaction from Tony, Nancy and I banged on the windows.

"He's not waking up!" Nancy said, alarmed.

I feared he never would.

Eighty-five

In desperation, I hefted one of the five-foot boards Tony had moved.

"What are you going to do with that?" Nancy asked.

"Watch!" Using the plank as a battering ram, I bashed the passenger side window and the glass exploded into crystal shards.

With a gloved hand, I reached in and unlocked the door. When the interior lights sprang on, I saw Tony's arms were covering his face. I gently shook him, and his arms dropped away, exposing his cold, dead expression and lolling tongue.

Nancy yelped once, then stumbled away.

I didn't have that luxury. With care, I examined his body. There was no blood that I could see. No visible wounds. And no notebook. I glanced at the ignition. The keys were gone.

"What happened to him?" Nancy asked.

"It looks like he was poisoned, just like Mason, but I don't see any gummies around."

I reached a gloved hand under the car seat. Then I checked the sunscreens and the back seat. There was still no sign of the notebook. I popped the trunk and searched it with no luck.

Steeling myself, I took another look at the corpse. Tony wasn't wearing his blue hoodie, but something else was missing from his usual wardrobe.

"Nancy?"

"Yes," she replied in a choked voice.

"Tony's vest is gone. Remember? The one with all those pockets. He always wore it. Do you remember what he kept in those pockets?"

Nancy sniffed and wiped away tears with her sleeve. "His keys, his wallet, and his portable card reader. He put his two phones in the big pockets with the zippers. He kept a lot of candy and energy bars, too, and a little pad he wrote in when he stopped for gas."

I closed the car door.

"Did he get robbed?" Nancy asked.

"I don't think so. It makes no sense. Why would a thief take the keys and leave the car? And why would a thief lock the car after the robbery or poison their victim when a gun or knife would be quicker and more efficient?"

Suddenly, my phone buzzed, a cacophony on this silent street. With shaky hands, I checked the screen.

Tucker was reporting in.

"I just talked to Dina Nardini," he said breathlessly. "She doesn't have the notebook. She says Lachelle LaLande had it last. I called Esther to tell her, but she didn't answer. She must be with Lachelle at the First Class Club already."

He paused to catch his breath. "Have you found Tony?"

I told Tucker exactly what we found.

"Listen, Tuck, I'm going to have Nancy stay here at the crime scene and call 911. I'm texting Dante to come here quickly and join her. He knows Tony better than any of us and can help with answering questions for the first responders."

"What do you want me to do?" Tuck asked.

"I want you to meet me at the First Class Club as soon as you can get there. If Lachelle has the notebook, I'll take it straight to Detective Russell and this nightmare will be over."

EIGHTY-SIX

@@@@@@@@@@@@@@@@@@@@@@@@@@@@@@@@@@

THERE were several trendy speakeasies in New York, and they all had hidden or unmarked doors. The First Class Club was no exception.

The exclusive watering hole was located on West 18th Street between Google's New York headquarters and Bathtub Gin, a popular speakeasy that hid its entrance inside a busy café. The First Class Club was easier to find since its front door was on street level.

I knocked and a window slid open.

"Reservation?" asked a deep male voice.

"I'm here to see Lachelle LaLande. It's important."

"That's not the password," the disembodied voice replied.

"I don't know the password."

"You would if you'd made a reservation."

"Please," I said, "this is a matter of life or death. If you care about Lachelle LaLande, then you'll open this door!"

After a moment, the door swung inward. A giant man in an impeccable suit stuffed with enough muscles to win a WWE match peered down at me.

"You better not be yanking my chain, little lady, or I'll bounce you."

"I won't be here long enough to bounce," I promised and was about to surge forward when he blocked me with his huge arm.

"Phone," he demanded.

"What?"

"You can't board the aircraft without putting your phone on airplane mode. FAA rules. And I've got to see you do it. That's FCC rules."

"FCC?"

"First Class Club."

"Fine! See, I've done it!" My phone disabled, I hurried down a short hall that perfectly matched the interior of a jet bridge. It led up to a faux airplane door where a pretty flight attendant in a uniform of Pan Am blue greeted me.

"Welcome to First Class. Have you reserved a table?"

I asked for Lachelle, and the young woman pointed to the bar at the far end of the club. As I moved through the crowd, I realized the long, narrow space replicated the interior of a wide-body airliner with curved walls and "windows" on either side. The windows were actually HDTV screens displaying synchronized images of blue skies, passing clouds, and the earth far below.

In the corner, a DJ in a pilot's uniform was spinning house music. A tune ended, and he purred into the microphone, "Ladies and gentlemen, this is your captain speaking. Take a peek through the portside windows as we fly over the world's tallest waterfall, South America's Angel Falls . . . Now relax and enjoy some angelic beats . . ."

The window screens moved in sync, making this fake plane feel as if it were tipping one wing toward the falls. It all seemed so real that, if I had more time, I would have grabbed a window seat myself.

A diverse mix of tech workers, hip-hop artists, and trendy singletons swamped the bar. I spotted Lachelle serving up cocktails in a flight attendant's outfit. Squeezing between the meet-and-mate mob, I sidled up to the bar's counter and called out to her.

She saw me and waved. "What are you doing here, girl?"

"I'm looking for Esther. Did she make it here?"

"You just missed her. She came for Tony's notebook," Lachelle said as she continued mixing drinks. "Seems like everybody is hot for that notebook lately."

"What do you mean?"

"A few days ago Howie offered me money for it."

"Howie?" I said. "Howie knew about the notebook?"

That bothered me. Until tonight, Nancy was relatively clueless about the details of our notebook search. Howie, on the other hand, had overheard me, Esther, and Tuck discussing the subject on more than one evening, yet he'd never said a word to us.

"Why did Howie care about your notebook?"

"He wanted into our group. He tried pressuring Tony to let him join. When Tony said no, Howie followed me down the block and offered me a Benjamin to lend him the notebook overnight. I told him I didn't have it on me and even if I did, he should find another project." She shrugged. "Tony was *very* serious about keeping things secret, and I didn't want to risk being booted from the group. Dina told me Howie tried the same thing with her." She rolled her eyes. "Talk about obsessed—"

"Listen to me," I said. "I have some bad news. Is there somewhere we can talk in private?"

"I already know about Mason. I feel terrible that she overdosed like that—"

"It wasn't an overdose. I believe she was murdered, and I'm here to keep the same thing from happening to you."

Lachelle read my grave expression and flashed five fingers at the other bartender.

"I have five minutes, Clare. Come on. Follow me."

She led me around the bar to a door in the back marked *FLIGHT CREW*. We entered a typical employee break room with utility tables and chairs, a snack machine, and lockers on one wall. I spoke fast.

"Tell me what you know, Lachelle. You said Esther was here and asked about the notebook?"

Lachelle nodded as she took her phone out of a locker. "It was a real quick conversation. I told her that I didn't have it. Tony dropped by my place this afternoon and picked it up."

The air rushed out of my lungs, and I sank into a chair, thinking the notebook was gone for good.

"Clare? What's wrong?"

"Tony doesn't have the notebook, Lachelle. Not anymore."

I told her about finding Tony's body in the West Village, but Lachelle's reaction was unexpected.

"That's impossible," she said. "After Esther and I came back here to talk, I told her I'd call Tony for her. I was just about to do it when I got this text from him. Tony is in Midtown right now, talking with a Hollywood agent. And I was spitting mad because my manager wouldn't let me leave!"

I read the message.

LACHELLE! DINA!
I HAVE A HOLLYWOOD AGENT IN MY UBER WHO WANTS TO REP
OUR MURDER MYSTERY. HE IS READY FOR A GROUP PITCH
ABOUT THE MULTIMEDIA ANGLE. GET HERE ASAP. WE WILL ALL
HAVE A DRINK AND GET RICH! MEET ME AT 217 WEST 44TH
STREET

"Lachelle, your manager may have saved your life. Tony really is dead. Whoever ended his life took his vest and is using Tony's phone to lure you into a trap. This text came from his killer!"

Lachelle looked horrified. "We have to warn Esther! She went to catch a cab out front. She's on her way to that address!"

Immediately, I tried to call, only to realize my phone was still in airplane mode. But when I reactivated it, my desperate call went to Esther's voicemail.

"Why doesn't she pick up?" I cried. "We all agreed to keep in touch!"

"She probably forgot to turn off airplane mode just like you did," Lachelle said. "Customers do it all the time."

"If Esther can't get calls, I've got to get to her!"

I shot through the club and out the front door. As soon as I landed on the sidewalk, I saw Tucker at the curb, exiting a yellow cab.

"Get back inside!" I cried. "We need that taxi!"

Eighty-Seven

〰〰〰〰〰〰〰〰〰〰〰〰〰〰〰〰〰〰〰〰〰〰〰〰〰

I TOLD the cabdriver our destination. Then I faced Tuck.

"Do you know where we're going?" I asked.

He blinked. "Didn't you just give the address to the driver?"

"Yes, but I don't know what we'll find there!"

"It's the Theater District, near Shubert Alley—" He plugged the exact address into the map on his phone. "Wait a second. This makes no sense. There's *nothing* at that address."

"What do you mean?"

"I mean, it's not a bar or restaurant. It's a parking garage next to a loading dock in back of the Minskoff Theatre."

"The Minskoff? Isn't that where Howie works as an usher?"

"Yes, but don't expect him to be around to help. All the Broadway theaters are dark by now."

Suddenly, some pieces fell into place.

"I agree," I said. "Howie Johnson is done ushering tonight. He's too busy working his new side hustle . . ."

Tucker stared. "I know that tone. What are you getting at, Clare?"

"Howie's a guy who's never off duty. All those side jobs. He seems desperate for money, but how desperate?"

"You think Howie is involved in something shady? Where is this coming from?"

"Lachelle told me something strange at the bar. She said Howie was intent on getting into their 'secret project' group, but Tony said no. Then Howie offered one hundred dollars to Lachelle and then Dina for the chance to borrow the notebook overnight."

"He offered them money? That doesn't make sense."

"It would if Howie knew he could spend a small amount of cash to get a bargaining chip for a much bigger payoff."

"What are you saying?"

"You saw for yourself that Joan Gibson seemed especially interested in Howie's pitch the day that she visited the Writer's Block Lounge—"

"Yes, his con man story."

"And what about that story? Howie supposedly worked closely with a con man in Queens and never suspected the con. Is that likely? Or . . ."

"Or what?"

"Or did Howie play a more active part in ripping off those people? Was Howie really a victim of the con man or was he the man's partner? Maybe he was both, Tuck. After all, Howie's clearly broke. He could have been a willing partner who got conned himself and was left holding the bag with no money in it. Anyone fleeced like that would turn bitter fast, even desperate."

"That's all conjecture on your part, Clare. What about Ethan Humphrey and his theory about his aunt and cousin framing him?"

"I do think Ethan was framed. But would an aunt who took care of her nephew for decades suddenly set him up for a murder rap? Would a woman who stepped up to shelter a vulnerable old friend after he was released from a psychiatric facility—would a woman like that want to see her granddaughter become a cold-blooded killer who frames her own cousin?

"Or does it make more sense that an icy cool executive who is willing to twist a mentally unstable old man into betraying his benefactor, a woman who would use an unsolved murder to threaten and likely blackmail a former friend—doesn't it make more sense that she would hire a side-hustle guy like Howie to help her find and steal a notebook?"

"Okay," Tuck said. "If that's true, when did she hire him?"

"I'll bet it began the day Joan appeared in our Writer's Block Lounge. Joan could have seen Howie bussing tables and decided he'd make the perfect paid snoop: cheap to hire and, in her arrogant mind, easy to order around."

Tucker continued to shake his head in denial, but I kept going, putting things together . . .

"Think about it. The night Esther was mugged, Howie saw us poring over Mr. Scrib's brainstorming notebook. He overheard our conversation while he was mopping up. That's the night we hired him to dig up info on Ace Archer. Howie left a good thirty minutes before Esther did. Suddenly, she gets mugged and Mr. Scrib's notebook is stolen!"

"This is all circumstantial," Tuck insisted. "It could be coincidence."

"Mike Quinn always questions coincidence when a crime is involved."

"You're not suggesting Howie murdered Joan, are you?"

"Remember the timing. Esther's stolen notebook held the keys to Mr. Scrib's apartment. If Howie did mug Esther, he likely would have taken the notebook to Joan the next morning; that same morning Joan visited Mr. Scrib in the ICU and heard the words that Esther did: 'behind the duck.'"

"But why would Howie kill Joan, if she was paying him?"

"When he brought her the wrong notebook, she could have asked for his help searching Mr. Scrib's apartment for the right one. She could have told him about her true crime publishing scheme, too. Joan blabbed way too much to me. She bragged she had an 'ace in the hole' to manipulate Addy—Ace as in *Ace Archer*. She probably talked too much to Howie, too, because she didn't know who he really was. I think Howie decided that he could make a lot more money if he got rid of Joan and blackmailed Addy himself."

Tuck looked stricken. "If that's true, I might have helped Howie make that decision."

"What are you talking about?"

"The day you and Esther had brunch at the House of Babcock, I was bragging to Howie about how you were rubbing shoulder pads with this big author who created this cool television show. He probably looked up Addy's history at the Performing Arts Library and found out Ms. Babcock is a multimillionaire. He could find everything ever written about Addy, her show, summaries of every episode of *She Slays Me*—it's all right there at his fingertips."

"Do you believe me, now?"

"I don't know. I do believe Esther's in trouble, and we've got to get to her before—"

The cab jerked to an abrupt halt, throwing us against the Plexiglas partition that separated driver and passengers. I heard a crunch of metal as the car in front of our cab slammed into an MTA bus. Our quick-thinking driver steered around the stalled bus, but we promptly hit another snag.

As the horns blared and traffic on Eighth Avenue slowed, I thought about Howie's state of mind. He was getting rid of anyone who knew about the contents of that notebook. Anyone who could dilute the value of his blackmailing scheme. Anyone who knew he was interested enough in that notebook to pay plenty of money to see it. And kill Tony to get it. That text message on Lachelle's phone told me he was ready to kill again.

I glanced at the nearest street sign. We were almost there when traffic came to a standstill.

"Make a right! Make a right!" I urged the driver.

"I can't, ma'am, the light turned red."

Then it's up to me to make a right, I decided, *and make things right!*

I popped the door and took off running, leaving Tucker behind to pay the fare. Turning the corner, I headed down 44th Street toward that loading dock behind the Minskoff. At this time of night, the theaters were dark and the crowds were gone. Few pedestrians were on the sidewalks and none on my side of the street.

More ubiquitous New York City scaffolding lay ahead. Though I was half a block away, I spotted a zaftig silhouette standing in the dim light under the scaffolding. It looked like Esther, and she appeared to be waiting for someone.

"Tony?" I heard her call out. "Where are you? Lachelle sent me!"

Before I could shout a warning, a tall figure wearing a black ski mask and Tony Tanaka's vest grabbed her by the throat and—in a silent, terrifying blink of an eye—dragged her off the sidewalk and into the shadows.

Eighty-Eight

〜〜〜〜〜〜〜〜〜〜〜〜〜〜〜〜〜〜〜〜〜〜〜〜

Once again, I made like a rocket, shooting past the parking garage and flying into the loading dock where the killer had pulled Esther. The dark, deserted driveway went back at least twenty-five feet.

In the shifting shadows, I heard scuffling, rushed toward the sound, and saw the tall, ski-masked figure with one steel arm encircling Esther's throat. She was clawing at the arm with both hands, desperately trying to free herself, but the killer continued to choke the life out of her while dragging her deeper into the shadows.

If I didn't do something *right now*, she could die in a matter of minutes!

"LET HER GO!" I shouted, my voice echoing in the darkness of the loading dock's recessed empty space.

My voice surprised the attacker enough to reduce the pressure on Esther's throat. She gasped for breath and began to thrash wildly.

That's when I surged forward with Madame's pepper spray.

"CLOSE YOUR EYES, ESTHER!" I shouted.

Esther was in the line of fire, but I had no choice and reached for the trigger. Thank goodness she realized what I was about to do and slammed an elbow with all her might into her attacker's midriff.

He grunted and relaxed his grip enough for her to drop to the ground. As she did, she sucked in a bucket of air and let loose with a deafening scream she must have rehearsed down by the river!

Before the attacker could grab her again, I let him have it. The pepper spray hit him squarely in the face. I feared the toxin wouldn't penetrate his woolen mask, but I needn't have worried.

"YAAAAAHHHHHHHHHH!"

The booming scream matched Esther's in decibels. The attacker ripped the pepper spray–drenched mask off, revealing what I'd already suspected: the face of con artist Howard Johnson.

Howie stumbled backward, slamming into a dumpster. His gloves were equally polluted with the burning substance, and he ripped them off, too.

"You bitches!" he raged, fighting the fumes that choked him. "The perfect con and a pair of glorified waitresses screw it up!"

Esther was gasping and coughing on the ground as fumes of the pepper spray reached her. Her eyes were squeezed shut, and I dropped down to help her.

"GET UP AND RUN!" I urged her.

That's when I realized the pepper spray had rattled Howie but failed to put him down. He was coming toward me fast, and there was something shiny in his hand—a knife? No, a hypodermic! With one thumb, he popped the safety cap off to expose the deadly needle.

"You like espresso shots, bitch?" he rasped at me. "Well, I got a shot for you!"

A vision of Mason Dunn's corpse flashed through my mind, and I knew that was not the way I wanted to go. I hit the trigger on the pepper sprayer again, but after a tiny sputter, it died.

Howie laughed and lunged toward me.

Suddenly, a flying figure body-slammed the man, sending Howie and his poisonous needle soaring in opposite directions.

"DON'T YOU DARE HURT MY FRIENDS!" Tucker cried as he pinned Howie face down on the concrete.

In the struggle, Esther's messenger bag, which Howie had slung over his back, burst open. A number of items spilled out—red gummies, keys, and two thick spiral-bound notebooks.

The first was the one Esther found in our shop after Mr. Scrib's mental breakdown. The second displayed the words TRUTH REVEALED in large cursive letters on its cover.

I reached for the TRUTH, just as an army of uniformed cops appeared on the scene. Tuck had called 911 before he jumped into action, and the police seized everything they found, including the notebooks.

I was told that the property would be returned to its rightful owners eventually. Right now, it was evidence—and away it went, along with the answers I'd been searching for.

A̶f̶t̶e̶r̶ paramedics on the scene treated us for pepper spray exposure, we gave our statements to the police. Mine included some theories for the detectives to consider that would answer a few puzzling questions, like . . .

Why was Howie wearing Tony's vest? And why did he choose an area full of security cameras as a murder site?

Ultimately, both questions would have the same answer. With the ski mask hiding his face and hair, Howie had planned to frame Tony Tanaka for the murders of Lachelle and Dina. After he killed the two women, he was going to put the vest and gloves back on the corpse in the car, fabricate poor Tony's suicide note, and use his phone to put it on social media.

In the days following Howie's arrest, I learned more about that evidence found in Esther's stolen messenger bag. There were leftover toxic gummies from the batch he'd fed to Tony, after visiting him in his car for a "friendly chat."

Police also found the keys to Tony's car and Mr. Scrib's apartment. The latter were found to be stained with Joan Gibson's blood. More of Howie's DNA was recovered from under Joan Gibson's fingernails from the fight she put up during her strangulation.

In a confession that Howie made as part of his plea bargain, he claimed Joan's murder was not premeditated. They'd argued in Mr. Scrib's apartment when Joan (as I suspected) had blabbed too much to Howie about the details of her blackmailing scheme.

He demanded a bigger cut. She arrogantly insulted him, and he decided to find the notebook himself and extort a big payoff from Addy. After he strangled Joan, he set up Ethan, "the passed-out drug addict" in the apartment across the hall—and it would have worked, too, Howie whined, except for that "nosy coffee lady" at the Village Blend.

During the plea bargaining process, police even uncovered the real story of the Queens con man. Howie had been in on the theater troupe con from the start, just as I'd guessed in my taxicab confession to Tucker.

When Howie's partner stole the money in an attempt to cut Howie out, Mr. Side-Hustle caught up with him, and reacted the same way he

did when he learned about Joan Gibson's blackmail scheme. Howie strangled his treacherous former partner, just as he'd done with Joan. But instead of finding someone like Ethan to frame, he hid the man's corpse in
the subbasement of the theater they'd rented to con the community.

Of course, we didn't know any of this on the night of Howie's arrest.
As we commiserated at that loading dock behind the Minskoff Theatre,
Tucker was devastated by Howie's betrayal.

"I brought a killer wolf into our cozy fold, and it almost destroyed the
Village Blend."

I assured Tuck that it was not his fault, that Howie conned everyone.

"Look at me, Tuck. I was so convinced that he was an asset—with a
capital *A*—I was ready to offer him a full-time position."

"I still feel guilty," he said.

"You shouldn't. In the end, your body slam saved the day."

Then I gave him and Esther a hug and reminded them of the most important dictum of the service industry and a truth even more universal:

"*Good* help is hard to find."

Eighty-nine

~~~~~~

Shortly after the curtain came down on Howie Johnson, I received an unexpected request from Addison Ford Babcock. Written in her own elegant hand, Addy invited me to a private meeting to "clear away any and all misunderstandings."

I accepted. On a cold but bright afternoon, I traveled to Brooklyn Heights. This time there was no long wait amid the potted palms. No formally dressed Addy swanning down her staircase for a grand entrance. Instead, I was given a warm hug by Addy's beautiful granddaughter.

Blair took my coat and led me up to a sun-room adjoining Addy's private office. When Addy saw us arrive, she immediately rose from her desk to embrace me. She wore no makeup or jewelry, just a plain pair of slacks and a simple sweater.

Blair stepped out and Addy invited me to sit at the cozy table set for two with my chair facing the wall of windows. As I admired the view of the promenade, the river, and the awe-inspiring Manhattan skyline beyond, Addy poured us freshly brewed coffee from a thermal carafe.

"It's your excellent Rwandan," she said with a wink. "It seems I have a new weakness."

"Thank you."

"No, Clare. I must thank you. My Ethan is no longer facing a ruined life—or circumstances where he might have taken his own. I can't commend you enough for what you've done."

"I'm glad I was able to help."

Addy fell silent for a moment, then said, "I understand when Ethan escaped from custody, he went to you for help. Would you share what he told you that night?"

It was an uncomfortable question, but I answered it. "Ethan believed that you and Blair set him up. That you engineered the death of Joan Gibson and pinned it on him because you were fed up with his behavior."

Addy looked away. I thought she might be angry, but when she spoke again, I realized she was choking back tears. "I feel terrible that Ethan could think such a thing, though I understand why. You had to know it wasn't true."

"I do now."

"Please believe me, Clare. I would never do anything to hurt my son."

"Son?" I blinked. "I'm sorry, did you say—"

"Yes, Ethan is my son."

I sat back, my mind reeling. I'd imagined many secrets that might have been revealed in Mr. Scrib's still-unseen manuscript. This was not one of them.

"Ethan never knew, but he finally does. I told him last night. You see, my sister and her husband raised him from birth. In gratitude I bought them a beautiful home, made sure Ethan attended private school and a fine university. Even though I couldn't acknowledge him, I wanted my son to have a good life."

"I don't understand. Why couldn't you acknowledge Ethan?"

"So many reasons. I had planned to tell him eventually, then I married and kept the secret from my husband. I had a daughter—how could I tell her she had a half brother? Then came my granddaughter, and the situation became even more complicated—"

Addy paused. "You see, when I realized I was pregnant, I knew I couldn't raise Ethan, but I chose to give birth to him because his father would never get another chance to have a child."

"I don't understand why—"

"I'm telling you this, Clare, because of something that happened at the very last meeting of the Writer's Block Lounge decades ago. It's something you need to hear. Only the core group was there that night. Bobby Briscoe, Ace Archer, Jensen Van Dyne, Peter, and Juliet—"

"So, Juliet was real?" I pressed.

"Yes, Clare, she was," Addy admitted. "We were supposed to be having a celebration. Instead, terrible things happened."

"You mean the death of Ace Archer?"

"That, and more . . ."

Addy went on to tell me that for a year leading up to that night, she'd worked with Ace Archer to develop a special project—a television pilot. The protagonist was to be an American version of James Bond, the secret agent with a license to kill. Once they sold the show, Ace planned to pitch himself as the star.

One of their fellow Writer's Block Lounge members (Wall Streeter Peter) had a connection with a network executive in LA, which gave them an "in." Ace and Addy decided to submit their material under a single gender-neutral pseudonym.

Their pilot script and episode outlines relied on clever assassination techniques, and Ace handed Addy the key to making their show unique, a notebook that was left to him by his late father, an old stage magician who performed under the name "The Amazing Stephano."

"The book was filled with secrets of his trade," Addy said, "tricks, gadgets, sleight-of-hand techniques, all of which I adapted into unique methods of assassination for the twenty-three script outlines of the proposed full season of our TV show."

According to Addy, as the work progressed, Ace began to slack off, but she kept on writing.

"Ace was a compulsive womanizer," she said. "He had dalliances inside the group and out. Joan Gibson was one of his conquests, only she took their tryst as something more. When Ace straightened her out one evening, she fled the group in tears."

"You and Ace were lovers?" I guessed.

"Not even once," Addy said. "Ace and I were creative collaborators, that's all, though because of our late nights working together, the group thought we were more than that. I was never jealous of Ace's women. What I resented was the time he spent with them instead of on our work.

"Anyway, with Ace off gallivanting, I began leaning on another member of the group for moral support. I cared for him, though he was secondary to my ambition. My focus was on the writing. It never wavered. Finally, I sent the finished pilot script and episode outlines to the network executive under the pseudonym that Ace and I agreed to use.

"Two months later, that pseudonym received a telegram. The network was hot to produce our pilot. Executives wanted to meet with 'the creator' as soon as possible. Ace and I made plans to depart for Los Angeles that night.

"I waited at the Village Blend with the group for a final toast and goodbyes. Ace was late—he'd gone to a travel bureau to pick up our tickets for the red-eye out of JFK. I couldn't wait to leave New York behind. I even had my suitcase with me.

"It was Bobby Briscoe who warned me what was coming. Bobby was a bartender when he wasn't peddling drugs. He even created our group's signature drink: an Americano mixed with chocolate liqueur, Kahlúa, and a splash of vodka. He called it a Kismet—"

I tensed, remembering the frantic ranting of Jensen Van Dyne that day in our shop: *Stay away from the Kismet!*

"Go on," I pressed. "What did Bobby say?"

"He'd overheard Ace ordering only one ticket from the travel agent. Bobby said he was disgusted by what Ace was about to do and he handed me an envelope. He said if Ace tried to 'screw me over' after all the work I did, I should 'mess him up' by putting 'a couple of these' in his drink.

"Inside were dozens of hits of LSD. Windowpanes, they were called, little squares of gelatin, each one laced with a megadose. I never used drugs and I didn't have a clue what he'd handed me or what they did.

"Minutes later, Ace showed up and completely shattered my world. He informed me that he was going to Los Angeles alone. As he saw it, he'd created the show's premise and provided his father's magic manual as the key inspiration.

"Ace pointed out the word 'creator' in the telegram, saying the network people expected to meet one person, not two—and since he was going to be the star, that person should be him. He planned to start over in LA with a clean slate. No one needed to know about his bad notices in New York. He even ordered the airline ticket under our joint pseudonym. He said he would find a seasoned television writer to pen the full scripts based on my detailed outlines. He said he'd send me money to pay for my time as a 'hired writer,' but Hollywood always rewrites things anyway, so I shouldn't expect much."

"What a cruel betrayal," I said.

"At that moment, Clare, I was broken. For a year, I poured my heart into the writing, and it didn't matter to this man, who I thought was my friend. Ace treated me like his thrown-away lovers. I was so stupid, so caught up in chasing my dream that I failed to protect myself. I had no contract with him. My name wasn't on any of the work, and I had no money for a plane ticket to follow him to California—"

"What did you do?"

"I didn't do anything. I sat there in shock. It was Jensen Van Dyne who stepped in to protect his Juliet."

"Wait, slow down. Are you saying that *you* were Juliet?"

"Yes, my name was Juliet, but not for much longer. Ace and Jensen got into a shouting match, and the Village Blend's big Italian barista ordered them to take their fight to the alley. The whole group went down the back stairs to see the outcome. But I stayed behind; I didn't care what happened. I decided even death was better than being stuck forever in that soul-sucking law office. I was devastated by Ace's betrayal, and I hated myself for being so gullible. I decided an overdose would free me from the Circle of Hell I was suddenly cast into. I dumped the entire contents of the envelope—thirty times a normal twelve-hour dose—into a cup of Kismet, but I never got a chance to drink it.

"Jensen reappeared with blood on him. I asked him what happened . . ." As Addy spoke, tears filled her eyes. "Jensen said he killed Ace. He handed me the airline ticket. 'This is yours now,' he said. I'll never forget that moment. There was blood on that ticket."

Addy took a ragged breath. "That's when Jensen reached for the cup of Kismet sitting in front of me. I stopped him. I told him I'd poisoned it, intending to take my own life.

"'Good,' Jensen replied. 'Because I'm not going to prison.'

"He swallowed the poisoned Kismet in one gulp."

Addy shook her head. "I begged him to go to the hospital, but he refused. He told me to go to LA and forget him, forget Ace, forget everything. Then he fled.

"That's when Bobby Briscoe stepped in. He promised me that he would take care of Jensen and insisted I go. 'Get out of here while you can, before the cops come,' he said and pushed me out the door.

"So, I left," Addy said. "I flew out of New York City using the name on the ticket and on the script. That night Juliet died and *Addison Ford Babcock* was born. For hours on the plane, I cried. Then I went into a kind of numb state. By the time I arrived in Los Angeles, I was changed, hardened. I decided to be strong and move forward. I legally changed my name, and I changed something else, too. Without Ace pushing to star in our show, I told the network that I wanted to do something revolutionary for the time, turn *He Slays Me* into—"

"*She Slays Me*," I said.

"That's right, Clare. I turned *Steven* Slay into *Stephanie* Slay, and television history was made."

"Then you never saw what happened in that alley. Or found out who moved the body."

"Not back then. I only knew what happened to Jensen. Death by LSD poisoning is rare; mental illness is not. Jensen has been diagnosed with hallucinogen persisting perception disorder. HPPD is a clinical term for flashbacks. Jensen suffers recurring bouts of hallucinations and seizures."

"There's no cure?"

"None. That's why I've taken care of him all these years."

"When did you find out?"

"Two months after I arrived in LA, with my career taking off, I discovered that I was pregnant. I would have happily handed the baby over to his father to raise, but I learned that Jensen was institutionalized—as he would be for decades."

I blinked again. "Wait. Jensen Van Dyne is Ethan's father? Not Peter? Not Bobby?"

"It was Jensen. Ace had lost interest in our project. He chose to play Casanova. But Jensen cared. He brought me food when I worked all night; he checked my progress every day. Jensen was devoted to his Juliet. Though my feelings were never as strong as his, I always cared about him. I was determined to protect him from harming himself."

I considered her declaration. "Then all along you feared that Jensen's memoir was a confession—and he would be prosecuted for it. You were trying to protect *him*. Not yourself."

She nodded. "In the end, none of us, not even Joan Gibson, knew the real truth, and that's where my confession to you today takes another turn . . ."

Addy handed me the photocopy of a letter addressed to Jensen Van Dyne. The return address was Sicily.

"The DA's office said this letter was found in the back of Jensen's notebook. Because Jensen couldn't recall the details of what had happened in that alley or who moved Ace's body, he wrote to the two people who were there that night—and still alive."

I sat back, astonished. "How did he get their addresses?"

"Apparently, Joan's assistant Kenny tracked down the information. Then Jensen wrote to them, begging them to write back with whatever they could remember. Bobby Briscoe never replied. He lives in Portland now, where he operates a successful marijuana dispensary. Clearly, he didn't want to stir up trouble for himself. But when Jensen contacted the big Italian barista who served our group, Nero responded."

With trepidation, I quickly read Nero's letter . . .

In his bold handwriting, he confessed that he knew drug dealing was going on in the Village Blend alley. At that time, there were zero tolerance laws, and the discovery of a dead body could have resulted in the Village Blend's closure.

As someone who'd worked for the Allegro family for years, Nero refused to allow Madame or the coffeehouse to be hurt. So, he called "a friend" in Brooklyn who owed him a favor. This unnamed friend moved Ace Archer's body, and Nero lied to Madame to protect her.

Nero had one more shocking truth to reveal. He told Jensen that if he was writing a confession about murdering the actor, then he would be wrong. Nero witnessed their clumsy fight, which was mostly wrestling around. Then Ace grew frustrated, wanting to end it, and he swung as hard as he could. But Jensen was smaller and quicker, and he ducked the blow.

It was Ace's own merciless momentum that sent him careering into a metal dumpster, and it was that crack to the head that killed him.

"Jensen didn't murder Ace?" I whispered.

"He felt responsible for Ace's death, but he didn't kill him. Ace killed himself."

I sat with that for a long moment, considering all the awful dominoes that fell from one actor's tragic fall.

"What's going to happen now?"

"The DA's office reviewed the original autopsy, which didn't contradict Nero's account. And because the statute of limitations expired on the crime of moving a body, they declined to press any charges against him. The case of Ace Archer was officially closed."

Addy refilled our coffee cups, and she thanked me again for what I'd done.

"There'll be no more secrets now," she said before we parted. "And in that spirit, Clare, there's one more thing I want you to know. What happened to Ace, and my own part in the cover-up, was something I never wanted to face."

"But the circumstances were extenuating—"

"Don't try to excuse it. I hid the truth for all these years, even if I did it to protect Jensen. And the fact is, Ace and I were partners in the original creation of the show that launched my career. I was wrong to deny him credit. That's why I'm fixing it now."

"How?"

"As I told Joan's associate Kenny earlier this morning, now that the truth is out and Jensen has been exonerated, I'm giving my approval to the reboot of *She Slays Me* and to the series of Stephanie Slay novels that Joan wanted to publish, but with one condition: that Ace's real name be added to all credits as cocreator. Because he has no next of kin, I'm pledging half the profits in his name to the Actors' Equity Foundation and Broadway Cares. Appropriate, don't you think?"

Given the tragic end of Elmer "Ace" Archibald Stephano, it sounded right to me.

"So many secrets, so much pain," I told Mike as we relaxed after dinner that evening.

"Everyone has reasons for keeping secrets," Mike said. "Sometimes they're good reasons. But most secrets won't stand the test of time. Sooner or later the truth will out."

As we talked, I remembered something Tucker told me in the wake of all the chaos. He said he'd seen plenty of young people come to New York with ambition, but ambition is a dream with a rocket attached. If your aims aren't pointed in the right direction, eventually you'll crash and burn—"and I don't mean as a star," he said, "but as a human being."

I thought of Howie Johnson, now destined for a life behind bars. He'd crashed and burned right into Dante's Inferno. And on the way he took the lives of Joan Gibson, Tony Tanaka, and Mason Dunn.

"I wasn't able to save them," I said. "That's what pains me most."

"You did what you could," Mike replied. "That's what good detectives do. With the help of Tucker and your baristas, you stopped a cold-blooded killer. And in the process you cleared one innocent man of murder charges and another who believed he was guilty of murder."

"But I couldn't save everyone."

"None of us can. But Esther, Ethan, and Mr. Scrib are grateful for what you did. You saved them, Clare. And despite all the troubles ahead, I have faith you'll save your Village Blend, too."

"We'll see," I said.

And with that, my very long day ended.

It was finally time to get some rest.

EPILOGUE

In the days that followed, our shop passed its health inspection, and my baristas and I reopened our doors, but we couldn't stop worrying. Would the customers return? We prayed and waited. After two agonizingly slow days, word got out, and our tables were filled again.

"We're back!" I triumphantly told Matt near the end of that week.

It was after closing, and we'd settled in by the fireplace to wait for Madame to stop by. She was out on a date with the man her son had dubbed "Mr. Space Invader."

To pass the time, I told Matt what he'd missed during his trip to Baltimore, which he'd extended to a visit with our daughter in DC.

I didn't begrudge him the time away. In fact, I was happy Joy got to see him on this rare touchdown on US soil. Despite his globe-trotting and gallivanting, Matt Allegro had always tried to be a good father. That's why I thought he'd appreciate the news I'd recently heard.

"You're telling me that old Mr. Scrib just learned he has a six-foot-two, one-hundred-ninety-pound bouncing baby boy?"

"At thirty-eight, Ethan no longer needs a diaper," I said. "That's a plus."

"Yes, but from what you told me, he needs parenting. Is Scrib up to it?"

"He has a strong paternal instinct, Matt. You should have seen him talk about the lost duckling he found in a storm drain, and how he raised it himself . . ."

I recounted the day Mr. Scrib was released from the hospital. He'd fully recovered physically, though he had no memory of the incident that landed him there. Esther and I brought him home and Ethan greeted us, after he made sure the apartment was ready.

To his delight, Mr. Scrib was reunited with Wacker, and the duck seemed happy to see him, too.

Esther packed a basket with treats, a thermos of Village Blend coffee, and a stack of disposable cups. She placed the stack on the desk and asked what number Mr. Scrib wanted that day.

"Three," he replied. "To honor my three wonderful friends."

Wacker let out a string of quacks.

"Fine," Mr. Scrib relented. "Make it four."

The excitement of his long-anticipated homecoming tired Mr. Scrib, and Ethan put him to bed.

"I'll stay with him tonight," Ethan told us. "In case he needs anything . . ."

"That was a nice thing for Ethan to do," Matt said when I finished catching him up. "Though I don't know how much of a bargain Scrib's human son is going to be. But at least Ethan doesn't have feathers."

"He doesn't use drugs anymore, either. The arrest scared him straight, and he's completing his outpatient rehab with flying colors."

"Well, that's good news. And did you say they're going to Paris together?"

"For six months. Ethan wants to study art, and Mr. Scrib has never traveled, so they're going on their first father-and-son adventure. First of many, I suspect."

A cloud crossed Matt's face. "How did my mother take all the revelations about what happened in the alley?"

"Better than I thought. I made dinner for her and Captain Siebold and conveyed the whole story. She said she knew in her bones that something bad had happened all those years ago. Finally hearing the truth was a relief, though distressing in its details."

"I know what Nero did was wrong," Matt said. "But I understand his reasons. Nero and my father were like brothers. After my dad died, he would have done anything to protect us."

"Your mother said that, too, but she also said if she could turn back the clock and change things, she would have done it in a heartbeat. Anyway, after she dried her tears, the dinner went well. The captain was a comfort to her, and I could see she was glad 'Mr. Space Invader' had invaded her space."

"You didn't bring up the whole Cody Wood thing, did you? I hope you didn't try to undermine me, Clare."

"I did not," I answered honestly. "I'm leaving that to you. Lay it all out when she gets here. Then I'll make my argument. Let the Driftwood chips fall where they may."

"Wow," Matt said. "You're really being a good sport about this. After the shop was closed by the police, are you starting to see things my way?"

"Not at all. Like I told you, our traffic is back, and it's been solid so far. The Writer's Block Lounge is alive and well."

Matt expressed skepticism about how long that would last, but before I could argue the point, Madame buzzed my phone with a text. Her car was arriving.

Matt's dark gaze hardened. "Remember your promise, Clare. You're going to let me lay out the whole business deal before you jump in, right?"

"Go for it, Gordon Gekko."

"I will," he shot back. "'Greed is good.'"

When I opened the door, Matt embraced his mother. She was dressed casually tonight after enjoying "the cinema and a bistro" with her Golden Ticket Captain. She had just dropped him off to attend our private meeting.

Matt sat his mother down by the crackling hearth and laid out a line of papers and documents in front of her. As she sipped his superbly sourced and my lovingly roasted coffee, he presented Cody's proposal.

Madame sat very still, her expression frozen. I was surprised—and a little worried—that she didn't object to the plan immediately. Instead, she listened intently to her son.

Matt confidently pontificated, stressing all the good that comes with a huge chunk of change in the bank, and all the bad that could go wrong with retail sales.

When he was finished, Madame focused her bright violet gaze on me.

"Clare, you've been strangely quiet through my son's speech. You made no objection, no argument. Do you have one, my dear?"

"I do. And I'd like you both to hear it."

I displayed my phone and played the secret recording that Esther had made on the night I confronted the Driftwood CEO in the street. I played the whole thing, including Cody Wood's shameless job offer to me, and his contempt for Matt's global sourcing—

. . . You're the talent and the brains, Clare . . . Come work for Driftwood . . . stop slaving over a balance sheet like a dollar-store manager . . . Matt's whole approach . . . it's fine dining when people are perfectly content to consume fast food . . . Who needs small indigenous farmers when we can cut costs with mass production . . .

With each new phrase, Matt's slow simmer morphed into a red-faced boil. By the end of the recording, I thought his head would explode.

"That son of a—"

What followed was a colorful string of curses in languages mostly heard in the high-grown coffee regions from Bolivia to Indonesia.

As her son raged, Madame rose from the table, gathered up all of Cody's documents, and with one great swipe threw them into the hearth.

Then she turned to me. "To be honest, Clare, your little recording didn't change my mind. I was against the whole scheme the moment I heard Driftwood was involved."

"I admit you had me worried. You listened so patiently."

"Boys," she said, rolling her violet eyes. "Sometimes you simply have to humor them. They usually come around to the right decision. Look at my Matt. You've changed his mind."

Matt wasn't listening. He was still blowing off steam. We heard a crash as he kicked a wrought iron chair.

"I suppose I did. But if he doesn't come down to earth soon, I'm going upstairs to fetch my fiancé's handcuffs—though I'd prefer to slap them on Cody Wood."

Madame's expression turned serious. "From the tactics that man used, I can tell you, Mr. Wood won't be giving up easily."

"You think he'll cause more problems?"

"Keep the handcuffs handy, dear, and remember what I taught you."

She didn't have to remind me. At the Village Blend, it was part of our caffeinated credo: *Survive everything. And do it with style.*

Recipes & Tips
From the Village Blend

Visit Cleo Coyle's virtual Village Blend at
coffeehousemystery.com
for a free, illustrated guide to this section
and even more recipes, including:

Cinnamon-Sugar Doughnut Muffins
Baileys Irish Cream and Caramel Nut Fudge
Chocolate-Stuffed Peanut Butter Cookies
Easy Vanilla-Cinnamon Iced Coffee Caress

7 Tips from the Village Blend's Writer's Block Lounge

Welcome to our special space for caffeinated creation. Here are 7 tips from our staff to help you reach your writing and productivity goals.

1) Follow your flow. For optimal productivity, a friend of the Village Blend (and former NASA mission specialist) suggests following your "ultradian rhythm" cycles. To prevent burnout, work in 90-minute sessions. Break for 30 minutes to reboot brain and body before beginning a new 90-minute session. Phone use is strongly discouraged in the lounge. Stay focused. No doomscrolling!

2) Refresh to de-stress. Physical activity boosts energy and sharpens cognitive abilities. During your work break, join our resident slam poet Esther for River Scream. Too shy for scream therapy? Come anyway for fresh air and a walk to the Hudson River Greenway. Twist and stretch, take 10 deep breaths, and return reinvigorated. Then enjoy a cup of our freshly roasted writer's fuel. Caffeinate and create!

3) Take smaller bites, and not just from the goodies in our pastry case. Big goals can feel intimidating. Consider smaller targets (word counts, page counts) with shorter, timed intervals. Request our free 15- or 30-minute personal timers or use our barista proctors. They love to poke and provoke!

4) Thought playgrounds. Feeling stuck in a rut? Our resident thespian Tucker reminds us that actors and directors use improvisation to explore characters and enhance dialogue. In that spirit,

try mixing things up to spark your imagination. Throw an unexpected challenge at your cast, make them face their biggest fears, or narrate from a new perspective. Additional writing prompts provided upon request.

5) Brainstorming journals. Our oldest member, "Mr. Scrib"—who just secured a publishing contract for a collection of his witty and poignant poems (congrats, Jensen!)—suggests carrying a notebook with you to scribble ideas, observations, and random thoughts: "Capture those elusive feathers of inspiration before they take wing."

6) No gain with shame. A first draft does not have to be perfect. Try freewriting. Spend a session without checking spelling or grammar. Edit later. Instead, tap into your inner voice and let it flow!

7) "Personal best" is best. Don't sabotage yourself by obsessing over what others may or may not be doing or achieving. Focus on making your creation the best it can be. Find joy in your journey. That's your golden ticket to success, and we're not talking money and fame . . .

True success is found by those who continue to love the work, despite setbacks, and never stop learning and growing as writers and as human beings.

Good luck and good writing!

CLEO COYLE RECIPES

Juliet's Kisses

Shakespeare's *Romeo and Juliet* was inspired by the fire-and-ice history of two feuding families in Verona, Italy. The first mention of the Montecchi and the Cappelletti is found in the Purgatory section of Dante Alighieri's epic poem *The Divine Comedy*. The English-speaking world would come to know them as the Montagues and Capulets when, hundreds of years after the fact, Shakespeare transformed this feud into a tragic romance between Romeo and Juliet, the fictional offspring of these two families.

It's no wonder this timeless story also inspired a sweet kiss of the culinary kind. In Verona, the *Baci di Giulietta* (Juliet's Kiss) can be found in almost every bakeshop as a tribute to these legendary lovers. The traditional Juliet's Kiss consists of two chocolate cookies sandwiched together with a chocolate filling. The bakers in Italy add almonds and hazelnuts to their cookies. And, yes, there is a Romeo counterpart, which is usually vanilla. Some bakers also mix the two, sandwiching a Juliet with a Romeo for a vanilla-chocolate kiss.

In that same culinary spirit, Clare Cosi created her own tribute to the story of these star-crossed lovers by developing two versions of the chocolate Juliet's Kiss for her Village Blend pastry case. Her recipes follow. Enjoy!

Juliet's Mocha Blossom Kisses

The Juliet cookies in this recipe are kissed not once but twice. The first kiss comes from espresso powder, which creates a light mocha flavor. The bigger kiss comes at the end in the form of an unwrapped Hershey's Kiss pressed into the center of the freshly baked cookie. Hershey's Kisses come in different flavors (milk, dark, almond, and more). Choose the one that appeals to you or mix them up to create a variety of kisses on your dessert or party tray. To see a photo of these cookies, visit Cleo Coyle's online coffeehouse at coffeehousemystery.com, where you can download an illustrated guide to this recipe section.

Makes about 34 cookies

1½ cups all-purpose flour (spoon into cup and level off)

½ cup unsweetened cocoa powder

¼ teaspoon espresso powder

½ teaspoon salt

½ teaspoon baking powder

½ teaspoon baking soda

1 cup (2 sticks) unsalted butter, softened

½ cup granulated white sugar plus ¼ cup, for rolling

½ cup light brown sugar, lightly packed

1 teaspoon vanilla extract

1 large egg, whisked with a fork

34 unwrapped chocolate Kisses (milk, dark, almond, etc.)

Step 1—Create batter: First, preheat your oven to 350°F and line a baking sheet with parchment paper. (Note: The parchment paper not only prevents sticking but also helps protect cookie bottoms from burning.) In a mixing bowl, whisk together the flour, cocoa powder, espresso powder, salt, baking powder, and baking soda. Set the dry ingredients aside. In a second bowl, combine the softened butter, ½ cup granulated white and ½ cup light brown sugar, and vanilla. Using an electric mixer, beat until creamy. Add the fork-whisked egg and continue beating until well mixed. Add dry ingredients gradually and continue blending on low until a smooth batter forms, but do not overmix.

Step 2—Chill it, baby: Cover the bowl with plastic wrap and chill the dough for about 15 minutes in the refrigerator. Chilling will make the dough easier to handle, but don't chill longer than 15 minutes or the dough will become too hard.

Step 3—Roll and sugarcoat: Place the remaining ¼ cup of granulated sugar in a shallow bowl. Using clean fingers, roll the dough into balls of about 1 inch in diameter. Drop the dough balls in the bowl of sugar and lightly coat. Place balls on your lined baking sheet, leaving room for spreading.

Step 4—Bake and kiss: Bake for about 12 minutes on the middle rack in your well-preheated 350°F oven. Within 1 minute of the cookies coming out of the oven, give them a kiss! Gently press an unwrapped chocolate Kiss into the center of each cookie. Carefully transfer the cookies onto a cooling rack. Hot cookies are fragile when handled. Allow them to cool and set; otherwise, you may find out (you guessed it) how the cookie crumbles.

Tip for cookie baking: Always allow your baking sheets to cool before putting more dough on them. A hot baking sheet will cause any cookie to spread immediately and alter its proper baking time. You can speed up the cooling process by running cool water over the back of your baking sheets. (Dry before continuing to use.)

Juliet's Chocolate Kisses
(Chocolate-Filled Sandwich Cookies)

To make these cookies: Follow the directions for the previous recipe, Juliet's Mocha Blossom Kisses, but leave out the espresso powder. Once the chocolate cookies are baked, do not press a chocolate Kiss into them. Instead, transfer the baked cookies to a rack. When they are completely cooled, sandwich two cookies together using the Chocolate Filling (in the recipe that follows). Put the cookies down carefully on wax paper to allow the filling to cool and set. Now brew up some fresh coffee or espresso and share your kisses with the ones you love.

Chocolate Filling

To make the filling: Place 9 ounces of semisweet chocolate chips or about 1½ cups semisweet chips into a microwave-safe bowl with about 6 tablespoons of unsalted butter. Burned chocolate is awful and cannot be fixed, so don't rush this process. Heat the chocolate and butter in your microwave for 1 minute only. Whisk with a fork. Return to the microwave for 10 to 15 seconds at a time, whisking between each session until the chocolate is completely melted. Whisk well until smooth and shiny. For a tasty variation, stir about ¾ cup finely chopped almonds or hazelnuts or walnuts into the filling before using.

Madame's Vanilla & Praline Sablés

Sablé translates to "sandy" in French, the name coming from the crumbly texture of this delicious cookie. Like a shortbread but more delicate, these tender, buttery, sugar-crusted rounds are perfect for coffee and tea breaks. The French have many variations (lemon, orange, almond). They dip them in chocolate and sandwich them together with jams. But Clare's favorite flavor is praline—and for good reason. Praline sablés were the cookies that Madame baked for her during her pregnancy. No surprise: They're a favorite of Clare's daughter, Joy, as well. To see a photo of these cookies, visit Cleo Coyle's online coffeehouse at coffeehousemystery.com, where you can download an illustrated guide to this recipe section.

Makes about 3 dozen cookies

Basic Vanilla Sablés

1 cup (2 sticks) butter, softened
½ cup confectioners' sugar
½ cup granulated sugar

1 large egg, whisked with a fork
2 teaspoons vanilla extract
2 cups all-purpose flour
½ teaspoon finely ground sea salt (or table salt)
1 egg white
⅓ cup coarse finishing sugar such as sparkling or turbinado

Step 1—Make the dough: Using an electric mixer, cream the butter and sugars. Add the fork-whisked egg and vanilla and beat until smooth. Add the flour and salt. Switching to a spoon or spatula, mix everything until the dough comes together in a sticky ball. Take care not to overwork the dough or your cookies will be tough instead of tender.

Step 2—Form logs: To make the sticky dough easier to handle, cover the bowl with plastic wrap and chill for 15 minutes (but no longer). Divide the dough in half and form two 8- to 9-inch logs on separate sheets of wax paper, using the paper to help shape and smooth the logs. Wrap the logs tightly and chill in refrigerator until very firm (at least 3 hours or overnight). Logs can be refrigerated for up to 1 week or wrapped a second time in foil and frozen up to 1 month.

Step 3—Prep for baking: Preheat oven to 350°F (give it at least 30 minutes of preheating time). Line a baking sheet with parchment paper and make an egg white wash by whisking 1 egg white in a bowl with a little water. Unwrap your dough logs and use a pastry brush to apply the wash all around the logs' exteriors. Next, roll the logs in the coarse finishing sugar. Using a sharp knife, cut the logs into slices of ¼ to ½ inch in thickness (your choice), and place the cookie slices on the lined baking sheet.

Step 4—Bake cookies for 15 to 20 minutes, rotating pan once for even baking. Cookies are finished when their edges are light golden brown but the centers are still pale. Remove from oven and slide the parchment paper to a cooling rack.

Praline Sablés

Follow the previous recipe for Vanilla Sablés, but in Step 1, fold ½ cup Crushed Praline (recipe follows) into the dough before shaping and chilling. You'll also want to replace the coarse finishing sugar (in Step 3) with ½ cup or more of crushed praline, pressing lightly to make sure it sticks to the egg-washed dough logs.

Crushed Praline & Foolproof Almond Brittle

Praline is a popular ingredient of French pastry chefs made with caramelized sugar and nuts. New Orleans pralines are another variety, softer and creamier, but that's not what we're making here. This hard candy praline can be served as nut brittle; ground up and used for flavoring; or chopped more roughly for use as a garnish over ice cream, tarts, custards, and cakes. Traditionally, the first step of a French praline recipe is to make the caramel. This recipe is not purely traditional because of the bit of lemon juice added to the water, but that's what makes this recipe nearly foolproof. It's a snap to make, and the first stage is a delicious nut brittle.

Makes 2 cups

⅓ cup water

¼ teaspoon lemon juice (to prevent caramel from crystallizing)

1¼ cups granulated sugar

1⅓ cups slivered almonds, toasted

(See tip on how to toast nuts on next page)

Step 1—Make the nut brittle: First, cover a baking sheet with parchment paper. To make the caramel, combine water, lemon juice, and sugar in a 2-quart saucepan. Place over high heat and stir constantly with a wooden spoon or silicone spatula. After 10 or so minutes of continual boiling and stirring, the mixture will turn light golden. Just as the color deepens to a darker golden, remove pan from heat (if it darkens too much, it will burn). Add almonds and stir well.

Step 2—Cool and finish: Carefully pour this very hot mixture onto your prepared baking sheet. Flatten into an even layer. As it cools, it will harden. You have just made a delicious almond brittle! If making crushed praline, break the brittle into pieces. Place the pieces into a resealable plastic bag and crush them into a coarse powder with a rolling pin or kitchen mallet. (Who needs anger management?) For easy cleanup, fill your pan with water, add utensils, and boil to melt any crusted caramel.

Tip on how to toast nuts: Preheat your oven to 350°F. Spread the nuts in a single layer on a baking sheet and bake for 8 to 10 minutes. Stir once or twice to prevent scorching. You'll know when they're done because your kitchen air will become wonderfully redolent with the aroma of warm nuts.

Clare Cosi's Crunchy Almond Biscotti (Easy Food Processor Method)

Like the gelato makers of Sicily, Clare developed this recipe with the goal of making her culinary creation taste exactly like the star ingredient. Bite into these crunchy, twice-baked cookies and the fragrance and flavor of almond will envelop you. Dip them in chocolate and your mouth will believe it's filled with chocolate-covered almonds. Although the Village Blend uses a professional baker to create these biscotti for their retail pastry case, Clare is happy to share this easy food processor method, which she uses in her home kitchen. Dip them in chocolate for an even richer treat (directions follow). To see a photo of these cookies, visit Cleo Coyle's online coffeehouse at coffeehousemystery.com, where you can download an illustrated guide to this recipe section.

Makes about 2 dozen finger-sized biscotti

½ cup whole, shelled almonds (skins on)

1 cup all-purpose flour

⅓ cup granulated sugar

¼ teaspoon baking powder

¼ teaspoon baking soda

Generous pinch of finely ground sea salt (or table salt)

1 large egg + 1 egg yolk

1 teaspoon pure vanilla extract

1 tablespoon vegetable oil

½ cup sliced or slivered almonds

1 egg white

Step 1—Make the dough: First, preheat oven to 350°F. Line a baking sheet with parchment paper and set aside. Place the whole almonds into your food processor and pulse until texture resembles sand. Add flour, sugar, baking powder, baking soda, and salt into the food processor's bowl and pulse gently until well mixed. Add egg, egg yolk, vanilla, and oil. Gently pulse the food processor until a dough forms. Transfer the dough onto a flat surface, knead, and shape into a disc. Add ½ cup sliced or slivered almonds and knead with your hands until the nuts are mixed in.

Step 2—Shape into logs and bake: Divide the dough in half and roll to create 2 long cylinders. Place these cylinders onto your lined baking sheet, leaving plenty of room in between. Now flatten them, shaping into long rectangles. Whisk your egg white with a little water to make a wash. Use a pastry brush to apply the wash to the top and sides of the dough rectangles—this will help to prevent crumbling and create a nicer crust. Bake for 20 minutes and remove pan from oven. While warm, the logs are fragile; handle carefully. The best way to transfer them is to slide the parchment paper off the pan and onto a cutting board or another flat surface. Allow the logs to cool for 15 minutes. Reduce oven temperature to 300°F.

Step 3—Add the "bis" to biscotti by baking again: Using your sharpest knife, slice the logs on a sharp diagonal into finger-thick cookies, about ½ inch. No sawing. Slice down hard in one motion to cleanly cut through any almonds. Reusing your parchment paper, place the cookies on their sides on the baking sheet and bake for an additional 10 minutes. Flip each cookie and bake for another 10 to 12 minutes. Remove from oven. The cookies will become crispier and crunchier as they cool. Store in a plastic container. No refrigeration is needed, but you must allow biscotti to cool completely before storing or the cookies will end up soggy from condensation.

Chocolate-Dipped Almond Biscotti

Bake up Clare's Crunchy Almond Biscotti in previous recipe. Dip half the almond biscotti cookie (lengthwise) into melted chocolate, so it can be tasted in every bite. To make the melted chocolate, place 6 ounces of chopped semisweet chocolate (or 1 cup chips) into a microwave-safe bowl. Add 4 tablespoons of heavy cream and stir well with a rubber spatula. Heat for 20 seconds and stir again, repeating until chocolate is melted. Chocolate burns easily, so heat slowly and take care.

Clare's "Cozy" Beef Stew for Two

"Your beef stew smells heavenly," Clare told Matt in the loft kitchen of his Brooklyn warehouse. "It's your recipe," he told her, which was true, but it began with his. Early in their marriage, Matt made a version of this outstanding beef stew for Clare, using coffee as a meat marinade and flavoring agent. During his sourcing trips, he enjoyed cooking it up for large groups of friends. When Clare made Matt's recipe, she found the large portions time-consuming to cook, so she shrunk the yield for a cozier dinner and made a few additional tweaks, including replacing the coffee with red wine for a lovely beef bourguignon flare. Port, Marsala, or your favorite red wine can be used in this recipe—experiment with your own taste. For extra flavor, be sure to marinate the beef pieces in your red wine of choice for 2 hours before starting the dish. You can also try Matt's original version and replace the wine with brewed coffee. Either

way, the result is a "cozy" beef stew for two, brimming with rich and hearty flavors. To see a photo of the finished stew, visit Cleo Coyle's on-line coffeehouse at coffeehousemystery.com, where you can download an illustrated guide to this recipe section.

Serves 2 (with leftovers)

For the Beef Prep

1 pound beef chuck steak, cut into 1½-inch pieces
Enough red wine (or port or Marsala or brewed coffee) to marinate

For the Seasoned Flour Mix

2 tablespoons all-purpose flour
1 teaspoon sea salt
1 teaspoon dried crushed rosemary
1 teaspoon dried thyme
½ teaspoon sweet paprika
½ teaspoon freshly ground black pepper

For the Stew

2 tablespoons olive oil, add more if needed
3 tablespoons butter
1 cup chopped white or yellow onion
1 stalk celery, chopped
1 teaspoon minced garlic
1 tablespoon balsamic vinegar
2½ cups beef broth, stock, or beef bone broth
1 cup red wine, port, or Marsala (Matt's version uses brewed coffee)
1 tablespoon Worcestershire sauce
1 bay leaf

½ pound baby Yukon Gold or baby red potatoes (or a combo of both)
2 large carrots
1 medium white or yellow onion (for the finishing step)

Step 1—Prep the beef: Cut the beef into 1½-inch pieces. Marinate the pieces in enough red wine (or port or Marsala or brewed coffee) to cover for about 2 hours before starting the stew. Do not marinate longer than 2 hours.

Step 2—Coat with seasoned flour: In a bowl, whisk together the flour and seasonings (salt, rosemary, thyme, paprika, and pepper). Pat the beef pieces dry and roll them in the seasoned flour mix, coating as evenly as possible.

Step 3—Brown the beef pieces: In a Dutch oven or deep pot (3 to 4 quarts in size), warm the olive oil over medium-high heat. To avoid overcrowding the pot, brown the beef pieces in batches. Add more olive oil, if needed. Set aside the browned beef pieces in a bowl to catch the juices.

Step 4—Start the stew: Add butter to the pot and sauté the chopped onion, chopped celery, and minced garlic until soft. Deglaze the pot with balsamic vinegar. Add browned beef pieces (and all the accumulated juices) back to the pot. Add the beef stock (or bone broth), 1 cup of your red wine (or port, Marsala, or brewed coffee), Worcestershire sauce, and the bay leaf. Bring to a boil. Reduce heat to low, cover, and let stew simmer for 90 minutes or until beef is fork tender.

Step 5—Add veg and finish: Cut the baby potatoes in half. Peel and chop the carrots into thick rounds. Julienne the remaining onion. Add your vegetables to the stew. Bring the liquid to a boil for 2 minutes. Reduce the heat to low, cover, and simmer for 30 minutes or until the carrots and potatoes are fork tender. Uncover and continue to cook over low heat until the liquid thickens slightly. (See "tip on thickening" on the next page to speed up the thickening process or create an even thicker stew.) Once finished, discard the bay leaf and serve piping hot with crusty bread to sop up the delectable beef broth.

Tip on thickening: As an option for speeding up the thickening stage in any stew or gravy, place a little cornstarch (1 teaspoon) into a small bowl and mix with a small amount of cold water to form a smooth paste. Gradually stir this paste into your hot liquid, continuing to stir as you bring the liquid to a boil for 1 full minute. If more thickness is desired, repeat the process. To avoid cornstarch flavor in your dish, add only the smallest amount needed.

Clare's Pan-Roasted Baby Potatoes

If you're a meat-and-potatoes kind of person, welcome to the club. This recipe is a great way to combine those flavors using a simple, once universal but currently underutilized ingredient. Tallow (rendered cow's fat) is a natural source of vitamins. It's great for the skin, and it has anti-inflammatory properties. Grass-fed tallow is the best for health and flavor, which is what Clare recommends for this recipe. It has a high smoke point and, more importantly, it imparts wonderfully savory flavor. Clare always uses tallow when cooking hamburgers, steaks, and these mouthwatering potatoes. To see a photo of these golden beauties, visit Cleo Coyle's online coffeehouse at coffeehousemystery.com, where you can download an illustrated guide to this recipe section.

Serves 4

1½ to 2 pounds baby Yukon Gold potatoes
4 cups water
1 tablespoon finely ground sea salt
2 to 3 tablespoons grass-fed beef tallow
½ medium onion, chopped
Ground pepper and additional salt to taste

Step 1—Parboil the potatoes: Rinse and drain baby potatoes but do not peel. Cut each potato in half and place in a single layer in a large, ovenproof skillet or sauté pan. Add enough water to cover and a tablespoon of salt. Over medium-high heat, bring the water to a boil and reduce the heat. Simmer for 15 to 18 minutes or until the potatoes are fork tender. DO NOT let the potatoes overboil or they will be mushy, and under-boiling will result in an apple-like crunch. To ensure the perfect texture, after 10 minutes of simmering, test a potato every minute or so until you're getting the perfect al dente result.

Step 2—Sauté and sear: Drain the pan of all excess liquid, transfer the parboiled potatoes to a bowl, and wipe the pan dry. Preheat the oven to 375°F. Using the same ovenproof pan, melt the tallow over medium-high heat. When the fat is hot, add the potatoes back to the pan, and stir to coat them as evenly as possible with the melted beef fat. Sauté for 3 to 5 minutes. For flavor, sprinkle in the chopped onions. Cook for a few more minutes, gently mixing the onions in with the potatoes and coating them in the tallow. Then place the pan on the middle rack of your hot oven for 5 to 8 minutes, or until the cut sides of the potatoes turn golden and the edges have browned.

Step 3—Finish and serve: Add pepper and more salt to taste and serve hot. They make the perfect side with steak, roast beef, meat loaf, burgers, chicken, turkey, or pork chops. Leftovers are wonderful the next morning, reheated for breakfast with eggs, bacon, and/or sausage.

Clare's Sautéed Pork Chops with Caramelized Onions

Pork is still a bargain when compared to other meats, and Clare enjoys the simple process of making this one-pan dish. The caramelized onions are buttery sweet, and cooking the pork in their rendered juice keeps the chops moist while adding another layer of flavor. They are so tasty that Clare cooked them up to welcome Mike back from the Sunshine State. To see a photo of this dish, visit Cleo Coyle's online coffeehouse at coffeehousemystery.com, where you can download an illustrated guide to this recipe section.

Serves 4

4 center-cut, bone-in pork chops, thick and well marbled (See tip on page 341)
1 teaspoon finely ground sea salt
½ teaspoon ground white or black pepper
1 tablespoon poultry seasoning (or ground sage)
3 large onions (white, yellow, Spanish, Vidalia, or a mix)
4 tablespoons salted butter, divided

Step 1—Prep the meat: Remove the cold pork chops from your refrigerator, rinse them off, dry them well with paper towels, and sprinkle each side with sea salt, white or black pepper, and poultry seasoning (or ground sage). While you work on the next step, rest the chops on plates outside of your fridge. By the time you finish with Step 2, the chops should be at room temperature and ready to cook. (Never place cold meat in a hot pan.)

Step 2—Caramelize the onions: Julienne your 3 onions. Over medium-low heat, melt 3 tablespoons of the butter in a large ovenproof skillet or sauté pan. When the butter is melted, add the sliced onions, and cook over medium-low heat, stirring occasionally, until golden brown (35 to 45 minutes). If needed during the cooking, add a bit more butter to the pan to prevent scorching.

Step 3—Cook the chops: Preheat your oven to 365°F. Keeping your pan over the heat, use a slotted spoon to transfer the onions from the pan into a bowl, leaving as much of the sweet onion juice behind in the pan as possible. Bring up the heat to medium-high, add another 1 tablespoon of butter to the pan. When melted, add the chops and cook for 3 to 4 minutes on each side, then pop them into the preheated oven for 18 to 20 minutes (flipping once during this stage). Chops are finished with this stage of cooking when the fat appears golden brown.

Step 4—Finish on the stovetop: Taking care not to burn yourself on the hot handle, transfer your pan from the oven back to the stovetop. Add the cooked onions back to the pan. Cook the chops and onions together over low heat for about 3 more minutes (or until the onions are reheated well and the chops reach an internal temperature of 150°F). Remove the pan from heat and allow the chops to rest with the onions for at least 10 minutes before cutting. This final resting period is important to preserve the wonderful juiciness of your delicious chops. Serve with crusty bread and eat with joy!

Tip on picking pork chops: Bone-in, center-cut pork chops are what you want for this recipe. Look for chops at least 1 inch in thickness. The thicker the cut, the juicier the results. Loin chops are too lean, and boneless chops tend to be dry. For the best-tasting, juiciest chops, also look for well-marbled meat with a layer of visible fat around the edges. As most chefs will tell you, fat means flavor.

Asparagus Roasted with Lemon & Garlic

Addison Ford Babcock's gourmet luncheon posed some challenges for poor Esther, but this delightful dish wasn't one of them. The roasting method is quick and easy, creating a sophisticated side bursting with bright flavor. While thinner asparagus spears are always more tender, thick-stemmed asparagus works fine in this recipe as long as their woody parts are removed—the directions (below) tell you how.

Serves 4

1 to 1½ pounds fresh asparagus
3 tablespoons extra-virgin olive oil or avocado oil
1 teaspoon sea salt
3 cloves garlic, minced
1 lemon

Step 1—Prep oven and pan: Preheat oven to 425°F. Line a sheet pan with parchment paper or aluminum foil.

Step 2—Prep asparagus: Rinse asparagus, drain, and dry thoroughly with paper towels. If asparagus is thick, slice off the woody ends and (if necessary) use a vegetable peeler to peel the bottom half of the thicker stalks to remove their tough exteriors.

Step 3—Coat and flavor: Mix the oil and sea salt in a large bowl. Add the spears and, using one clean hand, gently toss to coat thoroughly with the oil. On your lined baking sheet, lay out the spears in a single layer. Scatter the minced garlic evenly over the oiled stalks. Finally, wash and dry the whole lemon. Slice into thin rounds, remove any seeds, and lay the lemon slices over the oiled stalks. For lighter lemon flavor, use fewer slices.

Step 4—Roast until tender: Timing is tricky on this dish. Thinner asparagus stalks will be finished cooking in 4 to 9 minutes. Thicker stalks may take up to 14 minutes. Be vigilant and check every few minutes to achieve the desired tenderness.

Optional finishing flavor: Clare Cosi sometimes adds an Italian touch to her asparagus spears by sprinkling grated Romano or Parmesan cheese over the stalks as soon as they're removed from the oven. With cheese or without, these roasted garlic and lemon spears are delicious.

Individual Cherry (or Berry) Clafoutis

A simple but classic French dessert that originated from the Limousin region of France, Cherry Clafoutis is a delight of sweet crepe batter poured over fruit and baked into a crustless, slightly custardy tart. It was a favorite of the late Christian Bodiguel, who served for years as the executive chef of the Venice Simplon-Orient-Express (VSOE), *a rolling museum featuring gorgeously restored carriages from the original line, dating back to the 1920s and '30s. Addison Ford Babcock remembered how much she enjoyed these adorable individual versions aboard the posh train, and she proudly presented them to Clare and Esther at their gourmet brunch. This recipe is slightly adapted from Chef Bodiguel's original, which he shared with the public. If you don't have fresh cherries available, you can substitute frozen. Though not traditional, blueberries will (in an American pinch) work wonderfully, as well. May you eat (and travel) with joy! To see a photo of this dessert, visit Cleo Coyle's online coffeehouse at coffeehousemystery.com, where you can download an illustrated guide to this recipe section.*

Makes 4 servings

Softened butter for greasing ramekins

1½ cups roughly chopped sweet cherries (or whole blueberries)

1 large egg + 2 large egg yolks

3 tablespoons + 1 teaspoon whole milk

4 teaspoons heavy cream

½ teaspoon pure vanilla extract

2 teaspoons kirsch (or cherry juice or Pom juice)

1 tablespoon + 1½ teaspoons melted butter (use entire amount for batter)

⅓ cup confectioners' sugar

3 tablespoons all-purpose flour

Whipped cream or ice cream (for topping)

Step 1—Prepare: First, preheat your oven to 300°F. Generously butter four 4-ounce ramekins. Rinse and thoroughly dry your fruit. If using cherries, de-stem, pit, and roughly chop them. Blueberries should be left whole. Measure out the proper amount of fruit and divide it among the ramekins.

Step 2—Make the batter: Melt the butter, measure out exactly 1 tablespoon + 1½ teaspoons, and set it aside to cool before adding it to the batter. In a mixing bowl, whisk your egg and egg yolks well. Whisk in the milk, heavy cream, vanilla, and kirsch (or juice). Measure out the melted (and cooled) butter and add it to the bowl along with the sugar and whisk until dissolved. Finally, whisk in the flour, making sure it's fully incorporated. The batter will be loose.

Step 3—Bake and serve: Divide the loose batter evenly among the ramekins. Place the ramekins directly on your oven's center rack. Bake for about 30 minutes. Serve lukewarm with a topping of whipped cream or ice cream. The combination of warm fruit dessert and cold, creamy topping is pure delight.

The Village Blend's Double-Chocolate Espresso-Glazed Loaf Cake (Melt & Mix)

A special treat from the Village Blend pastry case, these rich chocolate loaves are delivered to Clare's shop every morning by her baker. The chocolate flavor is to die for, which is why the slices from these loaves always sell out. Clare developed the recipe years ago for her "In the Kitchen with Clare" column, one of the part-time jobs she held in New Jersey while raising Joy as a single mom. These glazed chocolate cakes are versatile, too. Enjoy slices as a snack with coffee. Or fancy them up for dessert service by plating them with a side dollop of sweetened whipped cream or gelato. To see a photo of the finished cakes, visit Cleo Coyle's online coffeehouse at coffeehousemystery.com, where you can download an illustrated guide to this recipe section.

Makes 2 cakes using loaf pans of 8½ × 4½ × 2 inches

¾ cup (1½ sticks) unsalted butter, sliced into small pieces

½ cup vegetable oil

2 cups granulated sugar

6 ounces semisweet chocolate, chopped

½ cup brewed coffee or espresso

½ cup whole milk

3 cups all-purpose flour

½ cup unsweetened cocoa powder

2½ teaspoons baking powder

½ teaspoon baking soda

¼ teaspoon finely ground sea salt (or table salt)

¾ cup sour cream (full fat)

2 teaspoons pure vanilla extract

3 large eggs, room temperature, fork-whisked
1 cup semisweet chocolate chips
Chocolate Espresso Glaze (recipe follows)

Step 1—Prep oven and pans: First, preheat oven to 300°F. Butter bottom and sides of 2 loaf pans (size 8½ × 4½ × 2 inches) and create parchment paper slings. The handles of these slings will be used to lift the baked cakes successfully out of their pans. To make the slings: Trim a length of paper in each pan so that the bottom is covered and the excess paper extends beyond the long sides to create handles. The butter will help the paper stick to the pan's sides. For a tight fit, put sharp folds in the paper where it hits the pan's corners.

Step 2—Easy "melt-and-mix" method: Into a saucepan combine the sliced-up butter, oil, sugar, chocolate, coffee, and milk. Stir over low heat until chocolate is melted and all ingredients are smoothly blended together. (Do not allow this mixture to boil or you'll end up with a scorched taste to your chocolate.) You can also use a microwave to melt these ingredients, but be sure to use a microwave-safe bowl and heat in 30-second bursts, stirring between each burst to prevent the chocolate from burning. Set aside to cool.

Step 3—Finish batter: Into a separate bowl, sift together the flour, cocoa powder, baking powder, baking soda, and salt. Stir in the cooled chocolate mixture from Step 2, along with the sour cream, vanilla, and whisked eggs. Beat with an electric mixer, scraping down the bowl until all ingredients form a smooth batter. (Do not overmix.) Finally, fold in the chocolate chips.

Step 4—Bake and cool: Divide the batter evenly between your 2 lined loaf pans. Bake for about 70 to 80 minutes (time will depend on your oven). Remove from oven. Cakes are done when toothpicks inserted into the centers come out with no wet batter clinging to them. Allow cakes to cool 10 minutes in the pan and then use the parchment paper handles to lift the cakes out. Let the cakes cool on a rack for at least a full hour before slicing. Do not glaze until completely cool.

Step 5—Glaze and serve: While the cakes are cooling, mix up the Chocolate Espresso Glaze (recipe follows). Spoon generously over each completely cooled cake top. Use the back of your spoon to spread the glaze evenly. Be sure to push excess glaze over the edges for a nice drizzly effect down the cake sides. Enjoy as a snack cake or serve slices on dessert plates with a generous dollop of sweetened whipped cream or a scoop of gelato on the side.

Chocolate Espresso Glaze

This glaze pairs beautifully with chocolate, mocha, and vanilla cakes as well as croissants. Spoon the glaze over the tops of your cakes and cupcakes to "frost" them or use a fork to drizzle the glaze back and forth across your pastry. Either way, it makes a delicious finish to your baked goodies.

Makes about 1 cup

> 1 cup semisweet chocolate chips (or 6 ounces of block chocolate, chopped)
> 1/4 cup brewed coffee or espresso
> 2 tablespoons unsalted butter
> 1 teaspoon pure vanilla extract
> 1/2 teaspoon espresso powder
> 1/4 teaspoon finely ground sea salt (or table salt)
> 1 tablespoon corn syrup (light or vanilla)
> 1 cup confectioners' sugar

Place chocolate chips (or 6 ounces of chopped block chocolate) into a mixing bowl and set aside. Over low heat, bring the following ingredients to a simmer in a small saucepan: coffee or espresso, butter, vanilla, espresso powder, salt, and corn syrup. Pour the simmering liquid over your chocolate chips (or chopped chocolate) and stir with a rubber spatula until all chocolate is melted and the liquid is smooth. Finally, add in 1 cup of confectioners' sugar and whisk until the glaze is completely smooth and shiny (with no lumps). You can spoon it over your cake and use the back of the spoon to smooth the glaze into an even layer. Or you can use a fork and a back-and-forth motion for a drizzling effect. Glaze will be wet at first and should set in about an hour.

The Village Blend's
Twinkie Tribute Cupcakes

A Twinkie Tribute Cupcake is a terrible thing to waste, but that's exactly what happened when an annoying ringtone set everyone off in the Writer's Block Lounge. The ball of tender golden cake with the gooey marshmallow filling was hurled at another patron who, despite being splattered, couldn't help but enjoy the cake-plosion's deliciousness. A retaliatory fling caused collateral damage, which soon escalated into the kind of food fight rarely seen outside of school cafeterias. Fortunately, the US Navy—in the form of a retired captain—ended the campaign. After warning commands were issued, Captain Siebold mellowed the situation with a lecture on smooth rhythms to inspire calmer seas for the lounge's future. Now you too can create your own edible tribute to the classic Twinkie treat. Clare developed this recipe years ago for her "In the Kitchen with Clare" column. With a cake mix starter, these spongy golden cupcakes with marshmallow filling couldn't be more foolproof to make. (Just don't throw them!) To see step-by-step pictures of this recipe, visit Cleo Coyle's online coffeehouse at coffeehousemystery.com, where you can download an illustrated guide to this recipe section.

Makes 12 cupcakes

For the Cupcakes

1 box yellow cake mix (*see note on next page)

1¼ cups water

⅓ cup vegetable oil

4 egg whites (room temperature is best)

For the Marshmallow Filling

(Double this recipe if you'd like a frosting, too)

6 cups (one 10-ounce bag) mini marshmallows
2 tablespoons corn syrup (or vanilla-flavored corn syrup)
½ cup confectioners' sugar
2 tablespoons unsalted butter, softened
1 tablespoon milk
½ teaspoon vanilla extract (use clear vanilla for a whiter filling)

*A note on the cake mix: Use any plain yellow cake mix (not butter yellow) for this recipe. Just be sure to pick up a mix that lists oil in the directions and has "pudding in the mix" as a feature. When you use oil in a cake recipe, your cake will stay fresher for a longer period of time.

To make the cupcakes:

Step 1—Prep oven and pan: Preheat oven to 350°F and spray a 12-cup muffin tin with nonstick spray or line with cupcake liners and set aside.

Step 2—Mix the batter: Into a large mixing bowl, combine cake mix, water, and oil. Beat with an electric mixer for about 1 minute until a smooth batter forms. Be sure to scrape down the bowl as you mix. Place in the fridge until you complete the next step.

Step 3—Beat the egg whites: In a clean and dry glass, metal, or ceramic bowl (do not use plastic, which holds grease), beat egg whites until soft peaks form.

Step 4—Fold the eggs into the batter: Using an electric mixer on a low speed, fold the egg whites into the cake batter. Do not overbeat; mix just enough to smoothly incorporate the egg whites. You should no longer see white, just the yellow batter.

Step 5—Fill the pan and bake: Fill each cup with ¼ cup batter. Then go back and add 1 tablespoon more to each cup. Do not fill cups to the top. This should give you 12 cupcakes with a little batter left over for a 13th cupcake (if you want a baker's dozen). When you fill the cups as described, they should bake up uniformly with little golden domes. Bake for 15 to 17 minutes. Transfer pans to a cooling rack and allow the cupcakes to cool in their pan.

To make the filling (and frosting, if doubling):

Step 1—Create the marshmallow crème: Place mini marshmallows in a large, microwave-safe bowl, drizzle the corn syrup over them, and heat in your microwave for about 30 seconds (adding 15-second increments if needed). Do not completely melt the marshmallows. Watch for them to become very soft. Then stir them up and voilà, you have made marshmallow crème (aka Fluff). Set this mixture aside to cool.

Step 2—Mix the filling (and frosting, if doubling): Once your marshmallow crème has completely cooled, add the remaining ingredients to the bowl: confectioners' sugar, butter, milk, and vanilla extract. Using an electric mixer, beat the filling until smooth and blended, scraping down the bowl as you mix.

To assemble the cupcakes:

Step 1—Unstick the cupcakes: If you are not using cupcake liners, carefully run a knife around the outside edge of each cupcake to free it from the metal pan. Then place it right back into the well for stability.

Step 2—Cut the hole: Using a small, sharp knife, cut a cone-shaped hole into the top of each cupcake. Remove the cone and fill the hole with the copycat Twinkie filling. To prevent sticking, lightly coat your spoons with nonstick spray. You can also use a pastry bag for this job. Or create one in a pinch by spooning the filling into a ziplock bag and snipping off one corner with scissors.

Step 3—Fill and finish: Slice off the top of your cupcake cone and place it back on the filled cupcake. The filling is gooey and delicious. If you prefer a stiffer filling, simply chill the cupcakes in the fridge after filling. You can serve your Twinkie Tribute Cupcakes as is or frost the tops, as long as you doubled the filling, as directed. Or make a vanilla buttercream frosting, if you like—though this would be a departure from a pure "Twinkie Tribute," it would still be delicious.

Tip for the baker: What should you do with that extra bit of cake that you cut from the center of each cupcake? Are you kidding? Brew a pot of coffee and snack away!

Kismet

Kismet is a "spirited" coffee drink that was originally created for the Writer's Block Lounge decades ago by one of its members, a bartender named Bobby Briscoe. The word kismet *means fate, and the name proved prophetic on one momentous night when many lives took a fateful turn with this drink.*

To make your own Kismet, pour a shot of crème de cacao (white or dark) into a tall glass or mug for a hint of sweet chocolate flavor. Add a shot of Kahlúa to boost the drink's coffee spirit. Fill the rest of the mug with a premixed Americano, or you can substitute boldly brewed coffee. That's your Kismet!

To make an Americano, add a double shot of espresso (2 ounces) to a tall coffee cup. Pour 8 ounces of hot water (off the boil) over the top. No espresso machine? No problem. As mentioned above, substitute a boldly brewed cup of coffee. If serving as a dessert drink, feel free to pour a bit of steamed milk into your

Kismet or top with a dollop of sweetened whipped cream and a garnish of grated chocolate or dusting of cinnamon.

**From Clare, Matt, Madame,
Esther, Tucker, Dante, Nancy, and everyone at the Village Blend . . .
May you eat and drink with joy!**

Don't Miss Cleo Coyle's
Next Coffeehouse Mystery!

For more information about what's next for Clare Cosi
and her merry band of baristas, visit Cleo Coyle at her website:
coffeehousemystery.com

ABOUT THE AUTHOR

CLEO COYLE is a pseudonym for Alice Alfonsi, writing in collaboration with her husband, Marc Cerasini. Both are *New York Times* bestselling authors of the long-running Coffeehouse Mysteries—now celebrating more than twenty years in print. They are also authors of the national bestselling Haunted Bookshop Mysteries, initially written under the pseudonym ALICE KIMBERLY. Alice has worked as a journalist in Washington, D.C., and New York, and has written popular fiction for adults and children. A former magazine editor, Marc has authored espionage thrillers and nonfiction for adults and children. Alice and Marc are also both bestselling media tie-in writers who have penned properties for Lucasfilm, NBC, Fox, Disney, Imagine, Toho, and MGM. They live and work in New York City, where they write independently and together.

VISIT CLEO COYLE ONLINE

CoffeehouseMystery.com
 CleoCoyleAuthor
 CleoCoyle
 CleoCoyle_Author